SHE WAS THE MOST MAGNIFICENT WOMAN HE'D EVER SEEN . . .

Jenny rode low over the mare, the long curls at her back flashing in the sunlight like spun gold, her face flushed with excitement, her beautiful sapphire eyes sparkling. Hearing her laugh, Cole felt something deep within him stir.

"Rein in," he said.

Jenny didn't want to stop. Nor did the mare. Jenny thought about ignoring Cole's command, but there was an urgency in his voice that made her reconsider. She pulled back on the reins.

Cole brought his horse to a halt before Jenny. He swung down and hurried to her before she could dismount. "Oh, that was so exciting, so wonderful," Jenny gasped, as Cole lifted his arms to help her.

Jenny's breath caught as Cole's strong hands clasped her tiny waist. As he lowered her to the ground, her body slid against his, and Jenny was acutely aware of every hard muscle and tendon. When she reached his eye level, he stopped and just held her against him. The sheer maleness of him was overpowering. She found it difficult to breathe. She watched as his eyes darkened with passion to a molten gold, felt the heat of desire in his breath fanning her face. He's going to kiss me, she thought, and felt a wild thrill of a different sort seize her. Her heart raced. . . .

LAUREN WILDE

YANKEE ANGEL

ZEBRA BOOKS
KENSINGTON PUBLISHING CORP.

To Mark, with love, Mom.

One

A loud knock shattered the silence.

Lying sprawled on his stomach on the rickety hotel bed, Cole Benteen opened one eye and glared over his shoulder at the door where the knock had come, wondering who had the audacity to interrupt his nap. Deciding to ignore the knock, he closed his eye, but the summons came again, this time louder and more insistent. Cole growled, rolled over, and curtly called out, "Who is it?" Then remembering that he was in Mexico, repeated the question in Spanish.

"My name is Amos Wright," a voice beyond the door answered. "You don't know me, but I have something of the utmost importance to discuss with you."

Cole didn't know Amos Wright, but he had certainly heard of him. Wright was a Yankee carpetbagger who had wrested a large ranch from its Texas owner with the help of the Yankees' crooked tax assessors and punitive reconstruction laws. The Bar J, located north of Rio Grande City, was one of the

7

largest ranches in South Texas and had once been the *hacienda* of a wealthy and powerful Spanish-Mexican before the Mexican War when the border dispute between the two countries had finally been settled. Rather than live under the hated *gringo's* rule, the proud *hidalgo* had deserted his ranch and moved back to Mexico, and an enterprising Texas veteran of that war had claimed the ranch as his personal spoils. No one in Texas contested his claim. The ranch was in an area so far removed from civilization and so overrun with bandits, Indians, rattlesnakes and scorpions that no one else wanted it. But Cole had heard that Wright had made the ranch quite profitable, what with all the wild longhorns running in that country free for the taking and the trail drives to the new railheads at Dodge and Abilene. Cattle raising was rapidly becoming very important in the state of Texas, so much so that it had replaced King Cotton in the state's economy, a fact that left Cole feeling very sad. It was just another reminder that his previous life was gone forever and he was facing a very uncertain future.

"Benteen? Can I come in?" the rancher called from the hallway, breaking into Cole's thoughts.

Cole was tempted to tell the man to go to hell just on general principle. He had even more reason than most Texans to hate carpetbaggers. But Cole couldn't imagine what the Yankee wanted with him. He certainly couldn't have need of his gun. Wright had an army of gunslingers to protect him and his interests in that wild area that was commonly called the *brasada,* the brush country that bordered Mexico. But the more Cole thought about it, the more puzzled he became, and in the end, his curiosity got the better of him. He rose from the bed and padded across the floor on his stockinged feet.

Amos had just about given up hope of Cole answering the door when it was flung open with a suddenness that made the carpetbagger jump back in surprise. Finding himself face to face with the notorious outlaw, Amos sucked in his breath sharply. Before him stood a tall, broad-shouldered, lean-hipped man with a thick head of chestnut hair, a dark, three-day stubble of whiskers on his lower face, and a snarl on his sensuous lips. Amos had expected the gunman to look tough and mean, but not this overpowering aura of danger that seemed to hang over the man, or a dynamic presence that made the Texan seem bigger than life. He quickly glanced into a pair of glittering eyes that looked as if they were made of molten gold. A tingle of fear ran up the rancher's spine, and his mouth turned dry, while a strange paralysis seemed to overcome him.

"Are you coming in or not?"

The surly question broke the rancher's strange paralysis, but did nothing to dispel the feeling of danger that undulated from the gunman in powerful waves. Amos thought he would rather step into the devil's own lair than walk into this man's room. It took all of his courage to step across the threshold and close the door behind him.

"What do you want?" Cole demanded, coming right to the point without even the barest of amenities.

"Do you mind if I sit down?" Amos asked, shocked at how weak his legs felt. Then, not wanting the outlaw to know the strange effect he had on him, the carpetbagger quickly added, "It was a long ride down here, and I'm a mite weary."

Cole's golden gaze ran over the carpetbagger's stocky, heavy-set body before his eyes came to a rest on the man's face. He briefly wondered if Wright's face was sunburned from his long ride under the blazing sun, or if the Yankee was a natural *huerto,* what the Mexicans called a red-complexioned man. Pushing the thought aside, Cole looked at the rancher's eyes and found they were a dull brown, a lifeless color that did nothing to enhance the man's beefy looks. No, with his coloring, his droopy sandy mustache, and his short legs and pot belly, Amos Wright was far from impressive looking, and Cole was frankly disappointed. But then he reminded himself that the Yankee's reputation for being a powerful man was based on his money, his political influence with the hated Republican party in Texas, and his army of gunfighters who did his dirty work for him, and not his physical appearance. Cole motioned to a straight chair beside his bed and answered, "Suit yourself."

As Cole turned and walked to the window and away from him, Amos breathed a sigh of relief. He was used to dealing with hard-eyed, mean-tempered outlaws, but there was something about Cole's gaze that unnerved him. Somehow the strange golden eyes didn't seem human, but more those of a savage animal. Then, taking note of the gunman's lithe, effort-

10

less walk, and remembering the snarl that had been on his lips earlier, the rancher knew what animal Cole reminded him of. A fierce, dangerous cougar!

The realization did nothing to help Amos regain his composure. He walked to the chair, turned it around, then slung one leg over it so that he could rest his arms on its back. Hopefully, the position would not only support his trembling limbs, but give him a more relaxed, yet controlled appearance. Damn Benteen, Amos thought. No man had ever struck such terror in his heart—and the gunfighter wasn't even armed!

Instead of walking back to the bed, Cole walked to the window and absently gazed out. He'd be damned if he'd sit across from the carpetbagger and treat him like some honored guest. He was beginning to wish he hadn't even invited the despicable man into his room. Then remembering what had prompted him to do so, he once more asked curtly, "What do you want?"

"I'd like to hire you."

"For that army of gunslingers of yours?" Cole asked, turning from the window with a sneer on his face. "No, thanks."

"No, that's not what I wanted you for," Amos answered, resenting Cole's scorning his men. Christ, the outlaw was the worst thief and cold-blooded murderer in Texas. What right did Benteen have to look down on his gunmen?

"Then what?"

"I'd like hire you to rescue someone that the Red Robber is holding prisoner."

11

Cole's dark eyebrows rose in surprise. "Are you talking about Juan Cortinas?"

"Of course I'm talking about Cortinas!" Amos answered angrily. "Who else but that marauding Mexican bastard would have the audacity to hold an American woman against her will?"

"Woman?" Cole asked, even more surprised. "The person you want rescued is a woman?"

"Yes, Miss Jenny Daniels, the woman I'm engaged to and intend to marry."

"How did she get taken prisoner?"

"Did you hear about Cortinas' bandits attacking Nuecestown this past spring?" Seeing Cole nod his dark head, Wright continued, "Well, they attacked a stage coach going from Corpus Christi to Brownsville on their way back to the border, and Jenny was on that coach. After robbing everyone, they took her and two others with them as hostages, in hopes that the posse that was on their trail would give up the chase for fear they would kill them. But the bandits didn't leave Jenny at the border, like they did the other hostages. They took her to Cortinas' headquarters in Mexico."

"You let the woman you're going to marry travel overland from Corpus to Brownsville?" Cole asked in obvious disgust. "That was a dumb thing to do. It isn't safe to travel anywhere for up to two-hundred miles north of the border with Cortinas' bandits running amuck the way they are."

Cole's criticism irritated Wright all the more. "Goddammit, I know that! I didn't *let* Jenny travel from Corpus to Brownsville! It was her idea. She

12

was supposed to take the steamer, but it broke down when it docked at Corpus. She decided to take a stage to Brownsville, or so those who were traveling with her on it claimed. You see, Jenny doesn't know what the conditions are in South Texas, or about our bandit problem. She's from back east. And now the prettiest, sweetest, gentlest little lady in the whole world is in the hands of that crude, murdering bastard. She's been gently bred, a lady to the bone. Can't you imagine how terrified she must be?"

In Cole's opinion, the woman Wright had described didn't seem to match the thieving, unpolished carpetbagger either, and he bluntly asked, "Where did you meet a woman like that?"

There was no doubt in Wright's mind what Cole was insinuating. He might have become rich and powerful, but he was no more a gentleman than he had been the day he was born. The Yankee had gotten where he was by being tough, mean, and crafty, and he was still amazed that a lady like Jenny had agreed to marry a raw, uneducated, ill-mannered man like himself. If she hadn't come from a rich, influential family herself, he might have suspected it was his money and position that had attracted her. But whatever her reason, it wasn't this damn outlaw's concern. Amos glared at Cole and replied in a hard voice, "Not that it's any of your damn business, but I met her when I went back east on a business trip last winter."

As soon as the heated retort had passed his lips, Amos knew he had made a mistake. The look that came into the gunfighter's eyes was enough to make

13

the hair on the back of his neck rise, and Wright knew he had been foolish to rile the man. Hoping to salvage what he could of their rather shaky relationship, Wright quickly said, "Look, I'm sorry if I seem cross, but I'm at my wit's end. I've been to the army, and I've been to the law, such as there is in these parts. No one will help me rescue Jenny. They say they can't cross the border and attack the bandits on their own ground for fear it might cause an international incident — of all of the goddamnest, stupidest things I've ever heard! Seems to me that the law did plenty of crossing the border after criminals and bandits in the past."

"That was the Texas Rangers," Cole responded. "The reconstruction government disbanded them after the war. The Yankees thought an armed group of Texans too dangerous, remember?"

It was a jibe that the carpetbagger didn't miss, and Cole could tell by the man's face turning even redder than it's normal florid color that Amos knew he was telling him it was his own fault that there was no one to help him. Cole took a moment to savor the effects of his remark, then said, "You've got an army of your own. Why don't you go down to Cortinas' headquarters and rescue the lady yourself?"

"Cortinas has at least a thousand men in that bandit army of his. All I have is forty, and a good two-thirds of them wouldn't cross the border either. No, it's either a one man job or a couple of hundred."

"Then why don't you go?"

At heart, Wright was a coward. When he had

served in the Union Army, he had always stayed as far back in the attacking ranks as he possibly could, and had even turned and run in a few heated encounters with the enemy. He didn't like confrontations unless he knew he had plenty of armed men to support him, which was why he had his own personal bodyguard and an army of gunslingers. He was the kind of man who hired other men to take risks and perform dangerous tasks. But he wasn't about to admit that to Cole. "I don't know where Cortinas' headquarters is located. No one does. At least no one that's talking, that is. I've heard that he's threatened to kill any man who divulges that information to an outsider."

"So why do you think I can rescue this woman? I don't know where his headquarters is either."

"But you can find it. I've heard you know your way around northern Mexico pretty well and speak the language like a native. And with your deep tan and coloring, you're dark enough to disguise yourself as a Mexican and pass for one of them. I figured you could find Cortinas' ranch, sneak in and rescue Jenny, then slip back out again."

"You're crazy if you think it would be that simple."

"All right," Amos conceded irritably, "so it wouldn't be simple. But I figured any man who could plan and execute as many daring robberies as you have can figure out something. Maybe you would prefer to hire some men to help you. If so, I'll foot the bill and pay all of your expenses. Money is no object."

15

Cole was tempted to tell the carpetbagger that he had never planned or executed any robbery. For years, he had taken the blame for every robbery and cold-blooded murder in the state, a blame that was placed at his feet by his politically-powerful enemies. Other than killing the bastard that had started his flight from the carpetbagger law six years before, Cole had only killed in self-defense when he was challenged by some stupid gunslinger who was out to make a name for himself and thought he could out-draw him. But the news that he had been vindicated of all the crimes he both had and was supposed to have committed by Governor Coke hadn't reached this wild, desolate part of Texas yet, and Cole wasn't about to enlighten Wright. For the time being, everyone still thinking he was being pursued by the law suited his purpose very well and explained his presence in Mexico. Instead of correcting the carpetbagger's opinion of him, Cole answered, "Then if money isn't the issue, why don't you offer Cortinas a ransom?"

"I did! I sent word through the Mexican grapevine that I'd offer a handsome payment for Jenny's safe return, and I kept upping it. But it turned out that Cortinas wasn't holding Jenny for a ransom. The bastard is courting her. He wants to marry her himself!"

Cole knew Juan Cortinas from way back to his boyhood in Brownsville when the Mexican was just coming into his heyday as bandit chieftain. Called "the Red Robber of the Rio Grande" because of his red beard and ruddy complexion, Cortinas came

16

from one of the best Mexican border families. In his younger days Cortinas had been a powerfully-muscled man and superb horseman whose daring and sensuously cruel face had held a strange attraction for women. Even now, in his mid-fifties, with his thickening waist and graying hair, the powerful, insolent bandit king didn't lack for women who would gladly share his bed and gloried in his company. Cole couldn't imagine Cortinas being so infatuated with any woman that he would actually woo her with marriage in mind. Deciding the idea was preposterous, Cole laughed and said, "You must be mistaken about who is holding your intended, Wright. Cortinas isn't the marrying kind. It must be some other Mexican bandit."

"I'm not mistaken!" Amos answered with heat. "Cortinas' own sister wrote me a letter and told me so. She said she was doing it at his request, since he had been the black sheep of the family and had never learned to write. She wrote that Cortinas wanted me to stop hounding him about a ransom, that Jenny wasn't going to be returned to me under any terms, that her brother was honorably wooing her and intended to make her his wife." A look of total repugnance came over the rancher's face. "Have you ever heard of anything so disgusting in your entire life? An old man like him, a bandit no less, courting a young, beautiful girl like Jenny?"

Cole could have pointed out to the carpetbagger that he wasn't much younger and that he was just as much a thief, but the Texan didn't bother. Suddenly, he just wanted the despicable Yankee out of his

17

sight. He walked to the door, saying, "Well, that's your and this Jenny's problem, and not mine."

Amos was stunned by Cole's abrupt dismissal. And there was no doubt in his mind that the rugged Texan was dismissing him. The gunfighter was holding the door open. "Are you saying you won't take the job?"

"That's right. I'm not interested."

"But you haven't even heard what I'm offering," Amos objected. "I'll pay you five thousand dollars."

"No deal."

"Ten thousand, then."

The sum sounded like a fortune to Cole, and he was tempted to reconsider—particularly in view of his purpose for being here in Mexico—but his dislike for the carpetbagger overrode any weakness he felt. "No," he answered firmly.

Amos rose from the chair and walked dejectedly to the door, thinking that he had no idea where to turn for help now. Desperately grasping at a last possibility, he stopped before Cole and said, "If you won't do it for the money, then please do it out of compassion for the woman. Jenny is a fine Christian woman, as gentle, as sweet, as soft-spoken as any of your Southern women. She doesn't deserve to be in the clutches of that murdering brute. Why, if she continues to spurn his advances, as I'm sure she will, there's no telling what Cortinas might do to her. Why, he might rape her, or kill her!"

"Why in the hell do you think that would make any difference to me?"

"I was hoping that you might still have something

18

of the Southern gentleman that you once were in you."

Cole wondered how the carpetbagger knew that he had once been a gentleman. Just how much *did* the Yankee know of his past? Cole shrugged his broad shoulders and answered, "Well, you're wrong. That was a long time ago. Since then, I've learned that no woman is worth risking your neck for. Take my advice and forget her."

A vision of Jenny with her golden hair, her beautiful face, and her big blue eyes flashed through Wright's mind. "Jenny isn't the kind of woman a man forgets."

Cole almost felt sorry for the Yankee. God, he was really smitten, he thought. Then remembering his own vulnerability to a female in the past, he hardened his heart and said, "A man can forget any woman, if he puts his mind to it."

Amos felt a rising anger. He had practically gotten down on his knees and begged the low-down outlaw to help him, and the unfeeling bastard had callously dismissed Jenny's life as if it were worthless. Suddenly infuriated at himself for allowing Cole to humiliate him in such a manner, as well as provoked at the gunfighter's refusal to help him, he snapped, "All right then! Forget I even asked. I'll find someone else to take the job. You mark my words!"

Amos whirled and stomped angrily down the darkened hallway, making the spurs on his boots jingle wildly. When the irate Yankee reached the stairs, Cole couldn't resist getting in one last dig and called, "Maybe you will find someone to go after her.

There's a fool born every day. And going after that woman would take a colossal fool. It's nothing but a suicide mission."

Hearing Amos' angry gasp, Cole smiled in satisfaction and closed the door. He walked back to the window and watched through the grimy pane as Amos walked from the building and mounted his horse. Then the rancher and his half-dozen henchmen who had accompanied him wheeled their horses and rode away in a flurry of dust.

Cole dismissed Amos Wright from his mind and turned his attention to the town of Bagdad below him. The Mexican *siesta* time was over, and the population of the port town that sat on the Mexican side of the jungle-like delta that formed the mouth of the Rio Grande were stirring once more. Soon the sounds coming from the port would drift through the sultry air: wagon wheels clattering on the wooden piers, roustabouts shouting in Spanish at one another, steamers tooting, mules braying, cattle being loaded on the boats, mooing. During the Civil War, Bagdad had done a thriving business exporting Confederate cotton when the South had been effectively blockaded by the Union Navy elsewhere. At that time, the settlement which was perched beside the muddy waters of the Rio Grande had probably been the busiest port in Mexico. Then, after the war, there had been a lull for a few years before Bagdad returned to its former prosperity. But today there was hardly a bale of cotton to be seen in the town. That was a gentleman's crop, and if it was shipped from South Texas, it went through Port Isabel, the Texas port on the mouth of the river. No, what was being exported from Bagdad now, what was making her such a thriving port was hides and cattle on the hoof, and two-thirds of it wore Texas brands and had been stolen by Cortinas' bandits. Which was why Cole was in this steaming town with its swarms of flies and yellow fever-carrying mosquitoes. Contrary to what everyone thought, both Anglo and Mexican on both sides of the border, he wasn't just another *pistolero* seeking refuge from the *gringo* law in Mexico. If he had been, he would have found a better place to settle than this stinking hell-hole with its rotting fish and poorly scraped hides. No, he was here to investigate Cortinas' illegal activities at the request of Governor Coke, and after what the Governor had done to help him clear his name, Cole couldn't refuse him. Besides, Richard Coke was an old family friend.

Cole gazed absently out of the window and recalled the events that led to his being in Mexico on this mission. The activities of the Mexican bandits along the Texas border had always been brisk, for the Mexicans still refused to recognize the Rio Grande as the legal border between the two countries. They insisted that the border was the Nueces River, a good two hundred miles northward, and that the land that lay between the two rivers rightfully belonged to Mexico and had been stolen by the U.S. For that reason, many of the bandits rationalized that they weren't really stealing, but simply taking *"Nanita's* cattle"—their grandmother's cattle—that belonged to them by right of inheritance, or if not theirs, then

21

some other Mexican's grandmother. And so they raided across the Rio Grande with impunity, stealing cattle and horses, plundering and murdering. However, it wasn't until Cortinas appointed himself as their leader in the late fifties that the bandits became organized. At that time, Cortinas had claimed Texas citizenship and was operating out of his mother's ranch north of Brownsville, since he was wanted in Mexico for theft. He led a raid on Brownsville and held it for several days, killing five people and releasing all of the prisoners in the town's jail before he returned to his mother's ranch. A combined force of U.S. troops and Texas Rangers chased him up and down the Rio Grande for months, until he was finally driven across the river, but not before he had sacked Rio Grande City and left the entire border from there to Brownsville, 120 miles downstream, in ashes.

Then the Civil War had come, not just the war to the north, but in Mexico itself. For awhile, Cortinas was busy fighting in that war and received a commission as a general in the Mexican Army, having declared for Juarez in the ousted president's fight against Maximillian and the French. When the war to the south of the border ended with Juarez's victory, Cortinas was a power to be reckoned with. Not only was he supreme, uncontested bandit king of the border, but he held considerable political power, a man who had so much influence with the government in Mexico City that he made and unmade governors.

Cortinas had turned his full attention back to his

banditry, and Texas was ripe for plundering. There was no one to stand in his way. The Texas Rangers, the only force that could begin to deal with the bandits, had been disbanded, and the United States military forces, mostly made up of inexperienced Negro troops, were too busy reconstructing Texas citizens to do anything to protect them from depredations on either their property or lives, both from the Indians on the frontier and the bandits on the southern border. The *Cortinistas* raided South Texas with a ferocity and energy that knew no bounds, and the thievery was wholesale. Not only did Cortinas stock all of his ranches with stolen Texas cattle, but all of his friends' ranches, too, then made contracts for delivering hides and cattle to be shipped to Cuba.

The situation had only worsened during Governor Davis' tenure, although Reconstruction had officially ended. The Governor and his radical congress couldn't care less what happened in South Texas. They were too busy plundering Texas themselves. Now, the situation had reached the point where something drastic had to be done and soon. According to one of the area's biggest ranchers, Captain King, who Cole had talked to on his way to the border, 100,000 cattle had been stolen from him alone since the end of the war, and Cole didn't doubt King's claim. Since he had begun his investigation six weeks before, Cole had seen 20,000 cattle driven across the Rio Grande and just two days before witnessed the sale of over 4,000 Texas cattle by one of Cortinas' lieutenants to a Cuban buyer here in Bagdad. That the thievery was actually increasing was bad enough, but the raids were becoming more and more vindictive. That spring, the bandits had attacked Nuecestown, north of Corpus Christi, and cold-bloodedly murdered several people, and a year before had jumped and brutally murdered four men at Penascal. The two raids had the Texans inflamed, and rightfully so. It seemed the Mexicans were no longer content to just steal. They wanted blood.

Cole's mind wandered to Amos Wright and what he had said about Jenny Daniels. He still couldn't imagine Cortinas so infatuated with a woman that he could actually woo her for marriage, but if that were true and the woman continued to spurn him, would he kill her? As far as Cole knew the bandits had never killed a woman. Beaten them, yes, but never out-and-out murder. But they appeared to be getting more and more savage.

Cole recalled what Amos had said about Jenny Daniels being sweet, soft spoken, and gentle. Unbidden, the mental picture of Mary Alice flashed through his mind. With it, he felt the pain he always experienced when he remembered her, and the anger. But he was enough in control of his emotions that he could imagine how he would have felt if it had been his betrothed in the bandit's hands. Suddenly, Cole understood the carpetbagger's desperation, for despite what Amos had thought, he was capable of compassion.

Briefly, Cole wondered if he could possibly help Jenny Daniels. After all, he had planned on finding Cortinas' secret hideout and giving it a thorough surveillance as part of his investigation. It wasn't as if

24

he would be going out of his way to rescue the poor woman. She'd be right there for the taking. Then, remembering how dangerous his mission was and the blood-thirsty nature of the bandits he was spying on, Cole quickly tossed the thought aside. Hell, he must have been crazy to have even considered it for a second, he thought with disgust. It *would* be sheer suicide, and Cole wasn't ready to die yet.

Two

Two weeks later, Cole sat on his horse with his hands tied behind his back and his empty gun holster slapping against his thigh as the bandit in front of him led the Texan's mount through the little Mexican settlement that sat beside Cortinas' headquarters. Behind him rode two other fiercely mustachioed bandits with their six-shooters pointed at Cole's broad back. A score or more of Mexican women and children had left what they were doing and crowded around the small procession, watching with dark, sober eyes and wondering why the *gringo* was smiling and not afraid.

Cole was smiling because the bandits were playing right into his hand by capturing him and bringing him to their leader. They might not recognize his name, but there was no doubt in Cole's mind that Cortinas would, and hopefully, the bandit chieftain would believe his story. And just to give that story more credibility, Cole had let his beard grow and refrained from bathing so that he fit the part of a desperate outlaw seeking refuge and employment in

Mexico. With the shaggy, unkempt growth on his lower face and his filthy clothing, he looked like the Wild Man from Borneo and smelled to high heaven.

Cole and his captors came to a stop at the heavy wooden gates hanging from the high adobe walls that surrounded Cortinas' headquarters. While the massive gates were being pushed aside for their entrance, Cole took the opportunity to study the placement of the howitzers that were spaced at intervals along the top of the walls. Then, as the gate swung open and he and his captors rode into the wide cobbled plaza that surrounded the massive, sprawling, two story ranch house, he saw even more cannons that were tucked behind piles of sandbags here and there. There were even a few Gatling guns sitting on the flat roofs of the storehouses that lined the interior of the walls. Christ, Cole thought, a grim expression replacing his smile, the rumors were true. Cortinas' headquarters was as well defended as any fort, and no one would ever be able to blast the bandit king out.

The horses came to a stop at the front of the ranch house, and Cole was roughly jerked down from his saddle and shoved through another massive door at the front of the building. Cole found himself in a smaller courtyard with a tinkling fountain and huge clay pots filled with brightly-colored flowers. He glanced quickly around and, above him, saw the iron-grilled balcony that lined the entire second-story and surrounded the patio, then spied two women servants pulling bread from a huge mud oven over in one corner of the courtyard.

27

Cole was led across the courtyard and beneath the balcony to another door which opened into a small foyer that sat to the side of a spacious *sala*. There, he and his captors were brought to an abrupt halt by the startling sound of a woman shrieking at the top of her lungs, "You bonehead! Are you deaf, or just plain stupid? I've told you over and over that I will *not* marry you! I want absolutely nothing to do with you. You disgust me! I can't stand the sight of you! Do you hear?"

"Ah, Jeanita, *mi vita,* you know you do not mean what you say," a deep male voice crooned soothingly. "You only need more time to get to know me better."

"Don't call me *mi vita!*" the woman screamed back. "I'm not your sweetheart. And I've told you time and again my name is Jenny, not Jeanita. Just plain Jenny! And I don't want to get to know you. All I want is for you to take me back to the border, to turn me loose."

Jenny? Cole thought in utter surprise. Surely this couldn't be the sweet, gentle, soft-spoken woman Wright had been talking about? No, fishwife or shrew would be a more apt description. And was the man she was railing at Cortinas? It seemed almost impossible to believe. No one talked back to Cortinas or called him names. He was a man who struck terror in the hearts of the toughest, meanest men. But this Jenny didn't seem to be the least bit frightened of him.

"Ah, Jeanita," Cortinas replied, apparently not in the least repulsed or angered, "why would you want to go back to Texas? Have I not given you everything your heart desires? A lovely apartment all your own, personal maids, breakfast in bed, a magnificent mare?"

"I don't want your damn horse! I told you I can't ride. I don't want anything from you but my freedom!"

"And you will have your freedom," the bandit king answered with just a hint of steel coming into his voice, "the day you become my wife."

"Hell will freeze over before I will become your wife, General!"

"Cheno. Please call me Cheno. That is what all of my friends call me, and what I would like for my betrothed to call me."

"I am *not* your betrothed! I'm Amos Wright's intended, and I demand that you take me back to Texas and him!"

"Amos Wright?" Cortinas asked in a scornful voice. "Why would you prefer that *gringo* to me? I am much more charming, much more generous, much more. . . ."

"You're old enough to be my grandfather!"

"No, no, *mi vita,*" Cortinas corrected gently. "Think of my years in terms of maturity, not age. Besides, that *gringo* is almost as old, and crude, while I am a gentleman. In my veins flows the finest Spanish blood in Mexico."

"I don't give a damn what kind of blood flows in your veins, you dumb ox! For the last time, I won't marry you, and that's final!"

"Then I will give you more time. I will ask again next week."

There was a long moment of silence in which Cole could imagine Jenny staring at Cortinas in utter disbelief, before he heard her shriek in exasperation, "You bastard! You haven't listened to a word I've said. You're impossible! Utterly impossible!"

A split second later, Jenny tore from the *sala* and ran right into Cole, almost bowling him over and knocking the breath from her. Without even thinking, Cole said, "Hey! Watch where you're going!"

Jenny's eyes widened at the rebuke, for the English had been spoken without the slightest hint of a Mexican accent. She gave the man a closer scrutiny. What she could see of the man's skin beneath his bushy, ill-kempt beard was deeply tanned, but not near as dark as the three Mexicans standing next to him. "Why, you're an American!"

"That was a brilliant deduction," Cole drawled sarcastically.

Jenny's blue eyes flashed. "Well, you don't have to be so hateful about it! I was just surprised to find you here."

"Maybe I'm being hateful because you're standing on my foot," Cole answered with a growl. "Would you mind stepping back?"

Jenny glanced down and saw that she *was* standing on one of the man's booted feet. She stepped back, and Cole got a really good look at her. What he saw took him by surprise. He could hardly believe that the shrew he had heard and the young woman standing before him were the same. With her shiny golden hair arranged in a mass of curls on the top of her head, her blue, blue eyes, her creamy complexion, her turned up nose, and her sweetly shaped mouth, Jenny looked like an angel stepped down from heaven. Even her slim, small-boned stature gave the impression of innocence and sweetness, although all the womanly curves were certainly there, Cole mused as his eyes lingered on her full, high breasts, then slipped to the gentle curve of her hips, then back to her breasts.

Jenny was all too aware of Cole's golden eyes on her. She was accustomed to men staring at her, even undressing her with their eyes, but there was something about this man's gaze that unnerved her. Perhaps it was the aura of danger than seemed to hang over the stranger, she thought. Maybe that explained why her heart was suddenly racing, why her stomach was fluttering so strangely. But deep down Jenny knew differently. She wasn't a person who frightened easily. No, it was the stranger's utter maleness that was making her feel so peculiar. She had never been so acutely aware that she was female. Feeling a little twinge of fascination, she, too, looked closer, then noticing that his hands were tied behind his back, blurted out, "Why, you're a prisoner, too!"

Before Cole could make any response, Cortinas walked from the *sala* and, seeing the group standing in the foyer, came to a halt, his grey-green eyes coming to rest on Cole. Cole was surprised to see the bandit king was dressed in a Mexican general's uniform, his chest covered with so many medals that they would have dragged a smaller man to the ground. Other than that, and his graying beard and hair, Cole noted that the Mexican had changed little

31

since he had seen him some fifteen years before. Cortinas was still a powerful, vital man who carried himself with a self-assurance that bordered on cockiness.

Shooting a fierce, oblique look at one of Cole's captors, Cortinas asked sharply in Spanish, "Who is this man, and why have you brought him here?"

"We found him sneaking around one of your herds and captured him. He claims he is a friend and insisted that we bring him to you," the man answered in Spanish.

"I have never seen him before in my life," Cortinas answered, then becoming aware of Jenny watching everything, Cortinas turned to her and said, "Please forgive me, *mi vita,* but I have business to attend to now. I will see you tonight at dinner."

Jenny had been filled with curiosity about the tall American, but her knowledge of Spanish was so limited that she hadn't been able to follow the exchange between the two Mexicans. Now she knew Cortinas was dismissing her. Feeling both frustrated and newly-irritated at his persistence in calling her *mi vita,* she lashed out, "The devil you will! I'll starve before I'll dine with you one more time, you bastard!"

Jenny turned and rushed from the foyer. Cortinas chuckled and turned back to face Cole. "I'd never allow a woman to talk to me like that," Cole commented in Spanish.

Cortinas wasn't particularly surprised at Cole's use of Spanish, since many Texans spoke the language fluently. However, he was surprised at the *gringo's* lack of an accent and his audacity to speak up so boldly. "Wouldn't you?" Cortinas asked in the same language, suddenly curious about the *gringo* with the strange golden eyes. "Why?"

"Why?" Cole asked as if it were the most stupid question he had ever heard. "Because a woman should be seen and not heard. She should keep her mouth shut, and stay in her place."

"Ah, so you are just like my men, who believe women should be meek and submissive," Cortinas answered with a nod to the two Mexicans who were still frowning at Jenny's heated retort. "I'm afraid I do not agree. I admire spirit, in both a woman and a horse. It is the sign of intelligence and good breeding."

"Good breeding?" Cole asked with a scoff. "She called you a bastard."

"She did not mean it. She only called me that because she is angry. It amuses me when she calls me names. No one has ever done that to my face before. She is a brave woman."

"If I stood here and called you a bastard, would you think I was brave?" Cole asked.

The ghost of a smile that had been playing at Cortinas' lips disappeared. A hard glint came to his eyes. "No, *señor*," Cortinas answered, suddenly switching to English, "I would think you are a fool, and I do not like fools." Cortinas paused, gave Cole a penetrating look, then asked in a clipped voice, "Why did you tell my men you are my friend? I have no *gringo* friends."

"Because it was the only way I could get them to

33

bring me to you. And in a way we are friends, or at least *compadres*. We're both thieves."

It was the second time the American had spoken out boldly, calling him a thief to his face, and Cortinas was again curious. He cocked his head and asked, "Who are you?"

"Cole Benteen. Have you heard of me?"

"Sí, I have heard of you. They say you are a mean *hombre.* What are you doing here?"

"Things got too hot for me on the other side of the border."

"I am not talking about here in Mexico. I am talking about here on my ranch."

"I was on my way to see you when your men jumped me."

"They say you were snooping around one of my herds."

Cole had been investigating one of the herds, checking to see how many Texas brands were on the cattle, but he answered smoothly, "Ah, hell, I was just riding through it and got down to exercise my legs. Had a cramp in my ass from riding so long."

"And why did you want to see me?"

"To ask you for a job."

"As a *vaquero?* What do you know about cattle?"

"Hell, no. I'm no goddamned cowhand," Cole answered with genuine disgust. "I want to hire on as a bandit."

"You are a highwayman and a bank robber. What do you know about stealing cattle?"

"What's there to know?" Cole answered with a shrug of his broad shoulders. "You find yourself a herd, kill anyone who's guarding it, then make a run for the border. It doesn't take that much talent."

Cortinas bristled and answered indignantly, "You are mistaken! It is not that simple. A raid must be carefully planned. You must be sure that there are no troopers in the vicinity to follow you and that the herd is not too well guarded. And then there are the posses to contend with. They are worse than the soldiers. They do not give up so easily. Sometimes we must hide to escape them. You would need to know all of our secret places. And there are not many fords on the Rio Grande that you can drive a large herd of cattle across. The river is full of quicksand and in some places infested with nests of water moccasins. No, *señor*, it takes more talent and skill than you think."

These were just the things that Cole wanted to find out: Cortinas' secret camps in Texas and the river crossings he used. "All right, so I was wrong," he conceded. "It takes more planning than I figured. But I won't be running the show, just riding along with the rest of the *peons* you hire."

"You are a leader, not a follower. You had your own gang of thieves." Cortinas paused, then said, "By the way, what happened to them?"

Cole had never had a gang. He had always been a loner, almost constantly on the run, hunted by Davis' henchmen with a vengeance. Again, it was another man's crimes he had been blamed for. "Most of them got shot up in that last bank robbery. Someone in the gang must have blabbed. The army was waiting for us when we rode into town. What was left of the gang scattered and lit out on their own. I high-tailed it for the border. Didn't get there any too soon, either. Took a bullet in my hat. Made me madder than hell, too. I'm kinda fond of this hat."

Cortinas glanced up and saw the hole that Cole himself had put in his black hat. Then looking back over the gunfighter, he noted that the man was dressed entirely in black: black pants, black boots, black vest and shirt, even a black silk scarf that was knotted at his neck. The only break in the drab color was the silver dollars that were sewed to the man's hatband. "Do you always wear black?"

"Yeah."

"It is the color of death."

A one-sided smile came to Cole's sensuous lips and a gleam to his golden eyes that made him appear very sinister. "Yeah, I know," he drawled in a voice that throbbed with menacing undertones. A tiny tingle of fear ran up Cortinas' spine, taking him by surprise, for the bandit king was a fearless man. Once again, Cortinas' eyes swept over the tall, imposing frame of the outlaw. He was just the kind of man the Mexican recruited for his ranks: ruthless, cold-blooded, and lethal with a gun. But the Texan lacked the first and primary requirement, an ignorance and blind loyalty that would make him manageable. It was of the utmost importance that his men follow his orders without question. He was the leader, the only leader. Could he trust this *gringo* to keep his place?

Cole was aware of the speculative gleam that came into Cortinas' eyes and knew he was being judged.

"Well?" he asked, not wanting to the give the Mexican too much time to think it over. "What do you say? Will you hire me?"

"I have not decided yet. I do not know if I can trust you."

"Why? What are you afraid of? That I'll lure some of your men away from you and form a bandit ring of my own down here? No, Cortinas, I'm not that stupid. I know what happens to anyone who tries to compete with you. They find themselves at the end of a rope, or with a bullet through their heart. I know the lay of the land. It's either work for you, or not at all, and since honest labor isn't to my liking and I still have to eat, I'll play the game by your rules."

When Cortinas remained grimly silent, Cole said, "Look, I'm not a threat to you. I just want a job until things cool off up north. When that happens, I'm heading back, and since you and I don't deal in the same kind of stealing, we won't be in competition. You can have your cattle rustling. Personally, I can't stand the animals. They're dumb and clumsy and stink to high heaven. And driving them is too damn much work for a steady diet. Robbing stage coaches and banks is much easier."

A minute ticked by, then another, while Cortinas studied Cole thoughtfully. Then he said, "I will still think this over."

"What do you have to think over?" Cole objected.

"I told you. I do not trust you. I do not trust any *gringo*."

"But you hire them. I know that for a fact."

"*Sí,* outlaws running from the *gringo* law, like you. But I still do not trust them. And I trust you even less."

Cortinas turned to the bandit standing next to Cole and said in Spanish, "Take him to the storage shed and lock him in."

"Lock me in?" Cole asked in surprise. "But why?"

"Because I am not so sure you only came here looking for a job, that you are not here to spy on me. Until I decide what your intent really is and if I will hire you, I will keep you locked up."

"And how long will it take you to make up your mind?" Cole snapped, not liking the turn of events.

"You will know my decision by tomorrow morning."

The two bandits on each side of Cole took one of his arms and roughly shoved him towards the door. Cole wrestled himself free and turned to Cortinas, saying, "At least tell them to untie my hands. My wrists are rubbed raw."

"No, they will stay tied. That way it will not be so easy for you to escape."

"Why should I try to escape?" Cole asked, his anger rising. "Dammit, I told you I came here of my own free will, looking for a job."

"And my men claim you were snooping. Until I decide who to believe, you will stay tied."

As Cortinas motioned for his men to continue, Cole once again jerked his arms free and whirled around. "And what happens to me if you decide to believe them and not me?"

A smile crept over Cortinas' ruddy face that made

Cole's blood run cold before the bandit king calmly answered, "Then I will kill you. I cannot take the risk of letting any of my enemies learn the location of my headquarters. You, of all people, should know the importance of secrecy."

"All right," Cole conceded, taking another approach, "so I was looking around out of curiosity. But that doesn't mean I was spying on you or that I had any intention of telling anyone else what I saw or where your hideout is. For Christ's sake, I'm a wanted man myself. I'm not going to rat on you. Suppose I promise never to divulge anything I've seen down here to anyone."

"And why should I believe you?"

"Haven't you ever heard of honor among thieves?"

"*Sí*, there are some bandit *jefes* here in Mexico that believe in it. However, I do not. I believe it is what you *gringos* call a pile of . . ."

As Cortinas' voice trailed off and he stroked his graying beard thoughtfully, Cole prompted, "Shit?"

The bandit king's blue-green eyes lit up with recognition. "*Sí!* How could I forget? Your *gringo* word is so expressive, is it not?"

"Yeah," Cole answered, with no enthusiasm. "It sure as hell is."

A few moments later, Cole was shoved roughly into a small wooden shed that sat to one side of the courtyard. Stumbling over a small box on the dirt floor, he fell flat on his face on the ground and jarred his shoulder painfully. Then the door was slammed shut and darkness surrounded him. Hearing the padlock on the door being snapped shut,

Cole rolled to his back and struggled to sit up.

Totally disgusted and frustrated with the unexpected turn of events, he stared into the darkness and uttered the only word that could truly express his feelings.

"Shit!"

Three

Cole shifted his weight, trying to find a more restful position, but it was a wasted effort. He couldn't get comfortable leaning back against the wall of the shed with his hands tied behind his back. His fingers felt numb, and his shoulder, where he had hit it when he fell, was throbbing. To add to his misery, it felt as if his stomach was rubbing against his backbone from hunger, while his mouth felt like someone had shoved a wad of cotton into it. It seemed that at least Cortinas could have fed him or given him a drink of water. Even a condemned man deserved that much.

The thought reminded Cole of the fate he might be facing the next morning. But he'd had a long time to think things over, and he didn't really believe Cortinas would kill him. In the first place, the bandit king had no reason to be suspicious of him. Just looking around his ranch wasn't proof that Cole had been spying, nor had Cole offered any resistance when Cortinas' men had captured him, as a guilty man would have been prone to do. No, he had decided that Cortinas was just testing him. If he tried to escape, the chieftain would assume he was either guilty of deliberate spying or had bolted because he was frightened, and Cole reasoned if he remained calm and did nothing to try to secure his freedom, he would not only convince Cortinas of his innocence, but impress Cortinas with his coolness under fire, so to speak. Certainly, the *jefe* didn't want a man who panicked working for him. That kind of a man could ruin an entire raid if something unforeseen should unexpectedly appear. Besides, even if he managed to get out of the shed, Cole seriously doubted if he could get past the gate and those high walls that surrounded the *casa*. Surely Cortinas had posted sentries on those walls and had guards at every gate. What the hell! He might as well sit tight and hopefully call Cortinas' bluff.

Cole wondered what time it was. Well past midnight, he judged from the absence of the noises coming from the courtyard outside. Apparently, the *casa* had settled down for the night. Then hearing a slight sound at the door, he stiffened and listened closer. Someone was tampering with the lock. But who?

Before the thought had barely formed in his mind, Cole heard the click of the lock and the squeak of the hinges as the door was cautiously opened. He strained his eyes in the darkness, but all he could make out was a shadowy outline stepping into the hut and closing the door. Had Cortinas sent someone to slit his throat while he slept, Cole wondered, since the intruder was acting with such stealth. But why in the hell would Cortinas do that? It would be easier and simpler to just shoot him.

Then Cole caught a whiff of a sweet scent and knew who it was. He'd smelled that perfume that afternoon. What in the hell was Jenny doing here?

Before Cole could react to his startling discovery, Jenny whispered, "Hey, mister. Where are you?"

"What are you doing here?" Cole asked sharply.

"Sssh," Jenny cautioned. "Keep your voice down. Someone may hear you."

Leaning forward, Jenny groped in the darkness in the direction Cole's voice had come from, then stumbled over his long legs that were stretched out before him. She fell heavily on top of him, loudly slamming his shoulder against the wall of the shed before Cole slid to the ground on his back with Jenny laying full-length over him.

For a moment, both were perfectly still and listening intently for fear someone outside of the hut might have heard. Then Cole became aware of Jenny's sweet scent engulfing him, a scent that left his senses spinning. The realization that the smell came from the woman herself, and was no perfume, was even more unsettling, and the memory of her golden loveliness flashed through his brain. Fast on its heels, Cole became acutely conscious of Jenny sprawled on top of him. Her soft breasts pressed against his chest, and her every breath seemed to tease and tantalize him. And he knew from her warm breath fanning his face that her lips were just inches away from his. To his horror, he found his body responding to the feel of her womanly curves and his manhood stirring.

43

"Get off of me!" Cole demanded in a voice born of sheer mortification.

Jenny misinterpreted the panic she heard in Cole's voice for anger. "Well, you don't have to get so testy about it," she retorted, struggling to sit up and lift herself from where she was lying. "I can't help it if I tripped over you. It's dark as Hades in here. Besides, this position isn't exactly to my liking either. My God, you smell like something the cat dragged in. Haven't you ever heard of bathing?"

Jenny's remark about his odor didn't improve Cole's disposition in the least, particularly in view of her smelling so sweet and clean and arousing him against his will. As soon as she removed herself and sat up beside him, Cole struggled to a sitting position. Then, feeling Jenny's hands running down the length of his arms, he asked, "What in the hell are you doing?"

"I'm trying to find your hands. How can I untie them if I can't find them?"

While she had been talking, Jenny had scooted behind Cole and begun fumbling with the bonds around his wrists. Cole jerked his hands away and snapped, "Cut that out!"

"Why?" Jenny asked in astonishment.

"Because I don't want them untied."

"Are you crazy! How can you escape if I don't untie your hands? Why, you'd be as helpless as a baby."

"I don't want my hands untied because I don't want to escape," Cole ground out between clenched teeth.

"Don't want to escape?" Jenny asked in disbelief.

"Are you loony or something? Mister, don't you know who these men are? They're a bunch of bandits. They're dangerous!"

"I know who they are!" Cole answered in exasperation. "But I don't want to escape. I let them capture me on purpose."

"On purpose? Why did you do a crazy thing like that?"

"Because I want a job with Cortinas and that was the only way I figured I could get to him."

"You'd join up with a bunch of murdering rustlers?"

"Why not? I'm an outlaw myself. That's why I'm down here, looking for a job. Things got a little too hot for me back in Texas."

Cole couldn't see Jenny's reaction, but he could almost feel her shock. There was a long moment of silence. Now she hates me, and she'll beat it out of here so fast it will make my head spin, Cole thought, feeling a strange twinge of regret. But to his utter surprise, Jenny said, "It looks to me like you made a bad miscalculation, mister. You're still being held prisoner."

Jenny calling him "mister" grated on Cole's nerves. "The name is Cole Benteen, and I'm only being held prisoner until morning, just until Cortinas decides if he's going to hire me or not."

"And what makes you think he's going to say yes?"

"I'm too good with a gun to turn down," Cole answered with a matter-of-factness that convinced Jenny it must be true. "You see, he's only trying to see how far he can trust me, if I try to escape or not. And you've damned near ruined it with your butting in."

Jenny gasped in outrage, then said, "Well, that's a fine how-do-you-do. I risk my neck trying to help you out and all I get for thanks is your accusing me of butting in."

Cole realized she had taken a big risk and felt a twinge of guilt that quickly disappeared when he remembered how she was jeopardizing all of his carefully laid plans. "I didn't ask you to rescue me," Cole reminded her bluntly. "Besides, getting me out of this shed isn't rescuing me. I still can't escape. There's no way I can get past that gate out there."

"Sure you can."

"It's guarded. There are probably sentries posted all over the place."

"You're right. There are. But I happen to know the man who guards the back gate has a fondness for hard liquor. He takes a bottle of it with him every time it's his turn to stand guard. Oh, he doesn't get so drunk he passes out, but he does some heavy sleeping on the job. I've watched him from my window enough times. He's there tonight, and that's why I thought we could make our escape. It should be real easy to slip up on him and knock him out."

"We?" Cole asked in surprise.

"Of course, we! You wouldn't be so ungrateful as to leave me behind, not after I helped you escape, would you?"

Cole didn't honestly know if he would or

wouldn't, and it didn't matter. "But I'm not escaping," he pointed out.

"Yes, I know that now," Jenny answered tightly, wishing he'd stop reminding her of her mistake. It made her look foolish, and she didn't like that. How in the hell was she to know he had some crazy plans of his own?

"I'm curious about something," Cole said. "If you think it would be so easy to get past that guard, why haven't you tried to escape?"

"By myself, all alone?" Jenny asked in astonishment. "Are you loony? Why, I'd get lost out there! I'm a city girl. I need street signs to find my way around. Besides, even if I knew my way out of here, it wouldn't do me any good. The general's men would catch up with me in no time, with me on foot. And that's how I'd be. On foot. Like I said, I'm a city girl. I don't know the first thing about riding a horse. But I figured if I escaped with you, I could ride behind you and hang on."

Well at least she had enough sense to recognize her shortcomings and not to try to escape by herself, Cole thought grudgingly.

"Are you sure you won't change your mind?" Jenny asked hopefully.

"No, I'm staying, and I'd appreciate it if you'd get out of here before someone comes to check up on me." A sudden thought came to Cole. "By the way, how did you get your hands on the key to that lock?"

"I didn't. I picked it with my hairpin."

"Where did you learn that trick?"

"That's none of your business!"

47

Seeing Jenny's dim outline moving towards the door, he called out softly, "Wait!"

Jenny turned and said, "I thought you wanted me out of here."

"I do, but I have some questions I'd like answered first."

"Like what?"

"Like who are you?"

"Jenny Daniels."

"I find that hard to believe."

There was a long, pregnant silence before Jenny asked, "Why did you make a remark like that?"

"Because you don't seem at all like the Jenny Daniels Amos Wright described to me."

"You know Amos?" Jenny asked in surprise.

"Not personally, no. But I've seen him recently. He came to me and tried to hire me to rescue you, but I turned him down."

It took a moment for Jenny to recover from the unexpected news. "Why? Didn't he offer you enough money?"

"Oh, he offered me enough, I guess, but I had better things to do."

"Like join up with a bunch of low-down, murdering bandits?" Jenny asked.

Cole heard the contempt in Jenny's voice and felt like a first-class heel, but he couldn't possibly tell her his real purpose for being here. He didn't know if he could trust her, particularly in view of the fact that she obviously wasn't who Amos thought she was. "Rescuing you—which I'm still not convinced can be done—would be a onetime job. Hiring on with Cortinas could lead to big things for me. Besides, I'm not a nursemaid. I can't think of anything worse than trying to drag some fool female back to Texas through that desert out there."

"I'm not a fool female!" Jenny answered, feeling highly insulted.

"The hell you aren't! If you'd stayed on that steamer in Corpus, like you were supposed to, you wouldn't be in this mess. And your sneaking in here to rescue me wasn't very smart either. You could have gotten us both killed."

Cole's remark about her lack of intelligence infuriated Jenny. She had lived by her wits her entire life and thought she had done quite well, considering the circumstances she'd had to overcome. Then remembering something Cole had said, she asked, "Why did you say I didn't seem to be the same Jenny Daniels Amos described to you?"

"Because that Jenny Daniels is supposed to be a lady."

"And who says I'm not a lady?" Jenny asked hotly.

"I do," Cole answered calmly. "No lady shrieks at the top of her lungs like a fishwife, calls people ugly names, particularly a bastard, or picks locks. My guess is you're an impostor."

Jenny gasped, for Cole's guess was too close to the truth for comfort. True, she wasn't an impostor in the strictest sense. The name was really hers. But when she had presented herself to Amos Wright, she had been impersonating someone else, a woman who didn't really exist. But she'd be damned if she'd admit anything to the hateful outlaw. "I'm no such

49

thing," she denied adamantly. "Even a lady can become so frustrated that she can forget her manners, you know."

Cole laughed harshly. "And now you're a liar, too."

Jenny was furious. "Damn you! I don't have to stand here and let you, an outlaw—the scum of the earth—insult me. I'm glad you didn't take Amos up on his offer, and I'm glad you refused me. I wouldn't go anywhere with you . . . you . . ." Jenny tried, really tried not to say it, but her temper had gotten the best of her. ". . . You stinking bastard!"

With that, Jenny opened the door, stepped outside, and closed it. Just as she started to rush away she heard Cole call softly in an urgent voice, "For Christ's sake, don't forget to shut the lock."

Jenny was sorely tempted to do just that and let the rude, ungrateful gunslinger face the music when Cortinas found the shed unlocked the next morning. But to her credit, Jenny couldn't do that. She had done some pretty sneaky things in the past, but she had never endangered a man's life, not even one as low-down as she considered Cole. Quickly she snapped the heavy padlock closed, then turned and rushed away.

Inside the shed, Cole heard the distinct click of the lock and breathed a sigh of relief. Thank God she was gone, he thought, and thank God no one would know she had tried to help him escape. It had been a fool thing to do.

Cole leaned back against the wall and closed his eyes, hoping to get a few hours sleep before morning.

He tried to shake Jenny from his mind, but with her sweet scent still drifting in the air, it was impossible. He wondered who she really was. She obviously wasn't any high-class lady, nor was she the angel she appeared to be at first glance. He strongly suspected that the petite blond was a designing gold digger using her beauty and feminine charms to lure Wright into matrimony, and the unsuspecting bastard had offered a small fortune to have her returned to him. If the rancher knew the truth about her, he would probably drop her as fast as a hot poker. Or would he? Cole wondered. Jenny's temper and sharp tongue hadn't disenchanted Cortinas. The bandit king had admitted that it was Jenny's fiery disposition that had attracted him. But somehow, Cole felt such would not be the case with Wright, that the rancher wanted a woman who was not only beautiful but would be a social credit to him, and yet know how to stay in her place. In that, Cole was prone to agree with the carpetbagger. He wouldn't want a shrew for a wife either, or a busybody who couldn't mind her own business, no matter how beautiful and desirable she might be. The last thought startled Cole, but he found he couldn't retract it. It had been years since he had taken note of a woman or had one stir any emotion in him. He had thought himself immune to feminine charms in any form or manner, but he couldn't deny he was physically attracted to the little spitfire. Yes, as much as he hated to admit it, she was a woman who could heat any man's blood.

At the same time Cole was thinking of Jenny, she was pacing the floor of her bedroom, still fuming at his insults. It didn't matter that what he had called her was true. No, it was his snide tone of voice that angered her, a scorn she would have found hard to tolerate from anyone, much less the likes of him. All right, so she wasn't a true-blue lady, she thought. So what? It wasn't any of his business.

Jenny came to a sudden halt. Would he make it his business? she wondered with a deep frown. Would he tell Amos his suspicions and ruin everything for her? Damn! She'd kill him if he did, Jenny thought recklessly. She'd worked too long and too hard to get where she was. Marriage to a wealthy and influential man had been her lifetime goal.

Then, remembering the gunslinger had told her that he'd come here to get a job with the bandits, she realized there would be little likelihood of his and Amos's paths ever crossing again, no more so than there should be any reason for Amos to come face-to-face with Cortinas, which is why she had felt no need to pretend to be a high-class lady in front of the Mexican. Without a doubt the bandit and the rancher didn't travel in the same circles, despite the fact that Cortinas was apparently very wealthy. Nor was she worried that Amos might try to rescue her himself and thereby give Cortinas the opportunity to reveal her true colors. She knew Amos was a coward. She could read men like a book. But it didn't matter. Bravery wasn't one of her prerequisites for a husband. No, she assured herself, her secret was safe. Amos would never know the truth.

Jenny's thoughts lingered on the rancher. She wondered if he was still trying to hire someone to rescue her. If so, she fervently hoped Amos showed better judgment in choosing the next man than he had the last. Jenny would rather take her chances on escaping and finding her way back to Texas alone than have to be in the company of a low-down, crude gunslinger like the one down in the shed.

The insulting bastard! She hoped he rotted down there.

Four

Two months later, Jenny stood on the balcony beside her bedroom and gazed out. From her lofty viewpoint, she could see not only everything going on in the plaza below her, but over the high walls surrounding the *casa* to the squalid little village that sat beside the ranch headquarters. There, in the flimsy huts made of mud and mesquite limbs called *jacals,* the *vaqueros* and bandits who worked for Cortinas made their homes. The general had taken Jenny on a tour there one day, and what she had seen had depressed her and brought back painful memories. Entire families were crowded into tiny, one-room homes that had no furnishings other than a rickety table and chair or two, no beds, no curtains or shutters over the windows, no floor, not even a fireplace. The cooking was done over open fires in lean-tos made of dried corn stalks. The dreary homes smelled of mold, mingled with the odor of spicy food and unwashed bodies, the dust was so thick you could hardly breathe; the roofs had gaping holes in them; and the place was infested with rats,

54

spiders, and snakes that wandered in from the desert. Other than the latter, which was thankfully one horror Jenny had not had to contend with in the city, the place reminded her of her childhood home in the slums of New York City. The only difference was that there was more than ample sunshine here beneath the searing sun, while Jenny had lived in a dim, shadowy world where the only sky she could see was a thin strip of blue between the roofs of the tenement buildings.

Despite the fact that the village brought back painful memories, Jenny continued to gaze at it. She did so because it helped her firm the resolve she had made years ago while still a child, a promise to herself that somehow, some way, she would escape that dreary, hungry, cold world and never be poor again. Never! And Jenny had quickly discovered that for a woman born in poverty there was only one way to accomplish that. She couldn't "go west" to seek her fortune, like her brothers had slipped off and done. That would be much too dangerous for a lone woman. Nor had she any hopes of pulling herself out of the miserable morass she was in by working her way out. Even the men who shared her plight had little hope of that. No, the only way to escape was through marriage, marriage to a man of some means or, better yet, a man who was downright wealthy. Why should she settle for being comfortably well off, when she could have luxury? she had reasoned. Nature aided Jenny to some degree, in that she was unusually pretty and desirable, but it had been up to Jenny to put herself in a position where

55

she might meet such a man. That's why she had joined the theater. She knew actresses often drew wealthy admirers. But she wouldn't accept the position as their mistress, she had promised herself. That relationship lasted only as long as the woman's looks. No, it would be marriage, or nothing, and had it not been for Cortinas' interference, she could have realized her goal by now and been married to Amos. Damn the Mexican bastard! Jenny thought, slamming her fist against the wrought-iron rail she stood beside. Why, of all times, had he decided to make a visit to the border to check up on his rustlers the same day she was brought in? If he hadn't, he would have never spied her and gotten that ridiculous idea in his head that he wanted to marry her. Then she would have been released with the other hostages.

Every time Jenny thought about being freed she thought about Cole and cursed him for not being willing to help her. In her estimation, he had become lower than low. He had become slime. She knew he had been released. She had been watching when they had brought him from the shed the next morning and untied his hands. Apparently, Cortinas *had* been bluffing when he had threatened to kill the outlaw, because she had later seen Cole ride off with the bandits. Since then she had spied him several times in the distance, always driving in herds of stolen cattle with his new cohorts.

Jenny's active mind took another twist. She wondered if Amos had tried to hire anyone else to rescue her. Whenever she noticed a new face among Corti-

56

nas' men her hopes rose, but no one had made any move towards her, and Jenny was beginning to get desperate. Besides being bored to tears with nothing to do and no one but Cortinas to talk to, she was beginning to worry about how much longer she could hold the bandit king at bay. Lately, he had been insinuating that there were ways he could force her to marry him, and while he had behaved so far in an amazingly gentlemanly manner—other than one totally repugnant kiss he had bestowed on her—Jenny sensed his patience was beginning to wear thin. More and more she was entertaining ideas of trying to escape by herself, despite how risky it might be. She feared Cortinas' thin civilized veneer might break any minute and he might force himself on her.

"What are you thinking about so hard, *mi vita?* I have been standing here for a good five minutes and you have not even noticed me."

Jenny jumped at the sound of Cortinas' voice. She turned and saw him standing beside her on the balcony. "I was just . . . daydreaming."

"And can you find nothing better to do than daydream?"

"Like what? I can't talk to anyone. You're the only one that speaks English. At least daydreaming gives me something to do."

"You could read. There are books in the *sala.*"

"They're in Spanish!" Jenny reminded him bluntly. "Besides, even if they were in English, I don't read all that well."

Cortinas chuckled and said, "That is what I like about you. You are so honest. And now, I will be honest with you. I cannot read at all."

"Then why do you have all those books?"

"They impress others, and some day, perhaps I will learn. But I am not the one who is bored. You are. Do you like to sew? My sister passes many hours embroidering. She has made the most beautiful altar cloths."

Jenny could only stare at him, thinking the world had gone insane. He led a band of murdering thieves, while his sister sewed linens for the church?

"Well, do you?" Cortinas prompted.

"Do I what?"

"Do you embroider?"

"No, I never learned and, quite frankly, I don't care to. I'd much rather do something more active."

"Ah, *sí*, more active. Of course. A woman as spirited as you would not enjoy such sedate pursuits. It is a shame you cannot ride. There is nothing more in . . ." Cortinas' bushy eyebrows almost met as he strained to remember the rest of the word.

"Invigorating?" Jenny supplied.

"*Sí!* Riding is a delightful pastime, particularly in our beautiful country."

Jenny's gaze swept over the landscape beyond the walls. The only thing to be seen clear to the horizon was a desert dotted with cactus and stunted mesquite. And the fool Mexican thought that was beautiful? she thought in disgust. Why, it was that very desolate, inhospitable land that was keeping her from escaping. Then a sudden thought occurred to Jenny. If she knew how to ride, she just might be able to pull it off. Not only would she have an animal to bear the burden of crossing that desert, but surely it would have enough sense to find water. With transportation and water made available to her, Jenny's two biggest worries would be eliminated. Then all she would have to do would be point the horse north. Yes, by God, with a horse she could do it! Her lagging spirits soared.

Schooling herself not to reveal her excitement, Jenny said, "You're probably right, General. I probably would enjoy riding, if I knew how." Jenny paused, then pretending to have just thought of something, said, "Maybe you could teach me."

Cortinas scoffed and answered, "Not I, my beautiful *gringa*. But not because I am not an excellent horseman." He stuck out his barrel chest. "I am the best in Mexico! But teaching you to ride will take some time, and I am much too busy with managing my business. You know, I have not only this ranch to look after, but several others, also."

And all those raids across the border to plan, too, Jenny thought bitterly, her face registering her genuine disappointment.

Seeing her look, Cortinas said, "No, *mi vita,* do not despair. I will get one of my *vaqueros* to teach you. And you will be taught by the best," Cortinas added expansively. "No one in this entire world can ride as well as a Mexican. No one! It is in our blood." Noting the doubtful expression coming over Jenny's face, Cortinas made his own assumption and asked, "You do not believe me? You think I am just bragging for the sake of bragging?" Before Jenny could correct him, he continued, "No! I will show you just how well we Mexicans can ride. I will take you to the weekly races my men have every Sunday afternoon. Then you will see for yourself what superb horsemen we are."

"I wasn't questioning your men's skill," Jenny informed him, feeling irritated at his making assumptions about her thoughts. "I was doubting if I could learn to ride from someone who couldn't even speak English. How would I know what he was telling me, if I can't understand him?" Jenny paused, then questioned hopefully, "Unless you have someone in mind who can speak English?"

"No, I am afraid not," Cortinas answered, shaking his head. "Not at this ranch. On one of my ranches closer to the border, I have several men who can speak a few words of the *gringo* language, but not here."

Jenny's spirits sank to a new low and tears of frustration stung her eyes.

"Do not look so disappointed, *mi vita*. Perhaps I will think of a solution. In the meanwhile, I will still take you to the races tomorrow. That should relieve your boredom a little."

Jenny didn't think watching a bunch of men race their horses was going to make her feel any better. If anything it would be like rubbing salt in an open wound, only reminding her of inadequacies that were keeping her a prisoner here. "No, thank you. I think I'll just stay in my room and . . . rest."

The smile on Cortinas' face froze, and his blue-green eyes glittered like splintered ice. "You misunderstand, Jeanita," he said in a voice throbbing with menacing undertones. "This is not an invitation. It is a command! You *will* go to the races with me tomorrow."

More and more, Cortinas was revealing this side of himself to Jenny, the hard, dangerous side. That was why she was becoming so desperate to escape. Jenny was stubborn, but she wasn't foolish. She knew sometimes it was more prudent to back down in a confrontation, particularly if it was one where brute strength might come into play. However, Jenny was equally determined she wouldn't cower. "If you insist," she answered coldly.

"I do."

For a moment, the two stared at one another in a silent contest of wills, then, once more demonstrating his unsettling mercurial personality, Cortinas laughed softly and said, "Forgive me, *chiquita,* if I seemed a little overbearing. It is the Mexican in me. We men take great pride in being *macho,* in controlling our women. But it is only because we know what is best for them." He paused for a response, but Jenny knew she was being baited and remained silent.

Cortinas bowed slightly, then said, "Until tomorrow, then. *Buenas dias.*"

Jenny watched as Cortinas turned and walked down the balcony to the stairs at one end of the building, her blue eyes flashing fire. Control her? she thought in silent fury. No, hell would freeze over before any man did that, she vowed. And she was becoming very weary of Cortinas' silly cat and mouse games.

61

The next afternoon, Cortinas drove Jenny into the countryside where the races were to be held. His shiny black buggy was the same vehicle that he had used to transport her from the border, and the bandit king was very proud of it, not only because it was identical to the one the late President Juarez had owned, but it seemed there weren't too many buggies or private coaches in northern Mexico, even among the wealthy. Jenny would have been tempted to try to steal it for her escape if she'd had any idea of how to go about hitching the horses to it. Not only would it have made for more comfortable traveling, but Jenny would have dearly loved to deprive the general of his prized possession out of pure spite.

A crowd of Mexican spectators had already arrived at the open area where the event was to take place and were lined up on both sides of what Jenny assumed must be the racetrack. As Cortinas drove up to one side, the people standing there cleared the way for him to drive through. Jenny assumed he was going to drive to the other side, but to her surprise, he stopped midway in the track and handed her a leather pouch, saying, "While I drive up and down the course, you throw out the coins in this bag."

"Why?"

"Because in the last contest, after the ordinary races are finished, the riders will be using the money to exhibit their riding skills. Instead of who arrives at the finishing line first, the winner will be whoever can pick up the most coins while riding at full speed."

"Are you saying they reach down and pick up coins from the ground as they race by?"

"*Sí.*"

"Isn't that dangerous?"

"*Sí,* very dangerous, but that is what makes it so exciting. They are pitting their skills against death."

Jenny reached into the bag and pulled out a handful of coins. Peering down at the writing on one copper disk, she asked, "How much is a *centavo?*"

"It would be the same as a penny in your money."

"And you allow them to keep what they collect?" Jenny asked in a voice heavily tinged with sarcasm.

"Of course," Cortinas answered magnanimously.

Cheapskate, Jenny thought, knowing there couldn't be but a few dollars worth of coins in the sack.

After Jenny had thrown out the *centavos,* Cortinas drove the buggy back to the sidelines, and from there, they watched the races. The Mexicans apparently took their racing very seriously, urging their choice of rider on with enthusiasm and cheering loudly when the winner crossed the finish line. When Jenny asked Cortinas what the winner received for his efforts, Cortinas informed her that the victory itself was enough reward, only confirming her estimation of his tight-fistedness.

Then came the time for the final event, and as the riders positioned their mounts at the starting line, Jenny noticed a slouched hat that stood out in the sea of broadrimmed *sombreros* the others were wearing. Instinctively, she knew who that hat belonged to. Cole. "What's *he* doing here?" she asked, his unexpected appearance triggering her anger at him.

"Who?" Cortinas asked.

"*Him!*" Jenny answered, nodding at the riders.

"Are you talking about the *Tejano?*"

"Well, that depends. What's a *Tejano?*" Jenny asked, thinking if it meant "low-life" it was totally appropriate, for she had noted the contempt in Cortinas' voice when he had said the word.

"A Texan."

"Well, I don't know if he's a Texan or not," Jenny answered. "Nor could I care less," she added, her blue eyes spitting sparks. "But I do know he's not one of your cowboys, so he shouldn't be here."

"He can participate. Any of my men can. And I will enjoy seeing him make a fool of himself. No *Tejano* can ride as well as a Mexican." Cortinas peered closely at Jenny, then asked, "Do you know that man?"

Jenny realized she had made the bandit suspicious. "No, of course not! The only time I've ever laid eyes on him was that day in your hallway."

"You seem to have a intense dislike for him. How can that be, if you do not know him?"

"I don't have to know someone personally to know they're nothing but low-down slime. I can tell by just looking at them." Jenny met Cortinas' gaze evenly. "I happen to be an excellent judge of character, particularly men's character."

Jenny realized her claim might make Cortinas think she was a "loose woman," but she couldn't care

64

less what his opinion of her was. In fact, she'd be more than willing to pretend to be just that, if she thought it would it cool his desire for marriage. But Cortinas wasn't in the least repulsed. He had already decided that Jenny was a "worldly" woman, and that did nothing to detract from her beauty and the feisty charm that the Mexican found so intriguing.

"You are right, of course," he answered. "The *Tejano* is the lowest of low. He was one of the worst outlaws in Texas. Which is why he is so valuable to me."

Jenny wasn't surprised at Cortinas' admission. From the very beginning, the general had not denied that he was a thief.

"Oh, I'll admit he is not very good at driving cattle," Cortinas continued. "But no one is faster and more lethal with a gun. It is said he has killed over twenty men, and not all were fair fights."

Jenny frowned. Cole had admitted he was an outlaw, and she had sensed an aura of danger about him, but she had never pegged him as a cold-blooded murderer. The image still didn't fit, and she was, in reality, a good judge of character.

Jenny's thoughts were interrupted by the sound of a gun being fired to signal the beginning of the race. She turned her attention to the score of men riding like demons out of hell, the *sombreros* tied around their necks flapping wildly in the air behind them and their horses' manes and tails flying. Then her eyes locked on Cole, the sunlight picking up the reddish highlights of his hair as the wind whipped it around his handsome face. From what she could tell, he was just as good a rider as any of the others. Then, as he leaned down from the saddle, his head perilously close to both the ground and the hooves of the horses running beside him, she sucked in her breath. She watched as he snatched up several coins, seemingly from right between the horses' pounding feet, then gasped in fear when he flipped over his mount's back to lean far over on the opposite side to collect a few *centavos* half-buried in the sand there, over and over like an acrobat, until she lost sight of him in the crowd of riders.

The spectators screamed encouragement as the riders swooped down for the coins while traveling at a breakneck speed and careening around clumps of cactus, then went wild when the group of horsemen bunched together and the contestants shoved and kicked at those riding next to them, then slammed their mounts into the other men's, trying their damnedest to unseat their neighbor. A man fell to the ground, causing a horse racing behind him to stumble and fall, sending his rider flying through the air, and until the swirling dust had cleared, Jenny couldn't tell if the riders had been injured by the flying hooves. It turned out that, miraculously, they hadn't, but Jenny thought risking life and limb for a few coins was nothing but pure insanity.

The air vibrated with the sound of the crowd's cheers and the pounding hoofs. Then suddenly it was over, and the crowd waited anxiously while the coins were counted. Because of the thick dust cloud that hovered over the racetrack, Jenny couldn't tell who the man was who mounted and rode his horse back down the track. She knew he must be the victor, but the line of spectators he passed as he rode towards her was strangely silent. Then as the grimy rider, looking very pleased with himself, cleared the dust cloud, Jenny knew why the Mexicans were showing no elation. The winner was Cole, and quite obviously, the outsider was not supposed to have won. Despite her anger at the gunfighter, Jenny felt a little thrill at his winning.

"The bastard!", Cortinas grumbled, scowling deeply. "Where in the hell did he learn to ride like that?"

Wisely, Jenny held her tongue and hid her secret approval, schooling herself to scowl just as deeply as Cortinas. Then, as Cole turned his horse and started to ride away, Cortinas' brow furrowed in speculation. After a quick glance at Jenny's frown, he stood and called out, *"Tejano! Alto!"*

Cole pivoted his horse and brought it to a halt. "Are You talking to me, Cortinas?" he called back.

"Sí. Come here."

Cole leisurely walked his horse back across the race track, ignoring the murderous looks being given to him by the other contestants as they rode past him. Stopping next to the buggy, he didn't even so much as acknowledge Jenny's presence, something that both Jenny and Cortinas noted, and asked, "What do you want?"

Everything about the Texan spoke of insolence to Cortinas and grated on his nerves. "Where did you learn to ride like that?"

Cole knew what the Mexicans' opinion of Texan

horsemanship was. The men he had been riding with had been rubbing his nose in claims of their superiority in that area for weeks. Which was why he had joined in the race. He'd had a belly full of their bragging and wanted to prove them wrong. "Oh, didn't I tell you? I'm really a Comanche in disguise."

Cortinas stiffened. He knew he was being baited. If there was anyone the Mexicans hated worse than their old enemies, the Texans, it was the Comanches, and if anyone was a superior horseman, it was those savage lords of the plains. "Do not be insolent!" Cortinas responded curtly. "Just answer me."

Cole knew he didn't dare tell the truth, that he had hung around the Texas Rangers stationed at Brownsville when he was boy, and that they, too, played that particular racing game. He shrugged his broad shoulders, then answered, "What the hell difference does it make where I learned? I just learned, that's all."

Cortinas gave him a long, penetrating look, then said, "I have another job for you, other than the one you have been doing. You will teach the *señorita*, here, how to ride."

Cole had only one more raid to make before he would complete his mission in Mexico, and now Jenny was interfering again. He sliced her a resentful glance, then asked, "Why me?"

"Because you speak English."

"Hell, no! I didn't hire on to play nursemaid to some sniveling female. Find someone else!"

"There is no one else, and if you want to continue to work for me, you will do what I say."

Cole's referring to Jenny as a sniveling female only added fuel to her anger. Before Cole could respond to Cortinas' ultimatum, Jenny interjected, "No, General! I'd rather die of boredom than take lessons from this rude, arrogant brute!"

"That suits me just fine!" Cole answered. "Now I can get back to what I was hired to do."

But before Cole could turn his horse, Cortinas said, "I'm afraid not. You will do as I said, or leave Mexico." Then before Jenny could speak, he turned to her and said, "I agree with you, Jeanita. He is rude and arrogant. But the fact remains that he is a good horseman and the only one who speaks English. And you *did* say you would like to learn."

"But . . ."

"No, Jeanita," Cortinas interjected in a tone of voice that brooked no interference. "The matter is settled. *Señor. . . .*" He hesitated, then remembering Cole's name, said, *"Señor* Benteen will teach you. It is not necessary for you two to like each other." In truth, Cortinas preferred that the two dislike one another. That way there was less danger of them forming any alliance that might threaten his plans for Jenny.

"I thought you said you didn't trust me," Cole reminded Cortinas, taking another track.

"I don't, and certainly not with the woman who will become my wife. For that reason, one of my most trusted *vaqueros* will always accompany you and keep watch so that you will not be tempted to endanger either her life, or her virtue!"

Cortinas inferring that he might force himself on

69

Jenny infuriated Cole, then as a sudden inspiration came to him, he beamed and said, "I think you're forgetting something. I don't know a damn thing about riding sidesaddle."

"Nor do I even own one of the silly things," Cortinas answered smoothly. "No, Jeanita will learn to ride as a true Mexican woman does, astride."

Astride a burro, you mean, Cole thought angrily, for he had never seen any Mexican woman of quality ride in that degrading position. But Cole knew he had no choice, not if he had any hopes of making one more raid and collecting all of the information he needed. Cortinas had effectively countered every argument he set forward. But how long was this foolishness going to delay his mission? he wondered. He sent Jenny a heated glance, then asked, "Just how proficient do you expect her to become?"

Assuming Cole was anxious to get back to rustling because he'd be missing out on his share of the loot, Cortinas said, "Do not fret, *señor*. This should not take but a few days. Just teach her the rudiments of riding. I do not expect you to make her an expert horsewoman. We both know that takes years of practice."

Cortinas picked up the reins and started turning the buggy. "You can begin the first thing tomorrow morning, while it is still cool. Jeanita is not accustomed to our heat, you know. Come to the *casa* this evening, and I will give you further instructions."

As they drove off, Jenny was aware of Cole glaring at her back. Once again, she started to object, despite Cortinas' strong dictate. Then she remembered the reason she wanted to learn and held her tongue. No, she decided, she would just have to tolerate the hateful Texan. That was the price she would have to pay for her freedom.

the reason she wanted to look pretty, and that her ought to like her looked, she would just have her to look at her, that was it, might also and have to pay for her beauty...

Five

Jenny was not at all happy when she was awakened early the next morning. Having worked far into the evening hours while she was an actress, she had become accustomed to sleeping late. She grumbled as she rose from the bed, then scowled even deeper as she donned the riding apparel Cortinas had sent her the night before to spare her pretty clothing. True, the simple *camisa* and long full skirt were much more practical for horseback riding than one of her expensive dresses, but having been procured from one of the servants, they were worn and faded. They certainly weren't garments that would enhance her beauty, and Jenny would have liked to look pretty that morning.

There was a reason why Jenny wanted to look pretty, a reason that irked her to no end. As much as she had tried to deny it to herself, she wanted to look particularly nice for Cole. For some ungodly reason, she had this strange urge to impress the rugged Texan, which puzzled her. The only men she usually

72

bothered to try to attract were wealthy gentlemen, and he was nothing but a low-down outlaw, rude, arrogant, unkempt, and undoubtedly as poor as a church mouse. The only reason she could fathom for wanting to attract him was so that she could have the pleasure of scorning him. Yes, that had to be it, she decided. She only wanted to insult him back, give the crude gunslinger a taste of his own nasty medicine.

Feeling relieved that she had found a logical reason for her peculiar feelings, Jenny quickly finished dressing, hurriedly ate the breakfast the maid had brought her on a tray, and walked out on the balcony. In the courtyard below, she saw Cole standing beside his horse and another reddish-colored one she assumed must be the animal she was going to ride. Then, noticing the Texan fidgeting impatiently, she hurried to the stairs at the end of the balcony.

Cole wasn't in a very good mood himself that morning. He still resented being forced into the position he found himself in and blamed Jenny. Then, seeing her walking across the courtyard towards him, his scowl deepened. Dressed in the simple Mexican clothing, with her long golden hair tied at the back of her neck with a ribbon, she didn't look at all like the lady of quality she usually did, for Cole had seen her standing on the balcony on several occasions when he had ridden in from a raid. He couldn't help but notice. Her glorious hair had shone like a beacon in the sunlight, and he had always thought, albeit grudgingly, that she looked regal and beautiful in her elegant dresses with their newly-fashionable bustles. But the Jenny he saw today had a much more disturbing effect on him. The simple clothing did nothing to detract from the woman herself, and he was acutely conscious of the graceful sway of her hips, a totally natural movement that seemed incredibly seductive and only served to draw attention to the rest of her curvaceous body.

Jenny was aware of Cole glowering at her. Any desire to please him disappeared like a puff of smoke to be replaced with renewed anger at his behavior towards her. As soon as she stepped up to him, she said, "Don't scowl at me like that! This wasn't my idea."

Her blue eyes flashing and her cheeks flushed with anger made Jenny look all the more desirable. Cole fought back a wave of pure lust, the unwanted emotion not improving his disposition in the least, and answered sourly, "Wasn't it? I thought you wanted to learn to ride."

"I do, but not from *you*. In case you're too dim-witted to have noticed, I don't like you."

Cole didn't like being insulted, and those who knew him well took care not to make that mistake. His eyes glittered dangerously, and a muscle in his jaw twitched before he brought his ire under control. "Good! That makes our feelings mutual."

For a moment the two glared at one another, then as a sudden thought occurred to Cole his dark eyes narrowed suspiciously. "Why all of the sudden interest in leaning to ride? You're not thinking of trying to escape by yourself, are you?"

Jenny didn't dare admit to the truth, for fear Cole

would tell Cortinas her plans. Undoubtedly, the bastard would do anything to get out of having to teach her. "Of course not!" she responded with an indignant toss of her golden head. "I told you, I'd get lost out there in that desert, and I'm too young to die. No, I'm just bored, that's all. Totally, utterly bored. Why, there isn't a soul to talk to, except Cortinas, and he's gone a good deal of the time. Not that I enjoy his company, of course. I've never met a more irritating egotist. But I *am* bored. I thought riding might occupy my time, since it appears I'm never going to be rescued," she added bitterly.

Cole felt a twinge of guilt at the last, then firmly reminded himself that any attempt to rescue Jenny would be pure suicide. And he imagined she *was* getting bored, confined to the *casa*. But dammit, he didn't like having his plans put on hold because of it. "Well, let's get on with it, then," he growled. "The sooner we finish this foolishness, the better. I've got more important things to do."

Cole's abruptness irritated Jenny all the more. "Of course you do. What could be more important than rustling cattle?" Jenny responded sarcastically.

Cole sliced Jenny a look so furious it made a shiver of fear run up her spine, then turned, grabbed the bay's reins and brought the animal forward. "This is your horse, a gift from Cortinas, I understand."

"Yes, he said something about buying me a horse," Jenny remarked, looking up at the animal apprehensively. The bay seemed awfully big and menacing, and she had never felt comfortable

75

around the animals since a dray horse had bitten her when she was young. It had been a very deep and painful wound, and she still carried the scar on her shoulder. "He's awfully tall, isn't he?" she commented, beginning to have second thoughts about learning to ride.

"It's not a he," Cole informed her. "She's a mare."

"Well, how would I know that?" Jenny answered sharply, hating to be made to look a fool. "I told you, I'm a city girl."

"There are ways of telling," Cole answered dryly.

Jenny glanced at Cole's horse and knew without a doubt that the animal was a stallion. A flush rose on her face, a spontaneous reaction that Cole didn't miss and puzzled him. Perhaps she wasn't quite the woman of the world he had pegged her for, he mused.

Turning his attention back to the mare, he said, "She's a fine piece of horseflesh, and I imagine Cortinas paid a pretty penny for her."

"If he even bought her," Jenny answered, remembering how stingy Cortinas had appeared the day before. "More than likely, she's stolen."

"Not from Texas," Cole answered, "although his men have been known to take horses along with the cattle every now and then. And I don't think Cortinas would allow his men to steal a Mexican horse and risk getting the *federales* after him. He's too smart to foul his own lair that way. No, I'd wager he bought her somewhere here in Mexico."

"But how can you tell she's a Mexican horse?"

"She's not branded. Both Texan and New Mexican

ranchers are branding everything nowadays." Cole would have liked to have gotten right down to the basics, but he knew if Jenny got injured in any way, Cortinas would have his hide. He took Jenny's arm and brought her closer to the mare, saying, "Since you're not used to horses, it might be a good idea for you and her to get acquainted before you mount. She's well-mannered enough, but it might make you feel more comfortable."

"How do you go about getting acquainted with a horse?" Jenny asked in puzzlement.

"The same as any animal. Pet her. Talk to her. Let her know you like her."

Jenny didn't like the horse. She was terrified of her. Carefully, very carefully, she reached out and stroked the animal's sleek neck, all too aware of the mare watching her from the corner of her eye. "Hello . . ." Jenny looked over her shoulder and asked, "What's her name?"

Cole shrugged, drawing Jenny's attention to his unusually broad shoulders, then answered, "I don't know. No one mentioned it. Hell, she's your horse. Name her yourself."

Jenny had never had a pet. Her family had been too poor. Oh, there had been plenty of cats in the neighborhood, drawn by the heavy population of mice and rats, but they really didn't belong to anyone. Secretly, she had always longed for a pet, something that she could call her own, and she had always thought if she had one she'd call it Prince or Princess, depending upon the gender. She turned back and stroked the mare's neck gently, saying,

"Hello, Princess. I'm glad to meet you. My name is Jenny."

Cole rolled his eyes in his head at Jenny speaking so formally to the animal. And he hadn't expected her to give the horse such a fanciful name. It seemed so childlike. Again, not at all what he would have expected from a worldly woman. "Scratch the back of her ears," he instructed Jenny. "All horses like that."

Jenny hesitated. The ears seemed terribly close to the animal's mouth. She jumped when Cole took one hand and placed it over the mare's ear.

"Christ, you're skittish," Cole commented in disgust. "Go ahead. Scratch her ear," he prodded.

Jenny's heart thudded in her chest from fear, but she complied. She'd heard the scorn in the Texan's voice when he had called her skittish. She was amazed at how soft the animal's ear felt, and just as Cole had predicted, the mare apparently loved it. Princess bent her head, pressing her ear into the palm of Jenny's hand in a silent appeal for more.

Jenny was just getting into really scratching the mare's ears when the bay suddenly thrust its head forward. Jenny cried out and jumped back, making the animal shy away.

"What in the hell is wrong with you?" Cole asked, catching the horse's cheek strap before she could rear. "You scared her."

"I scared *her?*" Jenny asked in disbelief. "What about me? Why, she tried to bite me!"

"Where did you get a fool idea like that? She was going to nuzzle you. That's how horses show affection."

78

"Are you sure?"

"Of course, I'm sure. Mules are bad about biting, but not horses. Only really mean horses bite, and this mare hasn't got a mean bone in her body. Now scratch her ears again and make up with her."

Jenny was still leery, and her heart was still racing from the fright she'd had. She decided not to risk it, saying, "No, I've changed my mind. I don't want to learn how to ride. Let's just forget it."

As she turned to walk away, Cole caught her arm and swung her back around. "Like hell we will! I'll be damned if I'll be a slave to your whims. First you do, then you don't. No, you've ruined my day, and by God, you're going to learn." Pulling the mare's head right up to Jenny's face, he commanded, "Now, scratch her ears."

There was a note of finality in Cole's voice that told Jenny he'd brook no further argument. It took all of her courage to obey. Her hand shook as she lifted it, but thankfully the mare didn't make any overt move, for she was just as wary of Jenny as Jenny was of her. It took almost ten minutes of petting and crooning to regain the animal's trust. The second time Princess tried to nuzzle Jenny, Jenny forced herself to stand still, a look of perfect horror on her face. Then feeling the softness of the animal's muzzle as the mare rubbed it on her neck, she laughed in a mixture of relief and amazement, then said, "Oh, that tickles."

The sound of Jenny laughing seemed to egg Princess on. The mare nickered and nuzzled the other side of Jenny's neck, and again, Jenny laughed.

Watching, Cole felt a little glimmer of warmth come alive within him. It seemed it had been an eternity since he had enjoyed something so spontaneous and natural as these two.

"She likes me! She really likes me!" Jenny said, totally forgetting her animosity towards Cole and turning to him with her eyes sparkling with pleasure.

Cole couldn't help himself. Her happiness was contagious. "Yes, I believe she does," he answered with a smile.

Even with the heavy shadow of a beard and his scowl, Cole had been a very attractive man, but with the smile on his face, he was devilishly handsome. Jenny's breath caught, and her heart raced with a different kind of excitement. She didn't even realize she had been staring at him until she heard Cole saying, "Well, I guess that's enough getting acquainted. Why don't you try to mount her now?"

Jenny looked around her and became aware of everyone in the courtyard watching them. She was used to performing before an audience, but not making a spectacle of herself. "Here? In front of everyone?"

"Why not?"

"Because I don't know how to get on a horse. I might make a fool of myself."

Cole admitted that was a possibility. The first time he had tried to mount a horse, he had fallen flat on his rear. But then he'd only been three years old. However, mounting in a skirt was going to be awkward enough without everyone gaping at her and making Jenny nervous. "All right. Let's go beyond the walls."

As they led their horses from the courtyard and out into the desert, Jenny noticed a paunchy man leading a horse following them. Seeing her glancing over her shoulder, Cole said, "That's Carlos, the man Cortinas sent to keep an eye on us."

With his *sombrero* pulled down low over his face, Jenny couldn't tell if the man was young or old, but she could feel his dark, piercing eyes on them and knew everything they did down to the smallest detail would be reported back to Cortinas. Suddenly, she highly resented his spying on them. She would have liked to be alone with the tall Texan. The aura of danger that hung over him excited her, and his utter masculinity appealed to something primitive in her. "Do you suppose he understands English?"

"Why?"

"I just don't like the idea of him eavesdropping on us. It's bad enough he's watching us like a hawk."

"Yeah, I don't like the idea of him tagging along either." But maybe it wasn't such a bad idea after all, Cole admitted silently. He was finding the little spitfire walking beside him more and more appealing, and any involvement with her could be very dangerous for him. He didn't doubt for one minute that Cortinas would kill him if he made any advances. Cortinas was a man who protected what he considered his with a vengeance. "But I don't think you have to worry about him understanding English. I was curious myself. I called him a coward and a woman right to his face, and he didn't even blink his eyes."

"Those were the two worst insults you could think of?" Jenny asked, feeling insulted herself.

"For a Mexican man, yes. They put great stock in their bravery and their masculinity." He gave her a meaningful glance and added, "It's a much worse insult than calling them a bastard."

If Cole was trying to shame Jenny for her use of foul language, she refused to rise to the bait. "Oh? That's interesting. I'll have to remember that."

When Cole had deemed them far enough away to be out of the servants' sight, he stopped, looked down at Jenny's hemline, and asked, "What are you wearing under that skirt?"

Jenny was completely taken aback. She was wearing her drawers, but that was none of the Texan's business. She drew up to her full height of five-foot-one and answered coldly, "That, sir, is none of your business."

Cole shook his head and said in exasperation, "I'm talking about your feet. I can't tell if you're wearing shoes or Mexican sandals."

"Oh," Jenny answered lamely, feeling very foolish. She stuck one foot out, saying, "I'm wearing my traveling shoes, since they're my most substantial, and I don't have any boots."

"Good," Cole answered, once again impressed with her good sense. "They should give some protection to your ankles, and the soles aren't as likely to slip on the stirrup as those flimsy sandals." He pulled her to the side of the horse and said, "Now, let's get you mounted. Grab hold of this horn," he placed his hand on the handle-like protrusion at the front of the saddle, "with your left hand and put your left foot in the stirrup, then as you pull yourself up, swing your right leg out and over."

"What if Princess moves when I try to get on?" Jenny asked nervously.

"She won't. She's as well-trained as she is well-mannered."

Jenny had to stand on her tiptoes to reach the horn. Then swallowing hard, she placed her foot in the stirrup. The top of the saddle looked a long way up.

"What are you waiting for?" Cole asked impatiently.

"Just wait a minute! I'm going to do it!"

As Jenny lifted herself, Cole decided to help by giving her a little boost. His hand barely cupped her bottom before she flew through the air, then swung her leg across the back of the horse as if she had been doing it her entire life.

Sitting in the saddle, Jenny glared down at him, then asked indignantly, "Just what to you think you were doing? How dare you fondle me!"

"I wasn't fondling you!" Cole answered in disgust. "I was trying to give you a boost. But you didn't need any help. You did it yourself."

Jenny hated men to pat or fondle her behind, not only because they were taking intimacies they had no right to, but because it seemed so sneaky. She had been so furious at Cole that she hadn't even realized she was actually sitting on the saddle. She looked

83

down, then around her in surprise. Then, even more surprising, she felt no fear. If anything, the height was exhilarating. Not even when she had been on stage, which sat considerably above the audience, or Cortinas' balcony had she had this feeling that she had command of everything she surveyed, and never had she been able to see so far in every direction. With the view totally unobstructed all around her, she thought she could see to the ends of the earth, the wide expanse of the desert awesome in its openness. For the first time, she realized it had a stark beauty of its own.

"The stirrups are too long," Cole said, breaking into Jenny's preoccupation with the scenery. "They need to be adjusted to fit your legs."

Jenny looked down and saw what he said was true. "Am I supposed to do that, or are you?"

"I'll do it. I just wanted to warn you if I happen to touch your legs, don't think I'm fondling you and get upset again. Remember Carlos is watching. We don't want him thinking there's something going on that isn't. I'd prefer to live a little longer."

Jenny frowned. "Do you think Cortinas would actually do you harm if he thought you were making a pass at me?"

"There is no doubt in my mind that he'd hang me from the nearest tree, and probably draw me, too."

"What do you mean, draw you?"

"Disembowel me. Haven't you ever heard of drawn and quartered?"

Jenny shivered. "People don't do those barbaric things anymore."

"They do here in Mexico."

Jenny was horrified, and all the more determined to escape. Then, as Cole's hands briefly brushed the bare skin exposed between the top of her high shoe and the hemline of her skirt as he adjusted the stirrups, she felt a thrill course up her leg and wondered what those long, slender fingers of his would feel like stroking and caressing the rest of her body. For Jenny, it was a shocking thought. She was never given to sexual fantasies. If anything, she found the entire sexual scenario, from kissing and fondling on, quite disgusting. Necessary perhaps, but disgusting.

When Cole had finished adjusting Jenny's stirrups, he handed her the mare's reins and said, "You might as well hold these while I lead your horse around a bit. After you've gotten used to the feel of the saddle, I'll teach you how to use them."

Jenny found she didn't mind the sway of the saddle in the least as Cole led the mare round and round in a wide circle. Not even the feel of the hot sun beating down on her bothered her. Her full attention was on, not the horse, but the man holding its cheek strap. At first it was his broad shoulders and back that drew her attention, the powerful muscles there straining at the material of his dark shirt. Then, drawn by the rhythmic slap of his gun against his thigh, her eyes dropped. She was mesmerized by his graceful walk and the sight of his tight buttocks contracting and relaxing in his snug pants at every step he took. She had never been aware of that part of a man's body, had never dreamed that it could have a sexual appeal. But then, she had never paid particular attention to any man's body before. It had always been the thickness of their pocketbooks that had attracted her.

"Alto!"

The loud command made Jenny jump. Then as Cole turned to see what Carlos wanted, Jenny blushed beet-red, afraid he might guess what she had been staring at so brazenly.

"He says it's time to go in," Cole explained after the Mexican had rattled off something. "It's getting too hot out here for you."

"But we haven't been out here but an hour or so. I'm not hot." Then realizing the reason she didn't want to go in was because she wanted to feast on the sight of Cole's muscular body a little longer, she flushed again.

"No, he's right. Your face is a little red. An hour is long enough to get burned in this sun, if you're not used to it."

"But . . ." Jenny's voice trailed off. She knew she couldn't object. Then Cole might ask why her face was so red, if she wasn't getting sunburned. "Okay," she agreed reluctantly.

Cole led the mare back to the gate of the ranch headquarters and helped her dismount. Jenny was very aware of his hand supporting her arm as she did so. "When will the next lesson be?" she asked when she had her feet squarely on the ground.

Cole frowned. They really hadn't accomplished much. "Tomorrow morning, I guess. But why don't you wear a hat of some kind. Then, maybe we could make some real progress. At this rate, teaching you to ride could take forever."

As Cole walked away, leading the mare and his horse behind him, Jenny watched bleakly. He didn't like her any better than he ever did, she thought. He couldn't wait to finish the lessons and get away from her. And what a fool she was making of herself, mooning over him like some silly, feather-brained female. She had better sense than that. What in the devil had gotten into her, anyway? She didn't need the Texan, except to teach her how to ride. Nothing else. Why should she care whether he liked her or not? To hell with him!

With that, Jenny turned and walked into the courtyard.

Six

Despite her vow, Jenny was up bright and early the next morning of her own accord and anxious for the riding lessons to begin. Typical of her nature, she still refused to admit that she was attracted to Cole. Such an admission would have been downright demeaning to her female ego, and Jenny had depended on her self-esteem, bolstered by a stubborn tenacity, to see her through life's hard times for a long while. Instead, she reasoned her anticipation had nothing to do with the rugged Texan but was only because the sooner she learned to ride, the sooner she could accomplish her escape.

Seeing Jenny coming across the courtyard a little later that morning, Cole looked at the straw *sombrero* on her head in surprise. When he had told her to wear a hat, he had expected her to show up with some flippant female head covering that would have given her little, if any protection at all, and certainly not a man's hat. Again she was showing her no-nonsense side, a side he still found difficult equating with her delicate appearance. He had never known a woman who looked so tiny and sweet, so totally helpless, to behave so self-sufficiently and so sensibly. Oh, there were independent women in the west: dance hall girls, ladies of the evening, widows who had taken over their husband's businesses, even a few women ranchers. The better part were hardened and coarse, and none Cole had seen had that delicate, angel-like appearance that Jenny possessed. Her looking one way and behaving another was unsettling to Cole, particularly in view of his inbred Southern beliefs of what a woman should be. Secretly, he wanted Jenny to be the sweet, defenseless woman Amos had believed her to be. That was the kind of woman that he could relate to, the kind of woman that men like him fell for. Then he wouldn't be so puzzled at why he was so attracted to her.

Jenny was aware of Cole staring at her hat as she walked across the courtyard and knew she must look silly. It was a role she hated, but she was determined she wouldn't let the Texan know. As soon as she stepped up to him, she snapped, "Stop staring! I know the hat looks ridiculous with my dress and all, but it *will* keep the sun off my face."

Cole noted the defensive tone in Jenny's voice and knew she had taken offense at his staring so hard. Not wanting her to know that it had been her, and not the hat, that he had been so engrossed with, he shrugged and said, "I wasn't staring. I was just wondering where you got it."

"I asked my maid through sign language to get me a *sombrero*. I know at least that much Spanish. I thought she would bring me a felt one, though, like what Carlos wears."

"Apparently her husband, or whoever she borrowed it from, isn't a *vaquero,* but just a *peon,* another servant."

"There's a difference?"

"There certainly is. Not only is a *vaquero* paid much better wages so that he can afford a felt hat, but he is also much higher on the social scale. Mexicans are very class-conscious."

So are Americans, Jenny thought bitterly. The more money a man had, the higher his position in society, and that was exactly why she was going to marry a wealthy man. She was just as tired of being looked down on as she was tired of being hungry.

Being reminded of her goal helped Jenny keep her mind focused on her lessons, and not Cole. That day, he taught her the use of the reins, and for well over an hour she practiced stopping, turning, and walking Princess. Then, mounted beside her, Cole coached her through a trot and then a canter, but before they could progress to a full gallop, Carlos once again called a stop, and motioned for them to return to the *casa.*

Jenny had actually been enjoying her lessons. Much to her surprise, she had discovered that riding was fun. "Why do we have to stop?" she asked Cole irritably. "I'm not getting sunburned. Not with this hat on."

"No, but it's hot as hell out here," Cole pointed out, "and you're still not accustomed to this climate. You could have a heat stroke. Besides, you've been in that saddle for several hours. You may not realize it now, but you're going to be sore. You're not accustomed to riding, either."

Cole's pointing it out made Jenny realize that her pelvis did feel achy and the insides of her thighs were burning a little. That, combined with Carlos' almost frenzied insistence, made her withdraw her objections.

As they rode back leisurely to the *casa,* Cole remarked, "If you can handle a full gallop as well as you did everything today, I'll consider our lessons finished. You've learned remarkably fast."

Jenny totally ignored Cole's compliment and cried out, "No! There's more that I need to learn."

Cole frowned. "Look, Cortinas said all I had to teach you was the basics."

"I'm not talking about riding."

"What, then?"

"I want you to teach me how to saddle Princess, too."

"Why? The servants will saddle her for you."

Not at night, when she planned her escape, Jenny thought. They'd be suspicious, and she feared Cortinas wouldn't let her ride alone even in the daytime without someone accompanying her, probably Carlos. But she knew she didn't dare tell Cole her reason. "I don't want the servants to do it for me. I want to do it for myself, or at least be able to if I want. She's my horse, isn't she?"

If any other woman had said that, Cole would have been suspicious, but he knew just how independent Jenny was. And determined. That was the reason she had learned so quickly.

"Besides," Jenny continued, "if I learn everything about taking care of her, I'd be able to spend more time with her. I've become quite fond of her, you know."

Cole knew, and the mare seemed to be just as taken with Jenny. But that was not what was on his mind. He scowled and asked, "What do you mean, take care of her? That entails grooming, feeding, a lot of other things. Cortinas didn't say anything about me teaching you all that. In fact, he didn't say anything about me teaching you to saddle her, either."

"But you could teach me at least that, couldn't you?" Jenny asked with her prettiest smile. "I'm sure he wouldn't mind."

Cole knew he was being manipulated in a manner as old as time. He wasn't a fool. His scowl deepened.

Knowing her ploy had failed, Jenny tossed her head and said, "All right, then, be stubborn about it! I'll ask Cortinas tonight."

Cole knew Cortinas would agree, as enthralled as he was with Jenny. The bandit would let her have anything her heart desired, particularly if it made him look better in her eyes. He had better quit while he was ahead, Cole reasoned, and all he'd have to do was teach Jenny how to saddle the mare. If she got to Cortinas, the Mexican might order him to teach her everything, and he could be detained another week or so. Then he'd miss out on the big raid Cortinas was planning for the end of the week. "That's not necessary!" Cole answered in disgust. "I know what he'll say. We might as well do it today and get it over with." Seeing the delighted expression coming over Jenny's face, Cole gave her a stern look and said, "But let's get one thing straight between us. All I'm going to teach you is how to saddle and bridle her. Nothing more! Agreed?"

That was all Jenny had really wanted. She'd worry about feeding and caring for Princess after she had escaped. "Agreed."

By that time, they had reached the main gate, but instead of stopping and letting Jenny dismount, the two continued to ride towards the stables at the back of the fortress. Following them, Carlos called out sharply, *"Alto!"*

"Christ! I forgot about that pest!" Cole grumbled. Cole brought his horse to a halt and turned in his saddle, then explained what he planned to the Mexican, telling Carlos that Cortinas had ordered him to teach Jenny how to saddle the mare.

Carlos didn't question Cole's claim. All the general had told him was to keep a sharp eye on the two and to see that Cole didn't keep the *gringa* out in the sun too long. But the Mexican wasn't too happy with the news. He had planned to take a long *siesta,* and he couldn't object, since the stables were covered and not much warmer than the *casa* at this time of the day. He shot Jenny a resentful glance, then nodded his head curtly for Cole to continue.

Cole and Jenny rode their horses to the back of the fortress-like building with Carlos following listlessly behind them on his mount. As they rode, they passed several smaller gates, but Jenny was unable to tell which was the one she had been contemplating using for her escape. Then, when they rounded the last corner, Jenny saw the stables for the first time. Constructed of the same gnarled mesquite limbs and covered with the same thick mesquite brush as the *jacals*, the stables were nothing but a long lean-to with several stalls built against the back wall of the *casa*. At the very end, she spied Cortinas' black buggy and assumed the structure must act as a carriage house as well as a place for his personal mounts.

When they reached the stables, a wiry stable boy hurried to Jenny to help her dismount and take her horse.

Cole waved the boy away and explained in Spanish that Jenny was going to unsaddle the horse herself and that they wouldn't need his services. Reluctantly, the lad retreated, shooting a look of doubt over his shoulder.

Cole swung down from his horse, saying to Jenny, "Dismount and bring Princess into the shade. Then I'll show you how to remove the saddle and bridle."

Jenny complied and removed the *sombrero* on her head, then stood for a moment relishing the coolness of the stables. The broad-rimmed hat had protected her face from the sun, but the tall crown had held the heat, and her hair was plastered to the top of her head with sweat. She watched while Cole undid the cinch and flank girth on the saddle and removed it and the saddle blanket, then carefully observed as he removed the bridle and bit. Neither appeared difficult. Then he reversed the process as Jenny watched.

"All right," Cole said, easily slipping the bit and bridle from Princess and handing it to Jenny. "Let's see if you can get her into this."

It turned out that it was more difficult than it appeared. The soft cartilage in the mare's ears seemed to have turned to stone, and Jenny was nervous about putting the bit into Princess' mouth, despite how well-mannered the bay had been and the animal's unusual co-operativeness in bending her head to her. For a good half-hour, she practiced the procedure over and over until Cole called a halt for fear the animal's tender mouth might be getting sore.

He turned his attentions to teaching Jenny how to saddle the mare, and it soon became apparent that it was a task Jenny wasn't going to be able to handle. She was simply too small to lift the heavy saddle, no matter how much tugging and pulling she did. Then hearing Carlos make some comment from where he was leaning against one of the other stalls, she shot him a hot look and demanded of Cole, "What did he say?"

"He says you're too little, that if you can't even lift it, you'll never get it on the mare's back."

"I'm not too little!" Jenny objected. "I'm no smaller than that stable boy over there. If he can do it, so can I."

"Carlos wasn't talking about your height, but your strength. That boy has been doing hard labor since he was five. You just aren't strong enough, and I agree."

Jenny couldn't stand the thought of her plans for escape being ruined by something as ridiculous as her not being able to lift the saddle. She wasn't one to give into any kind of weakness. She looked about her wildly, then spying Cole's saddle, said, "I could lift your saddle. It's not near as big and bulky as mine."

Jenny's saddle was a Mexican saddle, heavily studded with silver inlays, with a wide saddle skirt and massive leather toe-guards on the stirrups, while Cole's was a smaller western saddle. "That may be true," Cole answered in a hard voice, "but that's *my* saddle."

"I'll make a trade," Jenny offered. "You can have mine. Why, I'll bet mine is much more valuable, with all that silver."

"No! I don't like Mexican saddles. They're too ornate. Besides, I'm accustomed to my own. It's comfortable to me. I spent years breaking it in. I wouldn't give it up any more than I would my boots or my hat."

Jenny knew by the determined gleam in Cole's golden eyes that he wouldn't back down, no matter what. She frowned; then as a sudden idea came to her, she whirled around and asked the stable boy, "Do you have a saddle here like that?"

Even though Jenny was pointing to Cole's saddle, the stable boy didn't know what she was asking. He shot Cole a puzzled look.

"He doesn't know what you're talking about," Cole remarked.

It was a redundant statement that irritated Jenny all the more. "Then you ask him!"

"Why? It will probably be too heavy too."

"Dammit, will you just ask him?" Jenny asked exasperatedly.

Cole's eyes narrowed. "You've got a short fuse there, lady."

"Only when I'm dealing with someone incredibly hardheaded." Jenny knew instantly that she had made a mistake in calling Cole hardheaded by the dark look that came over his face. She decided to try to repair the damage by asking, "Please? Just ask him."

It wasn't just the "please" that soothed Cole. The pleading look in Jenny's beautiful eyes would have melted the hardest heart, and Cole pitied the man who was foolish enough to get involved with her. She'd make mush of his emotions. Cole directed the question to the boy and knew by the sudden sparkle that came to his dark eyes what the answer was going to be.

"*Sí, sí,*" the lad answered, then hurried to an empty stall and rummaged through a pile of discarded tack, pulling a battered *gringo* saddle from the bottom. With a victorious grin on his face, he carried it back to Jenny and set it at her feet, then before she could reach for it, dusted the dirt and cobwebs from it.

Jenny gave Cole an "I told you so," look, then bent to pick up the saddle. It took considerable muscle-power just to lift it and carry it over to the mare. She paused, trying desperately to summon the strength to toss it on the mare's back.

"Don't even try it," Cole said, seeing how red Jenny's face had become from her exertions.

"I can do it," Jenny objected through clenched teeth.

"You'll strain something."

"No, I won't," Jenny persisted.

Cole stepped forward and tried to take the saddle from Jenny. She swung it away from him and said, "I said I would do it, and I will!"

Cole admired determination, but in his estimation, Jenny had crossed beyond that and moved into pure pig-headedness, and that was something he didn't admire. "Why are you being so damned obstinate? Why risk injuring your back? Let somebody else saddle her. You can still spend time with her."

Even though it was a rational argument, it didn't apply in Jenny's case. She had to be able to saddle the horse to escape, or ride bareback, and that was out of the question. She shot Cole a murderous glance and summoned all of her strength, then with a mighty swing that did indeed strain muscles that had never been used so cruelly, tossed the saddle onto the mare's back.

"Bravo, señorita!" the stable boy cried out in approval.

The thrill of victory was sweet, but Jenny waited a moment for the protesting muscles in her arms and back to quiet before she turned. Beneath the shadow of his *sombrero,* for both men had kept their hats on despite the shade, Jenny could see Carlos' grudging smile. She pivoted fully to face Cole, a triumphant grin on her pretty face. But if she expected some sign of approval or admiration from him she was doomed to disappointment. His face was set in a deep scowl.

98

Damn little fool, Cole thought. She'd kill herself to prove a point. "I believe our saddling lessons are finished," he said curtly. He touched the tip of his hat with one finger. "Good day."

Jenny watched as Cole walked away, the heady thrill of triumph dwindling with each purposeful step he took. Damn him, she thought. He'd ruined everything with his sour attitude. All that remained of her achievement was a nagging backache.

The next morning, Jenny was waiting for Cole at the main gate with Princess. She saw him glance at the western saddle on the mare's back, but much to her chagrin, he made no inquiry as to whether she, or someone else, had saddled the horse. It appeared the Texan was bound and determined to ignore her accomplishment, and that hurt. Jenny wanted his approval very much.

Because she was riding in a different saddle, Cole took Jenny through everything he had taught her before he finally said, "All right. I guess you're ready for a full gallop now. Give the mare full rein, keep your head low, and remember to follow her rhythm. You don't have to worry about guiding her, not out here. Just give her her head. She isn't going to run into any cactus patches."

A tingle of fear ran through Jenny. "What if she doesn't want to stop when I do?"

"She will. But just to be safe, I'll be right beside you."

Jenny nudged the mare with her heel, then when she had reached a canter, leaned forward and said, "All right, pretty girl. Let's see what you can really do. Go!"

And Princess did. She took off at a speed Jenny had never dreamed the mare possessed. As the scenery flew past her and the wind rushing by her tore off her *sombrero,* Jenny felt another twinge of fear before she became caught up in the excitement of the race. The wind tugged at her skirts and sent them flapping, while the *sombrero,* still tied to her neck, whirled round and round behind her as if caught in a dust devil. She felt as if she were flying, and then did when Princess leaped over a ravine, then jumped a clump of cactus. It was the most exhilarating experience Jenny had ever had. She laughed from the sheer joy of it, and Princess whinnied in total accord.

Racing beside them, Cole once again thought that the two were the most beautiful, natural thing he had ever seen. The mare stretched out her long legs, the powerful muscles rippling beneath her reddish, damp coat, her ears laid back, her long mane and tail flying out like banners. Jenny rode low over the mare, the long curls at her back flashing in the sunlight like spun gold, her face flushed with excitement, her beautiful sapphire eyes sparkling. Hearing her laugh, a spontaneous tinkling sound that made his spirits soar, Cole felt something deep within him stir.

"Rein in," he said.

Jenny didn't want to stop. Nor did the mare. Jenny thought about ignoring Cole's command, but there was an urgency in his voice that made her reconsider. She pulled back on the reins. "Whoa, girl. Whoa."

Cole brought his horse to a halt before Jenny. He

swung down and hurried to her before she could dismount. "Oh, that was so exciting, so wonderful!" Jenny gasped as Cole lifted his arms to help.

Jenny's breath caught as Cole's strong hands clasped her tiny waist. As he lowered her to the ground, her body slid against his, and Jenny was aware of every hard muscle and tendon. When she reached eye level, he stopped and just held her against him. The sheer maleness of him was overpowering. She found it difficult to breathe. She watched as his eyes darkened with passion to a molten gold, felt the heat of desire in his breath fanning her face. He's going to kiss me, she thought, and felt a wild thrill of a different sort seize her. Her heart raced in anticipation.

Cole wanted to kiss Jenny, wanted it with a desperation he had never known. His lips ached to plunder the sweetness of her mouth, just as his manhood throbbed for the feel of her hot depths. Never had any woman brought him to such instant arousal. Yes, he wanted to kiss her, and much more. He wanted to throw her to the ground, kiss her until she was breathless, then make passionate love to her.

But at the fringes of his brain, Cole knew he didn't dare follow his instincts. He could hear the hoofbeats of a horse rapidly approaching, and knew it was Carlos. Damn the spying bastard! he thought. No, he didn't dare even a kiss, for fear it might be the death of him.

Jenny was stunned when Cole suddenly released her and stepped back. It wasn't until she spied Carlos riding up that she understood. But she wasn't prepared for the second shock when Cole stated flatly, "I believe that concludes our lessons. Goodbye, and good luck."

Jenny watched in utter disbelief as Cole walked away, mounted, then rode off, wondering if she had imagined what had transpired just minutes before. No, she knew he had wanted her, could have staked her life on it. But here he was walking out of her life as if nothing had ever happened. How could he run hot and cold like that?

Then the full impact of the finality of his going hit her. Jenny felt within her an unexplainable, terrible loss. Sudden tears sprang to her eyes. She had never felt so low, or so alone.

Seven

A week later, Cole rode his horse through the dark night and relished the feel of the cool desert air rushing past him. He had always enjoyed riding alone at night with a black canopy studded with stars over his head and the only sound that of his horse's hoofbeats. There was a peacefulness in that particular solitude that was missing in the light of day. At times like these, in the hush and stillness of the night, God's presence was almost palpable.

Then Cole spied another rider racing across his path, the vision shattering the serenity of the moment for him. Even though the horseman was still a good distance away, he knew instantly who it was. There was just enough starlight to pick up the glittering gold of her hair. "What the hell?" he muttered, then veered his stallion and took off after her.

Jenny heard the sound of a horse behind her and glanced over her shoulder. Since the rider wasn't coming from the direction of the ranch, she had no idea who it was racing after her. Terrified, she urged Princess on to greater speed, and the little mare readily complied, her long legs gobbling up the ground. But Cole's stallion was just a mite faster and, after a hard run through the night, finally managed to pull up beside Jenny's horse.

"Jenny! Rein in!" Cole yelled across the short distance that separated them.

Jenny could barely hear Cole over the thundering of their horses' hoofs and couldn't distinguish the voice as his. Nor did it dawn on her that the man must know her if he knew her name. She glanced across and saw a very sinister-looking man with his hair flying wildly around his face and his shirt flapping against his broad shoulders and chest. Thinking she must be facing rape, or maybe even death, she yelled back, "Leave me alone, you bastard!" then swiped at Cole with the end of her reins. Desperate, she pleaded with Princess to go faster.

The tip of Jenny's reins hit Cole at the corner of his eye, splitting the skin there and stinging like fire. "Goddammit!" he cursed, then moved his racing horse closer to Jenny's. Before she could lash out at him with her reins a second time, he reached over, snaked a long arm around her waist, and lifted her from the saddle.

Jenny was shocked when the man picked her up as if she weighed no more than a feather and swung her to his mount. She wouldn't have thought such a feat was possible at their speed. By the time he had placed her sideways on his lap, she'd recovered from her surprise, clawing furiously at his arm and spitting expletives. Feeling Cole's grasp only tighten in response, Jenny turned and beat on his broad chest with her fists, then reached up to scratch his face.

Cole had been in the process of stopping his horse before he had even fully settled Jenny in his lap, and it was a good thing. The little spitfire was fighting him so hard, she nearly succeeded in unseating them both. Then seeing her hand flying at his face with the nails bared, Cole jerked back his head, dropped his reins and wrapped both powerful arms around her, pinning her arms down at her sides.

Jenny felt as if a band of steel was wrapped around her. She squirmed and kicked out, then made a wild lunge to bite Cole's shoulder. But before her teeth could sink into his flesh, she heard him threaten, "You do, and you'll regret it!"

By that time Cole's horse had come to a halt and was making soft, blowing noises. Jenny froze. Without the sound of the pounding hooves, this time she recognized the man's voice. She looked up in disbelief and asked, "Cole? Is that you?"

"Well, who in the hell did you think it was?" Cole answered in exasperation.

"I didn't know. I couldn't distinguish your face in the darkness."

"I yelled at you," Cole reminded her angrily. "I called you by name."

He *had* called her by name, Jenny realized with a start. "There was too much noise."

Suddenly Cole became very conscious of their closeness. The warmth of Jenny's body, her intoxicating womanly scent wrapped itself around him like a lover's arms. Feeling his heat rise and a stirring of his manhood, he feared he would give himself away

105

with Jenny sitting in his lap the way she was. Damn her! he thought. It wasn't enough that he hadn't been able to get her out of his mind, that memories of her had tortured him throughout the entire ride to Texas and then back, but now, even when he was angry with her, even after the battering she had given him, she still aroused him. She was no angel. She was a temptress sent from hell to make his life miserable.

Cole leaned over and placed Jenny on her feet, then dismounted beside her. "All right, so you didn't realize who I was," he said grudgingly. "I guess I'll forgive you for damn near putting out my eye." He paused long enough for Jenny to glance at his eye and see the blood tricking from the small cut beside it, but before she could say the words, he cut across her apology with a curt demand. "Now I want to know what in the hell you're doing out here by yourself in the middle of the night."

Now that Jenny had recovered from her fright and surprise, she was rapidly getting irritated at Cole. What right did he have to be angry at her or make demands of her? she thought. He wasn't her keeper. In fact, the last time she had see him, he couldn't wait to get away from her. No, he didn't give a damn about her. All he was trying to do was stick his nose in her business. She bristled, somehow reminding Cole of an angry, wet hen shaking its feathers, then spat, "It's really none of your damn business, but I'm escaping."

"That's why you wanted to learn how to ride, wasn't it?" Cole asked with sudden insight, then realized he had been played for a fool. It didn't improve his humor.

"Yes, it was," Jenny answered candidly. "It appeared if anyone was going to help me escape, it was going to have to be myself."

"I credited you with better sense than that. You admitted yourself you'd get lost."

"I reconsidered and decided I wouldn't," Jenny countered. "I realized all I would have to do is travel north. Sooner or later, I'll hit the border."

"Then why were you traveling west?"

Jenny drew back in surprise. She had not realized she was going in the wrong direction. But her confidence came bounding back and she said, "I just got a little mixed up in the dark. By morning, when the sun comes up, I would have realized my mistake and corrected it."

"You crazy little fool!" Cole thundered, making Jenny jump at the loud noise. "You're bound and determined to get yourself killed, aren't you? Do you know what's directly north from here? Some of the most rugged, forbidding country in this world."

"Are you trying to tell me that Texas isn't north of here?" Jenny tossed back, highly resenting being called a fool. "Well, I know better!"

"Oh, it's Texas, all right, the part where it juts right out into Mexico. Why, that country is so dry and desolate, the only creatures that can live there are scorpions, snakes, and horned toads. It's riddled with bones bleaching in the sun, both animal and human, covered with scorching deserts and impenetrable mountains made of pure rock, and the water holes can be a hundred miles or more apart. If there was ever a hell on earth, it's that place."

"But Cortinas brought me here from someplace in Texas," Jenny objected. "It was dry, but it wasn't that bad, and there weren't any mountains. It was as flat as a pancake."

"The part of Texas that you're talking about is to the northeast, and there's a lot of desert between here and there, too. What were you going to do for water?"

"I thought Princess could find the water holes."

"Oh, animals are better than humans at finding water, I'll admit. But they can't tell good from bad, and there's a lot of bad in this country. Besides, did you really think you were going to have time to be wandering all over looking for water with Cortinas' men hot on your trail? And that's exactly where they'll be in a few hours, when the sun comes up and they discover Princess miss. . . ." Cole's voice trailed off as a sudden thought came to him. Jenny and Princess weren't the only ones whose absence would be discovered. "Dammit!" Cole said in fury, catching Jenny by the shoulders and shaking her lightly. "Do you realize the mess you've gotten me into?"

"What are you talking about?" Jenny asked in confusion, then jerked her shoulders from Cole's grasp.

"You're gone, and I'm gone. Naturally, they're going to think we disappeared together. They're going to be looking for me, too."

"Then you've left Cortinas and aren't out here riding herd, or whatever?"

108

Cole made a noise much like a snort and asked, "Do you see any cattle around?"

"Well, no! But I don't know what you were doing when you took off after me. There could have been a whole herd of them standing around." Jenny paused, then asked, "Why did you leave? I thought you liked working for Cortinas.

Cole wasn't about to tell Jenny that he had all the information on the bandit he needed and considered his job for the Governor finished. He didn't trust any gold digger. No, he'd let her continue to think he was an outlaw. "I could see there was no future for me with him. Besides, I like being my own boss."

"Then you're going back to Texas?"

"That's what I'd planned."

"I thought you said things were too hot for you there."

Cole shrugged. "There are places were the law doesn't venture. Lots of them. I'll just lay low until things cool off a little."

"Then you can take me with you," Jenny declared, her eyes shining brightly.

It wasn't what Cole wanted to do. He didn't trust himself around Jenny, and feared she'd wind him around her little finger just as she had Amos and Cortinas. Despite the fact that she wasn't his kind of woman, she seemed to hold a strange power over him. Nor had he changed his mind on how danger-ous helping Jenny escape would be. Cortinas would be furious when he discovered his little sparrow had flown the coop. The bandit king would come after them with a vengeance. "No, I won't take you with me. I told you I wouldn't help you from the beginning."

"But why not?" Jenny asked, with a hint of hurt in her voice. "You said you don't want to work for Cortinas any more, so it can't be that."

"Because it would be suicide for me, and probably for you, too, if he caught us together. Cortinas is one hell of a mean bastard when he gets riled, and he has an army at his disposal. From here to the Nueces River in Texas is going to be swarming with his men looking for you."

"Nueces River?" Jenny asked in puzzlement. I thought the Rio Grande marked the border."

"It does, but the Mexicans have never recognized it. They've always maintained the Nueces was the border and have kept things in so much turmoil between the two rivers that the area has become a lawless no-man's-land. So you see, unless you just happen to hit one of the small border towns, you'll have a long ways to travel before you're safe. No, the best thing for you to do is hightail it back before Cortinas discovers you missing."

"Go back to Cortinas? Go back to being a prisoner?" Jenny asked in astonishment. Her expression turned to one of fierce determination. "Absolutely not! I'm going back to Texas, with or without your help." She turned and started looking around for her mare, then spying her grazing on a patch of dried grass in the distance, started for her.

Before she could take two steps, Cole caught her arm and whirled her around. "Why are you being so damn foolish?" he asked. "So what if you were a

110

prisoner of sorts? You weren't starving or lacking for any comfort. You weren't mistreated. Is freedom worth risking your life? If you'd just bide your time, Cortinas would probably tire of wooing you and send you back."

"Oh? When? Three months from now? A year? By then Amos might have found someone else."

"Oh, so Amos is why you're in such a big hurry?" Cole asked in a biting voice, his dislike for the carpetbagger coming to the fore. "Why? Because you love him so much, or is it because you can't wait to get your hands on his money?"

"Why I'm anxious to get back to Amos is none of your damn business!" Jenny answered hotly. She tossed her head, then added, "Besides, there are other reasons why I'm anxious to escape."

"What reasons?"

Jenny hesitated for a moment then answered, "I was beginning to fear Cortinas."

Jenny's answer was just evasive enough to tell Cole that she feared Cortinas would force himself on her. Suddenly, his fury turned from Amos to the Mexican. He watched Jenny walk away to where Princess was standing in the distance. He followed her and asked in disgust, "You're determined to do this, aren't you?"

"Yes, I am, and thank you for pointing me in the right direction," Jenny answered coldly over her shoulder.

"You'll never make it to the border, even if you do stumble on good water. His men will catch up with you. They'll travel with a string of fresh horses, while

111

you have only Princess. You don't want to kill her, do you?"

Jenny whirled around so suddenly that Cole ran right into her. "No, I don't want to kill her, or myself! But I'm *not* going back, and that's final!"

Cole understood Jenny well enough to know she wasn't bluffing. No, once that pigheaded little spitfire decided to do something, she did it, come hell or high water. Which left him with two choices. He could leave her to her fate, a fate that she had brought on herself, he reminded himself grimly, or take her with him. He found he couldn't do the first. The thought of the light going out in those beautiful blue eyes was more than he could bear. And what the hell, he might as well do the latter. He was going to get blamed for her escape anyway. Cortinas would never give Jenny credit for having accomplished it herself, not a lowly woman. By the time Cole had made up his mind, Jenny was mounted. He called, "Wait!", then walked rapidly up to her.

"What for?" Jenny asked in a resentful voice. "More arguments? Sorry, I don't have time for them. I'm in a hurry!"

"Dammit, you are the most irritating woman I've ever met! The least you can do is wait to see what I have to say. I've changed my mind."

For a moment, Jenny wasn't sure she had heard right. Then she asked, "You'll help me?"

Cole took a closer look at Jenny's mount and noted that she had brought nothing with her, except the *sombrero* that was tied to her saddle horn. He wondered how in the world she had thought to survive with no food, no water, no weapon, not even a blanket to sleep under. It was a good thing he had decided to help her, he thought, then answered, "I'll take you with me as far as Rio Grande City, but no further."

"Just as long as it's in the United States," Jenny answered gratefully.

"It is. Just barely." Cole turned and whistled for his horse, then mounted the stallion when the animal reached him. Pivoting the stallion, he said over his shoulder, "This way."

"Wait!" Jenny called. "That's the same direction I was riding in."

Cole turned half-way in his saddle and answered, "That's right. We're traveling directly west."

"What's west of here?"

"Just more of Mexico, but that's the direction we're taking for the time being."

"But why?"

"Because Cortinas' men aren't going to expect that. They'll be looking for us in the opposite direction. By the time they figure out we aren't making a beeline for the Rio Grande and turn around, we'll have a few days head start on them. Then we'll circle back around."

"But that will take longer," Jenny objected.

Cole was in no mood for hearing any more arguments. In another hour or two the sun would be rising, and their absence would be discovered. Every moment was precious. "Look," he said in a hard voice, "I'm heading west. If you want to tag along, you can. But I'm riding now, so you had better make up your mind fast."

As Cole kneed his mount and rode away, Jenny only hesitated briefly. She followed, fearing the outlaw was her only means of escape, other than death. But deep down inside her, so deep Jenny didn't even know that part of her existed, there was another reason why she followed. Deep in her heart, she knew the Texan was the man destiny had marked as her soul mate.

Eight

Cole set a steady pace as he and Jenny rode through the night, just fast enough to lather the horses, but not fast enough to wear them down. Jenny was glad for Princess's heat in the cool night air, but when the sun rose and began to beat down on them in earnest, she began to perspire as freely as the mare, despite the *sombrero* that she had donned. Cole had never kept her out in the sun so long during her riding lessons, and she'd had no idea that it could be so unmerciful. On the trip to the border, she'd had the shade of the buggy, and while the broad-rimmed *sombrero* protected her face, its crown seemed to grip the heat. Beneath it, her hair was plastered to her head with sweat, while the exposed skin on her arms burned like fire, her lips were cracked, and her throat parched. Jenny refused to complain, however, knowing she had brought the misery on herself and not wanting Cole to think her an encumbrance after he had agreed to let her tag along. But by midday, Jenny was beginning to feel dangerously weak and dizzy and feared she would faint. As much as she hated to, she begged Cole to halt.

Cole had known Jenny was not faring well in the heat but had not realized just how bad her condition was until he helped her dismount. Alarmed at how flushed her face was, he carried her to the shade of a small mesquite, ignoring her feeble objections and cursing himself all the while for not paying closer attention. He had wanted to put as much distance as possible between them and Cortinas' men in hopes that by the time their pursuers had realized the direction he and Jenny had taken, their trail would be too cold for the Mexicans to readily follow. He had been so intent on his purpose that he had unwittingly put Jenny's life at risk.

As soon as Cole laid Jenny down beneath the shade, she muttered, "Water."

"In a minute," Cole answered, reaching for the hem of her skirt. "First, we've got to get you cooled off."

As he pushed her damp skirt up to hip level, Jenny rose to her elbows and cried out in alarm, "What in the devil do you think you're doing?"

"I'm trying to expose as much skin as possible to the air. You're burning up in that long skirt and that underwear."

Jenny was too weak to fight Cole. The world seemed to tilt crazily, then spin. She fell back limply while he reached under her skirt, deftly undid the tab that held up her drawers, then slipped them off. Vaguely, she realized that he had managed the feat without exposing her privates and was grateful, then was doubly grateful as she felt a blessed coolness on the skin of her bare legs. Not once did she think about the money belt that

116

was strapped to one thigh. She had completely forgotten it. But Cole noted it and thought it a confirmation of his estimation of Jenny.

Jenny didn't object when Cole stripped off her blouse, but when he started untying the ribbons that held her chemise closed, she caught his hand with one of hers and cried out, "No!"

"Cut it out!" Cole snapped, pushing her hand away. "This is no time to be modest. Whether you realize it or not, your body temperature is dangerously high. Besides, I've seen a woman's breasts before. Why do you think yours are so special?"

Again Jenny was too weak to fight him. Another wave of dizziness washed over her, and she closed her eyes, fearing she was going to pass out.

Cole sat back on his heels, whipped off his hat, and began to fan Jenny's body. But he soon realized that Jenny's breasts with their pert rosy nipples *were* special, or at least his body seemed to think so. The sight of them and her shapely legs were arousing him. He cursed his baser nature and deliberately averted his eyes, or tried to. They kept drifting back, repeatedly, to the loveliness that was revealed to him.

"Can I please have some water now?" Jenny muttered.

Cole started. Jenny had lain so still, he had thought she had fainted.

The dangerous beet-red color of her skin had faded. Cole rose and walked to his horse, then returned with his canteen. As he knelt beside her and lifted her shoulders, he noted that Jenny had pulled the chemise closed and thought with a wry smile that it was probably just as well. It might not benefit her heated condition; it would certainly help his.

Cole only allowed Jenny a few swallows of the water, telling her that too much too soon would make her ill. He took a drink himself, then gave each of the horses a handful, unsaddled them, and, stripping off his shirt, began to rub them down with it.

Watching from where she laying on the ground, Jenny asked, "Why are you doing that?"

"To wipe off their sweat. It's not good for a horse to cool down too fast."

As Cole rubbed down Princess, Jenny admired the powerful muscles on his back and found herself envying the animal. She'd like to have the Texan stroke her flesh that way. Then, realizing what she was doing, Jenny smiled. She must be getting better if she could entertain such an outrageous thought. A moment later, her exhaustion came down on her like a sledge hammer.

Cole was alarmed when he returned a few minutes later and found Jenny asleep, fearing she might have slipped into a coma. He dropped the bedroll he had carried back with him, knelt beside her, and placed his fingers against the side of her throat. Her heartbeat was slow and steady, and not racing the way it had been. Her skin had cooled considerably. He realized she was asleep. He opened the bedroll and spread the blanket beside her. For a moment, he wondered if he should place her on it, then decided against it, for fear it would disturb her sleep. He removed his gunbelt, wrapped the strap around the holster, and placed it at the corner of the blanket, then lay down beside Jenny. Within minutes, he, too was asleep.

* * *

Jenny was the first to awaken late that afternoon. She opened her eyes to an excellent view of Cole's broad chest as he lay on his side beside her. The sight of that obvious masculinity was startling, in view of the fact that Jenny had no idea where she was or how she had gotten there, and she had never slept with a man. Then, as the memory of everything came rushing back and she realized how exposed she was, she gasped, sat bolt upright, and quickly pushed her skirt back down.

"Was that to hide your legs or the money belt?" Cole drawled lazily, having been awakened by Jenny's gasp.

Jenny jumped in surprise at the sound of Cole's voice, then turned and faced him. "Both, I suppose. After all, you *are* an outlaw."

Cole frowned. He didn't like the idea of Jenny thinking badly of him, but he wasn't going to enlighten her. He still didn't trust her. "If I was going to steal from you, I could have done it while you were asleep," he pointed out as he sat up. He gave her a meaningful look, then said, "I'm surprised I didn't find a knife strapped to the other leg."

Jenny guessed what Cole was thinking. Ladies carried their money in their reticules, perhaps stuffed into their bodices, but not strapped to their leg. That was the mark of a street-wise woman, which she was. But she didn't deserve the comment about the knife. Only women who consorted with the lowest scum on the earth did that, and she wasn't that kind. "If I knew how to use one, maybe I would," she answered flippantly, not wanting him to know how deep his remark had cut. "So don't be sneering at my money belt. I'm

119

glad I thought of it. If I hadn't, Cortinas' bandits would have taken every penny I had. As it was, they got everything in my reticule and all of my jewelry. Why, those bastards even searched my luggage!" Jenny finished in renewed outrage.

It was then that Jenny noticed Cole's gaze and realized her chemise was open. She clutched it to her, turned her back, and reached for her blouse. As she donned it, she heard Cole say, "You're lucky they didn't search you. They've been known to do that, you know. Search women."

Or do a lot worse, Jenny thought, remembering how she had feared she was going to be raped for a few minutes. Thank God, their leader had decided they were in a hurry. "Well, they didn't, thank the Lord. If I hadn't had this money, I wouldn't have even considered escaping without any food or supplies."

"You were planning on buying those things?"

Jenny heard just a hint of sarcasm in Cole's voice and became defensive. "Of course!"

"Where? There aren't any towns out here, just a few little farms and goat ranches inhabited with *peons* and you don't even speak Spanish."

"I could manage with sign language, and I have money."

"American money, coins the average Mexican is unfamiliar with. More than likely, they wouldn't have anything to do with it. No, they'd be suspicious of both you and your money."

"Me?" Jenny asked in surprise. "Why me?"

"Because they'd wonder how in the hell a *gringo* woman came to be wandering around all alone out here in the middle of this godforsaken land. Was she running away from her husband, or was her husband killed by bandits, and were they pursuing her? Believe me, if the *peons* get any idea that *bandidos* are involved in this, they won't help you. They're absolutely terrified of the gangs of outlaws in this country."

"All right, so it wouldn't have worked," Jenny admitted reluctantly. "I guess it's a good thing I ran into you."

Good for her, but not for him, Cole thought bleakly. God, how had he gotten himself into this mess? he wondered. Just when he'd thought things were looking up for him, he found himself in a position where he was again a wanted man and on the run, only this time it was worse. He was dragging a woman with him. Did the gods of fate have something against him? Why him? "How do you feel?"

The question sounded more like a growl than a query. Jenny wasn't particularly surprised. She knew how Cole felt about the entire thing. "Thirsty and hungry."

"Not weak?"

Jenny did feel a little weak, but she didn't want to admit that to Cole. She didn't want to be any more a bother than she had already been, for fear he might change his mind about taking her along. "Not really."

"You can have some water, but not a lot," Cole said, reaching for the canteen and handing it to her. "That's all the water we have until we come across a stream, and we have to share it with the horses. And there's some goat *queso* and *tortillas* in my saddlebags. I'll get them."

Jenny had never thought such simple fare as goat cheese and *tortillas* could taste so good. After they had

121

eaten, Cole asked, "Do you feel strong enough to travel when the sun goes down? Even if we could get in four or five hours, it will help. Any distance we can get at this point in the game is to our advantage."

Jenny did feel stronger since she had eaten, but she was incredibly sore from being in the saddle for so long. Just the thought of putting her tender bottom on that hard leather made her wince in pain. "Yes, I think I can ride," she answered bravely.

"Good!" Cole answered, coming to his feet with a swift bound and starting to don his shirt. "Until then, I'm going to ride out and see if I can find a farm where I can buy a water bag and a blanket for you." He glanced at her hair, then added, "And a *rebozo,* if you're not going to wear that *sombrero* at night."

"What's a *rebozo?*"

"A big scarf Mexican women wear over their head and shoulders. You may not realize it, but even at night your hair stands out like a beacon. It's a dead giveaway you're not Mexican." Cole paused, then added, "But then you riding that horse is a dead giveaway too."

"Why?"

"Because peasant women don't ride horses when they travel. Most of the time they walk, or ride in carts. If they ride anything, it's a burro."

"Well, if I'm going to be so conspicuous as a women, why don't I dress like a man?" Jenny asked with startling logic.

Cole's rigid southern sense of propriety came to the surface before he could even respond to the practicality of Jenny's suggestion. "No!"

"Why not?"

"Because a woman wearing pants is . . . unseemly."

"Unseemly?" Jenny asked in disbelief. Then she laughed, saying, "My God, you'd think you were a preacher, instead of an outlaw. I've never heard anything so ridiculous. What's wrong with it? Why, I wore tights lots of times, when I was playing Shakespeare."

Jenny saw Cole's eyes narrow and knew she had let the cat completely out of the bag with her blunder. Before he had suspected she wasn't who she pretended to be. Now he knew.

"You're an actress?" Cole asked in a tight voice.

To Jenny's credit, she didn't try to gloss over her error. She met Cole's eyes levelly, and answered. "Yes, I am, and a good one, if I say so myself."

"Obviously. Your act fooled Amos."

Jenny could see the scorn on Cole's face and hear it in his voice. Briefly, she wondered if he scorned her simply because she was an actress, as so much of the public unfairly did, or if he scorned her because of what she was doing to Amos. Then anger came to her defense and she said, "Don't look at me that way, like I'm the scum of the earth. So I fooled Amos into thinking I was a lady and tricked him into asking me to marry him. So what? It's no more dishonest than what you've done. My God, you're a thief, an admitted bank robber. You're a fine one to cast stones. Talk about the pot calling the kettle black!"

Cole realized that he had nearly given himself away with his sanctimonious behavior. He wasn't supposed to be lily-white himself. "Is that why you're not afraid of me, because you think we're alike?"

"Maybe," Jenny admitted. "I never did believe that tale Cortinas told me about you being a cold-blooded murderer."

"Why not?"

"Because it didn't seem to fit. Oh, you're dangerous, and maybe you've killed out of self-defense, but not out of pure meanness. I'd stake my life on it, and I'm a pretty good judge of character."

Cole hoped she wasn't too good a judge. He didn't need her to see through his act. He'd have to be much more careful. He turned and walked to his horse, saying, "I think your suggestion to dress like a man might work, but we'd better change it to a boy. You're too small to pass for a man. I'll see if I can find some boy's clothing."

"But won't it look just as suspicious for you to be traveling with a boy?"

"Not if I was a *gringo* down here looking for a mining investment. They often have a *mozo,* a boy they've hired as a guide and a servant."

"You say *gringo* like you're not one."

"I'm not," Cole answered, picking up his saddle and swinging it onto his horse. "I'm a Texan, a *Tejano. Gringos* are greenhorns. They don't have any outdoors savvy, particularly Mexican outdoors savvy. They come down here looking for a fortune, thinking it's going to be like a hunting trip they went on back home. They usually find a little more excitement than they bargained for, and a lot more discomfort."

Cole swung into the saddle with the grace of a ballet dancer. "You're not afraid to stay here by yourself, are you?"

In view of the way it was said, Jenny felt she could give only one answer. "No, of course not."

He trotted his horse to the blanket, bent, and

swooped up the canteen. "Maybe I'll come across a stream or water hole where I can fill this." As he trotted his horse away, he called over his shoulder, "See if you can get a little more sleep before I get back."

Cole rode away, deep in thought. A part of him — that Southern gentleman part that he hadn't been able to shake — was very disappointed to discover that Jenny was not only a gold digger, but an actress. Christ, he thought, it was common knowledge that actresses were just as immoral as their sister "ladies of the evening." Yet there had been instances when Jenny had behaved almost maidenly, he remembered with puzzlement. Had that just been an act, too?

Then a smile crossed Cole's lips as he did a complete turn around and another part of him came to the fore. She sure did put him in his place, he thought with amused admiration, reminding him in no uncertain terms that he wasn't any better than she. In a way, it was a shame he wasn't who she thought he was. Then they would be kindred spirits. There was a lot of woman in that little spitfire.

Nine

Jenny was asleep when Cole crouched beside her a few hours later and tapped her shoulder. She bolted to a sitting position, swinging her arms wildly. Finally she looked around her, then distinguished who it was beside her in the dark, clamped her hand to her chest where her heart was racing, and exclaimed breathlessly, "Damn you! Why did you sneak up on me like that? You scared the hell out of me!"

"I didn't sneak up on you," Cole answered in annoyance, rubbing his shoulder where one of Jenny's fierce swings had clipped him and almost bowled him over. "I called your name. I can't help it if you're such a sound sleeper."

As she watched him rub his shoulder, Jenny asked, "Did I hit you?"

"Yes. You carry quite a wallop there, considering your size."

"I'm sorry. When I'm awakened from a sound sleep, I'm always a little confused and wild."

"Thanks for the information," Cole answered dryly. "The next time, I'll stand at the end of the blanket and yell."

Jenny laughed softly. Spying the white material he held in one hand, she recognized it as a pair of the pajama-like clothing the male peasants wore. "Are those my new clothes?"

"Yes. That's what took me so long. I had to wait until the family went to sleep before I could snatch them from the fence where they were drying."

He'd stolen from the poor, Jenny thought with strong disapproval. "Why didn't you just buy them? They couldn't cost that much."

"I was afraid it might rouse their suspicion. They might not think me buying a blanket, a water bag, and some food odd, but boy's clothing, particularly when I didn't have anyone with me?"

"So they might think it odd. So what?"

"They'd remember it, and if Cortinas' men came asking questions . . ."

Cole's voice trailed off and Jenny finished the sentence for him, saying, "They'd know to look for a man and boy, not a man and a woman." Then a sudden thought came to her, "But won't they be suspicious when they wake up and find the clothing missing?"

"There's no reason why they should suspect me. They saw me ride off, and the clothes certainly won't fit me. No, they'll assume some curious night animal dragged them off."

"There are night animals around here?" Jenny asked, glancing around her nervously.

"Yes. Coyotes, lobos, armadillos."

"What's an armadillo?"

Cole racked his brain for an apt description, then answered, "It's an animal about the size of a fat cat, completely covered with armor-like scales. If you saw

127

one, you'd know. There's nothing in the world quite like it."

It sounded like something out of the dark ages to Jenny. "Are they dangerous?"

"Armadillos?" Cole laughed, "God, no! They're frightened of their own shadow. If it wasn't for their hard shell, they probably would have disappeared from the earth ages ago. I had one as a pet when I was a boy."

Jenny took the clothing from Cole and rose, asking, "What part of Texas are you from?"

Cole saw no point in lying. He could tell her his beginnings without revealing his real identity. He came to his feet, saying, "I was born in Brownsville and spent my boyhood there. Then when my parents died from yellow fever, my brother and I went to live with an uncle in east Texas."

"Turn around, so I can change clothes," Jenny said.

Cole wondered what difference it made, since he had seen her in her drawers and chemise before, and even less, but he complied.

"Is that all you had, just one brother?" Jenny asked as she stripped off her blouse and skirt.

"There was a sister, but she died when she was an infant, before I was born." Cole didn't want Jenny asking any more questions, so he turned the conversation. "What about you? Did you come from a big family?"

"Big enough," Jenny answered evasively.

After she had put on the boy's tunic and pants, she walked around Cole, planted herself before him and asked, "Well? Do I look like a Mexican boy?"

Cole frowned. "Not up close. Your skin is too pale, and of course, there's still your hair. You can't cover it with a scarf, not if you're posing as a boy."

"I know. I thought I'd braid it and poke it up under my *sombrero*."

"You'll have to wear the hat when we're on the trail, then, and tuck your head down when we're around people, so they can't see your face."

"Won't that look suspicious, ducking my head?"

"No, not at all. All *peons* are very submissive, the children even more so. Remember to slump your shoulders, too, like you're beaten down. That will make it even more convincing."

Jenny was beginning to feel for the Mexican peasants. It seemed they were even more downtrodden than the poor were where she had come from.

While Cole picked up his blanket, shook the sand from it, and rolled it up, Jenny braided her hair and stuffed it beneath the *sombrero* as she put it on. She started following Cole to the horses, then remembered something, backtracked, and scooped the discarded blouse and skirt, thinking they might come in handy in the future. When she reached Princess, she saw Cole had already saddled the horse. She noticed the water bag hanging from the saddle horn and the blanket tied to the back of the saddle. She stuffed the blouse and skirt into the blanket, then something draped over the saddle caught her eye. "What's that?"

"That's a *serape*," Cole answered, reaching over her head and picking it up. "It's a kind of blanket-coat the Mexicans wear to protect them from the cold. Since it gets rather cool in the desert at night, I thought you might need it. Those clothes I brought you are long-sleeved, but they're a little threadbare."

Jenny was glad to see the cloak. She was already

feeling chilled. She accepted it from Cole and fumbled in the darkness for the buttons. Finally she asked in exasperation, "How does this damn thing open?"

Cole turned from where he had been checking his saddle cinch and laughed. "It doesn't. There's a hole in the middle to slip your head through." He took it from her and slid his hand through the opening, saying, "See?"

"Well, you could have saved me time and trouble and told me that," Jenny replied sourly, snatching the *serape* from Cole. Damn, she hated to look the fool in front of him, and it seemed that every time she turned around she was doing something stupid. He'd never come to admire her if she continued.

Cole didn't respond to Jenny's show of temper. He turned and mounted, while Jenny slipped on the *serape* and then replaced her hat. He turned his mount just as she was swinging into the saddle.

"I'll have to admit you do look like a Mexican," Cole remarked, when she had settled in.

"Yeah," Jenny agreed, looking down at herself. "I think the *serape* gives the whole costume the finishing touch. Now if I just had some of my stage makeup, I could darken my face and hands and look even more convincing."

"You'd still have to keep your head down. No Mexican has eyes your color, not that stunning deep blue. Maybe you'll find an occasional pair of eyes that blue among the pure Spanish around Mexico City, but not in this part of the country."

Ordinarily Jenny would have been miffed at anyone finding a flaw in her costume, but this time she smiled. Cole had called her eyes a "stunning deep blue," and there had been just a subtle drop in the timbre of his voice when he had said it. At least he admired something about her, she thought in secret delight.

They rode through the night in silence, and Jenny discovered two things that pleased her. One, the *serape* was long enough in the back that she could tuck the excess under her for padding, making her ride much more comfortable, and two, she could doze while she rode, as long as she was careful not to fall too sound asleep.

Because she was not as exhausted and uncomfortable as she had been the night before, Jenny noticed the stars disappearing from the sky one by one as dawn neared. Over her shoulder, she could see the morning star still burning like a bright lantern in the eastern sky. When she saw a pearly flush on the horizon behind her, she turned her horse and asked, "What's that light over there?"

"That's the sun rising."

"I don't see any sun."

"No, you see its light long before you see it, particularly out here on the desert," Cole answered, bringing his horse around to stand by hers.

"Can we watch?"

"The sunrise?" Cole asked in surprise.

"Yes."

"Why?"

"Because I've never seen one."

Cole couldn't believe his ears. "Everyone has seen a sunrise."

"I haven't. I told you, I was a city girl. A big city girl.

131

You can't see sunrises and sunsets there because of the tall buildings. You do good to see any sky, much less sun. Then, after I joined the theater and started doing some traveling, I was always asleep when the sun came up."

Cole frowned. There was something in Jenny's voice that made him believe she had missed out on a lot more than seeing a sunrise. "All right, we can stop for awhile. But I don't want to make camp here. I'd like to find someplace that will provide us with a little cover."

Jenny watched as the pearly flush on the horizon became more peach-colored, then rose-colored. The low-hanging clouds on the horizon took on a violet tinge, then turned a vivid pink as golden shards of light lit the blood-red sky and a blinding-white orb rose over the horizon, looking gigantic. All around her, on every cactus, on every yucca, on every lacy leaf of every twisted mesquite, the night dew sparkled in the light like glittering jewels, while rainbows danced on the spider webs. Suddenly, as if all nature had stood hushed for that breathtaking moment, the desert came alive with the joyous sounds of the desert larks, and high above them, an eagle shrieked, greeting the new day.

"That was the most beautiful thing I have ever seen," Jenny muttered in awe.

"Yes, it was," Cole agreed. "The most spectacular sunrises and sunsets I've ever seen have been in the desert. I think it must be because there is nothing to obscure the view. And no two are alike."

They rode for another two hours before Cole spied a line of trees up ahead of them. "We'll make camp up there. With any luck, there'll be a stream or a pond."

"Why do you think that?"

"Those trees are cottonwoods, not mesquites. Mesquites will grow anywhere, even on pure rock. But cottonwoods only grow around water. Let's just hope they left a little for us."

When they reached the trees and rode beneath them, they discovered that the stream was almost dry, but there was a small pool, its surface shimmering in the sunlight. As soon as she saw it, Jenny jumped from her horse and ran towards it, anxious for a swallow of fresh water for a change. Cole leaped from his horse and was right behind her. Reaching out, he caught her shoulder and swung her around, asking, "Have you forgotten what I said about water holes in this country? It may not be safe."

Jenny glanced back at the inviting pool. "But it looks safe."

"You can't go completely by that. You have to go by smell. If it's full of alkali, it will smell as bitter as it tastes. And if it's really loaded, you can feel it. It's slippery. If the water just smells bad, then it's stagnant, and there's a good chance it might be contaminated. Believe me, dysentery is no fun, particularly the Mexican variety of it. You stay here while I check it out, and keep your mare away," Cole added, seeing Princess coming towards them.

Jenny held Princess back by her cheek strap while Cole checked the pool. He walked back, saying, "It's safe. You can go ahead."

Jenny hurried to the pool, dropped on her knees, and scooped up a handful of water, while Princess drank noisily beside her. Shortly thereafter, they were joined by Cole and his horse. When their thirst had been satisfied, Jenny asked curiously, "Why didn't

133

your horse head for the pool, too, like Princess? Did he know he had to wait for you to check it out?"

Cole chuckled. "No, he's not that smart. I left him ground tied."

"What does that mean?"

"I've trained him so that when his reins are trailing the ground, he won't move from that spot, unless I whistle for him to come to me."

"That's amazing. Do you think I could teach Princess that?"

"I'm sure you could, if you're willing to spend the time on it. You're planning on keeping her, then?"

"Of course, I'm going to keep her!" Jenny answered with possessive outrage. "Why wouldn't I?"

"Amos might not like your keeping a gift from Cortinas."

"Then I won't tell him she was a gift. I'll tell him I stole her, that I just picked a horse at random." A sudden light came into Jenny's eyes. "Or better yet, I could say you stole her for our escape and gave her to me."

"Me?"

"Yes. You're helping me escape. You might as well collect the money Amos offered you. He doesn't have to know you didn't plan it that way all along."

It was a tempting suggestion. The money would go a long way to getting his plantation back on its feet. Then Cole remembered that he had to get his report to the Governor. As it was, Jenny was already delaying him. "No, I told you. Rio Grande City is as far as I'm taking you. I have things I have to do."

The only reason Jenny could fathom Cole turning down Amos' money was that he had something more profitable planned. Like robbing another bank. For that reason, she didn't argue with him, but she did feel a big disappointment at his decision.

Cole cleared an area in the underbrush to one side of the pool for their camp. After a breakfast of more *tortillas* and cheese, Jenny said, "I'd like to take a bath."

"Now?" Cole asked, in the process of spreading their blankets on the ground. "Aren't you sleepy?"

Since the day before, when she had sweated so profusely, Jenny had felt uncomfortable and sticky. "I think I'd sleep better if I felt clean."

"Go ahead. I might take one myself later."

"Do you have any soap?"

"Yeah, I have a bar or two in my saddle bags. Do you want to borrow some?"

"If you don't mind."

Cole knelt on one knee by his saddlebags and drew out a bar of soap. As he handed it to her, Jenny asked, "Do you by any chance have a towel in there?"

"I'm afraid not. I always use the clothes I take off for a towel, if I even bother with toweling off."

"Then put them back on wet?" Jenny asked, her nose wrinkling in distaste.

"No, I carry a few changes of clothing with me."

"Clean clothing?" Jenny asked, eyeing the saddlebags as if they contained gold bars.

"Yeah. Why do you ask?"

"Could I borrow a shirt?" Then seeing the frown coming over Cole's face, she quickly added, "Just to sleep in, just until this afternoon when my clothes are dry."

"You're going to wash everything, even the clothing I just brought you?"

"Why not? Who knows when I'll be able to do laundry again? And I promise I won't ask to borrow it after today. From then on, I'll sleep in my blouse and skirt. At least if I can't wash my other clothing, I can air it."

"All right," Cole agreed, reaching back into his saddlebags and pulling out a wrinkled, but clean shirt. "But just today," he reiterated.

Jenny took the shirt, saying, "Thanks. I really appreciate this." She turned, picked up the blouse and skirt which Cole had scattered on the ground when he had shaken out her blanket, and headed for the pool, veering off to one side where the brush would conceal her from Cole's eyes.

"Wait a minute!" Cole called, then hurried towards her.

"What's wrong?" Jenny asked as he approached.

"If you're going over there, you'd better let me check it out first."

"Check it out for what?"

"Rattlesnakes."

A horrified expression came over Jenny's face. She glanced down at the ground, looking nervously around her.

Cole passed her, picked up a big stick laying on the ground, and began shaking the brush with it, then when nothing came slithering out, moved on to the next clump of bushes, and on and on, until Jenny lost sight of him. Finally he returned, saying, "It's clear, but be careful when you step into the pool. Some of the rocks around the edge look slippery."

"You're sure it's safe?" Jenny asked.

"As safe as I can tell. If you're nervous about it, you can bathe right there." He pointed to the pond right next to their camp.

"No, I don't think so."

"I won't peek, if that's what's bothering you. I plan on going right to sleep."

Jenny was street-wise, but she was also modest. She couldn't bathe in front of anyone, much less a man, even if he had promised not to look. It would make her too uncomfortable. But she was afraid if she objected on those grounds, it would make her look silly in Cole's eyes. "No, I don't want to keep you awake with my splashing. I'll go over there."

As Jenny walked away, Cole stared at her back and once again wondered about her. Asking to borrow his shirt to sleep in had seemed bold, just as he would expect a woman of questionable virtue to behave, but her insistence on bathing in privacy told him differently. Over and over, she was giving him conflicting signals. He shrugged his shoulders in frustration, then turned and walked back to camp.

An hour later when Jenny returned, Cole was sound asleep. She placed what was left of the bar of soap next to his saddlebags, then tiptoed to her blanket, which he had spread a few feet from his, placed her shoes at the edge of it, and reclined. For just a moment, she relished the wonderful sensation of being clean and the cool shade of the tree over her. Even Cole's shirt was a source of comfort to her. Being long-tailed, it reached well below her knees and felt much like one of her nightgowns. The rustle of the leaves in the tree above her was a soft lullaby. With a dreamy smile on her face, she drifted off to sleep.

Ten

Jenny didn't know what had awakened her. She opened her eyes and gazed at the leaves dancing in the soft breeze above her, the sunlight winking here, then there, then here again as the leaves moved. Then she heard the splashing. Still groggy, she sat up and looked around her.

Her eyes caught and held on the sight of Cole wading from the pool beside the camp. It wasn't as if she had never seen a naked man before. She had. But she had never seen such a magnificent specimen of masculinity. With the powerful muscles on his arms and legs rippling, his smooth wet skin glistening in the sunlight, and the water drops caught in the dark hair on his broad chest glittering, he seemed more godlike than human.

She stared as if in a trance, trying desperately to keep her eyes away from what lay below the waist. But she couldn't seem to help herself. She glanced down and was shocked by what she saw. It appeared Cole was as well endowed there as he was in his unusual breadth of shoulder.

Then, as Cole came to a sudden halt, Jenny jerked

her eyes away and looked up. Seeing him watching her, she sputtered, "I'm . . . I'm sorry. Your splashing must have awakened me. I . . . I didn't mean to . . . to . . ." Her voice trailed off, and she looked away, a guilty flush rising on her face.

"That's all right," Cole answered calmly, picking up his pants and slipping them on. "I'm not offended, if you aren't, I thought it would be safer if I bathed right here, since you're such a sound sleeper. I wouldn't want anyone to slip up on you while I was away. I didn't realize you were awake."

What Jenny was feeling was not offense. Her heart was racing, her mouth had turned suddenly dry, and she was finding it difficult to breathe. For the life of her, she couldn't shake Cole's naked image from her brain. It stubbornly clung there. Jenny felt a heat rising that had nothing to do with guilt or embarrassment, a reaction that was as baffling as it was discomforting.

Cole noted Jenny's high color. Secretly he was pleased with her embarrassment, and a little amused. "You can look now. I'm covered."

Jenny risked a glance and saw it was true. Then she noticed something else. "You shaved!" she blurted in surprise.

Cole rubbed his chin and answered, "Yes, I did. Like you, I decided to start out fresh."

Jenny found Cole even more handsome with the beard gone. Now there was nothing to detract from his strong chin and sensuous lips. She stared.

"What's the matter? Cole asked. "Don't you like me clean shaven?"

Belatedly Jenny realized she was making a fool of

herself — again! "Oh, no, I like it," she answered nervously. "I really don't care for beards."

Neither did Cole, but he couldn't admit that. He had only neglected his shaving to make him look more the role he had been playing.

Jenny finally managed to drag her eyes away from Cole. "You've got a fire going," she said in surprise.

"Yes, I thought we could do with some fresh meat tonight. I shot a couple of rabbits and roasted them. Are you hungry?"

"Yes, but aren't you afraid someone will see the fire?"

"They won't. Cottonwood doesn't smoke when it burns."

She should have known Cole would think of that, Jenny realized. He thought of everything.

"But now that you mention it," Cole continued, "I've been considering something, and I think I'll do it. I noticed when I was swimming in the pool that one of these cottonwoods is pretty tall. I imagine you can see for quite a ways from up there. I think I'll climb it and have a look around while you're eating."

He turned and walked away, looking up at the thick green canopy above him for the tallest tree and saying over his shoulder, "I left a plate of rabbit by the fire. There's a pot of coffee there, too, and a cup. It should still be warm."

Jenny watched as Cole found the tree he was looking for, then scampered up as if he were part cat. Why did he make everything he did look so easy, so effortless? Jenny thought a little enviously. He didn't seem to have a clumsy bone in his body. She turned and walked to the fire.

Jenny was perched on a big rock and finishing the rabbit when Cole dropped to the ground and walked over to her. "Well?" she asked. "Did you see anything of interest?"

"No, there's not a soul out there, or even a farm to be seen," Cole answered, feeling a little puzzled by the total lack of civilization, "and I could see for well over fifty miles. That's one advantage of the desert. The air is so dry you can see distances you couldn't begin to see anywhere else. I guess we must have hit upon a little-traveled trail."

Jenny's hand stopped midway to her mouth. "Guess? Are you telling me you're not familiar with this country?"

"No, I'm not. I've never been this far west in Mexico. But don't get alarmed. We're not lost. I thought we could keep moving west tonight, then tomorrow, swing north."

"Will it be safe to move north that soon?"

"Safe, or not, I think we'd better. If we traveled much further west, we'd be in the mountains."

"I thought you said the mountains were to the north."

"Yes, the mountains in Texas. But we're still in Mexico, and here, there are mountain ranges everywhere. What isn't desert is mountains, or jungles, if you're around the coast."

Cole had come to rest before Jenny. She found herself eye-level with his broad chest and its mat of dark curls. She had the strangest urge to reach out and touch that very masculine hair, to see if it felt as soft and springy as it looked. Then, totally unbidden, the vision of him coming from the pool, nude and magnificently male, flashed in her mind and, to Jenny's discomfiture, remained. Again her heart raced, and a strange heat filled her. Her hands trembled as she set the plate with its bones down. Then rising on shaking legs, she stood and said, "I guess I'd better collect my laundry, so you can have your shirt back."

"That's not necessary. I have another clean one I can put on."

But Cole didn't move. As if mesmerized, he stared at Jenny, thinking with her shimmering hair hanging loosely around her shoulders and down her back, it looked as if she were standing beneath a golden waterfall. He became acutely conscious of her nakedness beneath his shirt, and the palms of his hands grew sweaty. His gaze shifted to Jenny's face and locked on her mouth, the lips soft and full, a mouth made for kissing.

Jenny watched as if in a trance while Cole's long arm slowly wound around her waist and his dark head dipped. Her heartbeat thundered in her ears. Then, when his warm lips touched hers, she felt a jolt of heat course through her and gasped. Thinking she was about to object, Cole tightened his embrace, and sealed his mouth firmly over hers, then nibbled at her lips. It made Jenny's legs feel like jelly, and her belly quiver. She stiffened when his tongue parted her lips and plunged into her mouth. She had never allowed any man to kiss her like that, so intimately. But Cole's kiss was so insistent, so masterful, so unbelievably exciting, that Jenny could only cling to him weakly, wondering dazedly where in God's name the outlaw had learned to use his tongue like that. It was a darting, teasing torment that seemed to sear her soul. It left her whimpering and clinging to him as if her life depended on it.

Abruptly, Cole broke the searing kiss and lifted his head. Through her dazed eyes, Jenny could see his were blazing with desire. Briefly, she felt some semblance of sanity, and muttered, "I'd better go."

But Cole didn't release her, and Jenny knew deep in her heart that she didn't want him to. Instead, he lifted her and brought her body full force against his, making her achingly aware of his hard male body pressing against her. He felt her breasts flattened against his naked, broad chest, his taut belly against her soft one, his muscular thighs against her rounded ones. He bent his head and nuzzled the soft crook of her neck. The warmth Jenny had been feeling turned to a fire that spread along nerve endings she had never known existed. She began to tingle all over. And then she became aware of the long, hard length of his readiness pressing against her thigh, scorching her with his pulsating heat right through their clothing. Shivers of raw excitement ran through her.

"You want me, don't you?" Cole asked in a husky voice, his lips against her ear. "As much as I want you."

Jenny had vowed years ago that she would never give her body to another man without a wedding ring on her finger. But she was incapable of keeping that vow, as helpless before Cole's strong sexual attraction as a fallen leaf was to the pull of gravity, as drawn as a moth to a flame.

"Answer me!" Cole demanded, molding her soft curves to his hard frame as if he intended to absorb her right through his skin, then taking her earlobe into his mouth and sucking on it.

143

"Yes," Jenny admitted breathlessly, then as his tongue darted into her ear, sending sparks dancing up her spine, whimpered, "Yes, oh, yes!"

Cole's mouth captured hers in a searing, demanding kiss that only fueled the firestorm that was raging in Jenny. With their mouths still locked in that hot, consuming kiss, he carried her the short distance to his blanket, then dropped her to her feet. Jenny clung weakly to his shoulders. The world spun around her while he unbuttoned the shirt, his fingers trembling with need. Impatiently, he ripped the last two buttons free; then as it fell open, pushed it back on her shoulders. Cole sucked in his breath sharply. Jenny was everything he had dreamed she would be, and more, every curve, every hollow perfection. He bent and buried his head in the valley between her breasts with their pert little nipples, breathing in deeply of her fragrance and muttering, "You're beautiful, so beautiful."

Cole fell to his knees, bringing Jenny with him and pushing the shirt down her arms as he lay her back. With his long body half covering hers, he bathed her face and neck and shoulders with kisses, his questing hands seemingly everywhere, smoothing over her hips and thighs, circling her belly, slipping around to caress the backs of her thighs, squeezing her buttocks, then moving back up, cupping and massaging her breasts. There seemed to be no part of her that didn't receive his ardent attention either from his skillful fingers or his mouth, except that part of her that was screaming with need. When he took one rosy, throbbing nipple into his mouth and suckled it, Jenny felt as if a bolt of fire had raced to that place between her legs. Desperately seeking something to assuage that terrible burning, she arched her hips and rubbed herself against the closest part of Cole she could find — his hip.

Cole knew what Jenny wanted, needed, but he hadn't gotten his fill of feeling her incredibly silky skin, tasting her sweetness, drinking in her fragrance. "Easy, spitfire," he muttered against her breast, gently pushing her away. "I'll give you what you want — eventually. Until then, this should help your hunger."

As Cole slipped one hand between her legs, then returned to his feasting at her swollen breasts, Jenny felt as if she were being drowned in sensation coming at her from every direction. Cole's slender fingers were a torment, as were his lips and tongue — teasing, taunting, titillating. Spasms of pleasure rocked her body, each more intense than the last. And still that terrible urgent need was there, clawing at her loins, making her beg for release. "Please, oh, please."

Cole could no longer deny Jenny. The feel of her damp heat beneath his fingers, the intoxicating taste of her skin, her excitement as she writhed beneath him had aroused him to an unbearable pitch. He unbuttoned his pants and slid them down, then moved over her. He cautioned himself to go slow, to remember how delicate Jenny was, to be careful and gentle with her, despite Jenny's frenzied pleading to hurry. But the moment his heated flesh touched hers, Cole felt an ungovernable urgency seize him. He plunged into her tight, hot depths, shuddering in reaction as she took him deeper and deeper.

Jenny cried out, part in pain and part in extreme pleasure at Cole's penetration, then marveled at the feel of his magnificent manhood filling her, throbbing in unison with her if they shared the same heart. When he began his movements, powerful, masterful strokes that took her breath away, she clung to him, urging him on, muttering over and over and over, "yes, yes, yes," then raking his back with her nails and moaning as the tempo increased. Then there was nothing but sensation, pure, unadulterated sensation as he made her feel, and feel, and feel things that she had never dreamed possible, until every nerve in her body was stretched taut, until she thought she would die from the exquisite pleasure, until a wild turbulence seized her and she exploded in a wondrous, glorious, terrifying burst of blinding-white light.

When Jenny recovered from her shattering experience, she was covered with a fine sheen of perspiration, her heart was still racing wildly, and she was left wondering what had happened. It had certainly never been that way before. With Stan, she could hardly wait for the act to be over. Why had it been so very special, so unbelievably thrilling with Cole? Then she knew why. Like everything else he did so much better than any other man, Cole made love so much more wonderfully.

Cole raised his head from where it lay between Jenny's breasts and asked in a thick voice, "Did I hurt you?"

"No."

"You cried out when I penetrated you," he reminded her.

Jenny remembered, and recalled urging him on just moments later, but Cole had been too engrossed with his own raging passion at that point to notice. "You didn't hurt me, not really," Jenny answered, which considering his immense size was quite astonishing, she thought. Then recalling everything, she whispered in awe, "No, it was wonderful. I never knew it could be so wonderful."

"Then you have no regrets?" Cole asked, wondering how he had let things get so badly out of hand. He usually had better control than that.

Jenny remembered her vow, but she couldn't regret what had happened. It was an experience she would never forget, like being given a glimpse of heaven. Once more, she didn't know if it would ever happen again. Their passion had just seemed to suddenly ignite, without either of them intending for it to happen. She stroked his damp shoulder and answered, "No regrets."

Cole smiled, vastly relieved that Jenny wasn't going to place the blame squarely on his shoulders now that her frenzied need had been satisfied. He knew most women would have done that — completely forgetting that they wanted it as much as the man, that they had spurred him on — or at least, pretended outrage. It seemed to be a game women played with men, one as old as time. It was a rare woman who would admit to pure and simple passion. He found himself admiring Jenny's honesty, and grateful that she wasn't going to put him through that pretense. "I'm glad you feel that way."

Cole looked around him and saw the light was rapidly fading. He kissed Jenny's forehead lightly before he lifted himself from her, saying, "We'd better break camp. The sun is going down."

They dressed and made their preparations to leave without a word, and they rode that night in silence, both knowing that their relationship had changed.

Neither wanted to bruise it in its newness by saying the wrong thing, nor did either have any idea of just what that relationship was, or dream of where it would lead them.

About an hour after sunrise, Cole was scanning the desert before him, looking for a likely place to make camp that day, when Jenny happened to glance back over her shoulder and saw a strange thing on the horizon. She turned half-way in her saddle and stared at it, trying to figure out what it could be, then asked, "What is that glittering back there? The sun hitting rocks, or something?"

Cole turned in his saddle and peered into the distance. Already the sun was making heat waves, making the desert look as if it was shimmering. In that shimmery haze on the horizon, he too, could see a strange glittering. Then suddenly it dawned on him what it was, and his blood ran cold. "Christ! That's a band of Apaches, and they've spied us!"

Jenny's heart seemed to leap to her throat. "Apaches?" she croaked. "How do you that's who it is?"

"Because that glittering is the light hitting their lances. Come on! Let's get the hell out of here!"

Jenny was terrified as they raced across the desert as if all the demons in hell were after them. She had never in her life dreamed horses could move so fast. They seemed to be flying, everything rushing past her in a blur. She risked a glance over her shoulder and saw the Apaches were close enough that she could see their red headbands and their long black hair flapping in the wind. It was a sight that struck terror in her heart.

"They're gaining on us," she yelled across to Cole.

"Don't look back," he answered, whipping his horse to greater speed with his reins. "Just ride like hell. That's our only chance, to outrun them."

Jenny followed Cole's lead, whipping Princess with her reins, begging the animal to run faster. But they seemed doomed. She could almost feel the Apaches' horses' hot breath on her neck. Then as a lance whizzed by her, the feathers tied to it fluttering wildly in the air, she called across to Cole, "I know we're going to die, but I want to tell you something before I do."

She picked the goddamnest times to try to carry on a conversation, Cole thought. "What?"

Jenny grinned sheepishly. "You're a damn good lover, and I wish we could have done it just once more."

Cole was taken completely aback by Jenny's compliment. He had admired her honesty, but sometimes she carried it to the extreme. Then he grinned and called back. "Thanks. So do I."

Cole realized he meant it. He had thought their coming together just a one-time thing, a slip on his part. But more than anything in this world, he wanted to make love to Jenny again, not another hasty joining where everything was lost in the passion of the moment, but leisurely, where he could savor every touch, every sensation. But more remarkable, he wanted to make it even better for Jenny.

Eleven

Shortly after Jenny had made her shocking announcement, some of the Apaches that were chasing them began to lose ground. By that time they had reached the foothills of the mountains, and Cole kept he and Jenny riding at the same rapid speed, despite the fact that both of their horses were beginning to make loud blowing noises. He saw no point in concerning himself over the animals' lives. If he and Jenny were captured, the horses would be slaughtered and eaten, since they were much fleshier than the Apaches' skinny mounts. They either all lived, or they all died.

Over one rolling hill after another, they rode, climbing higher and higher, the ground becoming more and more rocky, the hills steeper and more treacherous. The mesquite brush gave way to scattered cedars and an occasional stunted pine. Cole glanced back and saw that the last of the Apaches had finally dropped out, but nevertheless, he maintained their pace for another mile or so. Then he finally reined in on a rocky ledge at the side of the mountain they had been climbing. From that viewpoint, he could see everything below them and out into the desert. The Apaches and their exhausted horses were scattered all over the area.

Jenny turned her full attention to Princess. The mare was heaving to catch her breath, sucking in great drafts of air, and her mouth foamed. She dismounted and asked in alarm, "Is she going to be alright?"

Cole swung from his saddle and examined both horses. Thankfully there was no blood in either of the animal's spittle and both mouths could be easily opened. "They're not floundered from being overrun," he answered. "I think they'll both be okay." He turned and looked out over the ledge, saying, "Thank God those were Apaches and not Comanches. A Comanche's horse wouldn't have given out like those did, and we wouldn't have outrun them. Comanches appreciate horseflesh and know how to treat it."

Jenny was still concerned for her horse and thought it a shame that the animal was having to pay the price for their freedom. Why, a few more miles would have probably killed Princess. "I know we were outnumbered there at the beginning, but why didn't you shoot just those last few, since you're supposed to be such a damned good expert at it?" she asked angrily. "That would have spared these poor animals having to run those last miles."

"No, Jenny. My not killing any of them will probably be the only thing that might save our lives in the future. This way, they can just give up the chase and go home, without particularly losing face—after all, it was their horses that gave out, not them—but if I had killed any of them, they'd pursue us with a vengeance. Apache law demands that of them—a life for a life."

Since Jenny couldn't see over Cole's shoulder, she

glanced around him and saw that the Apaches were indeed withdrawing, for the most part walking their sweaty, weary horses away, while a few just left their collapsed mounts on the ground to recover by themselves. "Look!" she cried out excitedly. "You were right. They're leaving!" Then she squinted her eyes and peered closer. "What in the world are they doing to that one horse?"

Cole turned and looked out. "They're butchering it, since it's dead. They would have preferred ours, but—"

"They eat horses?" Jenny interjected in a shocked voice.

"Yes. I think they probably prefer the taste to beef. It wasn't just us they wanted."

Jenny turned away from the upsetting sight. "I'm sorry I criticized you," she apologized softly. "I should have known you knew what you were doing."

"I'm not positive they'll leave us alone, Jenny," Cole admitted readily. "I'm just hoping. Apaches are totally unpredictable. For that reason, as soon as our horses have rested for a few moments, we're heading further into the mountains. Since this range runs in a northerly direction, we'll follow it for a few days. We won't be sitting in the wide open, like we were down there in the desert." Cole paused a moment, then shook his head, saying in self-disgust, "The whole damn thing was my fault. I should have known when we found that perfect water hole and no one came near it all day, when the area was deserted all around, that we had blundered into Apache territory. It was stupid of me, but there's one consolation. I don't think we have to worry about Cortinas' men following us any more. They're bound to know what we didn't. They're probably counting us dead right now."

Jenny didn't know which was worse, being pursued by murdering bandits or being pursued by bloodthirsty Apaches. Like Cole, she could only hope that the red devils had completely abandoned their chase. Otherwise they had just jumped from the frying pan into the fire.

Jenny followed Cole as he led his horse up the mountainside, both she and Princess slipping here and there on patches of loose gravel. They followed a narrow ravine whose rocky walls went straight up, the bed of the stream that had cut the fissure in the earth's crust eons ago so dry that the ground had huge cracks in it. Jenny had thought she was glad to get out of the blazing sun, but discovered that there was no relief in the dark shadows of the canyon. Like the crown of the *sombrero* she had shed an hour before, the walls held the heat of the previous day like an oven.

It was well past noon when the ravine came to a sudden end in a small mountain valley that was cupped in the side of yet another jagged mountain. Jenny looked about in disbelief at the lush grass sprinkled with wildflowers, while Princess whinnied in appreciation, then pulled her reins loose and began grazing hungrily beside Cole's stallion. "Where did this come from?" Jenny asked.

"You find little valleys like this tucked here and there all over the mountains," Cole answered.

"I thought you said you have never been this far west," Jenny commented.

"I haven't," Cole answered, "but that's true in the

153

mountains in west Texas. I assume the same would be here, since all these mountain ranges are just an extension of them, or the Rockies." Cole looked around him saying, "There should be water here some place. There usually is in these valleys."

Water wasn't Jenny's prime objective. Relief from the heat was. She staggered to a small *piñon* pine and sat beneath its spreading boughs, relishing the shade and watching Cole as he walked around and looked for some sign of a stream. Then Jenny heard a tinkling sound behind her. She turned and peered at the solid rock wall of the mountainside about a hundred feet from her. There, among tangled vines growing up the rock, she spied the glistening water trickling down the facade. "I think it's back here," she called to Cole.

The waterfall was so small that it didn't flow into the tub-like basin that it had carved in the solid rock at its base. It dripped ever so slowly. And the cool water was the most delicious Jenny had ever tasted. After relieving their thirst and that of the horses, Cole and Jenny spread their blankets beneath the pine and slept. It was almost dusk when Jenny awakened to find a small fire burning and Cole lounging on his blanket.

"The coffee is fresh, if you'd like a cup," Cole said as Jenny sat up.

Jenny helped herself to a cup of coffee and as she drank it, Cole said, "I've decided we're not going to travel at night as long as we're in the mountains. It's too dangerous. The terrain is too treacherous in the dark, to say nothing of the risk of getting lost. We'll travel in the mornings, rest a few hours midday during the worst of the heat, then ride again in the afternoons. It will take us a little longer to get to Texas, but we'll stand a better chance of getting there in one piece."

Jenny had no objections, particularly not that day. She was still tired from the extended traveling they had done that morning, to say nothing of the emotional toll the Apaches chasing them had wrought. "In that case, I think I'll freshen up a bit. Can I borrow your soap again?"

"I assume you know you can't bathe or wash your clothes in that little pool. It's probably taken years to fill it up, and it's all the water we have."

"I know. I'm only going to use a little of it."

Cole slipped the soap from his saddle bags, and a battered small pot that Jenny hadn't known was there. He handed them to her, saying, "You can use the pot as your wash basin. Just rinse it when you've finished."

Jenny filled the pot with water, then slipped off into a wooded area beside their camp with the pot, soap, and her clean blouse and skirt in hand. She slipped off her clothing, draping it over several bushes to air out, then washed, and finally donned the skirt and blouse. When she returned a while later, Cole was frying bacon in a small skillet, equally as battered as the pot he had loaned her. Jenny helped herself to a cup of coffee and sat down on her blanket while Cole dished her out a serving of tinned beans, then slid several strips of bacon from the skillet onto the plate. "Here," he said, "you can have the plate. I'll eat out of the frying pan. You can have the fork and I'll take the spoon."

"You can share my coffee with me," Jenny offered, since there was only one cup.

"No, I already had a couple of cups," Cole answered, pouring the fat from the frying pan before

155

adding the beans.

They ate in silence, until Jenny noticed that the tin fork she was using had initials carved into its handle, as did the bottom of the plate. "Did you steal these from someone?" she asked.

Cole stopped with his spoon midway to his mouth. "What made you think that?"

"Because the initials carved in them aren't yours."

Cole laughed. "CSA stands for Confederate States of America. This is what's left of my old army mess kit."

"Oh, I guess that was stupid of me," Jenny admitted with a laugh of her own. "I wondered why anyone would bother to mark tin eating and cooking utensils. They certainly couldn't be valuable."

"Then it doesn't bother you that I served in the Confederate Army?"

Jenny swallowed the bite of food in her mouth before answering, "No. Why should it?"

"You're a Yankee. Supposedly, we're enemies."

"Not me. I never had any strong feelings against the South, nor did any of the people where I came from. We didn't want to fight you. Why, even our mayor was against it. He wanted to stay neutral, so the port could stay open. Then, after Lincoln started all that foolishness about freeing the slaves, we were even more against it. Why, there weren't enough jobs as it was, without having all of them swarming up north and competing for them."

Cole frowned, thinking Jenny didn't sound like any Yankee he'd come across. "Where are you from?"

"New York."

Cole remembered her saying something about the

port. "New York City?"

"Yes, except I never called it New York City. I don't think anybody that lives there does, even the snobbish rich. They always refer to it by the area they came from, and for me that was the Bowery. Have you ever heard of it?"

Cole knew as little about New York as Jenny did about Texas. He hadn't gone to college back east, even though that was common practice among the gentlemen planters of east Texas, where he had gone to live with his uncle after his parents had died. By the time he had come of age, the war was going hot and heavy, and the farthest north Cole had gone during the war had been Tennessee, where he'd sneaked off to join his older brother with Terry's Texas Rangers when he was barely sixteen. "No, I'm afraid I know very little about any of the east."

Jenny wasn't really surprised at Cole's answer. She'd figured he came from a poor family, and like herself had been forced by desperation into what he was doing, since he was making a living as an outlaw. No, he wouldn't have done any traveling, or had much of an education. That was why she felt she could be perfectly candid with him without fearing he would look down on her. "Well, I thought you might of heard of it, since it has such a bad reputation. Every day, the big newspapers have something in them about the Bowery, a riot, a brawl, a robbery, a murder. It's a rough place, but it isn't because the people are really mean. They're mostly Irish, and we Irish have a way of letting our temper get out of hand. And everyone who lived there was dirt poor. Seeing your family cold and hungry and sick all of the time makes a person desperate. You

157

know what I mean."

Cole had known hunger both during and after the war, and he knew what it was to be desperate, but he also knew nothing he had ever experienced could begin to compare to what Jenny was talking about. He'd heard of the slums in the big eastern cities, places where thousands and thousands of miserable human beings were crowded in tenement buildings that had been condemned as unfit for humans. They lived in poverty so abject it was almost inconceivable to people like him. Even the shantytowns of the South and the Mexican version referred to as "Chihuahua" in Texas and the Southwest couldn't begin to compare with those slums in filth and rampant disease, nor in sheer numbers. And Jenny had come from that hell? he thought in horror. Beginning to get some insight into what forces had molded Jenny's character, Cole wanted to know more and asked, "Is that why you joined the theater? To escape?"

"You're damn right it was! I saw my mother work herself to death, until she was nothing but skin and bone, and then drown in her own blood from consumption. I swore that wasn't going to happen to me, that I was going to get out, no matter what."

"And your father didn't object to your becoming an actress?"

"Why? Because of the reputation actresses have gotten, that we're all nothing but whores?" Jenny asked angrily. "That's not true, you know. Oh, there may be a few like that in the theater, but most actresses are just hardworking girls trying to make a living, and it sure beats working in one of those cold, damp workhouses. My mother did that, you know, worked in one of those hellholes making clothes. She was half-blind from sewing with no light and all hunched over by the time she was thirty. But you're right," Jenny continued, her mind returning to Cole's question, "my father would have had a fit if he'd known I'd joined the theater. He had all of those wrong ideas about actresses, too. But he was dead by then, killed in the war."

"And you still bear me no ill will?" Cole asked in surprise. The women he knew who'd had relatives killed in the war took a very personal hatred towards the enemy. To them, every Yankee was the man who killed their loved one.

"Because you're a rebel? No, I didn't blame the rebels for my father's death. If anything I blamed the Government, or my father."

"Why would you blame him?"

"I shouldn't have made that comment," Jenny said guiltily. "But my father didn't have to go to war. He was forty-seven, two years over the age limit. He wasn't even enrolled on the conscription list."

"Then he volunteered?"

"No, not exactly. One of those draft brokers came around. You know, the men representing the rich who had been drafted and wanted to buy their way out of it. He offered my father three-hundred dollars to go in some rich bastard's place. That's why I blame the Government. Buying exemptions was legal—but it wasn't fair!" Jenny added, her blue eyes flashing. "The poor couldn't buy their way out. They didn't have that kind of money. Only the well-to-do did. It meant the poor were doing the fighting, while all those wealthy men with their factories were getting richer and richer making uniforms and boots, guns and munitions. My mother and I begged my father not to do it, but three-hundred dollars sounded like a fortune to him. Both he and mother couldn't find work. The factory where my mother had been forced to work sixteen hours a day making uniforms at the beginning of the war had closed down, because there wasn't any material coming from the cotton mills any more. My father worked loading ships at the harbor, when his back was up to it. He'd injured it in an accident on the dock when he was much younger. But there wasn't much work at the harbor either, with the blockade and all, certainly not enough to go around. And my brothers couldn't help out. They'd taken off and gone west for parts unknown before the war even started." Jenny set her plate aside, gazed off for a moment, then said sadly, "No, I can't blame my father. He did what he had to do. I just wish he hadn't been so damn honest."

"What do you mean by that?"

"There were a lot of men who took the money to be a draft substitute, then jumped from the troop train as soon as it pulled out of the station. It was a fairly common practice. Of course, the Government sent bounty hunters after them, but a lot of them never got caught. But my father wouldn't do it. He was just too honest for his own good. Instead he ended up selling his life for three-hundred lousy dollars. And that money never did me and my mother much good either. A few weeks after my father had left, some son-of-a-bitch stole it from us, what was left of it after buying my mother's medicine, that is. Then I heard about my father being killed. She didn't last long after that."

Suddenly Jenny realized she had said a lot more than she had intended. She reached for the coffeepot, saying, "Sorry, I'm not usually such a chatterbox. I didn't mean to bore you."

"I wasn't bored," Cole answered in all honesty. "If anything my curiosity has been aroused. Just how old were you when you embarked on your acting career, if you don't mind me asking."

"No, I don't mind. I was twelve. But I told the manager of the theater group I joined I was fourteen. Of course, I didn't do much acting at first. I could lie about my age, but I couldn't hide my inexperience. I started out helping the costume lady and doing odd chores, but I watched every rehearsal and performance. Before long, I had all the roles memorized."

Cole wasn't surprised. He knew Jenny had a quick mind as well as fierce determination. And no wonder she was so tough and self-sufficient, if she'd been out on her own since she was twelve, he thought. My God, she'd been hardly more than a child!

Cole placed the skillet he had been eating from aside and stared at the fire, deep in thought. He reviewed everything Jenny had told him and found he could no longer scorn her for becoming an actress, not if it had been her only escape from the hell she was living in. He couldn't even fault her for being a gold digger. She was only trying to continue improving her lot. He didn't imagine an actress' life, traveling from town to town and living out of a trunk, very appealing to a woman, not if that woman was looking for security, and every woman seemed to have that nesting urge. And Jenny certainly wouldn't be the first woman to marry for money or position, Cole reminded himself bitterly. There were high-class gold diggers too. Mary Alice had proven that to him, dumping him as soon as she discovered he had lost everything and marrying a prosperous merchant from Waco instead. No, the only thing Cole could fault Jenny for at that moment was her choice in improving her lot in life. She deserved better than that coarse, middle-aged carpetbagger. Far better.

Twelve

Jenny drank her coffee in silence, since Cole was occupied with his own thoughts. She wondered if she
should have revealed so much about herself, particularly that part of her past that wasn't so pretty. She'd
never told anyone except her closest friends about that,
and then only after she had known Carla and John for
some time. But, strange as it seemed, she felt close to
Cole and wondered at it. Was it the nearness of death
that brought the barriers she usually kept around herself tumbling down? She hoped she hadn't made a mistake. She wanted Cole to like her as well as desire
her—if he still did. He'd made no other move toward
her.

She wondered if she should even let Cole make love
to her again, for it wouldn't change any of her plans.
She still intended to marry Amos, and she was sure it
wouldn't change any of Cole's plans either. Men were
like that. They could enjoy passion for passion's sake
and then walk away from it. Some women could do it,
too, but she'd never been one of them. She'd had only
one lover in her lifetime, if she could even call Stan

such a thing. For all of his conceit and polish and good looks, the actor had been terribly clumsy and inept. Jenny let her mind wander briefly to Cole's lovemaking the night before. She had never dreamed anything could be so wonderful. And she knew in her heart that Amos would never make love like that. As she had with Stan, she would dread the act with him. No, she was facing a lifetime of misery in bed, for Jenny had sworn she would never, never cheat on her husband. Despite everything she had done, she'd never sink that low. In exchange for his name and protection, she'd give him her all, including her fidelity. But she wasn't married yet, Jenny reminded herself. And if she was ever going to have a true lover, a man she mated with because she enjoyed it, and not because it was required of her, it was Cole. He was the only man who had ever physically attracted her, the only man who had ever aroused her passion. At least she'd have some memories to sustain her through the lean, bleak years ahead.

"Jenny?"

Jenny jumped at the sound of Cole calling her name. She looked at him in bewilderment.

"I asked you a question," Cole informed her. "Twice."

"I'm . . . I'm sorry. I . . . I must have been daydreaming," Jenny answered, a guilty flush coming to her face. "What did you ask?"

"I asked if there was any particular role you preferred."

"Why, yes, there is," Jenny answered, surprised that he should be that interested in her acting. "I loved playing Juliet." Jenny frowned, remembering Carla had always accused her of possessing a deep-seated

164

romanticism because of her choice, and Jenny had always hotly denied it, claiming she wanted nothing to do with love in any shape, form or manner, that love was a weakness, a folly.

"Then you played something other than boy's roles when you played Shakespeare?" Cole inquired, remembering what Jenny had told him about wearing tights.

"Yes, but not until I joined the Richmond Theater Troupe and met Carla and John Richards. They owned and managed the group and took me under their wing and tutored me, not only in my stage roles, but personally. They were a Southern couple who'd lost everything in the war and turned to acting to support themselves." Jenny laughed in remembrance, then admitted, "They were appalled at my speech and manners. Oh, I could play my roles very well, because I mimicked the other actresses, but otherwise I sounded, and behaved, like I'd just come off the streets. They smoothed out my rough edges, and taught me how to behave and talk like a lady. I owe them more than I can ever begin to repay them." Jenny paused, a scowl coming over her delicate face. "They must be worried sick about me. I promised to write as soon as the wedding was over. And I'm sure they could use the money I borrowed from them. They're probably wondering if they'll ever see it again."

"The money you carry strapped to your thigh?" Cole asked, his gaze falling.

Jenny laughed. "Not tonight. I tucked it under my blanket before I went to sleep. And I owe them a lot more money than that. They loaned me enough to buy an appropriate wardrobe and pay for my passage down here. I didn't have near enough in savings. Damn that Cortinas!" Jenny swore in remembered anger. "All that money for those expensive clothes totally wasted, and all my beautiful dresses gone. Why, I didn't even get to wear some of them."

"How did you plan on paying the couple back? Telling Amos you had an old debt to friends that needed settling after you were married?"

"Of course not! He thinks I come from money, and that they're my parents. I planned on just asking for money here and there and sending it to them. I don't think he'll ask where I'm spending it. He doesn't strike me as a skinflint, like Cortinas."

"Then your friends were in on this deception?"

Jenny shot Cole a sharp look at his calling her carefully laid plans a deception. "Yes, they were. In fact Carla was the one who noticed Amos in the audience that night. He was sitting in one of the boxes with another man and he wore a diamond ring and stickpin with stones so big they could knock your eyes out. She was curious about him, since she'd never seen him before, and asked one of the ushers to eavesdrop on him and his friend. He found out Amos was a wealthy rancher from Texas in town for a few days on business. That's when I got my idea. I thought if I could arrange a meeting with him, pretend I was a lady, and make him fall in love with me and propose before he left, he'd never be any wiser. I found out which hotel he was staying at, and talked Carla and John into helping me. We arranged to accidentally bump into him the next day in the lobby, and from there on it was simple. We told him we were visiting the city ourselves from upstate, so we wouldn't have to produce a home. Paying

166

for that hotel suite we occupied for three nights was expensive enough," Jenny complained.

"He didn't recognize Carla?" Cole asked.

"Not without her stage makeup. She was playing Lady Macbeth the night he saw her and looked really different.

"No, it all worked out perfectly," Jenny continued. "Amos proposed the night before he left, and I promised to join him as soon as I could collect a more appropriate wardrobe. Of course, my parents couldn't come for the wedding. My father couldn't leave his manufacturing business that long, and my mother's health was too frail for so long a trip."

"You had it all sewed up, all neat and tidy, didn't you?" Cole remarked.

Jenny heard the scorn in Cole's voice and exploded. "How dare you look down on me! How dare you call what I'm doing a deception! What I'm doing is no more dishonest that what you're doing. Do you think it's different just because you're a man? That your sex excuses you, but not me? Well, it doesn't work that way!"

"I really wasn't thinking about it from the standpoint of honesty as much as . . ." Cole's voice trailed off.

"As what?" Jenny prompted.

"Well, I guess I'm old fashioned. I believe you should love the person you marry."

Cole's mentioning love was like waving a flag in front of an angry bull. Jenny became only more enraged. She shot to her feet, shrieking, "Love? No, it will be a cold day in hell before I'll let myself fall into that trap again!"

"Again?" Cole asked.

"Yes! That's the line Stan fed me. He *loved* me, he was going to make me a great actress, we were going to get married and start our own troupe. The lying bastard! One day he just disappeared. Took off with another troupe heading south. Well, it only confirmed what I already knew. Only fools fall in love. That was what killed my mother. She could have married another man, a well-to-do merchant. But no! She had to marry my father, because she loved him, even if he was penniless, with no promise. Do you know when she was dying, coughing up her lungs, all she talked about was how much she loved him, after all those years of misery and deprivation and disappointment. Well, I'm not going to do that!" Jenny swore, her eyes glittering with fierce determination. "I don't need love, I don't want love, and I don't believe in love!"

Cole didn't believe *her*. Her denial was too adamant, too emotional. "You've been hurt and disappointed," he responded softly. "You're bitter, but the wound will heal in time. Some day, you'll love again." Cole frowned, wondering where all that foolishness had come from. He was a fine one to talk. He'd never forgive Mary Alice for betraying him, or make the same mistake again. No, no woman was going to trample on his heart a second time. But he did firmly believe what he'd said. If you married someone, you should love them.

"Love again?" Jenny retorted in a belated response. "I never loved Stan. I never said I did! I was infatuated with him. He was the leading male actor, and I was just a naive child. Because every silly female that saw him perform thought he was wonderful, I fell for all of his

168

smooth talk and let him manipulate me into bed. You're damn right, I'm bitter! But not because he broke my heart. Because he made a damn fool out of me, that's why!"

Cole wondered if Jenny had been a virgin when he'd made love to her because she'd been so tight and had cried out when he first entered her. Knowing the truth, he now felt disappointed. He would have liked to have been the first, he realized, then puzzled over his feelings. Why should he care? Those kind of proprietary feelings were reserved for the woman he loved and married, and Jenny was just another woman passing through his life.

Wasn't she?

Seeing the frown on Cole's face, Jenny realized she had revealed everything. Carla had always warned her never to tell all, to always keep some secrets, that men were fascinated by women who had an air of mystery about them. She sure had made a mess of things with her big mouth.

"Well, I guess there's nothing you don't know about me now," Jenny muttered dismally. "I can't blame you if you're disgusted with me, particularly after all that spouting-off I did about actresses being so virtuous."

"I'm not disgusted with you," Cole answered in all honesty. "If it's like you said, he took advantage of your youth and innocence, then he's the disgusting one, not you."

The look of utter relief that came over Jenny's face touched a cord deep within Cole. There was something about it that was almost childlike. She's vulnerable, he thought, despite all of her toughness and self-sufficiency.

"I'm glad," Jenny said, not aware she had given her true feelings away with her facial expression. "I know we didn't start off well, but I'd like for us to be friends."

Cole shrugged his shoulders and answered, "Why not?"

"Then why don't you tell me something more about yourself?"

"I pretty much told it all," Cole answered evasively. "I was born and raised in Brownsville, moved to east Texas when my parents died, lived with my uncle for a few years, joined the army, fought in the war, and came back in one piece."

Jenny waited for Cole to continue, then when he didn't offer any more information, asked, "Why did you become an outlaw?"

"I lost my land and . . ." He shrugged, leaving Jenny to make her own assumption.

"And you had to turn to robbing to live."

It wasn't a question, but a statement, and Cole left it there. It was certainly true for plenty of others in the South, men pushed to their limits and so desperate they turned to lives of crime to support their families.

"What happened to your brother and uncle?" Jenny asked. "Were they part of your gang?"

"No, they were never outlaws. My brother was killed in the war, and my uncle was . . ." Cole caught himself just in time. He had almost said "murdered," and *that* would have taken explaining things he didn't want to. ". . . killed accidentally."

As Jenny opened her mouth, Cole cut across what she was about to say. "No, Jenny, don't ask any more questions. I don't want to talk about myself. I don't want to talk, period."

"I'm sorry," Jenny said, sinking back down to the blanket she had been sitting on. "I don't know why I'm such a chatterbox tonight. I guess you want to go to sleep."

Cole's eyes drifted over Jenny's blond hair, gleaming like a golden cloud in the firelight, then locked on her beautiful face. "No," he answered in a husky voice, "that's not exactly what I had in mind."

Jenny's heart raced, and her mouth turned dry. For the life of her, she couldn't think of a thing to say.

Cole rose and stepped around the fire, then brought Jenny to her feet in front of him. "Do you remember what you said this morning when you thought the Apaches were going to catch us?"

Jenny's heart raced faster, and her legs trembled. "Yes."

Cole's eyes darkened. "Did you mean it?"

Jenny's heart pounded so hard she feared it would jump from her chest. "Yes," she barely whispered.

Cole smiled a seductive smile that promised heaven and made Jenny's legs feel like jelly. "Good. Because I meant it too."

He raised his hands and smoothed his palms over the silky mane that tumbled down each side of Jenny's face, then caught a handful of gold and raised it, burying his face in her hair and breathing deep of its fragrance. "Sweet, so sweet," he muttered. His warm lips brushed her temple as he wrapped his arms around her waist, and Jenny turned her head to him in breathless anticipation. His mouth closed over the tender shape of hers, his incredibly soft lips coaxing, nibbling, teasing unmercifully until Jenny was seething with hunger

171

and straining against him.

She whimpered in frustration and disappointment when he gently pushed her away and broke the kiss, then stood on her tiptoes and raised her head to him, her lips parting in silent invitation. Cole ran one finger across her trembling bottom lip, saying, "In a minute, spitfire. Then I'm going to kiss you until your toes curl. But first I want to see you."

Cole stripped off Jenny's blouse. His eyes locked on her well-molded breasts with their taut rosy peaks thrusting impudently, as if daring him to touch them, to kiss them. The sight sent a white-hot shaft of delight through him, making his manhood lengthen yet more, before he accepted the challenge, bent his head and kissed the tip of one flushed nipple. Jenny moaned when his tongue swirled around the peak, then whimpered as he took the swollen flesh into his mouth. She caught his head, her fingers tangling in his dark hair as she arched her back, glorying in what he was doing to her.

Her skirt fell, to puddle at her feet, and she found herself swept up into Cole's powerful arms. He took in the sight of her nakedness with deliberate slowness, lingering on the golden curls between her thighs so long that Jenny blushed in embarrassment. Then he raised his head and Jenny saw his eyes had taken on a smoky hue. "Did I tell you yesterday how beautiful you were?" he asked, his tongue thick with desire. "All gold and ivory."

He placed her on the blanket, then quickly stripped. Jenny watched enthralled as he bared his male magnificence to her, until he gazed at her again. Feeling a sudden pang of modesty, she dropped her eyes. Then he

172

was beside her on the blanket, taking her into his arms. The heat from his body engulfed her before she even felt his searing skin next to hers. Hot and cold shivers ran over her body.

Cole rained torrid kisses over Jenny's face, throat and shoulders, before he laved her breasts with his wet tongue, then nibbled on the soft skin of her belly and the curve of her hips, all the while his fingers stroking her creamy thighs. He raised his head and kept his earlier promise, kissing her deeply, sensuously, his strong tongue darting into her mouth, greedily seeking the sweetness therein, drinking deeply of her heady nectar. His tender violence wreaked havoc on her senses, spreading fire through her, sapping her strength, making her weak and yielding, and yes, curling her toes.

And as if that weren't enough wild, swirling sensation for Jenny, Cole's fingers had slowly inched upward to the junction of her thighs, his commanding mouth still taking that devouring, drugging kiss. He parted the soft, moist lips and found the core of her femininity with unerring sureness, slowly circling with tantalizing purpose. Then, when Jenny was quivering all over and her nails raked the muscles on his shoulders, he ventured more deeply and boldly than ever before and brought her to a glorious, shattering climax.

Jenny opened her eyes, wondering dazedly what had happened, then saw Cole rearing over her, huge and magnificent. Supporting himself on his forearms above her, he looked deeply into her eyes and whispered, "I think you liked that."

"Oh, yes," Jenny moaned, still floating on a sweet melting languor. "It was wonderful. Thank you."

He smiled warmly. "I'm glad to oblige. But I think

we can beat that."

Jenny gasped as she felt the searing, damp tip of Cole's erection brush across her thigh; then it seemed to be burning like a hot coal at her portal. Suddenly, the embers of her desire reignited.

"Look into my eyes," Cole commanded, and Jenny complied, finding he had taken on an intensity she had never seen. Then, locked in his compelling gaze, she felt him entering her slowly — ever so slowly — making her achingly aware of each magnificent inch of his immense manhood as it filled her. When he was buried completely inside her, a long shudder ran over his body. He lay his head between her breasts, muttering, "God, you're so sweet, so tight, so damn hot."

Cole ran his hands along her sides, then caressed her breasts. He raised his head from its silky pillow and placed a long series of little biting kisses on her soft mouth, then teased the corners with the tip of his tongue. Everything he did only increased the almost painful awareness of him inside her. His rigid flesh pressed against hers, seemingly scalding her. Every nerve ending in her sheath screamed for release as her thighs trembled uncontrollably. The anticipation was an agony.

"Do something!" she begged. "Please. I can't stand this!"

Cole chuckled, and she felt the rumble deep in his chest against her breasts. It only served to increase her frenzy.

"What do you want?" Cole teased, nibbling on her earlobe.

"You know damn well what I want!" Jenny answered, pounding her fists on his shoulders.

"This?" Cole withdrew his entire length and plunged back in.

Sparks danced up Jenny's spine and exploded in her brain. She couldn't answer. Her breath came in short, panting gasps.

Cole didn't need any further urging. The steely control he held over his passion broke, and he drove himself into her, setting a wild, primitive rhythm while his mouth ravaged the sweetness of her. Jenny strained against him, locking her legs around his narrow hips, her breath coming in little sobs, her body on fire with vibrant pulsating sensations. Electric shocks coursed through every fiber of her being. His immense power flowed over her, then through her, seeping into every pore, infusing her with the sweet unbridled fury of his passion, making her blood sing and filling her with sparks and bursting lights. Suddenly she was seized by a wild turbulence, her senses expanding until she feared her skin could no longer contain them. A tremendous euphoria filled her, and as she teetered on the brink, she felt as if she had attained immortality. Then as she was plunged into oblivion amongst a shower of exploding stars, a cry of sheer joy burst from her lips.

Cole followed Jenny in his own white-hot release just seconds later, his body shuddering uncontrollably with overwhelming delight and his hoarse cry of exaltation mingling with her joyous one, the sound shattering the stillness of the night and echoing through the mountains. He collapsed weakly over her.

They lay for a long while in the aftermath of their passion, still entwined, floating on a warm cloud, their muscles trembling with aftershocks. Jenny stroked Cole's shoulders, then ran her hands over the powerful muscles on his back, now slick with sweat from his exertions. Then her hands ventured further, to the rise of his buttocks. Remembering how they had flexed and relaxed in the throes of their lovemaking, a tingle of excitement ran through her.

Cole stirred and started to lift his body from her. "No, don't go," Jenny cried, tightening her arms about him, an instant before she felt a wave of shame wash over her. Why, she realized, she was practically begging him to make love to her.

"I'm only going to put some more wood on the fire. I don't want it to burn out. If there are any wild animals around, it will keep them away."

Jenny released him and rolled to her side, watching as Cole walked to the fire, squatted beside it, then placed several large branches on the glowing embers. While he waited for the wood to catch, Jenny drank in the sight of him hungrily, thinking he was truly beautiful with his splendid physique and inherent gracefulness. Then her eyes lingered on the sight of the damp hair on his chest, glittering in the light of the dancing flames.

When he rose and turned to her, Jenny again averted her gaze, not wanting Cole to catch her eyeing him as a hungry cat would a bowl of milk. That she had practically asked him to make love to her again was bad enough. She didn't have to make a complete fool out of herself.

When Cole reached the blanket, he dropped to his knees beside Jenny and sat back on his heels. The position placed his muscular thighs and his manhood lying at rest between them at Jenny's eye-level. She told herself to look away, if she had any semblance of modesty left, but she found she couldn't. She watched in fascination as his shaft hardened, lengthening inch by inch, then rose and stood proudly erect.

Tentatively, Jenny reached out with a trembling hand and touched him, the feel of his hot, throbbing flesh exciting her unbearably. His groan of pleasure gave her the courage to circle the rigid column with her hand and ask, "Does this mean we can do it again?"

Cole covered her hand with his and taught her the movements, before answering thickly, "It does."

Jenny thought she had died and gone to heaven.

Thirteen

Over the next few days, Cole and Jenny traveled northward through the mountains, doing more riding up and down the rugged terrain than forward. Surprisingly, Cole wasn't particularly disappointed with their lack of progress, even though he was still anxious to get his report to the Governor. He discovered that Jenny was a delightful companion. She was a fascinating story-teller, keeping him entertained for hours with tales of her adventures in the theater, many of them amusing. When she wasn't relating yarns from her past, she took a keen interest in everything around her. She was always asking questions. Had the questions been stupid or silly, Cole might have become irritated, but he was always amazed at her insight. The familiar sights became new and interesting to him through her eyes. And, to his relief, she avoided any more personal inquiries, saving him the trouble of having to evade them or out-and-out lie. Even the periods of silence between them were comfortable and not at all strained, as he would have thought they would be between a man and woman forced to travel together.

But then, they weren't simply two people traveling together. By tacit agreement they had become lovers. Every night, the two shared their blankets in the cool mountain air, and every night Cole made love to Jenny, tempering his raging desire with tenderness as he taught her to enjoy her sensuality to the limits of her capacity. He was rewarded for his patience and gentleness with Jenny when she eagerly gave of herself in total abandon, returning every pleasure he gave her two-fold, astonishing him with the depths of her passion.

On the fifth day, Cole decided to leave the mountains and begin their swing eastward toward Texas and, because Jenny had become more accustomed to the heat, stayed with their schedule of riding during the day. They camped that night in the rolling foothills, and while Cole hunted fresh game, Jenny searched for firewood, a chore she had elected to take over. She was waiting for Cole with a neat pile of broken branches when he returned carrying a couple of sage hens in one hand, and his hat, peculiarly bottom up, in the other.

Handing her his hat, Cole said, "We can munch on these while we're waiting for the hens to roast."

Jenny looked down at the tan pods laying inside the crown. They were about two inches in diameter and they didn't look like something edible to her. "What are they?" she asked.

"The fruit of a *pitahaya,* a strawberry cactus." Cole picked one up and demonstrated as he spoke, "You just peel this covering back and pop it into your mouth." Chewing, he said, "They're delicious."

Jenny was a little wary, but nonetheless, she followed Cole's lead. "Why, it *is* tasty!," she exclaimed in amazement. "But why do they call it a strawberry cactus? It doesn't taste like a strawberry."

"It's named for its size, not its taste. It's smaller than the other cactus tunas."

Jenny picked up another tuna and began carefully peeling it. "I didn't know cactus even bloomed, much less bore fruit," she remarked.

"They bloom mostly after a rain. Then the entire desert seems to come alive with blooms, not only all the cactus, but all the little succulent vines on the ground that you never even notice, as well as the sagebrush."

"Then that explains why I haven't seen a cactus blooming," Jenny remarked dryly. "I haven't seen rain since I came down here. I thought maybe it didn't rain at all."

"Oh, it does, mostly at this time of the year. So far, it's been an unusually dry fall. But when it does rain, it's something to behold. The storms are usually quite violent."

As Cole began picking feathers from one hen, Jenny gazed off thoughtfully into the distance, then asked, "Is all of Texas like that part I passed through on my way to the border, so dry and barren and desolate?"

"If you're wondering how it's going to be at Amos's ranch, yes," Cole answered, hoping to dissuade Jenny from marrying the carpetbagger. "And you're probably going to find yourself just as bored as you were with Cortinas. Amos's ranch is just as

180

isolated as his, and his workers are all Mexicans, too, except for that band of gunslingers he keeps, and they're hardly the kind of people you'd want to socialize with."

"I didn't ask you about that!" Jenny retorted. "I asked you what the rest of Texas looked like. I already knew what Amos's ranch is going to be like. He warned me that our social life might be a little lacking for a while."

"A little lacking?" Cole threw back sarcastically. "No, *nil* would be the more appropriate description. And what's this 'for awhile' business?"

"He said he was going to run for office and that we'd spend most of our time in Austin, or maybe even Washington, in time."

"I doubt that very seriously. The Democrats are back in power in this state, and things are going to stay that way, particularly if I have anything to say about it."

"Is that why you dislike him so much? Because he's a Republican?"

"Where did you ever get the misconception I dislike him?" Cole asked in a silky voice that throbbed with menace. "I hate the bastard! And not just because he's a Republican, but because he's a Republican carpetbagger, an opportunist of the worst sort."

"I don't see anything wrong with trying to better your life. Some people might call me an opportunist, too."

"Not *that* kind. Amos didn't gain what he has by simple dishonesty. He has blood on his hands. You don't, or at least I hope to God you don't."

The thought that Amos had blood on his hands was unsettling, but she didn't want anything to interfere with her plans, not even her own misgivings. She had set her course, and she was bound and determined to keep it, come hell or high water. "I don't care what Amos did in the past, or your opinion of him, so it's pointless for us to discuss him!" Jenny said angrily, jumping to her feet.

"Jenny —"

"No!" Jenny interjected. "I don't want to hear anything more about it!" She whirled around and walked rapidly away, heading for the clearing in the woods where they had staked the horses for the night.

"Where are you going?" Cole called.

"To visit Princess. Right now I prefer her company. She's smart enough to mind her own business."

Cole watched as Jenny disappeared in the trees, then finished dressing the hens and started the fire. He was angry and frustrated and trying to sort through his feelings. He wondered if he would resent it just as strongly if Jenny meant to marry any other man, or if his emotions were clouded by the fact that it was Amos, a man who stood for everything he despised. It was a question Cole couldn't answer. Then recalling what Jenny had said about Princess minding her own business, Cole grudgingly admitted to himself that he had stepped out of line. For the time being, he and Jenny would remain casual lovers and — he supposed — friends, although he had never counted a woman as a friend before. When they reached Rio Grande City, they would go separate

182

ways. That didn't give him the right to tell Jenny how to live the rest of her life, any more than it gave her the right to dictate to him. He had warned her. That was the best a friend could do. Wasn't it?

The conclusion Cole had arrived at wasn't very satisfying, but it was the best he could produce. He placed the hens on a spit over the fire. Noticing that the sun was going down, he went looking for Jenny. He walked into the woods and, as soon as the meadow where the horses were staked came into view, came to a dead halt. He sucked in his breath sharply at what he saw. Princess was rearing and whinnying shrilly, her front legs pawing the air frantically. About fifty feet from the mare, a huge black bull was standing, its massive shoulders swollen and bulging from aggravation, its head, with its wicked curved horns, lowered menacingly. The bull's eyes glowed with fury, and its nostrils dilated as it snorted. One hoof pawed angrily at the ground and sprayed dirt in a six-foot arc. Between the two animals was Jenny, waving Princess's saddle blanket at the bull and saying, "Scat! Go away! Leave her alone, you big bully! Go away!"

Cole was afraid to yell to Jenny to drop the blanket and freeze for fear the unexpected noise would startle her and make her move suddenly, thereby inciting the bull to charge. Nor could he get a clear shot at the bull with Jenny between him and the bull without risking shooting her. Slowly he drew his gun from its holster and eased up behind Jenny, his heart racing in his chest. He prayed she wouldn't see him in her peripheral vision and turn. His eyes never left the bull. When he was almost behind Jenny, Cole saw the bull tilt his head to one side, baring his master horn. The razor-sharp tip caught the light of the setting sun. Cole knew the animal was going to charge. He leapt forward, grabbed Jenny by the waist, and swung her around. Since a bull can run as fast as a race horse, a thousand pounds of animal fury came down on Cole so rapidly that he could only jump out of the way, firing his six-shooter rapidly as he and Jenny hit the ground.

Everything happened so fast that Jenny never knew what transpired. One minute she was flying through the air, and the next she was on the ground, face down. Cole landed on top of her. The thunder of the bull's hooves as it raced past and the roar of Cole's gun in her ears nearly deafened her. She struggled to rise, only to have Cole shove her back down. "Stay down!" he shouted. "I'm not sure I hit a vital spot."

Cole jumped to his feet and cautiously approached the bull, knowing he had only one bullet left in his gun. The animal was still on its feet, bleeding profusely from several wounds to its upper body, weaving from side to side. Finally the bull pitched forward and hit the ground so hard the impact shook the earth. Still Cole was cautious, knowing many a matador had been gored by what he thought was a dead bull, some fatally. Standing to one side over the prostrate animal, he shot the last bullet between the bull's shoulder blades, in the exact spot a matador placed his sword for the kill. The missile severed the huge animal's aorta. It was as sure, as quick, and as merciful a death as Cole could give it.

Cole turned and saw Jenny. She was standing. The fear he had been living with since he had first found her was replaced with fury. "What in the hell do you think you were doing, waving that blanket?"

"Why, I was trying to scare it away," Jenny answered, thinking her actions should have been obvious. "I was afraid it would hurt Princess."

"Scare it away?" Cole roared, making Jenny jump at the loud noise. "Do you know what that is?" He pointed at the crumpled animal.

"Of course, I know what it is," Jenny answered indignantly. She highly resented Cole shouting at her. "It's a cow."

"A cow? Goddammit, no! That's a *ladino,* a wild bull, the fiercest, most dangerous animal on earth! Do you see those ragged scars all over his hide? That's from running in the brush and being cut to pieces by thorns. That's an animal that doesn't fear pain or anything. You don't scare a wild bull away. All you succeeded in doing by waving that blanket was angering him. Movement incites bulls."

"Well, how was I supposed to know that?" Jenny asked defensively. "I'm a city girl. Besides, I don't know why you're so furious."

Cole's fear for her came rushing back like a gigantic wave. "Because you could have been killed, goddammit!"

"Stop yelling at me! It's not necessary. I'm not deaf. And your anger is uncalled for. I didn't get killed. I didn't even get hurt. I just made a mistake, that's all."

Cole realized that his anger *was* unreasonable and wondered at it. What he should be feeling was relief. He forced his fear down and said, "All right. I got a little carried away. I'm sorry I yelled at you." He glanced at the horses and saw both were restive. "Why don't you take the horses to the other side of those trees and tie them there? The smell of blood is making them edgy. Then gather some more firewood while there's still some light left."

"Why do we need more firewood?"

"Since I had to shoot it, I might as well butcher it," Cole answered, slipping his gun back into its holster. "At least get a few prime steaks off it to cook. That way, I won't have to worry about shooting any game for a couple of days."

"Can we have steak tonight?" Jenny asked, her mouth watering at the thought. She was sick and tired of game.

"Why not?" Cole answered with a scoff. "Those hens are probably burnt to a crisp by now." He cocked his head and said, "There's just one thing I want to know. Then I won't mention it again. Weren't you scared at all?"

Jenny glanced at the monstrous bull where it lay in a pool of blood and shuddered. "Of course I was. But I couldn't let it hurt Princess."

Jenny turned and walked away. Cole stared at her back for a long moment. Standing up to the bull when she was totally defenseless was not only pure folly, but the bravest thing he had ever seen a woman do. He turned back to the chore at hand. Cole squatted by the bull and pulled out his knife. He discovered his hands were shaking so badly he had to wait a few moments to begin skinning the animal. He realized that there were beads of sweat on his forehead. Cole had known fear before, both in the war and every time some fool called him out. The stark fear he had known when Jenny's life had been endangered was new to him. It had been an all-encompassing fear, so powerful that it had almost paralyzed him, then left him feeling incredibly weak and totally drained. He fervently hoped he never had to face that kind of terror again.

The next morning Jenny was awakened by a god-awful racket. It brought her bolt upright. She looked about her wildly in the grey pre-dawn light.

"There's nothing to be alarmed about," Cole assured her, having also been awakened by the noise. "It's just some burros braying."

"Are you talking about those little Mexican donkeys?"

"Yes."

"What are they doing out here, in the middle of nowhere?"

"You'll find herds of wild burros all over northern Mexico, and a good deal of the Southwest, too, particularly since gold and silver were discovered in the mountains there. They escape from the mines and the supply trains and go wild."

Again the noise came, a horrendous sound that grated on Jenny's nerves. It seemed unbelievable that such a small animal could make that much noise. "What in the devil are they braying about?"

"They're greeting the sunrise. A lot of creatures do that. Birds sing, coyotes howl, roosters crow, cows moo."

"But the sun hasn't even come up yet. It's still dark," Jenny objected, resenting having her night's rest disturbed.

"No, but they know it's about to happen, and since we're awake, we might as well rise, too," Cole said, throwing back the blanket.

At that moment Jenny could have strangled the burros with her bare hands for waking them so early. Of all of the comforts of her previous life, she missed sleeping late the most. But to her credit, she didn't beg off. She, too, rose and began slipping on her clothes.

That day they rode from the foothills and back onto the hazy Chihuahuan desert. Jenny looked about at the lush grass sprinkled with orange flowers that looked much like poppies in disbelief, then said to Cole, "I don't believe this. There are even wildflowers blooming."

"Enjoy it while you can, because it isn't going to last. I'm afraid there's a really bad part of the desert coming up. I'd go around it if I could, but unfortunately, we've got to cross it to reach the Rio Grande."

Two hours later, Jenny knew the truth of Cole's words. They entered a desert where there wasn't a blade of grass to be seen. There was nothing but an endless sea of sand dotted with clumps of cactus, an occasional dusty grey sagebrush, and Spanish daggers with their wicked looking leaves. The sun beat down on them unmercifully and was reflected by the sand, the shimmering heat waves making it look as if the desert floor was quaking. The only living things Jenny saw were a lizard sunning itself on a rock and a roadrunner streaking across the desert, making Jenny wonder where in the world the bird had gotten its energy, while hers seemed to be draining from every pore in her body.

Cole brought his horse to a standstill. He rubbed the sweat from his brow with his forearm, then said, "Something is wrong. It's too hot. Too damn close. A storm must be coming."

Jenny perked up and asked excitedly, "Do you mean rain?"

"Yes, but remember what I told you about storms in this country?" Cole said in an ominous tone of voice. "They can be very violent. We have to find shelter of some kind and a place where we can be assured of high ground, so we won't drown."

"Drown?" Jenny asked incredulously. "How can you drown in the middle of a desert?"

"This place is full of ravines and gullies that you can't even see until you're caught in one with a fifteen-foot wall of water coming down on you. It doesn't just rain out here. Almost invariably, it's a cloudburst."

Cole stood in his stirrups and gazed off into the distance, squinting to see in the blinding glare. Then, spying something to one side, he said, "I think there's a partially collapsed building of some kind over there. Come on!"

Jenny followed Cole across the desert, the heat becoming more unbearable by the second, and not a breath of air to be had. For a good mile, Jenny couldn't see what Cole had spied with his keen eyesight. Then she glimpsed what looked to be a pile of adobe with a half-burned corral to one side. She waited until they came to a halt beside the rubble and asked, "What was this place?"

Cole swung down from his horse, answering, "I'd guess it was once a *puesto,* a relay staion for a freighting company. I can't imagine anyone else building out here and we're somewhere near the Chihuahua Trail. They probably abandoned it after an Apache attack, and it must sit on high ground, since what's left of that corral is still here."

Cole began hurriedly unsaddling his horse. When he realized Jenny was still mounted, looking about at the ruins, he snapped, "For God's sake, Jenny, this is no time to dally. Dismount, and get your horse unsaddled. We've got to get these animals tied up to what's left of the corral and our things inside before that storm hits."

"Well, you don't have to be so testy about it," Jenny answered. "What's the big hurry?"

"That's the big hurry," Cole answered, nodding to the sky behind her.

Jenny turned in her saddle and gasped in disbelief. A line of towering black thunderclouds, laced with jagged bolts of lightning, was racing towards them, blotting out the sun and bathing the desert below in dusky-purple shadows. She had never dreamed that a storm could approach so rapidly or look so totally terrifying. She stared, mesmerized, as all the fury of nature came rushing down on them.

190

Fourteen

When Jenny didn't respond to his urgings, Cole muttered an oath, ducked beneath his horse's head, and swept Jenny from her saddle. He set her on her feet where she would at least be out of the way if she wasn't going to help. Jenny stood and stared at the approaching storm in mute fascination while Cole unsaddled Princess, took both horses and tied them firmly to a portion of the corral where they would get some protection from the storm, then tossed all of their belongings into a small area where the building had not collapsed.

By that time the wind preceding the storm had arrived. A strong gust caught Cole's hat, ripping it from his head. He barely caught it in time, tossed the hat into the shelter, then reached for Jenny's hand, pulling her back towards him, saying, "Come on. Get in before all hell breaks loose."

The wind was blowing sand and tumbleweeds everywhere and rattling a half-dead sagebrush nearby. It played with Jenny's hat. The wide-rimmed *sombrero* was twisting from side to side and twirling wildly where it was still tied, slapping Cole in the face several times before he succeeded in slipping the cord from around her neck. Then he sent it, too, flying into the shelter. As Cole pulled Jenny towards the remains of the *puesto,* she tore her hand loose and ran back into the storm.

"Jenny, come back!" Cole called, but the wind threw his words back at him.

He ran after her, his hair flying every which way and his clothing flapping, just as Jenny's were doing. When he reached her, he called over the wind, "Have you gone completely *loco?* Any minute the heavens are going to open up and you're going to be drenched."

"I don't care!" Jenny called back. "I've never seen a storm out in the wide open. I want to watch."

Jenny turned her face into the wind, avidly taking in the sights of the spectacular show nature was providing, despite the thrashing it was giving her hair and clothing. Lightning flashed against the dark sky, then forked, and forked again, looking like a giant silver spider web, and thunder rolled and crashed, deafening, shaking the ground. Huge black clouds rolled towards them like a giant locomotive, while a score or more dust devils danced across the desert. Jenny had never seen anything like this storm. Its beauty was wild and spellbinding; its power awesome and terrifying.

She turned to Cole and called out over the thunder and wind, "Oh, Cole, isn't this the most beautiful, exciting thing you've ever seen?" She raised her arms to heaven and lifted her head. "It's marvelous, exhilarating!"

Cole looked warily at the violence nature was dispensing. "Yes," he admitted grudgingly, "but it's too dangerous to stay out —" The rest of Cole's sentence was lost in a mighty crack as a bolt of lighting struck just yards away from where they stood, exploding in a blinding white flash that blasted them with a tremendous heat wave and left sparks dancing over the ground.

Cole threw Jenny to the earth, for fear they would attract yet another bolt. Laying over her, he said in her ear, "That's what I mean. It's too dangerous to stay out here in an electrical storm. You're flirting with death. Come back to the shelter."

As Cole started to rise, Jenny caught his shirt front and pulled him back down. "I'm tingling all over, Cole, just like I do when you make love to me."

Cole realized that his skin was tingling, too, from the electricity of the near hit.

"Make love to me, Cole. Right here in the middle of the storm."

While the seductive tone of Jenny's voice brought a spontaneous warmth to Cole's loins, his mind told him the proposal was absolutely foolhardy. "Not here, Jenny. Let's go back —"

Cole never got to finish his sentence. Jenny reached up, threaded her fingers through his wind-whipped hair, and pulled his head down, her lips capturing his in a fierce, passionate kiss that robbed him of all thought, stripped his will from him, and ignited his passion as if a torch had been thrown into an open drum of kerosene. He kissed her back, their tongues performing a wild, erotic dance that only fanned their raging desire. They were caught in an ungovernable urgency. They stripped each other, rolling in the sand as they impatiently tugged and pulled at the other's clothing, all the while dropping frenzied kisses and hot nips on the bare flesh that was being revealed to them.

When the last article of clothing was thrown to the wind, Cole pinned Jenny to the ground, spread her thighs with his hands and drove his rigid manhood into her hot, tight depths with one powerful thrust that was as true as one of his bullets. Jenny felt as if she had been impaled on one of the jagged, white-hot lightning bolts ripping across the sky above them. She dug her nails into the iron muscles of Cole's shoulders and arched against him, meeting each breathtaking, brain-searing, jarring stroke with one of her own, hot flames licking at every nerve ending in her body, setting her ablaze.

The pair became a part of the storm, and the storm a part of them. Lightning bolts struck the floor of the desert over and over, many dangerously close to them. Thunder crashed and shook the earth, the hovering black sky roiled, the wind howled, the sand swirled. Cole and Jenny were lost in a maelstrom as powerful and turbulent and terrifying as the fury nature had conjured. Their ragged breaths rasped in the air; a roaring filled their ears as their sweaty, gritty bodies strained, their hearts pounded frantically, and lights flashed in brilliant colors behind their eyes as they rode the searing edge of ecstasy. The first raindrops fell in big plops on the

194

sand beside them and made sizzling noises on their feverish skin.

Then the heavens opened and the rain came down in sheets of water that drenched them in seconds, but Cole and Jenny were oblivious. They were already drowning in incredible sensations of their own making, moving higher and higher from one plane of intense rapture to the next, until they were seized by a tremendous force that burst in consuming, agonizing fire which melted their souls as one and hurled them to the limits of the heavens.

Cole was the first to recover. Dazed, he looked about him, seeing the driving rain and hearing the rush of water in a nearby gully, but not yet understanding where he was and why. Then he became aware of Jenny sobbing beneath him.

"My God!" he exclaimed, as his memory came rushing back. He rose on his elbows and looked down on her. "Did I hurt you?"

"No," she sobbed.

"Are you sure?" Cole asked, remembering how fierce, how uncontrollable his passion had been.

"Yes . . . I'm . . . sure," she muttered between sobs. "I'm crying . . . because it . . . because it was so . . . so. . . ." Jenny's voice trailed off. There seemed to be no words that would adequately describe what she had just experienced. It had been more than wonderful, thrilling, exciting, glorious, frightening, beautiful. It had shaken her to the depths of her soul. She sobbed all the harder.

Cole didn't press. He, too, had been deeply touched by what they had shared. Just thinking

195

about it brought a strange twisting feeling to his chest. He smoothed the wet tendrils of hair back from Jenny's face, then tenderly kissed her tears, mingled with raindrops, from her long eyelashes. He knelt and picked her up, then carried her through the pounding rain to the shelter.

Once inside the dry, dim interior, Cole dried Jenny with one of his shirts, then wrapped her in her blanket to ward off the chill of the air. He slipped on a dry pair of pants, pulled her onto his lap and rested her head against his chest, rocking her until her sobbing ceased.

The blanket around Jenny gaped just enough that Cole could see the scar on her shoulder. He bent and kissed it, saying, "I'm been meaning to ask how you got that."

Jenny hiccuped before answering, "I was bitten by a horse when I was a child, a draft horse that belonged to the man who delivered kegs of beer to the saloon down the street from where I lived."

"It just bit you, out the clear blue?" Cole asked, thinking it unusual.

"No, some of the kids dared me to touch it. I didn't know the boys had been teasing it unmercifully almost every day and that it had snapped at them."

Jenny snuggled closer to Cole and lay her head in the warm crook of his neck. Exhausted by their tumultuous lovemaking and the unexplainable emotional upheaval that followed, she drifted off to sleep, feeling safe and secure.

Cole remembered Jenny jumping away from Princess in fright when the horse had tried to nuzzle her and realized she'd had good reason to be so afraid. But Jenny had risen above her fear, so much so that she had come to the mare's defense the day before, facing up to a wild bull. Both incidents were a testimony to Jenny's courage. It seemed that every day Jenny was unveiling yet another attribute to add to the growing list of things Cole admired about her. She was a hell of a woman, he admitted, strong-willed, determined, courageous, free thinking, deeply passionate, at times shockingly candid, infuriating one minute and fascinating the next—a woman who made all the other women he had ever known pale in comparison, including the woman he had once loved. It was an admission Cole could not retract. He finally realized that Mary Alice had been a weak, selfish woman, born and bred to be adored and pampered, a woman he had placed on a pedestal and thought the epitome of female desirability, then foolishly carried in his heart even after she had betrayed him. Yet she couldn't begin to hold a candle to Jenny with her strength, high spirit, fire, and fierce independence. It would be like comparing a meek, household canary to a fierce wild sparrow who had the heart of a hawk. Yes, Jenny was a lot of woman.

Cole sat and watched the storm until its fury was spent, deep in thought, a troubled expression on his face.

When Cole and Jenny rode away from the *puesto*

the next morning all signs of the storm had disappeared. The searing blue sky was perfectly cloudless, and the parched earth had absorbed most of the water. Only a trickle remained in the gullies where tons of water had rushed through during the night. But while there was little water to be seen, the evidence of the recent rainfall was obvious. Sagebrush that had looked limp and half-dead was flushed with life, and the creosote bushes emitted a strong, resinous odor. The freshly-washed leaves on the mesquite brush gleamed in the sunlight. Here and there Jenny began to spy blossoms on the various cactus, and by noon, the entire desert was splashed with reds, yellows, and purples. It seemed as if every plant, every bush, every tiny vine on the desert floor had had blooms just waiting for water to burst forth. Even the sage got into the act, the bushes covered with so many purple flowers you couldn't even see their grey foliage.

Jenny looked around her appreciatively, oblivious to the fierce sun beating down on her. Then a large plant with huge fleshy leaves that hung on the ground caught her eye. "Why isn't that cactus blooming?" she asked Cole.

"It isn't a cactus. It's called a century plant and only blooms every 10 to 30 years. It puts up a tall stalk that bears greenish flowers, then dies."

"Always?"

"Always. Its blooming marks the end of its life span." Cole glanced across at Jenny, then asked, "Why are you frowning?"

"I was thinking about that plant. It seems so sad. I

mean, it sits there year after year, jealously watching all the other plants bloom over and over, waiting and waiting for its turn, then when it does finally come, it dies. It seems like a cruel trick of nature." Jenny looked over at Cole and saw him staring at her intently. Suddenly she realized she had let him get a glimpse of that silly romantic side of her that she worked so hard to keep buried. Quickly she glanced about her, hoping to find something to distract him. She saw a line of trees up ahead and asked, "Do you think there's water up there?"

"There should be. If my calculations are correct, that should be the Rio Grande."

"Then we're almost to Rio Grande City?" Jenny asked, surprised that their long trip was almost finished.

"No, it's a little further downstream. We should get there by tonight, though."

A few moments later, they rode beneath the trees. They reined in beside the river, enjoying the shade for a moment before dismounting and leading the horses to the water for a drink. Jenny looked at the river. It was just as muddy as where she had crossed it.

"Does this river always look like this? So muddy?"

"On this end, it does, but if you go where it begins in the Rockies, it's crystal clear."

"Are we that close to the Rockies?" Jenny asked in amazement.

"No, the Rio Grande is a long, long river, almost two thousand miles long. It's the second longest river in the North American continent. Only the Mississippi is longer, and it's muddy as hell, too. In some places, this river is miles wide, in other places it narrows as it flows through deep canyons, filled with dangerous rapids, and in some places it just disappears in the summer time. You can walk completely across it without even getting the soles of your boots wet. You sure can't say that about the Mississippi. No, I doubt if any river in the world has as many faces as the Rio Bravo."

"Why did you call it that?"

"That's the name for it from this side of the river, the Mexican name."

"But why name it that? Doesn't *bravo* mean brave?"

"Yes, but it can also mean wild, and that's the meaning the Spaniards who discovered it had in mind when they named it. You see, it was flooding at the time, and when this river goes on a rampage, it's like nothing you've ever seen."

They followed the river downstream, staying in the cool shade of the cottonwoods and willows that thirstily hugged its banks. In some places the stream was obscured by towering canebrakes with silver plumes that fluttered in the breeze. In other places, the ground rose and the river flowed between chalky cliffs filled with small caves. Then the terrain flattened, and they saw their first sign of civilization in over a week—fields of corn growing on sandy stretches beside the river. Cole told Jenny the Mexicans called these *temporales,* because with the next flood they would be gone. Then both the corn fields and the trees disappeared, and they rode over what

200

seemed to be pure rock, the river beside them shining like a tin roof in the blazing afternoon sun.

"That's Camargo up ahead," Cole informed Jenny. "General Taylor began his invasion of Mexico during the Mexican War from that hellhole. Can you believe that his soldiers were wearing wool uniforms in this heat?"

Jenny didn't answer. The heat had drained her of all energy, and she couldn't care less about some insignificant Mexican border town they'd pass through or the part it played in history. Listlessly she stared at the squat adobe buildings gleaming in the bright sun. When she caught a glimpse of something white in the river, she asked in disbelief, "Is that a steamboat?"

"Yes. This is as far as they can travel, though. From here on upstream, the river is unnavigable. That's why Taylor used Camargo as his staging area. He shipped half of his troops upstream by steamboat, thinking it would be easier on them since they weren't used to marching in this heat. But he didn't know the Rio Grande. His losses were greater by water than land. Hundreds of soldiers were drowned in boat accidents. Even where this river is navigable, it's treacherous."

Jenny hardly heard a word Cole said. Her mind had zeroed in on a possibility that raised her spirits considerably. "Can we take a steamboat from Camargo to Rio Grande City?"

Cole chuckled. "That won't be necessary. A ferry should suffice. Rio Grande City, or Davis Ranch, as the Mexicans call it, is on the other side of the river."

They had arrived at their destination? Jenny thought in surprise. Why in the devil hadn't Cole just said so, instead of rattling on about Camargo? she thought irritably. She peered across the broad stretch of water at the Texas town, nestled between the river and some lightly-wooded hills. It looked much the same as its Mexican counterpart, except it had a few buildings made from lumber. It, too, was mostly crumbling adobe. And that was the biggest town in this area, the nearest to Amos's ranch? she thought in keen disappointment.

"Pull your *sombrero* a little further down on your head," Cole instructed her, then added, "and put on your *serape.*"

"In this heat? Why? I'll burn up in that hot thing."

"I think it might be a good idea if you continue to pretend to be my *mozo,* even after we cross over the river, and the *serape,* while a little warm, hides the curves those *hijo's* clothes don't. I don't think Cortinas' men are going to be looking for us here, but a woman dressed in boy's clothing riding out of Mexico is bound to gain attention and cause some speculation among the Mexicans. We don't want Cortinas getting wind of it."

It sounded reasonable to Jenny. "All right. I'll drop my disguise later, after I've contacted the authorities."

"Don't expect to find a sheriff in Rio Grande City. Remember, it's in the *brasada,* no-man's-land," Cole said while she removed her hat and donned the *serape.*

Jenny waited until her head had cleared the *serape*

before answering, "If I remember correctly, Amos said there was a fort nearby."

"Yes, Ringgold's Barracks."

"Then I'll go there," Jenny said, replacing her *sombrero* and pulling it down tightly over her head. "They'll get word to Amos for me, or maybe they'll even escort me to his ranch."

Cole didn't respond to Jenny's statement, nor did she notice the deep scowl on his face.

As they approached the outskirts of Camargo, Cole said, "Remember to keep your head down, and don't say a word, not even if someone says something to you. I'll do the talking."

"But won't that seem a little strange, that I don't answer?"

"I'll tell them you're mute." Cole glanced down at Jenny's hands. "And keep your hands under your *serape*. They're tanned from being in the sun, but not near dark enough."

Cole gave Jenny a sweeping appraisal, then reined in sharply and exclaimed, "Damn!"

"What's wrong?" Jenny asked apprehensively, bringing Princess to a stop, too.

"I forgot about your shoes. They might not be noticeable from a distance, but up close they are, and we're going to have ride right through town to get to the ferry."

"Isn't there someplace else we can cross?"

"No, the closest crossing is about ten miles downriver, at Las Cuevas, but even then we'd have to swim our horses across."

"Then I'll take my shoes off and ride barefooted."

"That might work if you get your feet dirty enough to hide their pale color." Cole maneuvered his horse so that it was between Jenny and the town and could act as a shield. Jenny dismounted and furtively removed her shoes, then ground her feet in the dirt until they were so covered with grime not a millimeter of skin showed. Cole shoved her shoes into his saddlebags.

A few moments later, the pair rode down the dusty main street of the sleepy little settlement, the town dogs barking and ferociously nipping at their heels, making Jenny, with her bare feet, very nervous. Mexicans leaned in the doorways of their miserable huts in hopes of catching a breath of fresh air and stared at them with dull, lifeless eyes.

The street ended beneath a huge mesquite at a ferry landing on the muddy river. They dismounted, and Cole dropped several coins into the hand of a wrinkled old man standing there. The Mexican untied the rope barring the ferry and stood back while Jenny and Cole led their mounts onto the bobbing flat boat. Their animals' hooves made a clattering sound on the wooden deck.

As the old man and a young boy who was his helper began to strain at the rope tied to two massive, gnarled mesquites on opposite sides of the river, the ferry moved forward with a jolt that frightened the horses. Cole and Jenny spent a good half of the ride across the river calming the animals, who didn't like the rocking sensation any better than the sudden movement. When they'd finally settled their animals down, Jenny turned her full attention to the little town squatting on the Texas side of the river. Suddenly, the full realization of where she would be shortly disembarking hit her and she was filled with excitement. She glanced over her shoulder to make sure the Mexicans weren't within hearing distance, then moved closer to Cole. She whispered, "It just dawned on me. That's the United States. We're home! Isn't that wonderful?"

When Cole didn't respond, Jenny looked up at him. He was gazing downriver, the expression on his face dark and brooding.

Fifteen

When Cole and Jenny left the ferry, they skirted the wharf where the steamboat company housed its offices and secured its vessels, then walked their horses down the dusty, deeply-rutted main street of Rio Grande City, which followed a portion of the long river road that ran from Brownsville to El Paso. Jenny forgot Cole's warning to keep her head down in her excitement. She looked from side to side and took in everything. Next to the river there was a fairly large building with a sign that read *cantina* on it, surrounded by a score or more of adobe huts that were little more than *jacals*. Then, almost as if they had crossed an invisible line, the Anglo part of town appeared. A wooden boardwalk lined both sides of the street where a general store, a barber shop, a hotel, a bathhouse, a jail, and three saloons sat. Jenny noted wryly that Rio Grande City was much like the Bowery in at least one respect — on a one-to-one basis, its drinking establishments far outnumbered the other businesses.

When they reached the hotel, Jenny expected Cole

to stop and tie their horses to one of the hitching rails in the street before it, but to her surprise, he kept walking. "I thought we were going to stay the night in a hotel," she remarked in disappointment.

"We are, after we stable our horses, and the stables are to the rear."

Cole turned at a dark alley between the hotel and a saloon. While the streets had been practically deserted, there was obviously a good business going on inside the saloon, judging from the loud noises coming from it. Through the walls, Jenny could hear boisterous male laughter, tinny piano music, muted voices punctuated by an occasional loud curse and a shrill female laugh, even the faint clink of glasses. They emerged from the alley into an open area where a large corral fenced with mesquite limbs sat next to a dilapidated shed.

A grisly old man sat in a rickety rocker under a small huesache tree that grew beside the shed. As they approached, he rose and limped towards them, and Jenny noticed that his shaggy grey hair and slumped shoulders were covered with yellow blossoms that had fallen from the tree, making her wonder how long he had been sitting there, waiting for some business to appear.

Cole asked the attendant what the fee was for one night. The old man spat a stream of tobacco juice to the ground and answered, "Two-bits a night for each horse. That includes a bucket of oats apiece, 'fore I turn 'em out with the other horses. If you're thinking of leaving your Meskin here overnight, it will be another two-bits for him to sleep in the shed."

"No, that's not necessary," Cole answered. "He can find a tree someplace to sleep under."

The sound of Jenny sucking in her breath sharply was audible, and Cole sent her a hard, warning look.

"Then that will be four-bits," the old timer answered, thankfully deaf enough that he hadn't taken note of Jenny's gasp. "In advance," he added, holding out his hand.

Cole paid the man, then removed his bedroll and saddlebags. Jenny followed his lead and removed her bedroll, taking care to expose as little of her hands as possible. The attendant took the horses' reins and led them into the shed.

As soon as he was out of hearing, Jenny said, "I'll be damned if I'll sleep under a tree!"

"I said we were going to sleep in the hotel, didn't I?" Cole replied in exasperation. "I only said that for that old man's benefit. You can share my room. But I'll have to sneak you in."

"Why?"

"Because Mexicans aren't welcome in this hotel, at least not as guests."

"You mean, they're not allowed?"

There was just enough bite in Jenny's voice for Cole to know she did not approve. "There's no law against it, if that's what you mean. It's just understood, that's all."

"Oh, I understand," Jenny answered bitterly, thinking there were a lot of places on the east coast where certain ethnic groups were not allowed either, including the Irish. In fact, feelings ran so high against her forebears in some places that she had changed her name from O'Daniel to Daniels at Carla's urgings. "They're good enough to work there, but not good enough to stay there."

"Dammit, don't go getting your Yankee dander up!"

Jenny's blue eyes flashed. "It's not my Yankee dander! It's my Irish dander! Maybe Irishmen aren't allowed there either."

Looking at Jenny's blazing eyes, Cole thought he knew why the Irish were called the "fighting Irish". If he had ever seen a person spoiling for a fight, it was her. "It doesn't matter what touched you off. The fact remains that Mexican servants do not stay at that hotel, and if we don't abide by that, we're going to arouse a hell of lot of animosity, as well as suspicion. Now, what's it going to be? Do we stay here, and I sneak you in, or do we go down the street to that *cantina* and get a room? But I'm warning you, the accommodations aren't going to be near as comfortable."

"I thought a *cantina* was a saloon," Jenny remarked.

"They are, but they rent out rooms, too, just like some of the saloons on this side of the river do, but in a *cantina,* you can take the room with, or without, a woman. On this side of the river, it's pretty well understood the woman goes with it."

Jenny was too street-wise to be embarrassed. "If we stay at the hotel, how are you going to sneak me in?"

"By that back staircase over there."

Jenny glanced over and saw the staircase coming

down from the second floor of the hotel. "Have you stayed here before?"

"No."

"Then how did you know about that staircase?"

"Because every hotel in this part of the country has one. How else are the crooks going to escape if a posse happens to come riding in?"

"Then the hotel owners build them with back staircases for that reason?" Jenny asked in amazement.

"No, I was just being facetious. Supposedly the staircase is there to make the stables convenient for their customers, but when you stop to consider that most of the hotel's customers in this area are outlaws, gamblers, con-artists, and traveling salesmen who aren't exactly on the up and up, it's pretty handy for making a quick escape, too."

"Have you ever done that? Made a quick escape by the back staircase?"

"Yes, I have," Cole admitted readily. He glanced over his shoulder to make sure the old-timer was still occupied in the shed, then led Jenny to the alley on the opposite side of the hotel. Hiding her behind some discarded boxes and barrels, he said, "Wait here until I come for you."

As Cole started to walk away, Jenny caught his sleeve and asked, "Will you ask them to bring up a bath when you rent the room?"

"What do you want a bath for? You got soaking wet yesterday."

"It's not the same. I want to sit in a tub of water and soak, then give myself a thorough scrubbing.

I've been dreaming about that for days."

"All right," Cole conceded, knowing once Jenny set her mind on something, he could move a mountain sooner than change it. "I'll see what I can do."

Jenny waited for what seemed like hours crouched in her dim hiding place. The stench from a near-by garbage pile made her feel nauseous and the flies it had drawn made a nuisance of themselves. Finally she heard Cole call softly, "Jenny? You can come out now."

Jenny crept from behind the boxes and barrels to where Cole was standing in the alley with his back against the hotel, watching the stairs from around the corner. When she reached him, he took her hand, looked both ways to make sure no one was coming, then said, "We'll make a quick dash up the stairs, then you'll have to wait while I make sure the hallway inside is clear. Ready?"

"Yes."

They sped up the stairs, then when they reached the top, Cole cracked the door and peered inside. "It's clear," he said, throwing the door open.

"Which room is it?" Jenny asked as she stepped past him into the dim hallway.

"The second on the right. I left the door unlocked."

Jenny darted down the hall, opened the door, and stepped into the room with Cole fast on her heels. As he closed the door behind them and swung the bolt shut, she said, "I had begun to think you had forgotten me. What took so long?"

"That damn bath you wanted!" Cole snapped in

211

remembered annoyance. "I had a hell of a time convincing them to bring me one. They couldn't understand why I just didn't go across the street to the bathhouse."

"But you did get it?"

"Yes, but only after I agreed to pay an exorbitant amount for it. Then I had to wait for them to deliver it, so you wouldn't be in the room when they came. It's over there behind that screen, but don't complain to me if it isn't hot."

"I won't, and I'll pay you back," Jenny said, already hurrying to the screen.

"Forget it," Cole answered, then stepped over to the dresser, unstrapped his gun belt, and placed the gun beside his saddlebags.

"Oh, Cole, it's one of those copper slipper tubs!" Jenny cried out in delight. "I never expected one of them. I'll be able to stretch out and really soak. Where do you suppose they got it?"

"They probably borrowed it from across the street," Cole answered dryly.

"Do you really think that's where they got it?" Jenny asked, stripping off her clothes.

"I think that's a very good possibility. And if that's so, just be glad today isn't Saturday. Then I couldn't have bought that bath for all the money in Texas. That's when all the cowhands come in for their weekly bath and night on the town. There's such a big demand, they're waiting in line in the streets for an empty tub."

Cole heard a splash as Jenny stepped into the tub, followed by a long sigh. He walked to the window, pushed back the lacy curtain, and opened it. The blast of hot air that entered did little to relieve the room's stuffiness. He walked to the bed, sat down, and removed his boots and socks, then stripped off his shirt and lay back on the bed, his arms folded beneath his head as he stared at the cracked ceiling above him.

For a long while there wasn't a sound in the room as Jenny luxuriated in the sensation of being surrounded by water. She could almost feel the gritty particles of sand floating from her pores. Then she set to work with a bar of soap scrubbing every inch of her skin with a vengeance. After she had removed the soapsuds, she peeked through the crack where the screen folded and saw Cole lying on the bed. "When I'm through washing my hair, you can have the tub, if you don't mind a little dirt in your water."

There was no answer from the bed, or even a sign that Cole had heard. Shrugging her shoulders, Jenny proceeded to wash her hair, lathering it twice and dunking her entire body into the tub. She stepped from the tub and picked up the towel laying on the stool, drying off her body, then attacking her wet hair vigorously until it was half dry. Wrapping the towel around her, she walked from behind the screen, saying, "I'm through, now, if you're interested."

Again there was no answer from the bed. "Are you asleep?"

"No."

When Cole continued to stare at the ceiling, Jenny wondered why he was acting so peculiarly. That was the second time that day that she had caught him brooding. "Do you mind if I borrow your hairbrush?"

"No, help yourself. It's in my saddlebags."

Cole rose from the bed, but instead of walking to the bath, as Jenny expected, stepped up to the window and stared out, his arms folded across his broad chest.

Not knowing what to think, Jenny walked to the dresser, removed the brush from Cole's saddlebags, and began brushing her hair, pulling the long tresses way out to the side to help dry them and watching Cole in the mirror. When he didn't change his position or say a word for well over fifteen minutes, Jenny set the brush on the dresser, turned and asked, "Is something troubling you?"

Cole turned halfway, his arms still folded across his chest, and looked her directly in the eye. "Yes, there is."

"May I ask what?"

Cole dropped his arms and faced her fully. "I'm finding it hard to believe that you're still going through with your plans to marry Amos, after what happened between us yesterday."

Jenny couldn't have been more shocked if Cole had tossed a bomb in her lap. When she recovered, every protective mechanism she had carefully nurtured came rushing to the fore. "I have no idea what you're talking about."

Cole crossed the room in two swift strides and caught Jenny's upper arms, saying in a hard voice, "Dammit, don't lie to me! Lie to Amos, lie to yourself, but not to me. Something happened between us

214

out in that storm, something special. We were no longer just a man and a woman joining, two people making love. We were one, not just in body, but in spirit. One identity, one soul, one everything. And I know you felt it, too. That's why you were crying."

Jenny had never felt so threatened. It seemed as if everything she had been working towards was in danger of crumbling. "No, it wasn't like that," she denied frantically, "It was just . . . just . . . just passion. We had fire and passion, but that's all."

"Fire and passion? That's all?" Cole repeated incredulous. "Christ, Jenny! You act as if that's an everyday occurrence. How many people do you think can honestly say that? Do you have any idea of how rare it is for a couple to achieve such heights, such ecstasy? And there was a reason for it. Something deep down inside us triggered it." His voice dropped an octave. "Love, or the beginnings of love." Cole shook his head in frustration at being unable to pinpoint the elusive emotion. "I don't know which, but something."

Jenny jerked away from Cole, saying furiously, "I told you I don't believe in love! It's a silly, weak emotion that can blind you to reality, that can rob you of all reason, that can destroy you. And I'm not going to let it destroy me!"

Jenny's denial was so intense that it bordered on hysteria, confirming everything that Cole had concluded about her. "I don't think you really believe that, Jenny, not deep down," Cole replied in a gentle, soothing tone of voice. "I think you believe in love, but you're just afraid of it. Loving someone means taking a chance, letting go, giving—"

Cole was getting too near the truth for Jenny's comfort. "No!" Jenny interjected violently. "You don't know me! You don't know anything about me! All we shared was passion. Nothing more! And that has nothing to do with my marriage to Amos."

Cole drew himself up ramrod straight. His facial expression was as hard as stone. "Then you intend to follow through with your plans as if nothing had happened?"

"Yes! Because nothing *did* happen!"

"I beg to differ with you," Cole said, his voice like velvet over steel. "Even if all we shared was an extraordinary passion, marriage to a man you have no feelings for is going to be very difficult. Every time you lay in Amos's arms, you're going to remember what it was like in mine. You're going to yearn for my kisses, ache for my touch, crave the ecstasy only I can give you. It's going to be hell, Jenny. Sheer hell."

There was an intensity in Cole's golden eyes that frightened Jenny. "No, it won't be like that!" she objected, stepping back.

His arm flew out with the speed of a striking snake and wrapped around her waist; then he yanked her to him so that her soft body was pressed fully against his hard, muscular one. His eyes glittered with fierce determination. "Yes, it will be, Jenny. You're going to be miserable with Amos. I've put my brand on you for life. And just to be sure you won't forget what you're missing," he said as he swept her

MORE PASSION AND ADVENTURE AWAIT... YOUR TRIP TO A BIG ADVENTUROUS WORLD BEGINS WHEN YOU ACCEPT YOUR FIRST 4 NOVELS ABSOLUTELY *FREE*
(AN $18.00 VALUE)

Accept your Free gift and start to experience more of the passion and adventure you like in a historical romance novel. Each Zebra novel is filled with proud men, spirited women and tempestuous love that you'll remember long after you turn the last page.

Zebra Historical Romances are the finest novels of their kind. They are written by authors who really know how to weave tales of romance and adventure in the historical settings you love. You'll feel like you've actually gone back in time with the thrilling stories that each Zebra novel offers.

GET YOUR FREE GIFT WITH THE START OF YOUR HOME SUBSCRIPTION

Our readers tell us that these books sell out very fast in book stores and often they miss the newest titles. So Zebra has made arrangements for you to receive the four newest novels published each month.

You'll be guaranteed that you'll never miss a title, and home delivery is so convenient. And to show you just how easy it is to get Zebra Historical Romances, we'll send you your first 4 books absolutely FREE! Our gift to you just for trying our home subscription service.

BIG SAVINGS AND FREE HOME DELIVERY

Each month, you'll receive the four newest titles as soon as they are published. You'll probably receive them even before the bookstores do. What's more, you may preview these exciting novels free for 10 days. If you like them as much as we think you will, just pay the low preferred subscriber's price of just $3.75 each. *You'll save $3.00 each month off the publisher's price.* AND, your savings are even greater because there are never any shipping, handling or other hidden charges—FREE Home Delivery. Of course you can return any shipment within 10 days for full credit, no questions asked. There is no minimum number of books you must buy.

4 FREE BOOKS

TO GET YOUR 4 FREE BOOKS WORTH $18.00 —MAIL IN THE FREE BOOK CERTIFICATE T O D A Y

Fill in the Free Book Certificate below, and we'll send your FREE BOOKS to you as soon as we receive it.

If the certificate is missing below, write to: Zebra Home Subscription Service, Inc., P.O. Box 5214, 120 Brighton Road, Clifton, New Jersey 07015-5214.

up in his arms, "I'm going to give you a loving you'll never forget."

As Cole turned and carried her to the bed, Jenny didn't know if he had made a threat or a sensual promise, if her heart was racing in fear, in excitement, or in intense anticipation. Somewhere in the back of her mind a voice cried out: fight him, he's dangerous, he'll make a slave of your soul.

Truly terrified of Cole's power over her, Jenny began to twist wildly in his arms. "Put me down!" she demanded. "Put me down this instant!"

To her dismay, Cole did just that. He dropped her on the bed so hard that she bounced and the springs squeaked in protest. Then, before she could roll away, he fell over her, pinning her down with his body, his hands holding her wrists by the side of her head. Jenny squirmed frantically, but the only thing she succeeded in doing was loosening the towel around her, baring her breasts to his magnificent chest, the crisp hairs there tickling her nipples and making them harden and rise in anticipation. She sobbed, half in delight and half in frustration.

She looked up at Cole, who was just lying there and looking down at her. "Let me go, damn you!"

"No. I'm going to make love to you," Cole replied, madly calm.

"You bastard! Rape me, you mean!"

Cole flinched at the ugly word, then replied, "No, Jenny. I don't want to hurt you. I don't want to cause you pain in any way. I just want to love you. I'm entitled to it, at least this once. It's going to have to last me a lifetime, too."

Jenny wished he would stop talking about love. Every time he said it, his voice dropped to a rich husky timber that washed over her like thick molasses and made her feel as if she were drowning. "I don't want this," she sobbed, knowing in her heart, just as Cole did, that it was a lie.

Cole didn't bother to answer. Jenny was trembling all over, and he knew it wasn't from fear. He lowered his head to drop soft kisses over her face, then when Jenny jerked her head to the side, nibbled at the silky skin on her throat that she exposed to him, his mouth descending slowly and leaving a trail of fire in its wake.

Jenny tried to block out the sensation of his warm lips, tried desperately, but his previous kisses and lovemaking had sensitized her to his touch. She was a willing slave to his mastery, his sheer artistry, her body, if not her mind, recognizing its mate and eagerly welcoming every kiss, every nibble, every tiny bite. By the time Cole reached the soft rise of her breasts, Jenny was a mass of quivering jelly. He released her wrists to smooth his palms down the length of her arms in a long, sensuous caress, then cupped a breast in each hand. As his lips closed over one soft mound, Jenny didn't use her freed hands to push him away, but folded her arms around his shoulders, arching her back to give him better access, making a deep purring sound in her throat at the wonderful things he was making her feel.

Jenny was so lost in sensation she never even realized when Cole shifted his weight from her temporarily and stripped off his pants. Only when she felt the feverish heat of his hot rigid shaft pulsating on her abdomen did she realize how far their lovemaking had progressed. But Jenny could no longer make any pretense of objecting. Her need for him was too great, too overpowering. She moaned and rubbed herself against him. Her silent but eloquent invitation brought a sharp gasp from Cole as his manhood grew yet longer and strained almost painfully.

But despite the demands being made upon him by his own lust, Cole was determined to delay this lovemaking, to savor it to its fullest extent. He pulled away, ceasing his feasting at her breasts, and explored her ribs and soft belly, kissing, nibbling, lathing her silky softness with his tongue. For Jenny, each kiss was ecstasy, and the feel of the hot tip of his manhood brushing her groin, teasingly close to where she wanted him, then her thigh as he moved lower and lower, was a fire that heightened her desire to a feverish pitch. When Cole stopped his explorations to pay homage to her tiny navel, his tongue lazily circling, then flicking, Jenny felt as if she would burst from need and cried out weakly, "Now, Cole! Please, do it now!"

Cole ignored her pleas as he continued his sensuous explorations, not missing an inch of skin on her lower abdomen, then dropping lower. The feel of his tongue teasing the sensitive skin on the insides of her thighs, then his lips nipping, was more than Jenny could endure. Her entire body felt as if it were a flaming torch. She trembled violently, so weak with need she could only whimper.

As Cole slid his hands under her hips and lifted

her, Jenny sobbed in relief and arched her back in anticipation of his lunge, knowing she would soon find relief from this terrible torment. Then when nothing happened, she lifted her head and looked down to see Cole sitting back on his heels between her thighs, still holding her poised for his entry. "What are you waiting—" She stopped in midsentence as a smile came over Cole's face and she sensed even before he lowered his head what he was about to do.

His intent utterly shocked Jenny. Frantically she squirmed away, but Cole only tightened his grip.

"No," she gasped. "Don't! Don't you dare do that!"

Cole lifted his eyes, and Jenny felt the heat of that smoldering look almost as if he had touched her. "Why not?" he asked thickly.

"It's too personal, too intimate. It's indecent!"

"There's nothing too personal, too intimate between people who love one another. This is just another way of showing that love."

There it was again, the word that left her feeling devastated. "No! Don't say—"

Jenny gasped as she felt the tip of his tongue against her. She reached down and grabbed his hair, pulling and crying out, "No! Stop!"

But Cole was determined to love Jenny so completely that she would never forget him, to place his brand on her for eternity. The taste of her sweetness there, the dizzying scent of her womanliness only made him more determined. Despite the pain she was bringing him, he held her hips firmly, his tongue laving her moist lips, before seeking the bud of her desire.

Jenny's eyes widened in wonder, then rolled back in her head. "My God!" she muttered at the feel of Cole's warm tongue circling, sensuously stroking, flicking like fire licking up a blazing wall. Every nerve in her body seemed to shift to that hard, throbbing bud; a roaring filled her ears. She parted her legs to him, and her hands fell limply to her sides as waves of pleasure flowed over her, each more intense than the last. Then when his artful tongue drove deeper to taste her essence, to tease and tantalize in the very center of her pulsating being, Jenny was rocked by powerful spasms of exquisite swirling sensations that took her higher and higher until she convulsed, crying out his name.

Jenny never knew if it was seconds, minutes, or hours later when she opened her eyes and saw Cole hovering over her and smiling down at her. He kissed her softly on the lips, then whispered, "That was for you, spitfire. Just for you. This is for us."

He entered her, then, achingly slowly, so that both could savor the sensation of their joining, he of her warm velvety heat surrounding him, her of his rigid strength filling her. Jenny had thought herself too drained to possibly feel any more sensation, but Cole didn't even have to move to arouse her. The feel of him deep inside her, his manhood pulsating, still growing, was its own stimulation, caressing her deep inside, making erotic promises of even more delights. She was seething with need long before Cole's mouth closed over hers in a deep searing kiss, then moved in slow, sensuous strokes. Each powerful thrust was an ecstasy, each retreat an agony. Cole's tempo increased, giving and taking, giving and taking, over and over bringing her to the quivering brink, until Jenny thought she would go mad if he didn't end this exquisite torture. Finally he did, bringing her to a glorious climax, then unbelievably fast on its heels, to yet another, before he allowed himself his own intense, shattering pleasure.

When it was over, Jenny again wept, not in uncontrollable sobs, as before, but quietly. Cole held her in his arms and kissed the tears away from her cheeks, knowing she cried from the wonder of it, the beauty of it. Once again, they had experienced that oneness, but the feeling of dying before being reborn hadn't been as intense as it had during the storm, and for that, Cole was glad. That had been such an utter loss of control that it had been frightening for him.

When Jenny finally stopped weeping, Cole said softly, "I love you, Jenny." The words were surprisingly easy for him to say. He had sworn he would never say those words to another woman.

Much to Cole's disappointment, Jenny made no comment. He had hoped to force her to admit to her feelings for him. He leaned back and looked at her, wishing he could see her face more clearly in the semi-darkness of the room. "Did you hear what I said?"

"Yes, I heard."

There was an iciness in Jenny's voice that made Cole's blood turn cold. "Then it changes nothing?"

"No, it doesn't. I still intend to marry Amos."

"And you still deny that you have any feelings for me?"

It took all of Jenny's fierce determination to force the words from her mouth. "It doesn't matter what I feel for you. I'm not marrying for love. I'm marrying for security, and you can't give me that."

Cole knew that what Jenny meant by security was material wealth, and it infuriated him that she placed more value on that than her feelings. Again, he had placed his love at the feet of a woman and she was trampling on it. He sprang from the bed, his movement so sudden that Jenny bolted to a sitting position in surprise.

Glaring down at her, Cole said, "You know, I had come to admire a lot of things about you, but I was wrong. You have got to be the coldest, most calculating woman I have ever met."

His harsh words cut Jenny to the bone. She had always thought of herself as being careful, not calculating, as being controlled, not cold. "Please, Cole, try to understand. I have—"

"Oh, I understand," Cole said, slashing across her words. "Amos's money is more important than my love."

Jenny realized she had hurt Cole, and that hurt her, too, bewildering her. She watched, feeling confused and miserable as he hurriedly dressed, then picked up his saddlebags and bedroll.

As he opened the door, Jenny asked in shock, "You're leaving? Now?"

Cole turned, the light from the hall shining on his face and showing Jenny the full fury he was feeling.

"There's no reason to stay."

Things were moving too rapidly for Jenny. Dazed, she muttered out of force of habit, "Well, good luck."

A wry smile crossed Cole's lips. "Thanks, but don't expect me to wish you the same in your venture."

As the door closed behind him, Jenny stared at it for a moment; she heard the sound of his sure footsteps moving steadily down the hallway. The full impact of his leaving hit her. She collapsed on the bed, sobbing uncontrollably.

Sixteen

After leaving Jenny, Cole stormed down the stairs at the back of the hotel and swiftly crossed the open area between them and the shed. He found the elderly attendant inside, sitting on a stool and eating a bowl of soup from a up-turned barrel that served as his table.

"I want my horse," Cole announced curtly.

The old man eyed him sourly, then said, "You ain't gonna get your money back. I already fed him those oats."

"I don't want my money back. I just want my horse."

"Can it wait until I finish my soup? I hate eating cold soup."

"No, it can't. I'm in a hurry."

The old-timer was used to men leaving town in a hurry, so much so that he didn't even bother to speculate why this one was making a quick getaway. Sighing in resignation, he rose, took the kerosene lamp hanging from a nail on the wall, and walked out a door at the back of the shed. Cole waited in the darkness until he returned with his stallion.

Handing Cole the rope from around the horse's neck, he said, "Your tack is over there. If you're in such a big hurry, you can saddle him yourself."

Cole didn't argue. He was anxious to get away and figured he could do it faster. As he slipped the bridle over his horse's head, the old man asked, "What about the mare? You taking her, too?"

Cole had forgotten about Jenny's mare. "No, I'll come back for her later," he quickly fabricated. He slipped his fingers inside his vest, pulled out a gold dollar, and handed it to the attendant. "Just hang on to her for a while."

A few minutes later, Cole raced from town and out into the countryside, hoping a good run in the fresh air would help cool his anger. All it really succeeded in doing was tiring his horse unnecessarily. Finally realizing this, he reined in, dismounted, and paced furiously, muttering oaths, then kicking a rock and sending it skittering across the ground. The flying rock frightened his horse, and seeing the animal shy away brought Cole to his senses. He walked to the stallion and patted its neck, saying, "I'm sorry, fella. I've been acting like I ate some loco weed, haven't I?" He looked around then said, "We might as well camp here for the night."

Later, sitting before his fire beneath a sky filled with glittering stars, Cole felt calmer. He realized his anger had been caused in the most part by the bruising Jenny's spurning had done to his ego. Once in a lifetime was enough for any man, particularly a man with Cole's innate pride, but twice had really made him look the fool. He reflected on everything that happened between him and Jenny and found he couldn't regret calling her cold and calculating, because in reality, she was. But that didn't stop him from still loving her. Accepting someone's frailties went along with the territory. And Cole still firmly believed there was a soft, tender spot deep down in Jenny, a part of her held prisoner by her fierce determination and cold reason that was crying out to love and be loved. He had only to keep chipping at her hard shell to free it.

Cole wondered if Jenny was worth burying his fierce pride for and pursuing. It was something he had never even considered doing with Mary Alice, and he knew Jenny wouldn't make it easy for him, particularly if she realized what he was doing. No, she'd put up all her bristly defenses to hold him at bay. She was like a beautiful cactus blossom, golden and delicate-looking, surrounded by prickly thorns. It would take determination and a lot of clever maneuvering to pick that prize, but Jenny was a prize well worth it.

Having decided to pursue Jenny, a frown came to Cole's face as he realized he was facing a timing problem. If he delivered his report in person to Governor Coke, by the time he got back Jenny could have reached Amos and married the carpetbagger. No, he needed that valuable time to woo her on the sly, or at least delay the wedding until she found out for herself just how despicable Amos was. But he couldn't put the governor's report on hold indefinitely either. Then Cole remembered that Coke had given him the name of a contact at Ringgold's Barracks to use if he ran into problems or needed any help. Determined not to ask for anything from the hated Yankee army, Cole hadn't paid much attention at the time, but now he struggled to remember the officer's name. What the hell, he thought. He might as well say to hell with his Southern pride, along with his male pride. He needed someone he could trust to deliver his report to the Governor.

Having made his decision, Cole slept for a few hours, then, about an hour before dawn, was in the saddle again, retracing the distance he had covered the night before and taking the river road to the fort. He arrived at Ringgold's Barracks with the sun, the rousing sound of reveille ringing in the air as he rode up to the gate.

He was stopped by a sentry, who asked him to state his name and what his business was.

Warily, Cole gave his name, then relaxed when the sentry showed no sign of recognizing it. "I need to speak with your commanding officer, Major Alexander," Cole said.

"He's probably at breakfast, sir," the trooper answered. "Is it important?"

"Not so much so that we need to interrupt his meal," Cole answered, being kinder to the soldier now that his anger had cooled than he had been to the old man the night before. "Is there a place where I can wait?"

"Yes, sir. The executive office is in that building directly across the parade ground."

"Thanks," Cole answered, nudging his horse forward.

The ride across the dusty parade ground was short, since the fort was very small, consisting mostly of just what its named implied, a few barracks. Cole dismounted in front of the small building, tied his horse to a hitching rail there, then entered. He told a very sleepy-looking first lieutenant who sat at a battered desk inside the same thing he had told the sentry at the gate. After a close scrutiny by the officer that made Cole a little edgy, he was directed to a small office off to the side where he waited for Major Alexander.

About fifteen minutes later, Cole heard the lieutenant talking to someone in a hushed, excited voice, then a deeper, muted voice answering, and felt a tingle of apprehension. He knew he was being discussed. A moment later, the door opened and the commanding officer walked in, finding himself face-to-face with Cole's drawn gun.

"Are you Major A. J. Alexander?" Cole asked the astonished officer.

"Yes."

"Did Governor Coke tell you about me?"

"Not directly. My orders came from General Ord, the Commander of the Department of Texas," the Major answered with a nervous little laugh. "Mr. Benteen, I'd appreciate it if you'd put that gun away. We're not going to attempt to arrest you, if that's what you're afraid of. I know the full story." He glanced at the lieutenant through the open doorway, then said, "However, my adjutant didn't. He recognized your picture from an old wanted poster. I had to tell him that you had been cleared of all charges and were working undercover for the Governor on the bandit problem. I hope you don't mind."

Cole glanced at the lieutenant and saw his face was beet-red with embarrassment. He slipped his gun back in his holster and said, "No, I don't guess it matters anymore. I've finished my surveillance. That's what I wanted to talk to you about. I was wondering if one of your couriers could carry my report to Austin and deliver it to Governor Coke for me. I have some urgent business here that demands my attention."

"Of course not, Mr. Benteen. I was instructed to be of any service I could to you. We have couriers riding to our headquarters at San Antonio almost daily with dispatches, and Austin is just a brisk ride from there. Is there anything else I can do for you?"

"Yes, loan me some paper and a pen, so I can write the report."

"Of course." He turned to his adjutant. "Lieutenant, will you see to that?"

"Yes, sir!" the lieutenant answered, snapping a smart salute, then hurried away to collect the items.

"You can use my office to write your report," Major Alexander told Cole. "And if there is any other way I can be of service, please let me know."

"Thanks."

The major turned, then pivoted quickly around and said, "I realize your report is confidential, but may I ask a question?"

"Sure."

"Do you think we're making any headway with these bandits?"

230

Cole knew the officer meant the army. "Absolutely not. The problem has just gotten worse."

"I was afraid you were going to say that," Major Alexander answered, a dejected look on his face. "But it isn't because the army hasn't tried. We have. We simply haven't got enough men to patrol this area."

"Well, maybe my report will remedy that, and you'll get more men."

"I'm afraid even that won't be good enough to eliminate the problem. There are so many places for the bandits to hide in the brush, and even when we do pick up a trail and chase them, they make a run for the border. I can't tell you how many times we've caught them at the river, their horses still dripping water and the stolen cattle running up the banks, and been stopped dead in our tracks. Why, one bastard even stood on the other side and laughed at us the other day. It's frustrating. Damn frustrating!"

For the first time Cole saw the army in another light. They were no longer Yankees, his old enemy, but men trying to do a difficult, if not impossible, job. "Maybe your superior officers will decide to let you cross the border and go after them. Sheridan did that in '73, when he ordered Colonel Mackenzie to cross the border and destroy those marauding Kickapoos' headquarters in the San Carlos Mountains."

"Yes, he did. And it did stop the Indians raiding into Texas, but it also brought a strong protest from the Mexican government, despite the fact that the Kickapoos were American Indians who fled to Mexico after the war so they wouldn't have to give up their Seminole slaves. Those Indians weren't even Mexican citizens. That's why I don't think my superiors are going to let us go after the bandits. They're afraid of causing an international incident that might precipitate hostilities. We're down here to protect American citizens' property, not start a war, as I have been so often reminded by General Ord."

Cole had always been in favor of going after the bandits, but the major's words gave him pause. The United States had entered the Mexican War for the sole purpose of gaining more land, for bringing the dream of Manifest Destiny to pass, but now they had more land than they knew what to do with. The government was practically giving it away in an effort to settle the wilderness. Besides that, the country was just recovering from a long, bitter war that had drained its resources and left it with a huge national debt. An entire segment of the country was still struggling to recover. It wasn't a time to destroy, but to build. "Well, I wish I could offer you a solution, but I'm afraid I can't," Cole replied in all sincerity, for the first time seeing all, not just part of the problem.

"I'm sorry," the major replied, looking a little sheepish. "I'm keeping you from your report. I guess I just had to get it off my chest to someone."

"Sure. I understand."

Cole watched as Major Alexander walked from the room, then set to work writing his report as soon as the lieutenant placed the pen and ink on the major's desk. A hour later, he was riding from the fort, following a column of blue-coated troopers going out

232

on patrol, their standard snapping smartly in the breeze.

When they reached the river road, the patrol turned to ride downriver, while Cole turned in the opposite direction towards Rio Grande City, his mind no longer on the bandits but on Jenny and how he was going to explain his appearance after storming out of her life just hours before. Finally thinking of a reason Jenny would find plausible without completely shredding his pride, he urged his horse to a greater speed.

It was just a little after eight when Cole rode into Rio Grande City, and the only living creatures to be seen were a hound dog sniffing at a horned toad skittering across the dusty main street. Cole dismounted before the hotel and tied his horse to the hitching post, then entered the building. Taking the stairs beside the front desk, he climbed them two at a time, then strode rapidly down the hall. Standing beside the door, he knocked softly, then when there was no response, tried the knob, thinking to rattle the door with it. To his surprise, the door was unlocked. "Damn!" he muttered under his breath, thinking Jenny had already left. He opened the door and stepped inside.

What he saw scared the hell out of him, not for what was, but for what could have been. Jenny lay sprawled across the bed, sound asleep and stark naked. Fury replaced the fright he'd taken. He slammed the door behind him, deliberately hard.

The loud bang had its desired effect. Jenny bolted to a sitting position and looked wildly about her, a terrified look on her face. When she saw Cole, she snatched the sheet up to cover her nakedness and snapped, "What are you doing here?"

Cole ignored her question, throwing one of his own back at her. "Why in the hell didn't you bolt that door after I left? Anyone could have walked in on you. You could have been dead by now!"

Jenny was used to sleeping in hotel rooms and had never been so careless, but she had been so upset after Cole left, she had cried herself to sleep. "What I do or don't do is none of your damn business! When are you going to get that through your thick skull? Now answer my question. What are you doing here?"

Belatedly, Cole realized he hadn't started things out on a good footing. Already they were butting heads. He shrugged, trying to make light of what had just happened and said, "I found I couldn't ride off and leave you here, in view of how things have worked out. I talked to the commanding officer over at Ringgold Barracks. He doesn't have anyone he can spare to escort you to Amos's ranch. He needs every man he has to patrol the area for bandits. So," Cole shrugged again, "I'll take you."

Jenny frowned at the disappointing news, then remembered her fear of his power over her. "No thank you," she said. "I'm sure I can hire someone here to take me."

"Hire someone?" Cole asked in a shocked voice. "Christ! Didn't you hear what I said last night,

234

about how this town is crawling with outlaws and other scum? You're going to put your life in the hands of somebody like that? Why, as soon as you get to the brush, he'd slit your throat and steal every cent you have—after he'd raped you, that is."

"You're an outlaw," Jenny pointed out. "You didn't do those things."

It occurred to Cole that he could tell Jenny the truth, now that his job for Governor Coke had been completed. But Cole wanted nothing less of Jenny than he was giving her. He wanted her to love him despite how low she thought he was, despite his faults, just as he loved her despite hers. "Yes, I am, and I guess that proves how lucky you were to hit on me, and not some other man. Don't push your luck, Jenny. Let me take you back."

Seeing Jenny still hesitate Cole thought it was just as he had feared it would be. She was going to make it hard for him. Well, so much for gallantry. He'd have to try another track. "All right, Jenny, I'll be honest with you. There's another reason I want to deliver you to Amos. I got to thinking about that money he offered me to rescue you. It'd come in handy until I could get another gang together, and I've already pretty much earned it."

"You didn't rescue me!" Jenny replied hotly, remembering how he had flatly refused to help her. "I escaped!"

"Dammit, Jenny, you know you would have never made it across that desert without me! And, you suggested yourself, that I collect from Amos," he reminded her.

235

When Jenny remained stubbornly silent, Cole sighed and said in disgust, "I never pegged you for being that unfair. Just because we had a misunderstanding last night, you're going to cheat me out of what's rightfully mine."

Jenny felt a twinge of guilt. "Are you sure that's the only reason you want to take me to Amos, to collect the money?"

"What other reason would I have?" Cole asked with pretended innocence.

"You could tell him who I really am and ruin everything for me."

Cole knew if he did a spiteful thing like that, Jenny would never forgive him. No, he wanted *her* to break the engagement, to come to him of her own free will. "I'm not going to do that, Jenny. I'm not going to take back what I said last night . . . my feelings haven't changed . . . but I'm not going to squeal on you. I may be a thief and an outlaw, but I've never sunk that low. Besides, you could do the same to me. Tell Amos I didn't really rescue you. It seems we're both vulnerable. I talk and you lose what you want, you talk and I lose what I want. We're both going to have to keep our lips sealed."

Cole's words put Jenny's fear of betrayal at rest, but reminded her of another fear, the fear that she might fall prey to the same emotions he had admitted to. He already commanded her body—the night before was proof of that—and she was in danger of losing her heart, too. Otherwise why would she have cried so long and so bitterly when she thought he had left her? She had to do something to protect

236

what was left, otherwise she'd end up just like her mother, selling her soul to the lowest bidder. "If I agree to let you deliver me to Amos to collect the money, you have to agree to something, too. From now on, our relationship will be strictly business. Our affair is over. You're not to lay a hand on me again — ever!"

Cole had expected Jenny's ultimatum. He knew as well as she, her defenses were lowest during their intimacy. While he had promised not to reveal her true identity in good faith, this was not a promise he intended to keep. Not indefinitely. Someday, she would be his: totally, completely, body and soul. It was a vow he firmly intended to keep, and if it took a little white lie to bring it about, he had no qualms. "If that's the way you want it."

Jenny frowned, knowing he hadn't given her a promise, but before she could demand an agreement, Cole changed the subject, saying, "I think you ought to change your disguise for our trip from here to Amos's ranch. I don't want to get into any more awkward positions like we did here at the hotel because you're pretending to be a Mexican. Besides, not being able to talk puts you at a disadvantage. I could pick you up some boy's clothing at that general store down the street."

"Why can't I just travel as a woman?"

"Because we'll be going through the *brasada,* a no-man's-land swarming with outlaws. I thought I told you that."

"You did. But is it that much more dangerous for a woman than a man?"

"Not if you're traveling with a troop of cavalrymen to escort you, or a band of armed guards, like Amos does. Otherwise, yes. The majority of those outlaws are woman-hungry, enough so that they'll kill for one, and they usually travel in gangs. I'm good with a gun, Jenny, but I don't know if I'm that good."

Cole didn't have to argue any further. His innuendos did it for him. Jenny didn't want him getting killed trying to defend her, nor did she want what would surely follow. There were better ways to die, cleaner and quicker. "All right," Jenny conceded, "I'll disguise myself again."

Relieved that he talked Jenny into letting him accompany her, Cole turned and walked to the door, saying over his shoulder, "I'll be back in about half-an-hour." He opened the door, then turned. "Don't forget to lock the door. Those same women-hungry men might be next door."

As the door closed behind him, Jenny shivered, then scurried from the bed to lock the door.

Seventeen

Cole was gone longer than an hour, much to Jenny's disgruntlement. Since she hadn't eaten the night before, she was starving, and every minute seemed an eternity. Then the knock on the door she was anxiously waiting for came. She hurried to the door as fast as she could with the sheet wrapped around her, and unlocked it.

Cole entered the room, carrying an armful of packages, which he promptly dumped on the bed. "What took you so long?" Jenny asked.

"I bought some supplies besides your clothes, among other things. What's your hurry?"

"I'm hungry. Unlike you, I've been confined to this room since yesterday afternoon."

Cole didn't bother to tell Jenny he hadn't eaten either. He handed her one of the packages and said, "Well the sooner you dress, the sooner we can get out of here."

Jenny took the package behind the screen and unwrapped it, finding a shirt, a leather vest, a pair of corded pants, a belt, and a pair of socks. "There aren't any underwear," she called to Cole.

"It's still summer. It's too hot for underwear."

That must explain why he didn't wear any, Jenny thought, then said, "It's October. That's fall."

"Not in South Texas, it isn't."

Jenny wasn't about to go without underwear. After throwing the sheet over the screen, she donned her drawers and chemise, then put on the clothing Cole had brought her. She walked from around the screen, saying in disgust, "Everything is too big and baggy."

"Yes, just exactly what you would expect to see in new clothing for a boy who's growing by leaps and bounds. You certainly wouldn't buy anything that fits, not if they're going to be outgrown that fast."

It was an argument Jenny couldn't dispute. She remembered her mother always buying at least one size larger for her brothers. "Then why can't I be a small man, instead of a growing boy, and get something that fits?"

"Because then you'd have to wear a gun, and that would drag you down. They're a little heavy, you know. Besides, I purchased the clothing for another reason, to hide your curves." Cole's eyes swept over her. "I see I've succeeded on the bottom half of you, but we've got to do something about the top. Your vest looks damn suspicious. How did you handle that problem when you were playing a boy's role in the theater?"

"I bound my breasts with torn sheets."

Cole glanced at the sheet hanging over the screen, then said, "I don't think the proprietor is going to like us tearing his sheets."

"I'm sure he wouldn't," Jenny agreed dryly. "I'll tear up that pair of Mexican pants you bought me."

Jenny stepped back behind the screen. A moment later Cole heard a ripping sound, followed by silence. "Do you need any help?" he called.

Jenny peeked between the crack in the screen and saw his big grin. "Absolutely not! I meant what I said about this being strictly business."

A few minutes later, Jenny appeared the second time, carrying her *camisa* and long Mexican skirt over her arm.

"What are you going to do with those?" Cole asked.

"I'm going to keep them."

"Why? I bought you a change of clothing."

"Who knows when I'll get more clothing, particularly women's clothing. I should have thought to have you buy me some dresses while you were at the store."

"And arouse suspicion? Why would I buy clothing for a woman?"

"Why would you buy clothing for a boy?" Jenny countered.

"I told them they were for my younger brother, back at our ranch."

"Well I don't suppose it matters what you told them, because you won't go back and buy any dresses, will you?"

"No, I won't. I wouldn't be caught dead buying a woman's clothing, and neither would any other man in these parts."

Jenny made an unladylike noise that sounded

241

much like a snort, then turned to the bed, asking peevishly, "Where are my boots?"

"They're in that package that's untied, along with your hat. He stepped up to the bed, and patted a second package, saying, "This has your change of clothing in it, a hairbrush, and some soap, and that package at the end of the bed is a pair of saddle-bags."

Jenny would have liked a towel, too, but thought Cole had done well, considering. She sat on the side of the bed and unwrapped the boots and hat, then asked in dismay, "Why didn't you buy new ones?"

"Those are new," Cole answered, walking around the bed. "That's one reason I took so long getting back. I had to take them out in the alley and work on them to make them look worn. I scuffed up the boots and got them good and dirty, then stomped on the hat a few times."

"Why in God's name did you do that?"

"Because a kid might need new clothes every now and then, but the likelihood of him getting a new hat and new boots at the same time is pretty remote. People don't have that kind of money out here, and I'm trying to keep from drawing attention to you. Besides, only greenhorns wear brand-new hats and boots. It's an advertisement for trouble. That's why when folks do have to buy brand-new, they do the same thing I did. Beat it up, so it will look old and worn."

Jenny thought she had never heard anything so ridiculous in her entire life. She slipped the boots on, then stood. "They're too big, too."

"They were the smallest size they had. There's an extra pair of socks in with the other clothes. Shove them in the toe to take up the extra room."

While Jenny finished dressing, Cole put her things in her saddlebags, then collected her bedroll. He stood and waited while she braided her hair, shook the excess dirt from the battered hat with a totally disgusted look on her face, then placed it on her head. As she shoved her braid beneath it, she said, "Well, at least this fits."

"Good. Because I want you to keep it on at all times, and pulled down as low as you can get it. No boy has a face like yours."

Jenny ignored Cole's oblique compliment. She was beginning to resent his bossiness. "Anything else?" she asked in a biting voice.

"Yes, remember to walk like a boy and lower your voice a little when you talk."

"You might have to tell me how to dress, since you Texans seem to have your own backward way of doing things, but you don't have to tell me how to act. I'm an actress, remember?" Jenny said with heat.

"Fine! Just don't come across looking like Romeo. This is South Texas, remember?"

As Cole walked out the door, Jenny followed, asking, "Do I have a name, if anyone should ask?"

"Well if you're my brother, I guess your last name will have to be the same as mine. You can pick your own first name."

"Okay. Call me Billy."

As Cole walked down the hall, Jenny wished he would slow down. The unaccustomed footwear was difficult to walk in, particularly when her foot kept sliding forward in the boot with every step she took. "Can we eat here at the hotel?"

"I hadn't planned on that . . ." Cole paused, then continued, "but it might be a good idea. That way we can put your disguise to the test. If it isn't going to work, I'd rather find out here, than out in the brush."

By that time, they had reached the stairs, and Jenny took them very carefully to keep from stumbling. At the foot, Cole turned to the left and led them into a small dining room. They sat at a table in the center of the room, where they could be easily seen by everyone.

Jenny glanced around her. Only two other tables were occupied, one with two men Jenny pegged as traveling salesmen because of their wrinkled coats and ties, and the other with three men who could have been cowboys or outlaws, for all she could tell. She noted that the latter were eating with their hats on and felt relieved, knowing she wouldn't be conspicuous from that standpoint. Apparently the headgear was like their guns in this part of the country. The men only removed them to sleep.

Jenny turned her attention to the table and looked about, but all she could see was the eating utensils already laid out on the tablecloth. Guessing what she was looking for, Cole leaned forward and whispered, "They don't have menus in these small hotels. They serve one meal all day long, every day of the year. Steak, red beans, and sourdough biscuits, with coffee."

Jenny was disappointed. She'd had her fill of steak from what Cole had taken from the wild bull and had been looking forward to bacon and eggs. A moment later a tall, skinny waiter with a grimy apron wrapped around his waist and a sour look on his face dumped two plates on the table before them. Jenny looked down at the biggest steak she had ever seen, so large it spilled over the plate. Picking up her fork, she lifted the meat and saw the beans filled the entire plate below it. Combined with the two steaming biscuits that sat to one side, she felt overwhelmed, until she took the first bite. Then she attacked the food ravenously.

As they ate, Cole looked around, noting that no one was paying the least bit of attention to Jenny. Apparently the disguise had fooled them, and he couldn't complain about her behavior either. The way she was wolfing down her food, Jenny looked just like a hungry male adolescent whose stomach was a bottomless pit. Cole watched in amazement, wondering where in the world she was putting it, as little as she was, then thought she was full of unexpected surprises. Life with her was never going to be dull.

The deduction brought Cole up short. He had never thought about the future, beyond making Jenny admit she loved him and break her engagement. Maybe the reason he had avoided it was just as she so coldly reminded him the night before: he had nothing to offer her. But that had changed, thanks to her forcing him to be as mercenary as she was, and he wasn't going to change his mind. The money Amos paid him was going to put his plantation back on its feet, and he had no compunctions about taking it. All he was being paid to do was deliver Jenny. What happened after that had nothing to do with the deal Amos offered him. Cole almost laughed out loud, thinking the carpetbagger would be giving him the means to give Jenny the financial security she craved. Of course, he couldn't offer Jenny the luxury Amos could give her, not yet, but it would come, that and a much more genteel life. Cole felt as if a tremendous weight had been removed from his shoulders, but he firmed his earlier resolve. He would tell Jenny nothing of his true identity, or his plans for the future, now that he had discovered there was one for them. It was paramount that she choose him for himself and nothing else. His battered pride demanded that much of him, and her.

When Jenny and Cole walked from the hotel a little later, he untied both his horse and the one next to it. Jenny looked at the heavily-loaded animal and asked, "Where did you get him?"

"I bought him to carry our supplies. We had to beat it out of Mexico pretty fast and travel light, but there's no reason for that now. Besides, it's a good idea to travel in the *brasada* with plenty of smoked meat, rather than rely on fresh game. The sound of a gun going off can travel a long way and draws too much attention."

"All that is meat?"

Cole chuckled. "No, there's some sacks of dried beans and cornmeal, some tinned milk and fruit, some coffee, a set of tin dishes for you, a couple of blankets."

As they walked to the alley next to the hotel, Jenny asked, "Why do we need more blankets? I thought you said it was still summer here."

"It is today. But you never know when a norther is going to blow in at this time of the year."

"A what?"

"A norther, a cold blast of air straight from the arctic. It can drop the temperature as much as thirty degrees in one hour."

Jenny thought that had to be a gross exaggeration, the kind Amos had warned her Texans were prone to make. She asked, "Just how far is Amos's ranch from here?"

Cole had been to Amos's ranch before. If you went as straight as an arrow, it was a two-day ride from here. But Cole intended to draw the trip out. "About a week's ride, or so."

Jenny frowned. "I could have sworn Amos told me it was closer to Rio Grande City than that. Are you sure you know where it is?"

"Positive. My gang and I passed by it one day."

Jenny had a niggardly feeling that he wasn't being completely honest with her. She shot him a penetrating look, thinking to find some sign of guilt or deception, but Cole looked completely at ease.

They walked from the alley and up to the shed by the corral. Spying Jenny, Princess whinnied and ran up to the railing, obviously happy to see her mistress and not at all fooled by the disguise. It was all Jenny could do to keep from running to the mare and hugging her neck, but she was afraid it wouldn't fit her new image.

The attendant was once more sitting beneath the tree in his battered rocking chair, watching them as they walked towards him, his full attention on Jenny. He frowned, wondering if he was getting senile. He could have sworn the young man had a Meskin boy with him the day before.

"I'll take that mare, now," Cole said as he came to a stop before the old-timer.

The old man rose and glared at Cole. "You told me to hang on to her for a few days. I ain't giving the money back."

"I don't want the money back. I just want the mare," Cole answered in exasperation, thinking the conversation sounded familiar and growing weary of the old man's testiness. "But this time you do the saddling. At least I can get what I paid for there."

Twenty minutes later Jenny and Cole were riding north, taking a cow trail through the brush, since there was no road. Jenny had seen mesquite thickets, but had never ridden into one. She was shocked at how dense they were. At least a dozen varieties of cactus grew everywhere, narrow-leaved, paddle-leaved, barrel-shaped, some hugging the ground and so small they could hardly be seen, and others in huge intimidating clumps, with chaparral, coma, and other briary bushes growing right over them and completing the layering. The mesquites formed a low canopy over all. It was a dim world of tangled, thorny vegetation that seemed to be reaching out from every direction to scratch or prick or puncture, so thick in places that you couldn't see three feet from you.

"Couldn't we have gone another way?" Jenny asked Cole, riding ahead of her. "My face and hands are getting scratched, and my new clothes ripped."

"It wouldn't have done us any good to skirt this thicket. We would have just run into another one. There's no way you can avoid them. That's why the cowhands in this part of the country wear gauntlets, heavy leather leggings, and wooden toe-guards on their stirrups, to protect themselves when they have to flush stray cattle from areas like these."

"I can't imagine why the cows would even come into something like this. There's no grass."

"No, but there are mesquite beans, and they love them."

Jenny looked about her, then asked, "What's that rustling noise?"

Cole reined in and listened. "I think it's some javelinas."

"What are they?"

"Wild pigs."

"Are they dangerous?"

"They can be, especially the boars. They have big tusks on them." Cole listened a moment, then said, "I can't tell which direction they're going. If you see them coming at you, just keep Princess still. They'll probably go right by you. They're as blind as bats. Whatever you do, don't go riding into the brush. It's more dangerous than they are."

"Then how can they go through it?"

"Their skin is as tough as nails. Now, be quiet a

minute, so I can listen."

Jenny held her tongue and looked nervously about her. The noise sounded nearer to her. Then she got a whiff of a terrible stench. Apparently Princess smelled it, too. The mare began to move about nervously, her nostrils dilated. Jenny bent forward and patted her neck, saying in a low, soothing voice, "Easy, girl, easy. Be still."

A moment later the noise began to fade. "They're heading away from us," Cole said.

"Did that horrible smell come from them?"

"Yes. Sometimes they stink worse than a polecat."

"Just what *is* a polecat?" Jenny asked as they began riding again.

"A skunk."

"Are there skunks out here, too?"

"It's a likely possibility."

"And what else?"

"Do you mean dangerous, or anything?"

"Dangerous, I suppose."

"Well, there might be a bobcat, but the biggest danger is probably rattlers."

Jenny looked around her wildly for any sign of the lethal reptiles. She saw something step onto the trail, and reined Princess in sharply. "Cole!" she called.

Cole brought his horse to a sudden halt at Jenny's fearful cry, reached for his gun, and turned in the saddle. Then seeing what she was staring at, he laughed.

Jenny assumed since Cole was laughing the creature was harmless. "What is it?"

"It's a porcupine."

"I assume it isn't dangerous."

"Not unless you touch it and puncture yourself on one of its sharp quills."

When the porcupine lumbered from the path in front of her and disappeared in the brush, Jenny nudged Princess forward to follow Cole. She felt a sharp sting as another thorny bush found its mark. So what's new? she thought wryly.

Eighteen

The thicket Jenny and Cole were traveling through eventually thinned, and they made camp that night beneath one of the live oaks that were scattered among the mesquites.

After they had unsaddled their horses and put them in a rope corral that Cole fashioned, Jenny helped gather wood for the fire. Although she took care when she picked up the dead mesquite branches laying all over the ground, she stuck a thorn from one in her thumb, the half-inch barb penetrating her flesh to its hilt. "Damn!" she muttered, jerking the limb away and dropping it, sucking on the painful wound.

Cole had been gathering wood right beside her. He lowered his load to the ground and took her hand, looked down at the wound, then pressed on her thumb with his thumb and forefinger, saying, "You need to make it bleed, to flush the poison out."

"Is that why it stings so badly, because the thorns are poisonous?" Jenny asked in alarm.

"There're not really poisonous from the standpoint

of making you ill, but mesquite punctures do stay sore for a good while, even if they don't fester." He took her tiny hands in his big capable ones and turned them over and over. "Christ, you *did* take a beating! They're full of scratches." He dropped one hand and lifted her chin, looking at her face. "Even your face. And they all look mean and red. I'll see if I can find something to put on these scratches after I have a fire going. The light is fading fast."

"You're carrying medicines?"

"No. What I'm talking about is growing out there in the brush, or at least I hope it is. That's why I want to start the fire first, before I go looking. It's easy to get lost in this brush in the dark."

After Cole had a fire going, he walked into the brush, disappearing completely from Jenny's view within a few minutes. She watched anxiously for his return, the flames of the fire casting eerie shadows over the woods and making them look spooky. Ten minutes passed, then fifteen, then twenty, the only sound the crackling of the fire. As she heard rustling to the side of her, Jenny remembered the javalinas earlier that day and turned, her heart racing in fear at what she might see.

Cole stepped from the woods. He stopped to tear away a persistent branch of coma that had caught on his pants leg. Jenny had not expected him to return from that direction and felt weak with relief, so weak that she sank to the ground.

Cole walked to her, then hunkered beside her and handed her a pulpy, narrow leaf. "This is aloe. Break it in half and smear the slimy end on your scratches.

253

It will not only take away the fierce sting, but seems to help the healing."

Jenny knew nothing of herbal healing and was wary. Seeing her hesitation, Cole broke the leaf, took one hand and rubbed the open end on her scratches. As the aloe juice soothed the burning almost as soon as he applied it, Jenny said in amazement, "It really works. How did you know about this?"

"It's pretty much common knowledge in this part of the country. I don't know who discovered it, the Mexicans or the Indians, but it's just one of the native cures that we Texans have adopted."

As Cole took her other hand and started to apply the juice, Jenny pulled it away and said, "I can do it."

"Fine," Cole answered, "but let me get those scratches on your face, particularly the one that's so close to your eye."

Jenny felt uneasy with Cole ministering to her. But it was more than just his nearness, which always had an unsettling effect on her. His actions seemed so tender, so caring, so loving. The only other person who had touched her so had been her mother.

When Cole had covered every scratch on Jenny's face, he handed her the piece of aloe, walked to the pile of supplies, and produced a skin sack that Jenny had never seen before. He poured its contents into a pot and set it over the fire. Seeing the puzzled look on Jenny's face, he explained, "That's our beans for tonight. They're hard as rocks and have to be soaked several hours before they can be cooked, preferably all day. Carrying a sack to soak them in while you're riding is a trick I learned from the Texas Rangers."

"You were once in the Texas Rangers?" Jenny asked in surprise.

"No, by the time I would have been old enough to join, they had been disbanded. There was a group that had their headquarters in Brownsville that I hung around with when I was a boy. They taught me a lot about survival in the wilderness that's come in handy since I've been on the run."

Cole made a pot of coffee, and while they were waiting for the beans to cook, they each sipped on a cup. Then Cole sliced some meat from a ham he unwrapped, opened a tin of biscuits, and dished them up along with the beans as soon as they were done. He handed a plateful to Jenny.

Cole had always done the cooking and serving, but there was something subtle in his manner that made Jenny acutely aware of his attendance. A peculiar warmth came to her chest, an emotion she knew had nothing to do with desire. A sudden suspicion came to her. Was he wooing her? It didn't seem to fit his tough image as an outlaw and gunfighter. That was a tender enticement that fit more into the realm of a gentleman, which the rugged gunman certainly wasn't. No, Cole's approach had always been more physical, more demanding, more elemental, more directly to the point. In the end, Jenny didn't know if Cole had an ulterior motive for being so kind and attentive, but she was determined that, if he did, he wouldn't succeed. Her resolve was firm. She wouldn't allow herself to fall in love with a man with no future, doubly so one who would probably end up at the end of a rope.

When Jenny finished eating, she washed her dishes in a basin of water Cole had provided for that purpose and asked, "Where are my blankets?"

"I'll get them for you."

"That won't be necessary!" Jenny answered sharply, before Cole could even rise. "I'm quite capable of making my own bed. Just tell me where they are."

Cole could think of only one reason for Jenny to become so independent so suddenly. She feared he wouldn't adhere to her "strictly business" mandate. She's just as prickly as that porcupine out there, he thought, then hiding his amusement, smiled blandly and said, "They're under the tarp, with the supplies."

When Jenny had fished out two blankets and was in the process of rising from the pile of supplies, Cole called, "Since you're up, do you mind bringing me one?"

Jenny was tempted to refuse. She didn't want to wait on him for fear he would misconstrue it, any more than she wanted him to wait on her. Then realizing that would only make her look childish, she slipped a third blanket out.

When Jenny reached where Cole was sitting, she tossed the blanket in his lap, then deliberately walked to the opposite side of the fire and spread her blankets. Before she even reclined, she saw Cole was spreading his bed out and felt a pang of disappointment, a spontaneous reaction she quickly squelched.

Cole lay down on his blanket, gazing up at the branches of the tree over him, seeing the wink of a star here and there between the leaves. Jenny did the same, her body rigid with expectation, fully prepared to do battle. The minutes ticked by, and when Cole made no move towards her, she relaxed. "I think this is the tallest tree I've seen in Texas," she said.

"Live oaks grow considerably taller than mesquites, but then almost everything does. They're a poor excuse for a tree."

"Oh, I like the mesquites, too. When they finally become a tree," Jenny added as an afterthought. "But I'll have to admit, I'm not an authority on trees. Anything that grows more than four feet in the air and has leaves on it impresses me. We didn't have trees in the Bowery, you know."

No trees, no sunrises, no spectacular storms, Cole thought. God, it must have been a dreary place. He thought about the majestic oaks that surrounded his plantation house, magnificent trees that made this one look like a midget. He could hardly wait for Jenny to see them, them and the cotton fields that rolled out in every direction when the crop was in bloom, the delicate petals turning from white, to pink, and finally a reddish purple, blanketing the earth in color as far as the eye could see. There was only one sight that could match that spectacular beauty in Cole's estimation, the bluebonnets on the prairies in springtime. Undoubtedly, there were no flowers in the Bowery, either. Why, even the cotton fields when they were ready for picking were beautiful, looking like a fluffy cloud had drifted down from heaven and settled on the earth, startlingly white beneath a searing-blue sky, rose-hued beneath

257

the setting sun, and glowing with a life of their own in the darkness of night.

Cole smiled, remembering his uncle telling him he had more of his grandfather's planter soul in him than his father's merchant soul, for the brothers had come from Alabama, where their father grew cotton. And it was true. From the moment Cole had arrived on the plantation, he had loved the place—not just the beautiful home, but the land itself. He had followed his uncle around like a puppy and badgered the older man to teach him everything he knew, promising himself he'd have a plantation just like it someday. Cole had never dreamed his uncle would die so young, and the plantation would become his. Yes, he'd bring the plantation back to what it once was, Cole vowed. He owed it to himself and his uncle and to Jenny, whose life had lacked the beauty he'd had the privilege of knowing.

Cole had been silent for so long, Jenny thought he had drifted off to sleep. She jumped when he said, "I never did tell you what the rest of Texas looks like, did I?"

"Then it isn't all like this?"

"No. A lot of it is dry and arid, but not necessarily like this. Each area is a little different. The western part of the state is mountainous, but much more rugged and rockier than those mountains in Mexico we rode through. If you move eastward across the state from there, you'll travel over a high, dry tableland where the rivers flow through deep, narrow gorges, the water in them so alkaline in the summer that it can't be consumed by man or animal. Then gradually the land begins to roll, until you've reached the hill country. Some of the most beautiful rivers and streams in the state are there. They're spring fed, crystal clear and ice cold even on the hottest summer day, surrounded by towering pecan and other native trees. In some places they're deep and reflect the green of the trees around them, in others they're white with rapids, and in still others they dance over beds made of pure rock. From the hill country, past Austin, you come to some of the richest farmland in the south, the Black Prairie. It's a gently rolling land, much of it in the broad, fertile valleys of the Colorado and Brazos Rivers, lightly wooded, except around the rivers where it hasn't been cleared. Directly east is the timber line, where huge pine and hardwood forests grow, so thick with underbrush and twisted vines that it's almost impenetrable. Then finally, along the eastern border, the ground dips so low you'll find dark swamps, mysterious, brooding, ghostly, and to the south, along the Gulf, salt marshes where millions of birds winter."

To Jenny, Cole's description of his state sounded almost poetic. She had no strong ties to her birthplace, took no pride in her state. Her bonds had been to her family, not the land. Home had no real meaning for her. Her roots were shallow, if not nonexistent. She was both amazed at Cole's deep feelings and touched. As she became aware that Cole was waiting for some comment, she muttered, "It seems impossible to believe that's all in one state."

Cole laughed, answering, "I didn't even tell you about the panhandle—the great grassland—or the hundreds of miles of beaches along the Gulf." He paused, then said, "Yes, it's an amazing state, not only geographically, but in its makeup too, part Old South, part Mexican, part Western. It's even got a strong German flavor in the hill country. But then, it's a hell of a big state, no thanks to the radical Republicans. The bigwigs in the capital wanted to split it into several states so there would be more congressional seats for them to occupy. One idiot, Edmund Davis, wanted to divide it into three states, so that everything west of the Colorado River would become the State of West Texas, with San Antonio as its capital. Of course, he pictured himself as the governor. The press ridiculed his idea, calling it the state of Coyote since there were more of them than people in that area."

"But that didn't happen," Jenny pointed out.

"No, it didn't. But Davis got what he was conniving for. He became governor of Texas in an election where there were so many irregularities it was a farce."

Cole's voice had taken on a bitter edge. "You don't sound like you care much for the man," Jenny commented.

"Davis? Christ, no! I hated the bastard!" Cole realized he was on the verge of giving himself away by making his hatred sound so vehement and quickly said, "But so did almost everyone in Texas. He set up a separate state police force that consisted mostly of Negroes and scoundrels and included every law enforcement officer in the state, and made them answerable to him personally. They terrorized the people. They were so brutal and overbearing that even some of the radical Republicans in Congress couldn't abide them. For his entire term, and then some, Davis was a virtual dictator, corrupt, inefficient, extravagant—stupid! Unbelievably stupid. And if you don't believe me, here is an example of some of the moronic things that bastard did. After the army had finally run down the Comanches, captured two of their most powerful and influential chiefs and imprisoned them, Davis pardoned the chiefs and released them. It was an act so incomprehensible that even Sheridan, who has no love for Southerners, Texans in particular, was inflamed. He wrote Davis a letter telling him if the Comanches went on the warpath again, he hoped the Governor's scalp would be the first taken. Unfortunately, it wasn't. Predictably the Indians went on another bloody rampage and had to be run down again."

Even though Jenny knew nothing of Indians and their ways, she was in agreement. Davis's act seemed unbelievably irresponsible. "But he's not still governor, is he?" Jenny asked, remembering Cole saying something about the Democrats being in power.

"No, he isn't, but it isn't because he didn't use everything at his disposal to stay in power. He delayed elections for a full year, then when he was finally voted out by an overwhelming majority, he refused to give up his office. He posted his militia around the capitol and appealed to Grant to send him military aid, claiming—of all things!—that there had been voting irregularities. When Grant refused to intervene, an irate Texas crowd determined to see

261

the rightful governor inaugurated marched on the capitol, aided by Travis Rifles. Davis finally surrendered his office, slipped out a window one night, and vanished."

Jenny had never paid much attention to politics, but she could clearly see the terrible injustices Cole had presented. When he fell to brooding darkly, she sensed there was something more than what he had told her, something personal. She realized Cole was much more than he appeared, that there were facets to this man that she had never seen, that she might never be allowed to see. There were depths to Cole that she had never dreamed existed. He was an enigma, and for that reason, all the more fascinating.

The next morning there was a dense fog covering the brush. It left every bush and tree dripping with moisture. To Jenny, the woods looked as spooky as they had the night before with the firelight dancing over them.

She and Cole were sitting before the fire, having a last cup of coffee before they packed up, when Cole tensed and peered into the fog across from them.

"What's wrong?" Jenny asked.

"Ssh! I heard something." Cole listened closely, then hissed, "Someone's coming. Don't say a word and keep your head down."

Jenny couldn't see or hear a thing. Then, as if they had stepped from behind a wispy white curtain, three men on horseback appeared. As Cole rose to his feet, the man in the lead held his hands extended before him, saying, "Don't shoot, mister. We're friends, not foe."

"What do you want?" Cole asked curtly.

"We smelled your coffee, and were wondering if you could spare a couple of cups. We used our last bit last night, and I just can't face the day without coffee."

Cole had already been wary—he hadn't survived as long as he had in the brush without being careful—but now he was even more suspicious of the strangers. He remembered seeing these men in the general store in Rio Grande City, buying supplies. He found it hard to believe they would forget coffee.

"There may be a few cups left in the pot, but we only have two cups," Cole answered.

"We can share. Been doing it all our lives. We're brothers."

Cole wasn't surprised. The three looked alike, with black, bushy beards, eyebrows so thick they covered the bridge of their noses, thin lips, and black, shifty eyes. The only difference between them was that the one who had been doing all of the talking was heavier than the other two. Cole pegged him as the older of the three. In all, they were a mean-looking lot.

As the three men dismounted and walked towards the fire, Cole said to Jenny, still sitting on the ground, "Give me your cup, Billy. Then go load our supplies and saddle our horses."

It seemed a strange command to Jenny. She hadn't saddled her own horse the entire time she and Cole had been traveling together, because it was such a chore for her, much less saddled his and loaded a pack horse. She handed Cole her cup, rose, and walked to where the horses were corralled at one side of their camp, then pretended to begin packing up.

The older brother handed the cups Cole offered him over the fire to his younger brothers, then picked up the pot and filled them half full with coffee, saying, "We sure appreciate this. Of course, we'd do the same for you, seeing as how we're all cut from the same cloth."

"Oh?" Cole asked. "In what way?"

The stranger put the pot back down, answering, "Why, we're all stage coach robbers." When Cole made no response, his face looking as if it were made of stone, the man continued, "Pete," he motioned to the brother standing closest to him, "recognized you from a wanted poster. You're Cole Benteen."

Cole knew it would be pointless to deny it. He remained silent.

The older brother continued, saying, "We heard about that last bank robbery you did and how all your gang were killed. We thought maybe you might be looking for some more men."

"No, I'm not getting another gang together. I've decided to go it alone for awhile."

"And the kid? What about him?" the outlaw asked in a surly voice.

"What about him?"

"You'd take on a snot-nosed kid, but not experienced gunfighters?"

"Maybe I prefer to take them young and train them the way I want."

An ugly look came over the outlaw's face. His hand moved towards his gun. But Cole had been expecting it, and his draw was faster. Two gunshots rang out, the loud sound echoing in the woods' around them, both from Cole's gun. The first hit the outlaw in the shoulder just as his gun cleared leather, the second hit his brother's gun as he, too, drew, sending the weapon flying through the air. Cole, still crouched, spun his gun around to point at the third outlaw, who was reaching for his gun. "Don't try it!" Cole warned. "If you do, I'll blow your head off."

The man's hand stopped in mid-flight; his face turned ashen.

"Put your hands up," Cole instructed, but the man was frozen with fright. "Dammit, reach!" Cole yelled.

The man's hands flew up.

"For God's sake, Pete, help me!" the older outlaw cried from where he was writhing on the ground in pain and holding his free hand over the wound. "I'm bleeding like a stuck pig."

"I can't help you," Pete answered, staring down at his hand in horror. "I think my hand is paralyzed."

"Goddammit, that's just temporary!" the wounded man answered. "Help me. I think he broke my arm."

As Pete moved to help his brother, Cole said in a hard voice, "Leave him alone!"

"But—"

"No buts! Dammit, he asked for it! Now, move back from him. Move back, before I really lose my temper and blow all of your heads off!"

With Cole's golden eyes glittering with anger, Pete didn't doubt his threat. He looked very dangerous.

"Please, you ain't gonna let me bleed to death, are you?" the outlaw on the ground pleaded. "Help me."

Cole glanced at the large puddle of blood beneath the man and knew he must have hit a major blood vessel. He had shot to wound, not kill. "Billy, come up here!" he called over his shoulder.

Everything had happened so lightning-fast that Jenny was still in a state of shock. She rose and walked to Cole, her legs shaking badly. When she came to his side, Cole handed her his gun, saying, "Keep them covered, while I check that bastard's wound."

When Cole placed the gun in Jenny's hand she was shocked at how heavy it was. She was tempted to hold it with both hands, but feared that would give away her gender. She struggled to hold it while Cole walked around the fire and crouched beside the wounded outlaw, shoving his hand out of the way so he could look at the bullet wound, then ripping the scarf lose from around his neck.

"Why did you three really come here?" Cole asked as he bound the outlaw's shoulder with his neck scarf. "I know it wasn't to ask for a job. You wouldn't have pulled your gun on me for that." When the outlaw remained grimly silent, Cole tightened the scarf painfully, demanding, "Answer me!"

The outlaw cried out in pain, then muttered, "Okay, okay, but loosen that up a bit." As Cole relieved the pressure slightly, he said to the brother

266

standing next to him, "You tell him, Pete. I feel like I'm gonna puke."

The outlaw's face had taken on a greenish hue. Cole switched his attention from him to Pete. The man shuffled his feet nervously, then said, "We figured since you'd pulled off so many robberies and didn't have any gang left, you must have a fortune stashed away some place. We thought we could force you to take us to it."

"In other words, you planned to rob me?"

Pete's face drained of all color. "Yeah," he admitted. "We'd heard you was fast, but we didn't think you were that fast."

"Well, I guess now you've learned differently," Cole remarked.

"Yeah," Pete answered lamely.

Cole rose, picked up the first outlaw's gun, then walked to retrieve Pete's, briefly putting his back to the third outlaw. The man had been watching Jenny's hands shake, and not knowing it was because the gun was almost too heavy for her to hold, thought it was out of fear. He decided to risk a draw.

Jenny saw his hand moving towards his gun, shouted, "Keep your hands up!" then pulled the trigger. The bullet shot the outlaw's hat from his head. Another bullet followed fast this time kicking up dirt between the man's feet.

"Godalmighty, kid! Cut it out! My hands are up!" the man yelled frantically, jumping from side to side.

Cole had swung around at the first shot and, realizing Jenny was shooting wild and could hit him, was just as nervous. "Easy, kid," he said in a soothing voice, then not wanting the outlaws to realize how bad a shot she was, added, "Stop playing around with him. He's going to behave himself."

Jenny had meant the first shot to be in the air as a warning shot, and the second had just happened as a result of her fright. Her heart raced when she realized how close she had come to killing someone. She struggled to calm herself.

Cole tossed one of the outlaw's guns aside, out of reach, then walked to the man who was still armed and shaking like a leaf to relieve him of his weapon. As he slipped the gun from the man's holster, the man whispered, "Jesus Christ! Who taught that kid how to shoot?"

"I did," Cole lied.

"What did you say his name was?" Pete asked, equally impressed.

"Billy."

"Billy who?"

"Just Billy."

Cole walked around the fire and stood beside Jenny, facing the trio. "Okay, get the hell out of here!"

"Without our guns?" Pete asked in alarm.

"Exactly."

"But we could get killed out there, without our guns," he objected.

"You should have thought of that before you got so greedy," Cole answered coldly, then glanced at the wounded outlaw who had passed out on the ground. "And you'd better try to get your brother to a doctor. That's a nasty wound he's got there. Without proper treatment, he could lose the use of that arm."

Pete shot Cole a furious look, then motioned for his brother to help him. Together, the two lifted their older brother, carried him to his horse, and draped him over the saddle, then mounted their own horses. As they started to ride away, Cole called, "And by the way, there is no stash. I gambled it all away."

Cole and Jenny watched until the three horses with their riders disappeared in the brush. Then Cole dropped the two guns he had been holding and relieved Jenny of his.

Jenny rubbed her aching arm and asked, "Is that true? You don't have any money hidden anywhere?"

"Yes."

"You actually gambled it all away?"

"No. There never was any stash. I just said that so they could pass that little bit of information around," Cole explained, thinking he'd be damned glad when he could get out of this lawless country and back east.

"Where did you learn to shoot like that?" Jenny asked, remembering how lightning-fast everything had happened. "Did the Rangers teach you that, too?"

"I picked up a few things about marksmanship from them, but I was too young to carry a gun. Rangers don't pride themselves on being fast on the draw. That's for gunslingers."

Before Jenny could ask any more questions, Cole changed the subject, asking her, "Were you scared?"

"I was terrified," she admitted. Then she started to laugh, saying, "But I wasn't near as scared as that bastard I shot at. That's the first time I've seen a grown man pee in his pants."

It was a classic example of something only Jenny would say, and for that reason Cole saw nothing outrageous about it. Her total honesty was a part of her charm. He joined her in her laughter, thinking she was a wonder and a joy.

Nineteen

Two days later Jenny and Cole rode from a mesquite thicket onto a gently rolling prairie that was liberally sprinkled with grass. Despite their exposure to the sun, Jenny was glad to see the open area, thinking she'd rather contend with the searing light than the wicked thorns and almost claustrophobic closeness of the brush. Besides, here she could ride beside Cole and feast her eyes on him, providing of course, she was careful not to let him catch her sneaking glances.

He sat straight as an arrow in his saddle. His striking golden eyes were focused on the distant horizon. Jenny had to admit that he was the most appealing man she had ever seen. It was more than his rugged good looks and splendid physique that drew her. She admired his superb confidence, every nuance of his mannerisms, his easy stride, his quick mind, his keen senses, his strength. Of all the things she had come to appreciate about Cole it was his strength that was uppermost in her mind, not just his considerable physical prowess, but the remarkable strength of character within him. It was a force that came from the wellsprings of his soul, a power she sensed was as indestructible as a rock. If not for her fierce will and determination, it would be so easy for her to fall in love with him.

Jenny dragged her eyes away from the man riding next to her and sighed deeply, fearing she had already fallen a little in love with the gunfighter. It was something she had resolved she would never do, fall in love with the wrong man. She'd never thought she'd be so weak, so foolish. Well, there was nothing to do but harden her heart towards him, she decided. It was something she had to do for her own survival. But it would be so much easier to do if she wasn't in constant contact with him. Then maybe she could forget.

A rumbling noise that sounded much like thunder broke into Jenny's thoughts. She glanced up at the sky and saw there wasn't a cloud in sight. She noticed Cole had turned in his saddle and was peering at something behind them.

Jenny turned and looked. All she could see was a thick cloud of dust in the distance. "Is it a storm of some kind?"

Cole finally got a glimpse of what was bearing down on them. "No. It's a herd of stampeding mustangs."

"What are they? Cattle?"

"No, but I wish the hell they were. You can stop stampeding cattle if you get in front of them and turn them. But those are wild horses, and once

272

they start running nothing on this earth can stop them or make them change their course. And we're right in their path." Cole glanced quickly around them, then said, "Come on! Let's see if we can make it to that line of brush over there."

The line of brush Cole was talking about was over a half-mile away. As they raced diagonally to the rushing herd, Jenny finally saw the mustangs. She was both shocked and astonished. She had never seen so many horses, hundreds and hundreds of every color of horseflesh in the world, stretching as far as she could see, all running at breakneck speed with their long manes and tails flying. Closer and closer they came, no matter how much she urged Princess to greater speed and the valiant little horse responded. A solid wall of horses came thundering down on her, and Jenny knew she was looking death in the eye as thousands and thousands of pounds of wild, terrified horseflesh came rushing at her, so close now she could see the whites of their eyes and their dilated nostrils.

"We're not going to be able to outrun them!" Cole yelled over the horrendous sound the herd was making. "Veer in front of them and join them. Whatever you do, don't try to fight them. Just go with the flow."

Jenny had barely turned Princess when she felt the hot breath of the lead mares on the back of her neck. Then she seemed to be swallowed by the herd, as the front wave of horses pulled up beside her, then overtook Princess. The gallant mare couldn't outrun the wild horses because of the weight she was carrying. Jenny was rapidly surrounded by racing horses. The tremendous heat they generated made her sweat profusely. She was soaking wet within minutes. She no longer guided her mount. Nor did Princess have any control of where she went. The lead mares had complete mastery of the entire herd, and it veered first to one side of the prairie, then the other, then back again, in a sweeping undulating motion.

The earth shook from the tremendous beating. The sound of pounding hooves reverberated in the air until it was a pulsating, deafening roar. Jenny's head began to ache, and every breath she drew in was a struggle. Her heart beat so fast and hard from fright that she feared it would jump from her chest. The smell of horse sweat was so strong it was overpowering, making her nauseous. Several times, the horses around her crowded so close that she felt their hot, slick flesh pressing her legs. She feared she would be crushed. The stampede had become a horror that seemed would never end.

Jenny looked around, hoping to spy Cole, but with the exceptionally long manes and tails of the mustangs whipping about, it was impossible to see much further than a few horses away. Past that, everything was a blurred image of flashing movements. A horrifying thought came to her. Had he not completed his turn before the herd overtook him? Had he and his horse been bowled over and trampled to death beneath thousands of razor sharp hooves? Tears came to Jenny's eyes, and a lump the size of her fist formed in her throat.

It was the sound of Princess's shrill whinny that drew Jenny's attention away from her morbid thoughts. There was an unmistakable pained quality to it. She glanced over her shoulder and saw a big black horse was nipping at Princess's flank, its lips drawn back revealing large sharp teeth. The sight enraged Jenny. Mindless of her own safety, she turned in her saddle and took a swing at the horse. She almost lost her seat, and grabbed frantically for the saddle horn.

A moment later Cole appeared, riding right next to her. To Jenny, it looked as if he had been dropped there out of the clear blue sky. Before she could recover from her surprise, he called over to her, "The herd is slowing down, probably to cross a river. If that's the case, we'll make our break then. As soon as you come out of the water, head for the woods to the right. And drop your reins while you're crossing. Princess will have a hard enough time carrying you over without having to contend with them pulling on her head. If you should get some space between you and the next horse, slip off her back and hang on to the saddle horn, so she can tow you across. It will make it a hell of a lot easier for her."

Jenny never saw the river through the solid mass of horses before her and around her. Only by the splashing did she know they had entered it. Then, when they reached the deep part, she felt the dip

275

as Princess started swimming.

Jenny became alarmed when she saw how hard her mare was having to fight to stay afloat. She glanced around her, but saw not an inch of space to slip into, as Cole had done a few yards away. Princess's body sank dunking Jenny in water to chest level. The only part of the valiant mare visible was her head. Jenny swore as the mustangs swimming on both sides of Princess closed in, thinking they would hamper her mare even more. Then seeing the danger they posed for her, Jenny slipped her feet from the stirrups and raised her legs, fearing they'd break them. As Princess's head, neck and body rose from the water, Jenny realized what the mustangs had unwittingly done. They were buoying her horse with their bodies, so that Princess swam easier.

With the immediate danger lessened Jenny took the opportunity to look around her. Swimming horses filled the river, water thrashing as they kicked their legs. She spied a colt being towed across the river by its mother, the foal's head laying on her back as she did all the work. The colt looked so sublimely relaxed and unconcerned that Jenny laughed.

"Jenny, get ready!" Cole called, slipping back into the saddle the second his horse's hooves touched bottom.

As she and Princess came out of the river, dripping water, Jenny lowered her legs, grabbed Princess's reins, and turned her, but not before she was given a shower by the two horses still hovering close to her mare as they shook the water from their coats.

Half-blinded by water drops, Jenny followed Cole and his horse, weaving around horses that were emerging from the river, then breaking into a gallop when they reached open ground. She didn't look back until they came to a stop at the brush line. She looked back and saw the herd was leisurely grazing, instead of continuing their wild run as she had half-expected. The scene was so peaceful looking that Jenny found it hard to believe that those were the same dangerous horses that had been so life-threatening just moments before.

Cole's eyes quickly swept over Jenny to assure himself that she had not been injured in any way. She looked none the worse for her wild ride. Her face was flushed, only making her more beautiful. He was proud of the way she had handled herself. A lesser woman would have panicked, and that would have created big problems for him. They both could have been killed. Yes, she was a hell of a lot of woman, well worth fighting for.

Unaware of Cole's complimentary thoughts, Jenny asked, "What made them stampede?"

Who knows?" Cole answered. "Maybe something spooked them, or maybe they just felt like a good run. Mustangs have got to be the runningest creatures on earth."

"Where did they come from?"

"They're descendants of some Spanish horses

that escaped after a shipwreck off the Texas coast. You'll find herds of them all over Texas, but particularly in South Texas. Some people call this area Mustang Desert for that reason."

"I never dreamed there were that many horses in the entire world."

"That's just a small herd. Some of them have ten thousand horses or more." Cole looked around and said, "I think we ought to camp here and give our horses a rest. They're not accustomed to that kind of abuse."

Cole's mentioning abuse reminded Jenny of what had happened to Princess. She turned in her saddle and saw the mare's flank was covered with ugly tooth prints, one oozing blood. "Look what one mean horse did to Princess!" she cried out angrily. "It was biting her."

"Yes, I know. I saw him. He probably thought Princess was one of his mares. That's how the stallions drive their mares by nipping them on the flanks to make them run."

"Why in the devil would he think that?"

"In a stallion's eye, a mare is a mare. It doesn't matter if they're tame or wild."

"Your stallion doesn't treat her that way," Jenny pointed out.

"He doesn't have strong herding instincts like the mustang stallions do. However, if he took a fancy to your mare, he might get a little rough in his courting. Biting people is the mark of a mean horse, but biting mares in the heat of passion goes

278

along with mating." A slow grin spread over Cole's lips, giving him a boyish charm that wrenched Jenny's heart. "Of course, sometimes, the female bites back."

Jenny knew by the grin that Cole was no longer talking about horses. He was reminding her of a particularly deep bite she had placed on his shoulder during one of their more torrid lovemaking sessions. A spontaneous flush rose on her face, but she refused to respond verbally. Instead she dismounted.

Cole followed suit, and their horses shook the water from their coats, making the reins and the stirrups rattle, sending a spray of glittering water drops flying everywhere. There was nothing either Cole or Jenny could do but endure another shower. Then they set to work unsaddling the animals.

Jenny was still thinking about how meanly Princess had been treated. "Did you see those horses crowding Princess when she was about to go under in the river? Why, they wouldn't even give her room to swim."

"No, that's not true, Jenny. Princess was hampered by both your weight and her flank girth. It's hard for a horse to kick its back legs with that around them. Even without my weight, my horse was having a time of it. The mares beside Princess knew she was having trouble, so they lent her support. They didn't know that it was the saddle and you that were making it so difficult. A horse heavy with foal does the same thing."

"Then it wasn't just coincidence that they helped her? It was on purpose?"

"Yes. It's one of those amazing survival techniques that nature instilled in them."

"Like the colt laying its head on its mother's back and letting her swim it across?" Jenny asked, smiling in remembrance.

"Yes, a colt isn't near strong enough to swim a stream that size. Horses can swim, but it's not their strength."

Jenny yanked the saddle from Princess's back, then removed the soaking wet saddle blanket. She stepped back to view the ugly bites on her flank, then asked, "Do you think some aloe might help these?"

"I've never heard of aloe being used on a horse. I'd suggest steeping some creosote leaves in water and washing the wounds with it. It seems to cleanse the wound and keep them from getting infected, and right now that's all Princess needs."

"Does it sting?"

"A little."

Jenny didn't want to do anything that would cause Princess more pain, but she didn't want the bites to get infected either. She had seen rat bites that had gotten infected back home, and knew one little girl who'd lost her hand because of it. "Do you think we could find some creosote bushes in this brush?"

"I'll have a look in a minute."

Jenny turned and saw Cole's eyes were sweeping

the prairie across the river. "Are you looking for something?" she asked.

"Yes, our packhorse. I had to let go of his lead rein so he could run free and lost sight of him. With all that weight he was carrying, he was probably at the very back of the herd. I was hoping he might have broken free when we reached the river. If not, I don't know how he could have made it."

Jenny felt a twinge of guilt. She had not even thought about the packhorse. She craned her neck and looked, too, but there was no sign of the animal.

Well, I guess he's at the bottom of the river, the poor bastard," Cole muttered, "along with our supplies." He turned and glared at the mustangs; then his eyes widened in surprise. "Well, I'll be damned. He made it across the river."

Jenny whirled around. "Where is he?"

"On the other side of the prairie, by that line of brush."

Jenny strained her eyes, but she couldn't see the horse. Her vision was simply not as good as Cole's. "Are you going to go get him?"

"I'll wait and see if the herd is going to move on or not. I don't want to start another stampede by walking into it."

"Why would they do that?"

"Because I'm human, and they're afraid of humans."

"They weren't afraid of us when they almost ran us down," Jenny pointed out.

"They were beyond noticing by that point. Besides, it's our human scent more than anything that frightens them. They couldn't smell us for the stench of their own sweat."

Cole and Jenny corralled their horses and searched for firewood. Since Cole had not been able to fold his saddlebags over his saddle before entering the river, everything in them had gotten wet, as had everything in Jenny's, and he was forced to start the fire Indian-fashion, a tedious and time-consuming chore. While he was doing that, Jenny was spreading their wet clothing over bushes to dry. Finishing her chore before Cole, she turned and looked at the herd. "It doesn't look like they're going to leave," she remarked.

"No, I guess not, and I can't say I blame them. They've got water and good grass."

"Why did they do that? Bunch up into smaller groups?"

Cole added a few twigs to the flames he was nursing before glancing at the herd and answering, "Each one of those groups of mares and colts belongs to a separate stallion, and ordinarily they keep a fair distance between them. After the stampede, it took awhile for the stallions to gather their herds. If any one of those mares strays away from her group, the stallion will chase her back, and if any other stallion invades what he considers his territory, he'll attack him."

"Well, if he's so possessive, why doesn't the stallion take his herd someplace else?"

"There's safety in numbers. The bigger the herd, the less danger from packs of wolves,"

Cole placed a couple of branches on his fire, then rose and looked out over the prairie. "I see our packhorse is still over by that brush. I guess I'd better go and get him if we're going to eat tonight."

"You're not afraid of stampeding the herd?"

"I'll stay next to the river and skirt around them."

"While you're gone, I think I'll look for a creosote bush."

Cole frowned, thinking it might be too dangerous for Jenny to go into the brush by herself, then remembered what she had just been through. In view of that, he didn't think she'd accept his reasoning. "All right, but be careful. Rattlesnakes like to hide beneath them. And don't wander too far away from camp. It's easy to get lost in that thicket."

That night, there was a full moon, and Jenny sat watching the grazing herd. It was easy to pick out the stallions. They spent more time with their long, sleek necks raised in watchfulness than grazing.

"Are all male animals that protective?" she asked Cole.

"No, very few are. Usually, they disappear as soon as the mating is over. It's the females that protect the young. But mustang stallions are constant, if you can overlook the fact that they keep a harem, so to speak. Once he has brought a mare into his herd, the stallion protects her as long as she lives. Of course. the mares usually outlive the stallions, since there's always a younger, stronger stallion around to challenge the older one."

Jenny continued gazing at the peaceful scene. "They're really beautiful, aren't they?"

"Yes, they are, even more so when they're running. Unfortunately, you couldn't see them from where we were, but a herd of mustangs running is something to behold. They sweep across the prairie, wild and free, their stride so graceful they seem to be flowing, or flying, with their amazing speed. And they glory in their freedom. You can see it when they run. I don't know of any other wild animal that delights in its freedom as much, or goes to such lengths to protect it. You take away a mustang's freedom, and it's just not the same animal. The wild and beautiful spirit is gone."

There was a hint of melancholy in Cole's voice that caught Jenny's attention. "Why would anyone take away their freedom?"

"For the same reason the longhorns are being rounded up. For profit. With more people moving west, the demand for horses is high, too high for the horse ranches to supply. Besides, the mustangs are up for grabs. They belong to anyone who can capture them. Since the captor is spared the expense of having to raise them, you can see why mustanging is a very lucrative business right now."

Cole gazed out at the herd for a few moments, then said, "Ten, twenty years ago, there were twice as many wild horses as there are today. At the rate things are going, the scene we're looking at may well disappear in another twenty years."

"But they're so beautiful," Jenny muttered sadly, looking back out at the horses.

The moonlight gave Jenny's hair a silvery sheen and made her skin look as if it had been powered with stardust. Not near as beautiful as you, Cole thought, as he gazed at the ethereal loveliness across the fire from him, a sight that made him ache with love. It took every bit of his steely control to keep from reaching for Jenny.

When Jenny looked back a few moments later, she saw Cole had retired on his side of the fire. She lay down on her pallet and gazed up at the stars, thinking Cole cared about things that most people wouldn't even give a thought to. Strangely, his sensitivity didn't detract from his strength. It only enhanced it, making him all the more attractive, and Jenny all the more miserable.

Twenty

When Cole and Jenny left their camp the next morning, the herd was still there, the colts frisking playfully in the dew-covered grass while their mothers grazed and their fathers stood tall and kept their ever-constant vigil. As she and Cole moved along the fringes of the brush line and past the herd, Jenny kept her eye on the mustangs, thinking she had never known there were so many different colors of horseflesh: sorrels, bays, whites, greys, golden bays, red sorrels, blacks, pintos. Some horses had manes and tails that were different colored from their bodies, others had stockings, and many had white marks on their foreheads. No two seemed alike, and all were beautiful. When they finally left the herd behind, Jenny felt a sense of loss and wondered if she would ever see another herd as large or beautiful. Remembering what Cole had told her the day before, she wondered if she would ever see another at all.

The stretch of open prairie changed around noon to a lightly wooded area. Since it was so warm,

Cole called a noonday break. After eating cold ham and tinned biscuits, Jenny stretched out on the blanket they had placed beneath a hackberry tree, while Cole wandered into the woods. He returned with a hat-full of orange-red fruit that Jenny had never seen before.

As he lowered himself to the blanket Cole said, "I thought I spied some wild persimmons when we rode up. If you try to eat these when they're not ripe, they're so sour they'll make your lips pucker, but this late in the year these ought to be ripe." He extended his hat. "Try one."

Jenny took a persimmon, bit into the golden flesh, and juice squirted everywhere. One drop hit Cole in the eye. The surprised look on his face made her laugh.

"How is it?" he asked.

"Delicious. Just a little tart, but not too much."

As they sat eating their fruit, Jenny said, "I saw some narrow, red pods an inch or two long on a bush yesterday. I've noticed them before. Are they edible?"

"Is the skin waxy looking?"

"Yes."

"They're edible, but believe me, you don't want to put them in your mouth. They're *chiltipiquins,* Mexican wild peppers, and they're hot as hell. Even the cattle won't eat them. But the turkeys love them. That's why it's a waste of time to kill a turkey in these parts at this time of the year. The meat is so hot, you can't eat it."

As Jenny helped herself to another persimmon, Cole studied her, then remarked, "You know, you've handled this trip surprisingly well, considering you're not used to this heat or riding. I would have thought you'd have been exhausted by now."

"Well, I guess my traveling around with the theater group toughened me up."

"How did you travel? By stage?"

"Sometimes, but mostly it was by train. Have you done much railroad traveling?"

"No, I can't say I have. I blew up a lot of railroads during the war, but I've never ridden on one. Railroads just recently came to Texas."

"Well, take my word for it, traveling by railroad in a third-class car is worse than traveling by stage. The seats are wooden, with no pretense of padding, and the springs are so worn they're almost nonexistent. The movement of the train jars you so bad, you ache all over, and your bottom is black and blue. And you have to watch out for sudden stops. One of the women in our troop broke her arm flying into the seat in front of her, and all because some fool cow stepped on the track. If it's summer, you have to ride with the windows down to get even a breath of fresh air. Then the hot cinders get you. Practically every dress I owned had tiny little holes it in from those damn cinders, and my hands and face would be covered with tiny little burns, which thankfully didn't leave scars. But the winters were worse. Then you froze, because there was no stove in the third-class cars."

"The worst trip I ever took was one winter when we got stranded in a snow storm. We sat there for over twenty-four hours with no heat, because the conductor wouldn't let us go into the next car that had a stove. They wouldn't even let us go to the baggage car and get our luggage, so we could put on extra wraps. One man got frostbite on his toes. It wasn't until the men in our troupe threatened to rip out the seats and set fire to them that they finally allowed us to go where there was heat, and then, guess where it was? The caboose! They didn't want their first and second-class passengers being contaminated by us," Jenny finished bitterly.

"Because you were theatrical people?"

"No, there were some immigrants back there with us. It was because we were poor. But we ran into plenty of prejudice because we didn't practice a so-called respectable profession." Jenny paused, then said, "No one could ever tell me why it wasn't respectable. We worked just as hard as anyone else, and we didn't cheat our customers, like some merchants and bankers did. We always gave them what our posters advertised. I finally decided it must be because we moved around so much. The public thought of us as vagrants. That, and what we offered the public made us unacceptable. Entertainment was something frivolous and unnecessary, certainly nothing one would take seriously as a means of making a living. Or at least, that's what a lot of people seemed to think."

"How long did you stay in one spot?"

"In some places, just one night. Oh, God, how I hated those one-night stands!" Jenny said with fervor. "It seemed like I barely stepped off one train before I was back on another, the milk train, so called because it stopped at every town, every little hamlet, every bend in the tracks throughout the night to deliver milk. Sleeping on the ground is a luxury compared to trying to sleep on one of those hard seats being jostled around, stopping and starting, stopping and starting. We all looked forward to longer engagements where we could sleep in a hotel. It didn't matter how bad the beds were, it was an improvement."

"Why didn't you spend the night in a hotel, instead of getting back on a train on those one night stands? Were your engagements that far apart?"

"No, that happened when I was with the first theatrical group. The manager was a skinflint, the biggest cheapskate that ever walked the earth. The train cost less than a hotel room, and then he didn't have to put out the expense for transportation the next day. The extra money went into his pocket. That was one of the main reasons I left that group and joined up with Carla and John. The last straw was when he booked a cattle car for us to travel in one day. That was the second most miserable ride I ever had. It was in the middle of the summer, and that boxcar was like an oven, to say nothing of the terrible stench. Those horses yesterday smelled like roses compared to it."

Jenny paused, then said a little sheepishly,

"Sorry, I didn't mean to complain. I was just trying to explain how I got to be such a good trooper, as we like to call each other in the theater. I'm used to hardships when traveling. Why, if I'd kept at it a few more years, I'd probably have callouses on my rump from those hard seats."

Cole thought it would be a shame to have anything mar Jenny's delightful little bottom. "Well, I'm glad you got away from it," he commented, renewing his vow to see Jenny had a much easier life.

There was silence while the two concentrated on eating their persimmons. Then Jenny renewed the conversation by saying, "You said you blew up railroads in the war. Does that mean you didn't do much fighting?"

Cole smiled wryly, answering, "Hardly. I served in Terry's Texas Rangers. We were a cavalry regiment, and I guess that's why we were sent on so many raids, because we could move around faster and easier, plus the fact that we were all good woodsmen and not likely to get lost. But those railroads were prime military targets and well guarded. We did plenty of fighting destroying them, as well as in regular battles. General Bragg particularly liked to use us for his cavalry charges. We had a wild, piercing yell that we borrowed from the Comanches. It scared the hell out of the enemy. That's why the Indians developed it. To strike terror in the heart of their enemies. Sometimes that's all we had to do, yell and charge, and they'd drop

291

their weapons and flee in confusion. But even when they didn't run, it wasn't much of a contest. We had six-shooters, and they had one-shot muskets and pistols. Once their bullets were gone, they relied on their bayonets, and if they were cavalry, all they ever had was sabers. You can't fight a six-shooter with those puny weapons. We never failed to break the enemy line, whether cavalry or infantry, the entire war."

"Did all the South have six-shooters?" Jenny asked, wondering if that was so, why hadn't they won the war?

"No, they fought with the same weapons the North did, but most of the Texas units carried them. The six-shooter had become a part of our lives, since most of Texas was still frontier, and for the better part, we fought with our own guns. Maybe that's why we came out of the war with fewer casualties than the rest of the South, because we had better weapons. It sure wasn't because we weren't in the thick of the fighting." And it was his experiences in the war that had prepared him for his life as a fugitive, Cole thought, subsisting on parched corn, living without tents, crossing and re-crossing rivers time and time again to raid Yankee supply lines, constantly on the move like a hunted animal.

"Were you drafted?"

"No, I volunteered."

"Because you were afraid you were going to be drafted?" Jenny asked, knowing a lot of men had joined for that reason, hoping to get shorter enlistments.

Cole didn't tell Jenny that he had been exempt from draft, because he and his uncle had been raising the most valuable crop the South had—cotton. It was through cotton sales that the South financed the war. "No, I joined of my own accord. I was sixteen and full of vinegar. I was scared to death it was going to end before I could get into it, and miss out on the glory and excitement. I found out what every other soldier since the beginning of time has learned, that war is hell. It's a lot of confusion, a lot of disillusionment, a lot of misery, a lot of death and dying, and no damn fun. I've wondered if war is ever worth it, even if you win."

Cole's words brought him up short. He wondered why he had said that to Jenny. His true feelings about the war were something he had never admitted to anyone, had hardly even acknowledged to himself, except recently. They had always seemed so disloyal, to Texas, to the unit he had fought with, to his brother who had given his life for the Cause. Disloyal, and somehow unmanly.

But if Cole feared Jenny would look down on him for his admission, he was very much in error. She was a woman to the core and had no use for the senseless violence called war. That was a man's folly, a man's stupid preoccupation that robbed women of their men and children of their fathers. No, all Cole's admission did was make Jenny admire him for his honesty. Men didn't often admit to mistakes, particularly mistakes as glaring as war.

"Well," Cole said, hoping to gloss over what he'd revealed to Jenny, "we'd better get back in the saddle if we're going to cover any distance today."

They made camp early that evening in a lightly wooded area beside a small creek so that Jenny could do some laundry. When she returned from that chore, she discovered Cole chopping underbrush and piling it in front the corral.

Seeing the puzzled look on Jenny's face, Cole explained, "I'm trying to make a quick windbreak for the horses before that norther out there hits."

Jenny turned and looked to the north, seeing a line of dark clouds moving towards them. "How do you know it's not just another thunderstorm?"

"Because of the bluish cast to those clouds. That usually signifies cold air. Also there's no lightning. Besides, ordinary thunderstorms don't come from the north in this part of the country."

Cole quickly built a lean-to with its back facing northward, then spread the tarp over it, and lashed it down, while Jenny piled the rest of the brush he had cut at each end of the structure. Before they had even finished, the wind was thrashing the bushes and blowing sand everywhere. The gritty particles stung their exposed skin and half-blinded them. They carried their saddles and supplies into the lean-to, then huddled at the back, and ate a cold supper, since it would be impossible to maintain a fire in that high wind.

Jenny had never seen anything like it. The norther came howling down on them with a speed and fury that seemed unbelievable. The wind didn't come in gusts, but in a steady blow that made the tarp crack and pop and rattled the limbs on the trees all around them. Darkness fell, and within an hour the temperature had dropped drastically. Jenny was freezing, despite the two blankets she had wrapped around her. She lay huddled in a little ball, then jumped when she heard something hitting the lean-to that sounded as if rocks were being thrown against it.

"It's hailing," Cole remarked, laying in his bedroll a few feet away.

"Is it going to snow?"

"In this part of the country?" he asked incredulously. "Not likely."

"Well, the temperature must be freezing," Jenny counted.

"No, I don't think it's really that cold. It's the strong wind that's making it seem that way."

After a few moments, the hail stopped, but the wind howled ever louder, steady and shrill. The cold cut through the tarp and brush as if they had no protection. Jenny's teeth began to chatter.

"Come over here with me, so we can share our blankets and body heat," Cole said.

Jenny remembered how Cole had stormed her defenses that night at the hotel and quickly reduced her a mindless, spineless creature with no will of her own. "Absolutely not!"

"Dammit, Jenny, I'm not trying to lure you into my bed to seduce you. You're cold, and I can warm you. Now, come here!"

Cole reached out and pulled Jenny into his bedroll, then quickly tossed her blankets over his. She tried to struggle, despite her shivering, but Cole held her fast, muttering something under his breath about animals having better sense. Finally, she stilled, but not because of Cole's tight embrace. His heat was surrounding her, seeping into her chilled flesh, a blessed relief from the misery she had been dealing with.

"Roll over, so you're facing me," Cole instructed.

"Why?" Jenny asked suspiciously.

"Damn, you're stubborn as hell when you get some fool notion in your head," Cole retorted. Holding her firmly, he said, "Press your face into the crook of my neck and put your hands under my arms. You'll warm up quicker."

Jenny was reluctant, but her nose felt like an icicle and her hands felt numb. She did as Cole told her, relishing his heat as drowsiness crept over her. Then an awareness of something brought her suddenly alert. She jerked back, pounded Cole's chest with one fist, and sat up. "You sneaky bastard! You *did* trick me!"

"No, Jenny."

"Don't lie to me! Just how stupid do you think I am? I could feel it!"

Cole knew what *it* was. His swollen, straining

296

manhood. "Jenny, just because I have an erection doesn't mean anything is going to happen. It may come as a surprise to you, but I have very little control over how that part of me behaves. It has a will of its own, which can sometimes be very embarrassing. However, I can control how I behave. I gave you my word, and I intend to keep it. Now lay down. You're letting the cold in."

Jenny was feeling chilled again without Cole's heat. Reluctantly she reclined, but not in the same position. Deliberately, she placed her back to Cole. Cole shook his head. Jenny had to be the most obstinate woman he had ever met. He folded his arms around her and pulled her against him. Immediately Jenny felt warmer, but she could also feel the long, hard length of him where his eager flesh was imprisoned against one of his legs. It pressed against the back of her thighs. She tensed her full concentration on that threat.

"For God's sake, Jenny, relax!" Cole said in exasperation. "It's not going to jump off me and bite you. Just ignore it and go to sleep. That's what I'm going to do."

Fifteen minutes later, Jenny knew by Cole's deep, steady respirations that he had fallen asleep. To her amazement, there was no change in his manhood, and for the life of her she couldn't ignore it. She could feel it pulsating even through their clothing, its heat seemingly searing her, so tantalizingly close to that secret part of her that had begun to throb and burn, too, that it was an agony. She remem-

297

bered the last time Cole had made love to her, the memories so vivid that she could almost feel him inside her, his magnificent shaft moving with a will of its own, even though he, himself, was still. The recollection only served to heighten the pitch of her craving. Her arousal became so acute that it was painful, but there was no relief to be had. That it was a torment she had brought on herself made it even worse. She was the one who had dictated they would no longer be lovers.

Eventually Jenny fell asleep, hating herself. The wind outside the lean-to offered her no comfort. It shrieked like a demented woman.

The next day, Cole circled back, heading directly for Amos's ranch. He'd decided that drawing their trip out so that he would have more time alone with Jenny had been a mistake. Not only was he endangering her by dallying in the *brasada,* but he couldn't go through another night like the one before. It had taken all of his control to keep from breaking his promise to her. Although the wind had died down considerably and the temperature was rising, he knew as soon as the sun set, it would plummet again, and he and Jenny would have to share a bed to ward off the cold. That was a hell he couldn't endure again, and he was determined to keep his word. Jenny's trust was as important to him as her love. He wouldn't let his physical need get in the way of gaining what he

298

wanted. One would give him only momentary satisfaction. The other was a prize to last him a lifetime.

While Cole considered the temperature to be warming, Jenny didn't. The wind still chilled her to the bone, despite the sun beating down on them from a cloudless sky. She rode with a blanket wrapped around her, wishing she had brought her *serape* along with her as well as her Mexican blouse and skirt. She glanced across at Cole, riding next to her in just his shirtsleeves and vest and looking totally comfortable. Didn't anything get him down? She felt a little annoyed at his stamina. Not the heat, not the cold. She was the one who should be going without a wrap of any kind, not him. She was the northerner.

When they came to a river, Jenny looked around her and asked, "Is this the same river we crossed the other day?"

Cole hadn't expected her to be so observant. He shrugged his shoulders and answered evasively, "It could be. The rivers out here do a lot of twisting and turning."

"We're not going to cross it, are we? As cold as it is? Why, I'll catch my death."

"It's not deep here. I doubt if it will come to our horses' bellies. They won't even have to swim it."

Jenny looked at the river doubtfully. The still-brisk wind was whipping up small waves, and it looked much deeper than Cole predicted. "There's not a ferry anywhere?"

"Not out here." Cole moved his horse towards the bank, saying, "I'll cross and prove to you how shallow it is."

Cole urged his horse into the water, followed by the packhorse. As they splashed across the river, the water rose steadily to a few inches above their hocks, then receded. Cole turned his mount when it reached the opposite bank and said, "See? Come on across."

Jenny urged Princess into the water and crossed, enduring the cold water drops the horse splashed on her. As the mare trotted up the bank, Jenny muttered, "I'm sorry, girl."

"What?" Cole asked, thinking she had said something to him.

"I was apologizing to Princess for making her go into that cold water."

"Apologizing to her?" Cole asked in disbelief. He shook his head, laughing. "Honestly, Jenny, you and that damn horse."

"Don't call her a damn horse!" Jenny replied hotly.

Cole sobered instantly beneath Jenny's anger. "I didn't mean it as an insult. It's just that sometimes you carry your fondness for her to extremes. You treat her like she's human."

"To me, she almost is. She's a better friend than most people I've known, and my only pet."

"You've *never* had a pet?" Cole asked in disbelief, for Texans and most Southerners had a weakness for pets. There was hardly a household that didn't have a dog, or a cat, or some wild animal that had been tamed for that purpose.

"No," Jenny answered, raising her chin defiantly in expectation of more ridicule.

"In that case, I'm sorry I said what I did. I had an ugly-looking hound when I was a boy that I thought was human. He went everywhere with me, even slept with me. He was my best friend. Damn near killed me when he died."

Jenny didn't even want to think about Princess dying. "How long do horses live?"

Cole smiled, knowing what Jenny was thinking. "Twenty, maybe thirty years if they're taken care of."

Cole turned his horse from the river, and Jenny fell in beside him. As they rode, Cole thought, Yes, Jenny had a soft spot deep down inside her, and if that horse could bring it forth, so could he. He was a hell of a lot smarter, and he hoped, just as worthy. Besides, he had something working for him that Princess didn't—the age-old appeal of the opposite sex.

An hour or so later, they came across a fair-sized herd of longhorns and skirted the group, rather than riding through them. Jenny was amazed at the cattles' horns. More than just a few stretched a good six feet from tip to tip and looked as if they weighed the animals' heads down. "There's not much meat on them," she observed.

"No, and they'll look even scrawnier by the time they've been driven to the railhead," Cole responded. "I understand the buyer at that end fattens them up before they slaughter them."

Jenny looked at one animal whose horns were twisted and looked particularly vicious. "Are they dangerous?"

"No, usually they're pretty placid, unless they've been stampeded by something. Then they're dangerous as hell."

"What about the bulls?" Jenny asked, wondering if that was why the bovine looked so threatening, and remembering her last encounter with the irascible male of that species.

"There aren't any bulls in that herd. Just cows and steers. Other than mating season, the bulls stay apart from the rest of the herd."

Jenny wondered what a steer was. She had asked so many questions that Cole must think her awfully stupid. But her curiosity got the better of her. "What's a steer?"

Cole grinned. "I was waiting for you to ask."

There it was again. That appealing smile that made her heart do crazy little flip-flops. "Oh? Then why didn't you just tell me, and save me the trouble?" Jenny asked irritably.

"Because I enjoy your questions. They bolster my ego."

Jenny thought that Cole was one man who didn't need his ego bolstered. She had never known a man so self-confident, so self-possessed. And right then, he looked downright cocky. "Well, are you going to tell me or not?" she snapped.

"A steer is a bull that's been castrated."

Jenny frowned, then asked, "You mean, like an eunuch?"

A surprised look came over Cole's face. Then he laughed and said, "Yes, but I didn't think you'd know about them."

"Well, I guess it's not a subject ordinarily discussed in polite company," Jenny admitted, "but sometimes we traveled with circuses — they couldn't afford anything better than third class seats either — and there was this very strange looking man, extremely fat, with a high, shrill voice with one circus. I asked Carla about him, since she was well educated and seemed to know everything. She said he played the role of an eunuch in the circus's belly dancing show. Then she explained what an eunuch was, and why it was done to a man. Of course, she didn't know if he really was one or not. But why do they do that to animals?"

"If you had that many bulls around, you'd have an awful lot of fighting going on, and not just at mating season. Bulls are just normally ornery. You saw that for yourself. Castrating them makes them more docile and easy to handle. They do the same to horses. They're called geldings."

Jenny was glad for the information Cole had given her. Those were things she needed to know if she was going to be a rancher's wife. Then she spied a structure in the distance. It seemed to pop up out of nowhere. "Look at those high walls over there," she remarked to Cole. "Is that a fort?"

"No, it's a ranch house, built very similarly to Cortinas' home, with high, protective walls around it. Many years ago, it belonged to a wealthy a *hidalgo,* as the upper-class Mexicans are known."

"Does anyone live there now?"

"Yes," Cole answered grimly. He turned in his saddle so he could face her. "That's your destination, Jenny. We've been on Amos's ranch for the better part of an hour, and that's his home."

Twenty-one

When Cole announced their arrival at Amos's ranch, Jenny was both surprised and strangely disappointed. It was the latter emotion that showed on her face, prompting Cole to ask somewhat smugly, "What's the matter, Jenny? I thought you were looking forward to being reunited with your betrothed."

"I was. I mean, I am," Jenny sputtered in confusion, still trying to sort through her ambiguous feelings. "But I thought you said it would take a week to get here."

"We made better time than I expected," Cole answered smoothly. He urged his horse to a trot.

Fifteen minutes later, Jenny and Cole rode through the open gate between the high walls of the compound and into its spacious courtyard. The sprawling adobe home with its many grilled windows and roofed walk-ways was covered with bougainvillea blooming in a riot of reds and purples. As they walked to the door, Jenny looked about her appreciatively, while Cole eyed the guard on top of one of the walls in puzzlement.

Cole knocked loudly on the massive, ornately-carved door. A moment later, it was opened by a chubby, middle-aged Mexican woman who Jenny assumed must be Amos's housekeeper. *"Buenas tardes,"* the woman said.

"Buenas tardes," Cole answered, then asked, in Spanish, to see Amos.

The housekeeper led them to a parlor and asked them to wait. Jenny looked around and saw the room was furnished with bulky leather chairs and couches. The only decoration on the walls was a set of longhorns and the only things gracing the massive claw-footed tables were plain kerosene lamps. It was an austere, masculine room in desperate need of a woman's touch. There wasn't a pretty thing in sight.

A moment later, Jenny heard the heavy tread of Amos's step coming down the hall. When he walked into the room, he barely glanced at her before he saw Cole, scowled, and asked, "What in the hell are you doing here, Benteen?"

"I decided to take you up on your offer. I've rescued and delivered your fiancee."

Jenny realized Amos hadn't recognized her in her disguise and swept off her hat, saying, "Hello, Amos."

Amos stared at Jenny in disbelief. "Jenny?"

"Yes, it's me," Jenny answered in a voice Cole thought sickeningly sweet.

"Oh, my God!" Amos stepped to Jenny and

hugged her tightly. "I can't believe it. You're here, safe and sound, my own little darling."

Jenny endured the bear-hug Amos gave her better than Cole did watching it. Seeing the angry frown on his face over Amos's shoulder, Jenny made a face at him, warning him to behave himself, then said, "Oh, I'm so relieved to be here, Amos. I was so afraid." Her voice caught with a little sob. "I thought I'd never see you alive again."

"My poor little dear," Amos crooned. "It must have been terrible for you. Terrible." He stroked her braid with one beefy hand. "My sweet, little darling, my angel. You're safe now. I won't let anything harm you."

The scene made Cole roll his eyes in disgust, not only at Jenny's acting, but Amos's making an ass out of himself in front of him. There was a time and place for endearments, and it wasn't in front of someone who was practically a stranger.

Amos stepped back and gazed at Jenny's face adoringly; then his eyes swept down Jenny's length. He scowled at her clothing.

"I know I look appalling, but . . ." Jenny hesitated just a heartbeat, shot Cole a hard, warning look, then continued, "Mr. Benteen thought it would be much safer for me to travel through that dangerous country if I was disguised as a boy."

Amos tried to cover his disapproval by quickly saying, "Of course, Benteen was right, my dear. Your safety came before everything, even propriety. I'm glad he thought of it."

Amos turned to face Cole. "I thought you turned me down?"

Cole knew why Jenny had called him mister. She didn't want Amos thinking they had been on too-personal terms now that she had slipped into her sweet, ladylike role, but he didn't like the new formality. He forced his mind to the question Amos had asked and answered, "I got to thinking about it and changed my mind. I assume you'll honor your end of the deal."

Amos drew up in affront and answered huffily, "I certainly will! I'm a man of my word."

"Then you didn't find anyone else for the job?" Cole asked, not able to resist baiting the hated rancher.

"No, no, I didn't," Amos admitted. "You said yourself you thought it would be suicide. Was it as difficult as you thought?"

"Well, the escape from Cortinas's stronghold went pretty smooth," Cole answered with a wry glance in Jenny's direction, "but Jenny and I had to travel through Apache territory to shake the party he set on our trail. It was nip and tuck there for awhile, when the Apaches were chasing us."

From the shocking report Cole gave him, Amos zeroed in on one thing, just as Cole had thought he would. "Jenny?" he asked in a hard voice. "You call my fiancee Jenny?"

There was a challenge in Amos's tone of voice, and Cole was more than ready to do battle in any shape, form, or manner. He looked the rancher directly in the eye and answered, "That's her name, isn't it?"

Amos was still a little afraid of Cole, and the gunfighter had a mean look on his face just then. Amos turned to Jenny, asking in an accusing tone of voice, "Did you allow this gunfighter to call you by your first name?"

Jenny could have throttled Cole. She knew he had deliberately riled Amos. She blinked back imaginary tears and said in a meek little voice, "Oh, please don't be angry, Amos. Under the circumstances, I didn't think—"

Cole couldn't stand to see Jenny cowering to Amos, even if it was nothing but an act. He cut across her words, saying, "Goddammit, Wright, stop acting so stupid! There's a time and a place for everything. It would have been ridiculous for us to travel together for almost two weeks and call each other mister and miss. That kind of formality belongs in a drawing room, not out in a desert where you're running for your life."

Again Amos zeroed in on one thing. "Have you forgotten there's a lady present?" he asked indignantly. "Watch your language!"

Cole flicked a glance at Jenny, rolled his eyes in exasperation, then muttered, "Excuse me." He turned to Amos, saying, "If you're going to take this out on anyone, Amos, take it out on me. I didn't give her any choice in the matter."

The carpetbagger's eyes narrowed suspiciously. "And was there anything else you didn't give her any choice in?" He whirled to face Jenny, asking, "Did this man overstep his boundaries in any other way?"

Jenny knew exactly what boundaries Amos was talking about. "Oh, no! He was a perfect gentleman."

The two men glared at one another over Jenny's head, and she knew the only way to diffuse the potentially explosive situation was to distract them, or at least one of them. She threw herself into Amos's arms, broke into the best stage tears she had ever produced, and pleaded pitifully, "Oh, please don't be angry anymore, Amos. I can't stand any more tension. This has all been so difficult, so trying for me. I'm a nervous wreck."

Awkwardly, Amos stroked Jenny's back, saying, "I'm sorry, darling. I was just trying to protect you. Please, don't cry. I can't stand to see a woman cry."

"I'll stop . . . if you'll stop arguing . . . with Mister Benteen," Jenny said between imaginary sobs. "He was . . . very kind to me. Why, if he hadn't rescued me . . . there's no telling what would have happened to me at the hands of that . . ." Jenny caught herself just in time. She had almost said bastard. ". . . that terrible old man."

Amos stiffened. "Did Cortinas do anything to you?"

Jenny dropped her eyes, as if to hide her shame, saying, "He forced a kiss on me. Oh, Amos, it was terrible! It made me feel so soiled. And he kept insinuating that he could force me to marry him, too. I could tell he was getting more and more impatient. I was so desperate I was even considering trying to escape by myself, even if it would have been the death of me. I'd rather have died than submit to . . . *that*," Jenny ended with an appropriate shudder.

"Damn, I wish I could get my hands on that bastard!" Amos exclaimed angrily, then realizing what he had said, muttered, "I'm sorry, Jenny. I shouldn't have used that language in front of you."

"That's all right, Amos. My father used to let a bad word slip every now and then when he was upset, too. My mother said that men just can't help themselves sometimes, so I don't take as much offense as a lot of ladies would," Jenny answered, thinking how apologizing for every slip of the tongue was going to get tedious for both of them.

"That reminds me," Amos said, stepping back from Jenny. "I telegraphed your parents with the bad news when you were abducted, but I never got an answer from them. I even sent a second telegram."

Jenny knew why Amos had never gotten an answer. The address she had given him had been fictitious. "Oh, my father had to leave the country suddenly, that's why," Jenny quickly fabricated. "He's probably still in Europe. And my mother went to stay with my aunt while he was gone, since her health is so poor. You see, my great-uncle was very ill, and my father was his only heir. Even though he hated to leave his business, he felt it was the least he could do, in view of the inheritance he would receive. Poor great-uncle Archibald," Jenny sighed, then wiped away another imaginary tear. "He must have died. I guess that's why my father has been delayed so long."

"I'm so sorry to hear that," Amos muttered, swallowing Jenny's story hook, line and sinker, while Cole shook his head at Amos's gullibility and wondered if Jenny couldn't have come up with a better name for her relative than Archibald. For Christ's sake! *Archibald?*

Amos led Jenny to one of the chairs, saying, "My goodness, my dear, you have certainly been through a lot. Kidnapped, rescued, now the loss of a relative." He sat her in the chair, although Jenny would have preferred to stand after her long ride. "As soon as we reach Rio Grande City we'll go to Ringgold Barracks and telegraph your mother at your aunt's residence. She must be worried sick."

"Why are we going to Rio Grande City?" she asked in surprise.

"Why, to catch the steamer to Brownsville, where the preacher is, where we're going to get married."

"We're not going to get married here at the ranch?"

"Oh, no, my dear. This is much too far for the preacher and our guests to travel, and in view of recent developments, entirely too dangerous for everyone." Amos turned to Cole, saying, "The Mescaleros are on the warpath."

"When did that happen?" Cole asked in surprise.

"About a month ago. They've been terrorizing this entire area, along with West Texas."

"Then that's why you have a guard on the wall in broad daylight?" Cole asked, the puzzle having been solved.

"Yes. Several ranches have been raided and set to the torch, and a few had their ranch hands attacked out in the open and their herds run off. In one instance, every man was murdered and scalped. Of course, all of my *vaqueros* carry guns, but they're cowboys, not gunfighters, and their aim is pretty poor. I've been sending armed guards out with them on the range, so they can concentrate on their work without fear of being caught by surprise."

Cole had brought Jenny to Amos's ranch because he feared the brush was too risky a place for her. He hadn't realized just how dangerous it *had* become. Of all the Apaches, the Mescaleros were the most fierce, the most cunning, the most daring, particularly since they were waging a desperate, last-ditch fight for survival in Texas now that the Comanches had finally been subdued and placed on reservations. But it so happened that the Indian activity might well aid him in his plans, Cole mused. He had thought to bury his pride and ask Amos for a job in order to have an excuse to stay close to Jenny. Now maybe he could manipulate the hated rancher into asking him.

313

"Well, that's a real shame, having your wedding delayed particularly after you and Jenny have had to wait so long already," Cole commented.

"What do you mean, delay my wedding?" Amos asked.

"Well, you'll have to wait until the Mescaleros have gone off the warpath and things are fairly safe again, won't you? Unless, of course, you've hired more gunfighters since I saw you, and you have enough to guard your interests here, as well as take with you on your trip to Brownsville."

Amos frowned. "Well, no, as a matter of fact, I have even fewer gunfighters. Several quit on me when the Mescaleros started cutting up. They were afraid to fight Indians—the cowardly bastards!" Amos finished in remembered anger. Then catching his error, he glanced quickly in Jenny's direction and saw her already smiling sweetly at him in forgiveness.

"I guess they weren't Texans, huh? Used to fighting Indians and all?" Cole asked.

"Why, no they weren't." Amos peered at Cole as if he'd just seen him.

"That's a shame," Cole remarked, "a dirty shame." Then pretending to just notice Amos's penetrating look, Cole asked, "Is there some reason why you're staring at me so hard?"

"Yes, there is. I was wondering if you're for hire as a gunfighter?"

Cole scowled and said, "No, I—"

"I'll make it well worth your while," Amos interjected quickly. "I'll pay you twice as much as my other gunfighters."

Cole laughed harshly, saying, "That still won't cut it. You'd have to pay me fifty dollars a day to make it worth my while."

Cole's price was much too steep, but Amos figured he could fire him as soon as they got back from Brownsville, and that was what he wanted him for, to protect them on their trip. Naturally, he'd take his best gunfighters along with him. "You drive a hard bargain, Benteen, but I really don't have any choice. I'll pay. Just don't tell the others what we agreed on."

"That goes without saying. I'm not stupid," Cole responded, then added, "But there's a little unfinished business between us. I haven't been paid for this job yet."

"I'll pay you just as soon as I've seen to Jenny's comfort," Amos answered sharply. The Texan's demanding attitude irritated him to the core. He turned to Jenny. "I know you must be exhausted after all you've gone through, my dear. I'll get Rosa, my housekeeper. She speaks a little English. She can show you to your room and get you anything you may need, until we can find you a maid."

Jenny wasn't the least bit weary but she knew she had a role to play. If Amos thought she should be tired, then she'd pretend to be. "Thank you, Amos. You're so considerate."

Amos had left the room to get Rosa, beaming

from Jenny's praise. Cole sauntered over to Jenny's side, bent over, and whispered, "My compliments, spitfire. Your acting was superb, a bit nauseating, but superb. You had him eating out of your hand."

"Well, you didn't do so badly yourself!" Jenny retorted. "Making him think it was his idea to hire you." She peeked around him to be sure Amos and his maid were not walking down the hall, then asked, "What are you up to, Cole? Why are you sticking around? I know you can't stand Amos."

"I'm not sticking around for Amos. I'm sticking around for you. I would have thought you would have realized that."

Jenny felt a little tingle of pleasure and hated herself for it. "I told you, it's over between us! I'm going to marry Amos."

Cole stepped in front of Jenny, placed his hands on the arms of the chair she sat in, and leaned over so that his face was just inches from hers. "That may be what you think, Jenny, but as far as I'm concerned, I'm still very much in the running."

His nearness had its usual effect on Jenny. Her heart raced and her breath quickened. "Then you're a fool! You're wasting your time."

Cole saw the racing heartbeat pounding at the base of Jenny's throat and knew his power over her. "No, Jenny, I don't think so. And deep down, neither do you. You don't want me to walk out of your life, not now . . ." That same infuriating grin spread over his face. ". . . not ever."

316

Jenny opened her mouth to fling back a retort, then heard Amos and his maid in the hallway. Cole heard them at the same time, rose, and stepped back from her just as Amos walked into the room.

"Jenny, this is Rosa," Amos said, then turned to his housekeeper and said, "Rosa, this is Miss Daniels, my future wife."

"*Senorita,* welcome," the Mexican woman said, her dark eyes shining with genuine warmth.

"Thank you, Rosa," Jenny answered, rising from the chair. "Do you think we could arrange a bath, before my nap?"

"*Sí, sí, senorita,*" Rosa answered. "Come with me."

"I'll see you this evening at dinner," Amos said as Jenny passed him. He dropped a kiss on her cheek. "I hope you have a good rest."

"Thank you," Jenny muttered.

As Jenny turned at the door into the hallway, she caught a glimpse of Cole standing beside Amos from the corner of her eye. Cole stood tall and straight, broad-shouldered, lean-hipped and flat-bellied, his presence radiating so much strength and raw masculinity that he completely overshadowed the pot-bellied, barrel-chested, shorter man next to him. It was almost as if Amos didn't exist, as if Cole had shoved him out of the room by his sheer power of being. The comparison made Jenny heartsick. And fast on the heels of that admission came another truth. She *was* glad Cole wasn't leaving.

Damn him! He was right again, Jenny thought,

317

feeling defeated and terribly frustrated. God, how it galled her when that smug bastard was right!

Two weeks later, Jenny was in the stables spending some time with Princess when Cole suddenly appeared beside her. A spontaneous burst of joy ran through her at the sight of him, irritating her no end and making her snap waspishly, "What are you doing here?"

Cole had trained himself to watch for the quicksilver expressions on Jenny's face that revealed her true feelings. He bit back a laugh and said, "That's a hell of a way to greet an old friend. Did you get up on the wrong side of the bed today?"

"What side of the bed I got up on is none of your business! Now, answer my question. What are you doing here? You're supposed to be out on the range, guarding Amos's *vaqueros*."

"We guard his stables, too, and today is my day for that job," Cole answered, but actually, Cole had paid the gunfighter assigned to stable duty to switch places with him that day in hopes of seeing Jenny.

"I've never seen a guard when I've been here before."

"We usually sit up on the roof."

"Then why aren't you up there?"

"Because I came down to say hello to you."

"Well, you'd better get back to work before Amos catches you shirking your duties."

318

Cole ignored Jenny's warning. His golden eyes swept her length, then made the return trip, stopping at her breasts. "That's a pretty outfit. Where did you get it?"

His gaze made Jenny very nervous. She pulled at the low neckline of the *camisa* then answered, "Rosa found it for me, along with several others. As soon as we get to Brownsville, Amos is taking me to a dressmaker there. She's going to make me an entire new wardrobe, including my wedding dress."

Cole's eyes took on a hard glint. "Then you haven't changed your mind about marrying Amos?"

"No. Why would I?"

"I thought when you got to know him a little better, you might find out what an ass he is."

"That remark was uncalled for," Jenny retorted. "You don't even know Amos." Deliberately, she turned her back to Cole and started petting Princess.

"I know him well enough to know he's not the man for you. You deserve better, Jenny."

Jenny whirled around, asking spitefully, "Oh, like who? You? A gunfighter? An outlaw?"

"Yes, me!" Cole answered angrily, feeling the sting of her insults. "I won't stifle you, Jenny. I won't set you up on a pedestal and say, 'stay there'. I'll give you room to be yourself, and love you for what you are, not for what other people think you should be. You're too damn good for him, Jenny.

You! Not that weak simpering woman he wants you to be. And do you know why he wants that kind of a woman? Because he's not man enough to handle a real woman, a woman like you."

"I don't want a man that can handle me. I want a man that can support me. Don't you understand that?"

"There's more to marriage than being given the physical comforts, Jenny. There's sharing—"

"I won't listen to any more of this nonsense!" Jenny exclaimed, cutting off Cole's words.

As Jenny started to rush from the stable, Cole caught her and whirled her around. He pinned her against the wall. "All right, Jenny, if you won't listen to reason, maybe you'll listen to this."

As he bent his head and his lips touched hers, Jenny jerked her head away. "You promised you wouldn't touch me again!" she said.

"I didn't promise anything, Jenny. I said, if that's what you wanted. But that's not what you want. You know it, and I know it." His mouth came down on hers, not in savage demand, but with fierce determination, coaxing, wooing, diffusing her anger with promises of sensual delight, until her lips parted. His silken tongue entered her mouth, drinking greedily of her nectar, caressing her with an ardor that left her weak. Jenny felt the familiar warmth steal over her and a tingle in her fingertips. She embraced him, clinging for dear life as her senses spun, making little mewing noises in her throat.

Still holding her a prisoner in his embrace, Cole dropped hot kisses on her face, her throat, the tops of her breasts, then returned to feast at her lips. Over and over he kissed her, long, sweet, agonizing kisses, then hot and demanding kisses, then sweet again, until Jenny was trembling and straining against him, the place between her legs burning fiercely for want of him. When his hand cupped one breast, Jenny moaned and a wetness slipped from her. It was then that she realized just how fully she had capitulated, how shameless she was in his arms.

She struggled feebly, and to her surprise, Cole released her. He stepped back. His golden eyes glittered with the heat of his desire, his breath came in ragged gasps. "Go, Jenny," he said thickly, "while I can still let you go. But remember what I said."

Suddenly, Jenny felt humiliated at how her body had betrayed her. She couldn't get away from Cole fast enough. She ran from the stables and across the cobbled courtyard as if all the demons in hell were after her.

"There's no need to run!" Cole called, seeing how wildly she was behaving. "I'm not coming after you!"

Deep down, Jenny wanted just that, not only for Cole to finish what he started, but to make her go with him, to take her by storm and just carry her off, forever. Sudden tears welled in her eyes, and her vision blurred. She tripped on a loose stone and fell, crying out as she felt her ankle turn.

321

Within seconds, Cole was there, squatting beside her, a concerned look on his face. "Go away!" Jenny cried out, pushing at his shoulders before she sat up and reached for her throbbing ankle.

"I'm sorry, Jenny. I didn't mean for this to happen. Let me help you." It was more the pleading sound of his voice than his request that made Jenny withdraw her objections. He examined the ankle, his touch surprisingly gentle.

"Is it broken?" Jenny asked.

"No, I think it's just twisted, but it's swelling pretty fast," Cole answered. He whipped off his neck scarf and wrapped it firmly around her ankle.

"I'm afraid you're not going to be able to walk for a few days," Cole said. Before she guessed his intent, he picked her up in his arms and stood.

"Put me down!" Jenny demanded.

"Didn't you hear what I just said? You can't walk on that ankle. If you try it, you'll just make it worse."

As Cole carried her across the courtyard towards the ranch house, Jenny wiggled furiously, repeating, "I said put me down!"

"Stop making such a scene," Cole hissed. "There are people watching. If you raise too much of a ruckus, they're going to get suspicious."

Jenny looked around her. People were coming from every direction, and one of them was Amos. Her heart sank.

Amos hurried up to them, asking in a hard tone of voice, "What's the meaning of this?"

322

"She twisted her ankle on a rock crossing the courtyard from the stables," Cole explained, not breaking his stride by one step.

Amos glanced down and saw the scarf Cole had wrapped around Jenny's ankle. "Are you sure it's not broken?"

"Reasonably sure."

Amos had to hurry to keep up with Cole's swift stride. "What in the world were you doing at the stables?" Amos asked Jenny. "I thought I told you I didn't want you riding with all the Indians about."

"I was just visiting my horse."

"Visiting your horse?" Amos asked in disbelief, then commented curtly, "I've never heard of anything so ridiculous."

"It's not ridiculous," Cole answered, coming to Jenny's defense. "She's become quite fond of that animal."

"Maybe not ridiculous for a child," Amos retorted, "but Jenny's a grown woman."

Cole saw Jenny flinch at Amos's thoughtless remark. He clenched his teeth and said, "That animal saved her life on several occasions. I think that changes things considerably."

There was a hard, warning tone to Cole's words that caught Amos's attention. It suddenly occurred to him that Cole might be attracted to Jenny, and that it was he, and not his employee, that should be carrying her. She was *his* fiancée.

Amos stepped directly in Cole's path and said,

"I'll carry her from here. You need to get back to your duties."

Cole was reluctant to surrender Jenny to the rancher, and Jenny knew it. Again she had to intervene in what could have become a nasty scene. She said to Cole, "Amos is right. I'm keeping you from your duties. Thank you."

Cole glared at Amos for a long moment, then looked down at Jenny and said, "You're welcome. I'm glad I happened along."

Amos took Jenny from Cole's arms, turned with a triumphant smirk on his face, and walked away. Cole glared with impotent anger at Amos's back, his look so murderous that several of the Mexican bystanders shivered and hastily crossed themselves.

Twenty-two

Over the next week, while she was recuperating from her twisted ankle, Jenny had a lot of time to mull over everything Cole had said, and that was what she was doing that afternoon as she paced the floor of her bedroom.

She admitted that she and Amos were not well suited. She had known that from the beginning, but somehow Amos's faults hadn't seemed so glaring back in New York, just as his physical appearance hadn't seemed so disappointing until she had seen him standing next to Cole. Amos was a poor conversationalist at best. His favorite topic for discussion was himself and his influential friends, and when he wasn't discussing that, he expounded at length on how much he hated the Mexicans, the Indians, the Negroes, the Jews, and the Southerners, particularly the Texans. It seemed that they were, either individually or collectively, the source of all the problems in the world. Jenny knew someday he would viciously attack the Irish, too, and she didn't know if she'd be able to keep her mouth shut. She hadn't realized he was so bigoted.

325

On several occasions, Jenny had tried to change the subject by asking questions about his ranch, something she was genuinely interested in. Unlike Cole, Amos didn't want Jenny asking questions. He always told her that was something she need not bother her pretty little head over, as if she didn't have enough sense to understand. Not only did Jenny feel her intelligence had been insulted, but she discovered she was even more bored than she had been at Cortinas's *hacienda*. There, at least she had the ongoing spats with Cortinas to liven things up, and she much preferred them to Amos's tedious, irritating monologues. Yes, she was bored to tears and found, much to her dismay, that she missed Cole's company as much as his lovemaking.

Yes, she missed his lovemaking. As shocking as the admission was, Jenny couldn't deny it. Every night she lay in her lonely bed yearning for his kiss and touch, tormented by vivid memories of his beautiful lovemaking. It was almost as if she had become addicted, her physical need for him so demanding that she tossed and turned for hours before she fell into an exhausted sleep. And, just as he had predicted, she couldn't stand for Amos to touch her, not even in the most casual manner. It made her skin crawl. His kisses, although chaste, sent shivers of revulsion through her. Jenny didn't know how she was ever going to live through the marriage act. She would just simply have to block it out of her mind, like everything else, she decided. After all, everything in life had its price. This was the price she would have to pay for her secure, luxurious life.

Jenny glanced around at her bedroom, thinking it wasn't exactly luxurious. Like the rest of the house, its furnishings were plain and practical. But Amos had already promised her she could do anything she wanted to the house after they were married, that cost was no object, just as it would be no object in picking her new wardrobe. And he had already given her several jewels. Obviously, he wasn't going to be stingy. And he had servants to wait on her every whim. She'd never have to lift a finger the rest of her life. Yes, marriage to Amos would definitely have its compensations.

Jenny was interrupted in her musing by the sound of footsteps in the hall outside her bedroom. Thinking it might be Amos coming to visit, she hopped into the bed from where she had been pacing the floor and reclined quickly, propping her ankle on the pillow just as a knock sounded on her door.

"Come in," Jenny called.

Rosa opened the door and walked in, carrying Jenny's supper tray.

"Oh, good!" Jenny cried out in pleasure. "I'm starving."

Rosa laughed. "You are always starving, *chiquita*. How do you stay so little?"

"Well, I don't always eat this much," Jenny fibbed, "but I can't resist. Your cooking is delicious," she said with all sincerity.

"*Gracias*. I enjoy cooking for people who like my cooking." Rosa looked down at her ample body, then laughed and added, "like me."

Jenny laughed. She genuinely liked the housekeeper and much preferred her company to Amos's. However, Rosa had a job to perform and couldn't spend as much time visiting as Jenny would have liked.

As Rosa placed the tray over Jenny's lap, Jenny asked, "Can you stay awhile?"

Rosa knew Jenny was not who she pretended to be. If she were the lady she claimed she was, she would not be socializing with the servants, but ordering them around and making demands on them. She also thought she knew why Jenny was marrying a man twice her age. His wealth. Rosa didn't condemn her for it. She had grown up dirt-poor herself, and might have done the same thing, had she had the opportunity. She just wished it had been someone other than *Señor* Wright. He had a mean streak in him that Rosa feared might some day turn on the girl, and if that happened she was going to need a friend. *"Sí,* for a few minutes."

"Good!" Jenny replied and motioned to a chair next to her bed.

As Rosa sat on the chair, Jenny said, "I've been meaning to ask you where you learned to speak English. Amos said you knew a little, but you know much more than that."

"El patrón and his wife taught me."

"Who's he?"

"He used to own this *hacienda*. We called him *el patrón* in the Mexican manner, although he was a *Tejano*. He made a house servant of me when I was a young girl, with the understanding that I would learn to speak English. Now I am glad he insisted. I

328

am one of the few who speaks the *gringo* language in this area, and the only woman I know of," Rosa said proudly.

Jenny thought Rosa had a right to be proud of her accomplishment. "Do you call *Señor* Wright *el patrón,* too?"

A closed expression came over the woman's face. "No, *señorita.*"

Jenny thought she knew why not. Some of the larger theaters had what they called patrons, too, people that aided and supported them. Of course, it all stemmed from appreciation of what the theaters were doing, and undoubtedly the Mexicans knew how Amos felt about them. Jenny decided to change the subject. "Are you married?"

"No, I am a widow, for ten years now. My husband was killed in a stampede."

"I'm sorry," Jenny responded.

"Gracias, but we know it is one of the risks our men take. Cattle ranching is very dangerous work. I have a cousin who broke his neck when his horse stepped in a prairie dog hole and threw him—it is surprising how often that happens—another who was attacked by a pack of *lobos* while he was standing night guard, a nephew who died of tick fever, and a brother who was gored by a cow that was *rabioso,* what the *gringos* call mad."

Jenny frowned. She didn't know cows could be rabid.

Rosa misinterpreted Jenny's frown and said, "I am sorry. I did not mean to frighten you. You need not worry about your *novio. Señor* Wright does not take

329

an active part in the work."

Jenny wasn't surprised to hear that, particularly if it was dangerous. "Do you have any children?"

Rosa's dark eyes lit up. *"Sí,* two sons and a daughter. My sons work here on the *hacienda* also. When my husband died, *el patrón* told me we would have a home here as long as we lived, or liked."

"Where is your daughter?"

Rosa hesitated for a long moment before she answered, "I sent her away to live with my sister in Mexico when *Señor* Wright hired the *pistoleros.* She was a very beautiful girl." Rosa left Jenny to draw her own conclusion.

"But surely, *Señor* Wright would not have allowed one of his gunfighters to harm her," Jenny objected.

A hard expression came over Rosa's face. *"Perdón, señorita,* but I do not agree. I do not think *Señor* Wright would have done anything if my daughter had been raped by one of those animals. She is a Mexican, a nothing. It would have been up to my sons to punish the man, and that in turn would have caused their deaths, if not by the *pistolero* they sought, then by a *gringo* posse. It is the way of things in this part of the country."

It was the way of things in many places, Jenny thought; the downtrodden had no rights. "I understand, Rosa. I'm glad you sent her away."

A look of tremendous relief came over the woman's face. *"Gracias.* I was afraid I had said too much."

"No, don't ever be afraid to be honest with me. I know how *Señor* Wright feels about your people, and unfortunately I can't change his feelings. But they're not my feelings."

"I sensed as much."

"Then we can be friends, at least on the sly?"

Rosa laughed. *"Sí, amigas* and conspirators, at least until I have to leave."

"Why would you have to leave?"

"Señor Wright does much talking of bringing in *gringos* to work his ranch. If my sons leave, I leave."

"But that would be foolish. Your people have been working this ranch for . . ."

"For well over a century," Rosa supplied when Jenny hesitated. *Sí,* there is no one who knows cattle as well as the *vacquero.* No one! It is in his blood."

"Maybe it won't happen," Jenny said, thinking if it did come to that, she'd fight Amos on it. Surely she could make him relent from the practical standpoint, if not from the human. He needed the Mexicans, with all their skills and expertise, for his ranch to be a success, particularly since he had no experience himself.

It was Rosa who changed the subject this time. "How is your ankle?"

"It's much stronger," Jenny answered. "I was up walking on it before you came in. It's ridiculous for *Señor* Wright to insist I stay in bed all this time."

"I do not think he plans on you staying in bed much longer. I heard him say he is planning on leaving for Brownsville tomorrow."

Without even inquiring if she was up to that long trip? Jenny was annoyed. "Are you sure?"

"Sí, I overheard him telling Ricardo, his head *va-*

331

quero, and then giving him orders on what work was to be done on the ranch while he was gone."

That sounded just like Amos, Jenny thought. He didn't know anything about it, but he'd give orders. Suddenly Jenny's appetite disappeared. She pushed the tray from her lap, saying, "Please take this, Rosa."

"But you have not finished."

"I'm not hungry any more."

"Are you sure?"

"I'm positive."

Amos came to Jenny's room an hour later. After greeting her, he paced the floor nervously. The coward, Jenny thought. He doesn't have nerve enough to bring up the matter. Finally, when she grew tired of watching him, she asked, "Is there something on your mind?"

"Why, yes, there is," Amos answered in a relieved tone of voice. He sat on the chair beside her bed and asked, "I've been thinking about our trip to Brownsville. Do you think you could travel tomorrow? You won't have to be on your feet, you know. You'll be traveling by wagon. If you don't feel like sitting up and dangling your leg quite yet, we could make a pallet in the wagon bed for you, but I would like to go ahead with our plans. I'm anxious to make you my wife."

Jenny knew why he was anxious. His furtive looks had become more and more lustful. The time to pay the piper had come, and Jenny wasn't one to renege on an agreement. "That won't be necessary. My ankle is much stronger. I can ride."

"Ride?" Amos asked in a shocked voice. "Certainly you don't mean in those boy's clothes you came in, astride?"

Being jostled in a wagon over a terrain where there wasn't even a road sounded too much like the train rides Jenny had taken back east, and she was going to do everything in her power to keep from going through that misery again. "Yes, I was thinking of that."

"I'm afraid that's out of the question," Amos answered tightly, striking a pompous pose that made Jenny all the more determined.

"If I remember correctly, you said my safety was more important than propriety. Have your feelings about that changed?"

"Of course not!"

"Has it ever occurred to you what would happen if I were riding in a wagon and we were attacked by Indians? A clumsy wagon can't move near as fast as someone on horseback. Not only would I be in more danger, but I'd also hold everyone else back."

It was an argument that even Amos couldn't dispute, but Jenny's voice had taken on a determined, hard edge that he didn't like. It was almost as if she were bucking him on this, not at all like the sweet, manageable woman he knew. He took a moment to mull this over, then said somewhat reluctantly, "You have a point there. And it would also save us from having to take time-consuming detours when the trail is too narrow for a wagon to pass through. Why, we

333

could probably shave off a day or two of travel that way."

Jenny wondered if she hadn't outwitted herself by suggesting a quicker method of travel. She wasn't looking forward to her wedding night.

Unaware of her thoughts, Amos continued, "Yes, I think in view of safety and the time it would save us, we could put propriety aside."

Jenny wondered who would see her? It shouldn't even matter how she rode. The brush was practically deserted, except for outlaws, who couldn't care less if she was properly dressed or not. Then a sudden thought occurred to her. "I hope this doesn't mean I'm not ever going to be able to ride Princess around the ranch."

Again there was that challenging edge to Jenny's voice that unsettled Amos. If he told her no, she couldn't, would she refuse to marry him? he wondered. Amos wasn't willing to take that risk. He had never been so hot for a woman as he was for Jenny. He was almost desperate. "No, of course not, my dear," he said in a silky voice. "You can ride, once we've purchased a sidesaddle and an appropriate riding outfit in Brownsville, and once the Indians have settled back down." Amos paused, then said, "I've been meaning to ask you about that horse. Ricardo, my overseer, said he thought she was a thoroughbred, a very expensive thoroughbred, and certainly not the usual ranch stock. Just how did you come by her?"

"Mr. Benteen stole her from Cortinas' private stables. He thought she might be expensive, too. That's why he took her, to thumb his nose at Cortinas."

It sounded like something the daring Texan would do, Amos thought, then laughed and said, "Good for him. And good for me. Cortinas may have some of my cattle, but I did him one better. I have his prize mare."

Jenny wondered just how Amos had gotten the idea that Princess was *his* horse. Then it dawned on her that he was counting them already married and her property as being his. Well, Amos might lay claim to her body, but he would never claim her horse, Jenny vowed. Princess belonged to her!

Amos leaned forward in his chair, took one of Jenny's hands in his and kissed it. The bristles of his mustache felt prickly on Jenny's knuckles. "Just think, darling. In a week, we'll be man and wife."

It was the hardest smile and most difficult lie Jenny had ever had to produce. "Oh, yes. That will be wonderful."

Early the next morning, Jenny walked from the ranch house and out into the courtyard where Amos and his party of bodyguards were waiting for her to join them. As Amos helped her mount Princess, Jenny looked quickly around and saw there were eight gunmen, including Cole. She wasn't surprised to see the rugged Texan. She knew Amos would take his best gunfighters along to protect him. His *vaqueros* could make do with second best.

As they rode from the courtyard and into the open, the guards surrounded them. Jenny was pleased to find Cole by her side. He smiled at her, making her insides feel like they were melting, and asked, "How is your ankle?"

Amos jerked his head around and saw Cole. "Her ankle is none of your concern!" he spat hatefully. "Go to the rear, and keep a sharp eye out for Apaches."

Cole was tempted to tell the carpetbagger to go to hell, but he feared Amos would fire him on the spot. He particularly wanted to stick close to Jenny on this journey, since there might be Indians lurking about. He placed the tip of his finger to the brim of his hat and nodded his head to Jenny, then wheeled his horse and trotted to the back of the group.

"It wasn't necessary for you to be so abrupt with him," Jenny said to Amos, throwing caution to the wind. "He was only being considerate in asking about my ankle. He was the one who found me, you know."

"What I know is that I don't like him nosing around you," Amos answered in a hard voice, his red complexion mottled with fury. "You're my intended, and he's my employee. He needs to learn his place."

The last sentence set Jenny's teeth on edge, knowing Amos would say the same of her if he knew the truth about her. She held her tongue and stared straight ahead.

Amos knew Jenny was angry at him and was perplexed. What had gotten into her? he wondered. Both last night and today, she hadn't acted herself. He wondered if he should apologize, then decided against it. Wives needed to stay in their place, too. This would be good training for her.

About thirty minutes later, they were riding parallel to a line of thick brush when Jenny heard a loud cracking of limbs. She turned to the brush, half-expecting to see a locomotive barreling out of it from the loud noises she was hearing. Then something did dart from the thick woods, a thousand-pound steer carrying enough mesquite branches on his horns to burn a good-sized fire, with a *vaquero* and his horse following in mad pursuit. The Mexican saw the group as soon as he cleared the dense brush and veered his horse away, but the longhorn ran straight for the party, looking for all practical purposes as if it were going to run them down. Its heavy horns made its head wobble from side to side as it ran. Jenny would have never believed that anything that big could travel that fast. Before she could even turn Princess and make a run for it, the steer tore across her and Amos's path, the tip of its razor sharp horn on that side just inches from their mount's chests and its passing making a whooshing noise even over the sound of its pounding hooves. Terrified, both horses reared and pawed the air, then Amos's horse tore off at a dead run, while Jenny hung on for dear life to keep from being thrown. Princess reared over and over, neighing shrilly.

When Cole had first heard the cracking noise, he had a good idea of what was coming. Even before the steer cleared the brush, he was riding towards Jenny, planning to steer her from danger. But his progress was impeded by the other gunmen turning their horses and racing away. About the same moment the steer passed Jenny's path, Cole's mount had arrived at the scene, and Cole hit the dirt running. Only a quick jump to the side kept him from being bowled over by Amos's runaway horse. Then he raced to the terrified mare, dodging her flying hooves, until he could manage to catch her cheek strap. But even then the wild-eyed mare tried to rear, jerking on the strap and thrashing her head. Cole held the strap firmly with one hand, despite the jolting she was giving his arm, and stroked her neck with the other, crooning, "Easy, girl, easy. Nothing's going to hurt you . . . Easy, girl. Easy does it."

As Princess finally began to calm down, Cole looked up at Jenny and saw her ashen face. "Are you all right?" he asked in concern.

"Yes," Jenny muttered, "just scared." She slipped from the saddle, shocked at how weak her knees felt when they hit the ground. She stepped up to Cole, and began stroking Princess's neck, too, asking, "Is she all right?"

"She's fine," Cole answered, scratching the mare's ear.

"Are you sure? That bull came so close I could have sworn his horn grazed her."

Cole didn't bother to tell Jenny it had been a steer. He examined Princess carefully and found no sign of injury. "No, she's fine."

"Why did she do that? Rear that way?" Jenny asked, still shaken. "I had no control over her at all. None! She's never been unmanageable."

"She did what every horse will do when they see

something dangerous coming at them. She tried to defend herself with her front hooves. That's pure instinct, and about the only defense a horse has, other than its speed."

Cole turned and looked out at the prairie, seeing the other gunmen riding back and Amos's horse still running hell for leather in the distance. "Well, at least we got rid of him for a few minutes. The damn fool should have known what was coming," Cole said, furious that Amos had not been able to protect Jenny. "Anyone who knows anything about ranching in this part of the country should. All that cracking of wood could only mean one thing, a brush popper flushing a cow out."

"A brush popper?"

"That's what the Anglos call cowboys in this part of the country, a brush popper, because of all the jumping and hopping and contortions his horse has to do to find and scare the cattle out of the brush."

"Was it my imagination, or were that bull's horns crinkled?"

"No, he's what they call a mossy-horn. All longhorn's horns get crinkled and scaly looking when they're over six years old. Only you don't see them that old very often. They're slaughtered long before that. That steer has probably been hiding in that mesquite for years and years."

Jenny noted that Cole had said steer and realized she'd made a mistake in judging gender once again. "If it wasn't a bull charging, why didn't it veer? It looked like it was going to run right into us. Are longhorns nearsighted or something?"

339

"Buffalo are, but I've never heard of cattle being nearsighted. But they aren't very smart, and hell, with horns that size on them, they're used to things getting out of their way. I guess it never occurred to him to change his course."

Jenny laughed, then asked, "How do you know so much about ranching? Did you work cattle at some time?"

"Hell, no! I can't stand cows. They're stupid and clumsy and smell to high heaven. They have none of the intelligence or nobility a horse does. But you can't go into a saloon or bar in this part of Texas without running into cowboys, whether brush poppers or *vaqueros,* and hear them talking. In fact, that's about all they can talk about, cows. It's disgusting."

"Well, Texas' future does seem to be in its cattle," Jenny pointed out.

"Maybe, maybe not. There are other things of value we can grow beside cattle." There was something in Cole's tone of voice that made Jenny think he wasn't just making an idle comment, but before she could ask him what he meant, his gaze slid over her and he changed the subject, asking, "How did you convince Amos to let you wear those clothes? More tears?"

Jenny didn't take insult at Cole's comment about her tears. She *had* used them as a means to get what she wanted. "No, believe it or not, I used reason. I pointed out that it would be safer for me if I rode, that I could move much faster on a horse, if we were attacked by Indians."

In Cole's estimation, Amos shouldn't have had to have that pointed out to him. He should have known it. He turned and looked out over the prairie, seeing Amos sitting on his horse and talking to the *vaquero* who had flushed the steer out of the brush. It was obvious that the carpetbagger was giving the hapless man a severe dressing-down from the way Amos was angrily waving his arms and the way the Mexican was hanging his head as he stood before him. The bastard, Cole thought, putting all the blame on the poor *vaquero,* who had only been doing his job. Why, he hadn't even come back to see how Jenny had fared before berating the man. And this was the man who claimed to love her?

Cole didn't bother pointing out Amos' insensitivity to Jenny. He gave her credit for having enough sense to see it for herself.

Jenny *did* see, but it didn't change anything for her. Sensitivity wasn't a requirement for her future husband, any more than bravery had been — or so she thought.

Twenty-three

By the time Amos returned from giving his *vaquero* a verbal thrashing, Jenny was once more mounted and Cole had returned to his position at the back of the column. Other than his eyes briefly skimming over her, the rancher gave no acknowledgement that Jenny had been in any danger or that Cole had come to her aid. He pretended that the entire episode had never occurred, signaling for the lead gunman to continue.

They rode in utter silence, the only sound that of the horses's hooves and occasional jingling of reins or squeak of leather. Jenny wondered if Amos was sulking or if he was always so taciturn when traveling. She wished it was Cole riding beside her. She was bored to tears. Then she heard a bird singing joyously somewhere in the brush beside them. Her eyes scanned the dense vegetation, but she could see no sign of it. The song went on and on and on, each note crystal clear and, amazingly, never repeated, from the highest high to the lowest low. Even when they had ridden quite a distance away, Jenny could still hear it.

The song of the mockingbird was the last distraction Jenny had until they stopped for their noonday break. As soon as she had dismounted, Amos said to Jenny, "After we've had a bite to eat, I'll have the boys put up the tent and you can rest for a while before we continue."

"What tent?" Jenny asked in surprise.

"I always travel with a tent, but it's at your disposal on this trip. A tent and a cot."

What happened to sleeping on the ground in a bedroll, like everyone else? Jenny wondered. "I don't think that's necessary. It's not at all warm today, that I might need to get out of the heat for awhile, and I'm not at all tired. Why don't we just go on and make camp a little earlier tonight?"

Jenny thought for a moment that Amos was not going to agree, and if that were the case, strongly suspected it would be because she had suggested it. Jenny might have blamed it on her being female, but she had noticed that he was man who resented suggestions of any sort from anyone. He was likely to do just the opposite in his determination to keep the upper hand, which to her was the height of obstinacy. She couldn't fathom how his ranch had been the success it was, unless his Mexican overseer was a master at diplomacy as well as an expert on cattle. However, after some thought on the matter, Amos did agree. After curbing their hunger with cold *tamales,* the group continued their ride uneventfully and made camp that evening in the brush beside a muddy creek.

When Jenny and Amos dismounted, one of the gunslingers stepped forward and took Amos's reins from him, then reached for Princess's. Jenny almost jerked them back, before she realized that the man must act in the capacity of a servant as well as a gunman and that he meant to water and bed the horses down for the night. Reluctantly, she placed her reins in his outstretched hand, but Princess refused to go with him, shying nervously, even threatening to rear. Jenny thought she knew why. Except for Cole, the gunfighters were a heavily bearded and unkempt lot. None of them smelled good, but this man's odor was particularly offensive. Jenny started to step forward to take Princess's reins when Cole appeared, took the mare's reins from the man, and said, "I'll take her. She knows me."

The gunfighter surrendered the reins gladly, having feared the mare would go wild like she had earlier that day and he'd have his skull split open. Hell, what was he doing acting like a goddamned groom, anyway? he wondered. He whirled around and hurried away with Amos's horse and his own mount.

Jenny watched as Cole took a different path to the creek, leading Princess and his stallion behind him. Then she smiled as Princess bent her head and nuzzled Cole's shoulder, whinnying softly as if she were thanking him for rescuing her.

"That goddamned horse!" Amos said from behind Jenny. "That's the second time she's cut up today. She's going to have to learn to behave herself, or else."

Jenny whirled on Amos, and he was shocked to see the fury in her blue eyes. "Don't ever curse Princess again! And she does know how to behave her-

self. It's your gunfighters that don't know how to behave, like bathing every now and then. My God, that
man stunk to high heaven! Princess probably
thought he was a polecat."

Amos didn't know what to say. This was a Jenny
he had never seen, a woman who looked angry
enough to scratch his eyes out. "I'm . . . sorry," he
stammered, totally unsettled by Jenny's anger.
"You . . . you really are . . . fond of that horse,
aren't you?"

Jenny realized she had lost control, but reasoned
she had gone too far to back down. "Yes, I'm afraid
I am."

"In that case, I'll ask Benteen to care for her on
this trip."

Jenny would have preferred to care for Princess
herself, but knew Amos would never allow that. It
would be beneath her dignity as a lady, a role that
was getting increasingly hard to play. She decided it
was time to try to repair some of the damage she had
done, as much as she hated to. She smiled sweetly
and answered, "Thank you, dear Amos. I know I've
been a little difficult lately. Knowing there might be
Indians lurking about has my nerves totally un-
strung. I really appreciate your patience with me."

Jenny's transition from fury to honeyed sweetness
was too swift for Amos. It took a moment for him
to accept the excuse she offered him for her behavior.
Then he smiled and patted her hand, saying, "That's
quite all right, my dear. The rigors of this country,
including the Indian threat, takes a little getting used
to. I understand."

After being "forgiven" by Amos, Jenny decided not to risk her luck any further and made a concentrated effort to do better at playing her role as an eastern lady of quality. As soon as the tent had been erected by several of the gunfighters, she retired to it, and waited for Amos to bring her dinner, which she ate alone, since it would have been improper for him to stay in the tent and eat with her, or so he said. Jenny didn't mind her solitude in the least, and not just because she didn't enjoy Amos's company. She had noticed several of the gunfighters snickering behind her and Amos and others had cast glances in her direction that left no doubt in Jenny's mind as to what their filthy thoughts were. She felt soiled without having even been touched, and was glad to be away from them.

When night fell, Jenny didn't bother to light the kerosene lamp that hung on the center tent pole. A half-moon had risen, its brilliant glow penetrating the thin canvas of the tent and giving the interior a subdued light. Jenny reclined on the cot on her side, fully dressed except for her boots, and stared at the eerie shadows the firelight cast on the side of the tent. She strained her ears to hear what the men were saying, but their voices were too muted to distinguish words. Again, bored to tears, she wished it were she and Cole sitting by the fire, but she knew there was no hope of that, for she had heard Amos tell Cole to take first watch, then seen him walk from the camp when she had carefully lifted the tent flap that served as a door and peeked out. The time crept by, seeming like an eternity, before Jenny felt even the stirring

346

of slumber, and then, just as she was finally drifting off, she was awakened by the sound of six men snoring loudly, the noise made worse by the fact that no two snores were in unison. For the rest of the night, Jenny tossed and turned, hardly sleeping a wink.

When Amos saw Jenny the next morning, he didn't find her appearance at all unusual. He expected her to look tired after trying to sleep on a hard cot, outdoors, perhaps worried that Indians might attack. However, when Cole delivered Princess to her, he knew better. He had never seen Jenny with dark circles under her eyes. As he helped her mount, he asked softly, "What's wrong? You look like hell."

Jenny didn't take offense at his blunt observation. She knew it was the truth. "Believe it or not, I feel even worse," she answered with a little groan. "I couldn't sleep a wink for all that noise."

"What noise?" Cole asked, for he'd been up the better part of the night keeping watch and heard nothing unusual.

"That snoring!" Jenny whispered hotly. "It was nerve-wracking."

"It wasn't me," Cole answered. "I don't snore."

Jenny looked down from her saddle at him and smiled. "I know."

It was a moment that Cole would remember and treasure the rest of his life, for Jenny's smile was so warm, so genuine that Cole felt it to the depths of his soul. Then the moment was shattered by a gunfighter running into the camp, yelling excitedly, "There's a spotted cat back there in the woods. Spied him up in the trees while I was pissing."

347

Cole stiffened at the man's crudity in front of Jenny, but Amos hardly noticed, too caught up with what the man was telling him. "How big was he?"

"Looked full-growed to me," the man answered, then asked, "Can we go get him, boss?"

"Yeah, boss," another gunfighter chimed in, "let's go get him! We've been taking bets on who's the best shot. This ought to settle it once and for all."

Amos was thinking it would take more skill in tracking than shooting expertise, and that might put him in the running. "Okay, it's every man for himself, except I get the skin, regardless of who shoots him. You're still in my employ."

"Oh, hell, who cares about the skin!" one gunfighter said in disgust. "Let's go get him!"

Their eyes glittering with excitement and their guns drawn, Amos and his gunfighters raced from the camp and into the woods, leaving Jenny and Cole by themselves. "You're not going?" Jenny asked Cole.

"Nope."

"Because someone has to stay behind and protect me?"

"Partly, but even if you weren't here, I wouldn't go."

They could hear the breaking of limbs and the men shouting back and forth. "There he is!" One man yelled. "I saw him up in those trees."

"Where are you?" another called.

"Over here, he's over here," yet another shouted, "on the ground."

The voices all came from different directions, telling Cole and Jenny that the men had scattered, and if they had all indeed seen the cat, the animal was giving them a merry chase.

Then the sound of gunshots split the air, followed by someone asking, "Did you get him?"

"Hell, no!" came the answer. "The bastard got away."

Another burst of gunshots was heard.

"Did you get him?" someone called.

"No, it was a goddamn owl!" was the disgusted answer.

"Those damn fools, shooting at everything that moves," Cole spat. "It will be a miracle if they don't kill each other. And, I hope to God that there are no Apaches around. With all those guns going off, they'd have our position fixed by now."

The sound of gunshots coming from every direction was making Princess edgy. Jenny dismounted and tried to soothe her, while Cole glared in impotent fury at the woods. Another burst of gunshots was heard, followed by a shrill animal cry, then a exultant cry, "I got him! I got him!"

A few moments later, the excited group returned to camp, carrying the dead cat between two men. As they laid it on the ground by the fire, Jenny was shocked to see how small it was. "Is it a dangerous animal?" she asked Cole.

"An ocelot? Hell, no! An adult male in this country rarely weighs over twenty, twenty-five pounds. I've seen some tomcats bigger than that."

"Does it present a danger to ranch stock?"

"I've never heard of an ocelot attacking stock, like

349

a *lobo* or cougar. They live off of mice, birds, rabbits, and rarely leave the brush."

"Can their meat be eaten?"

"I guess if you were desperate, yes. Men have been known to eat lizards and snakes, why not ocelot?"

Jenny had been staring at the animal all the time she had questioned Cole, thinking it was beautiful even in death, and how much more so it must have been in life, stalking the underbrush for food or gracefully leaping from tree to tree. Its background fur was a smoky pearl, its black spots ranging from mere dots on its feet to large, shell-shaped spots on other parts of its body. From its pink nose to its black-tipped tail, it couldn't have been much over thirty inches long. A quiet fury had been growing in Jenny, that burst loose as she asked Cole sharply, "If they didn't shoot it because it was dangerous, or for food, then why did they kill it?"

"For the same reason men traveled out to prairies by the train loads to kill buffalo by the millions. For the sport," Cole answered bitterly. "I guess that poor cat presented as much challenge as those dumb buffalo did."

"This was no sport!" Jenny retorted, tears coming to her eyes. "It was cruel, senseless killing!"

The shrill pitch of Jenny's voice had gained the attention of some of the men gathered around the cat while one skinned it. Cole stepped in front of Jenny to shield her from their curious eyes and answered, "And so was the killing of those buffalo. Unfortunately, there are some men who find killing exciting, regardless of whether it has any point to it or not. I don't understand it myself. Maybe it makes them feel bigger, more manly."

Cole saw Amos coming and stepped aside. The rancher shot him a resentful glance, then stepped up to Jenny, smiling broadly and saying, "The skin on that cat is absolutely beautiful, my dear. Got him right between the eyes, so there's plenty of skin to make a hat or a muff from. Would you like that?"

Knowing Amos had had some reason for killing the cat didn't change Jenny's feelings. It had still been brutal and senseless, and she strongly suspected that he would have savored the kill it even if its skin had had no value. She fought back the queasy feeling she was having and said angrily, "No, I would not! The skin was beautiful where it belonged, on the animal. I don't ever want to see it again! Not ever!" Jenny turned and rushed back into the tent before the tears came.

Amos turned to Cole and said, "Well, that's a woman for you. They just don't understand these things. I'll hang the skin on the wall in my office, where all my friends and business associates can admire it. It takes a man to appreciate hunting trophies."

Cole made no comment, but he didn't feel less manly for his feelings.

Twenty-four

That day, Jenny was very quiet and subdued. Amos had no idea just how upset she was with him. In his estimation she was behaving as a lady should, being seen and not heard. Cole, however, even from his position at the back of the column, knew Jenny was still angry. He could tell by the rigid set of her back, and while he regretted the cat being senselessly killed, he was glad Jenny had been given yet another glimpse of Amos's true character. The better she came to know her intended, with all his many faults, the better Cole's chances of winning her over were.

That evening, when Amos delivered Jenny's meal to the tent, he said to her, "It might be a good idea for you to retire early tonight."

Jenny had intended to do that anyway, since she had gotten so little sleep the night before, but just to be difficult, she asked, "Oh? Why?"

Amos frowned. Was it his imagination, or was there a hint of anger in her voice? "Well, I plan on breaking camp early tomorrow, before daybreak. I want to make sure we reach Rio Grande City in plenty of time to catch the noon steamer to Brownsville."

"Then we'll be going straight to the steamer?"

"Yes." Seeing the frown on her face, Amos asked, "What's wrong?"

"I was hoping to send a wire to my parents."

A look of annoyance came over the rancher's ruddy face. "I know I told you we'd send one from Rio Grande City, but the telegraph station is at the fort. I don't want to have to ride over there and back and risk missing the steamer. We'll do it when we get to Brownsville. After all this time, a day or so more shouldn't matter."

After Amos had left, Jenny thought what he had said was probably true. By this time, Carla and John probably thought she had skipped out on them and never intended to pay them back.

It was then that it dawned on Jenny they would be making the trip to Rio Grande City in a little over two days, while it had taken she and Cole much longer to get to Amos's ranch. Jenny was no fool. She knew there could be only one reason, and it wasn't because Cole had gotten lost. He knew this country like the back of his hand. No, Cole had deliberately drawn the trip out, but Jenny found she couldn't whip up any anger at him for deceiving her. She wouldn't trade those days, or any of the time she had spent with Cole, for all the money in the world. Those were precious memories that were going to have to sustain her for a lifetime.

* * *

The next morning, they broke camp several hours before daybreak and then rode into Rio Grande City around eleven in the morning. The town was nothing at all like the sleepy hamlet Jenny had seen on her last visit, but was bustling with activity and crowded with people. "Is there some kind of celebration going on?" she asked Amos.

"Not that I know of," he answered, looking about him in puzzlement.

As they made their way down the main thoroughfare, weaving in and out of the heavy horse and wagon traffic, Amos stopped a man going in the opposite direction and asked, "What's going on? What are all these people doing here?"

"Why, they came to see the Army and the Texas Rangers invade Mexico," the man answered with excitement. "Word's going around that it's going to happen any minute now."

Before Amos could respond to the shocking news, the man spurred his horse and rode away. "That's just rumor," a lanky, redheaded, middle-aged man said from where he was standing on the boardwalk a short distance away.

Amos gave the man a hard look, then maneuvered his horse up to the boardwalk and asked, "Aren't you one of the men who rides shotgun for the steam line?"

"Sure am, but the steamers aren't running today. There ain't no boat traffic going either way on the river, until this mess settles down."

Cole and Jenny rode up. Catching the tail end of what the man had said, Cole asked, "What mess?"

The man peered at Cole, then asked, "Don't I know you? Your face looks familiar. What's your name?"

Only because Cole knew the man was neither a law officer nor likely to challenge him to a gunfight, he answered. "Cole Benteen."

The man laughed, saying, "Why, no wonder you look familiar. Your pa used to run the general store in Brownsville, and you're the spitting image of him. I used to do business with him when I lived there. Thomas, I believe his name was."

"Yes, that was my father."

Jenny frowned. Cole's father had been a merchant? Where had she gotten the idea he came from farm stock?

"Yep, I remember you," the man continued. "You were always hanging around with the Rangers."

"Yes, I was," Cole agreed, then trying to steer the conversation back to its original topic, said, "but didn't you say something about a mess?"

"Sure did. Damndest mess you ever saw. Almost got ourselves into a war with Mexico. Still might, if something don't give."

"What are you talking about?" Amos demanded.

The man gave Amos a resentful glare, then asked Cole, "Is he with you?"

"Yes. I'm currently working for him."

The man gave Amos another withering glance, then said to Cole, "Well, we can't talk here. Too much noise."

"What about the hotel dining room?" Cole suggested.

355

"It's plumb full of people. So are all the saloons. I'll bet you every Anglo in South Texas and half the Mexicans are here, or down at the Las Cuevas crossing."

"Why there?" Cole asked.

"Because that's where the action is taking place." The man stepped down from the boardwalk and said to Cole, "Give me a hand up. I'll ride behind you."

After the man was seated behind Cole, Cole asked him, "Where are we going?"

"Ride down to the river. The steam line has me quartered in one of the empty warehouses, next to their offices. We can talk there."

As Cole and the guard rode off, Amos looked around him, not liking the curt manner in which the man had treated him and hoping to find out what he wanted to know from someone else. After his questions had been brushed aside by several people hurrying by, however, he relented and followed. For that reason, Amos, Jenny, and his gunfighters arrived at the steamboat offices a moment or two after Cole and his passenger.

As everyone in his party dismounted, Amos glared at Cole and the steamer guard, already walking up the stairs to the wharf where the offices and line of warehouses sat, then turned to his gunslingers and said, "You boys wait here. As soon as I find out what's going on, I'll let you know."

As Cole and the man walked down the wharf a good distance ahead of Amos and Jenny, the guard glanced over his shoulder, then asked Cole, "What're you doing working for that bastard? You're not riff-raff like those others."

"Then you know who he is?"

"Hell, yes! Amos Wright. The goddamn carpet-bagger is always trying to throw his weight around at the steamship offices, expecting to be treated special. We all keep hoping he'll fall overboard and drown."

"I'm acting as one of his bodyguards, but I don't plan on doing it much longer. Like you said, he's a little hard to take."

The guard gave Cole a long, penetrating look, then said, "I heard you got a bum deal, and Governor Coke straightened it all out for you. I'm glad to hear it."

So the news had finally trickled to South Texas, Cole thought in surprise. "So am I. But do me a favor, will you? Don't mention it to them," Cole said, motioning over his shoulder.

"Sure. Whatever you say."

Cole had been wracking his brain to remember the man's name ever since the redhead had recognized him. Suddenly it came to him. "Thanks, Joel."

Joel grinned and said, "Ah, so you finally remembered me?"

"Yes. Joel MacDougal. I'm sorry it took me so long."

"Well, I had an advantage over you. You were just a kid at the time. Kids don't pay any attention to adults." He paused, then asked, "Who's the little lady with Wright? She's about the prettiest female I've ever seen."

"Miss Jenny Daniels. She's his fiancée."

"That pretty little thing is gonna marry that son-

357

of-a-bitch?" Joel asked in an outraged voice.

"Not if I can help it," Cole answered.

Joel shot him a sharp glance, then chuckled and said, "So that's the way it is, huh? Why you're hanging around?"

Cole hadn't meant to divulge that information. His thoughts had just slipped out. "Yes, but let's keep that between us also."

By that time, they had reached a door to one of the warehouses. Joel produced a key, unlocked it, and held the door open while everyone walked through it.

Jenny squinted her eyes in the dim light and saw that the storage room was empty except for a bed, a chest with a lamp on it, a pot-bellied stove and a couple of barrels.

Joel pulled up a small barrel for Jenny, saying, "Here ma'am, you can sit on this. Sorry I don't have any real chairs, but all I do is sleep here. I know it ain't much, but I prefer it to the hotel. It's quieter here by the river."

"Thank you," Jenny answered, sitting on the barrel.

"You pull up a barrel, too," Joel said to Cole.

"That's not necessary!" Amos said impatiently. "We didn't come for a visit. We just want to know what's going on."

Joel looked Amos directly in the eye and said, "I don't recall asking you to tag along. I was talking to Cole, here. If you're in a hurry to find out what's going on, you can get. Or you can stay, but don't rush me. I don't like being rushed, and I don't like having to yell over a crowd."

It was all Cole could do to keep from laughing at the shocked expression on Amos's face. Joel was definitely a man after his heart, he thought.

Having put Amos in his place, Joel turned to Cole, saying, "Make yourself comfortable, son. This story is a mite long."

Cole straddled a barrel, while Joel sat on the side of his bed, then began his story, saying, "Well, the ruckus started three days ago, at nightfall, when a Mexican rancher rode into one of the cavalry's camps out the brush and told the officer there, a Captain Randlett, that bandits were driving a herd of stolen Santa Gertrudes cattle to Las Cuevas and would probably cross the Rio Grande the next day."

"Las Cuevas, the ranch?" Amos asked.

Joel nodded.

"Isn't that one of Cortinas' ranches?" Amos asked Cole.

"No," Cole answered, "actually it belongs to one of his friends and sub-chiefs, a General Juan Flores, but so many stolen cattle pass through it that many people think it's Cortinas' headquarters."

Joel frowned, wondering how Cole knew that. It wasn't common knowledge. "Well, anyway, to get back to my story, the captain wired Colonel Potter in Brownsville the news, and was ordered to follow the bandits, and if they caught them at the river, to follow them into Mexico."

This time it was Cole who interrupted. "Wait a minute, Joel. Are you sure you got that straight? Potter ordered his men to follow the bandits into

Mexico?"

"I'm sure, Cole. I ain't gonna tell you my contacts, but I'm sure."

"Then the army *has* invaded Mexico?" Amos asked in excitement.

"Well, I don't rightly know," Joel answered irritably. "You're getting way ahead of the story."

"Go on, Joel," Cole said, "tell it your way. We'll try not to interrupt anymore."

Joel shot Amos a heated look, then continued. "Well, Captain Randlett didn't head straight for the river the next morning, like he'd been ordered. He stopped to gather a bunch of Texans and Mexicans, then waited until he heard from a courier from Ringgold, which was sending troops, too. By the time he got to the river it was late in the afternoon, and sure enough, there the bandits were, pulling out some cattle that had gotten bogged down in the mud on the Mexican side. The soldiers killed two of the bandits, wounded a third, and the rest ran off into the brush. Then, instead of following, Randlett decided to wait for the reinforcements from Ringgold to arrive, and since they didn't get there until nightfall, decided to wait until the next day to follow. During the night, Potter ordered more troops out, from both Edinburg and Ringgold. Major Clendenin and his group from Edinburg arrived at the river first, but he wouldn't let Randlett cross, since the moment when he had caught the bandits red-handed had passed. Clendenin said it would be a war-like invasion that might trigger war with a country we were at peace with."

"That goddamed Randlett!" Amos exclaimed furiously. "Why didn't he do what he was supposed to, when he was supposed to! I've been waiting for years for the Army to get the guts to cross and give those bandits a thrashing, and that idiot ruined their only chance."

"Maybe not," Joel answered. "You ain't heard the rest of the story, and you ain't gonna, either, if you don't stop interrupting."

"I have a lot at stake here," Amos answered defensively.

"So does everybody on the border," Joel tossed back, then deliberately directing his words to Cole, said, "The officers wired Potter, and he told them to hold tight until Major Alexander arrived from Ringgold, and that he would be in command. Then lo and behold, who do you suppose showed up on the scene? Captain Leander McNelly of the Texas Rangers."

Cole frowned. The Texas Rangers had just recently been reinstated, and ordinarily he would applaud them, but he had mixed feelings about McNelly. The captain had served in Governor Davis's hated police force, and although Cole had never personally come into contact with him, that was generally enough to make him dislike any man. However, McNelly had also served brilliantly as a cavalry officer in the Confederate Army, and the post-reconstruction Texas legislature that had appointed him apparently held him in high regard. Cole was reserving judgment, at least for the time being. "I heard McNelly was taking enlistments for a group of border Rangers, and then I was out of touch for a while. How did he do?"

"He had those bandits running scared there for awhile," Joel answered with a big grin. "Caught a bunch red-handed at the old Palo Alto battleground outside of Brownsville and whipped the tar out of them. Killed the whole lot. From then on, the bandits didn't try to hold on to the cattle if they got caught. That taught them to let go of the herd and make a run for the border. Then McNelly had to go back home for awhile for his wife to nurse him back to health. He's consumptive, you know. He ain't been back long."

Cole had heard about the fight at Palo Alto and knew the Mexican side of the story. It was true the bandits no longer stood and fought after the trashing McNelly's rangers had given them, but they had never run scared. They had simply changed their tactics. "And what did McNelly do when he arrived on the scene?" Cole asked.

"He told the calvary that he'd collect his men, who had made camp some distance in the brush, and cross over into Mexico and bring those cattle back."

"Just like that?" Cole asked in disbelief. "How many men did he have?"

"About thirty."

"Is he crazy?" Cole asked. "He's going up against an army of two- or three-hundred bandits with thirty men? Or didn't he know how many bandits were at Las Cuevas?"

Joel was wondering how Cole knew how many bandits were at Las Cuevas. "I reckon he did. He has spies among the bandits. But I don't think he was really expecting to go it alone. The Army had promised to cover his return, and I think he read more into those promises than the officers meant."

"Why do you think that?" Cole asked.

Joel shot a sharp look in Amos's direction, then shrugged his shoulders and answered evasively, "It's just my opinion. Anyway, he crossed the river that night. Found a Mexican that had an old leaky canoe to take his men across, four at a time. Swam five of his horses over, but they had such a time pulling them out of that same mud the cows were stuck in that afternoon, he didn't have any more sent over. They attacked the ranch at dawn, with the five with horses leading the way. Caught the Mexicans chopping wood, and killed four men — "

"Wait a minute!" Cole demanded. "What happened to the palisade, what happened to the artillery?"

Again, Joel wondered how Cole knew so much about the bandit hideout. McNelly hadn't known about the artillery, himself, until he had encountered it. "There wasn't any of either, because they hit the wrong ranch. They attacked the Las Curchas, a little ranch between the river and Las Cuevas. When they realized their mistake, they rode the other half mile to Las Cuevas, but the bandits had been alerted and were waiting for them. They turned around and made a run back for the river."

"Who in the hell was their scout, to make such a stupid mistake?" Cole asked.

"Jesus Sandoval."

"*Casoose* is with McNelly?" Cole asked in obvious disgust.

"Yep, and up to his old tricks, now that McNelly reinstated *la ley de fuga*."

Amos had really tried to keep from interrupting, but his curiosity got the better of him. "Dammit, who's *Casoose,* and what's this *la ley . . .* whatever?"

"Sandoval is a Mexican Ranger, a sadistic brute who takes pleasure in torturing prisoners," Cole answered, "and *la ley de fuga* is an old Spanish law that provides instant death for any prisoner if a rescue attempt is made, but there have been times when the Rangers have stretched it to mean instant death, period."

Cole saw the shocked look on Jenny's face and turned the conversation away from the gruesome topic, asking Joel, "Did McNelly cross back over to Texas?"

"Nope. He retreated as far as the river bank and made a stand there. The bandits attacked him several times, but he repelled them. Killed General Flores in the first exchange. During one of the attacks, McNelly called across the river and pleaded for Captain Randlett to come help him. The soldiers said it sounded like the Rangers were being annihilated, so Randlett and about forty of his men crossed. McNelly tried to get them to go with him to attack the ranch, but Randlett refused. He told McNelly he'd stay with him on the river bank, but he wouldn't go any further until Major Alexander arrived and told him what to do."

"What did Alexander say when he got there?" Cole asked.

"He ain't got there yet, at least, not by the last report I heard."

"Why not?" Cole asked. "Las Cuevas crossing is just ten miles downstream from the fort. What's taking him so long?"

"I imagine he's waiting for orders from the big boy himself. And Sherman is probably waiting for Washington on the Potomac to tell him what to do."

"Then the Rangers and Randlett's troopers are still in Mexico?" Amos asked, his eyes glittering with excitement.

"Yep, just waiting for Alexander to show up."

"Dammit, I want to be there when he arrives!" Amos said with determination. "If the Army marches into Mexico, I want to be there to see it." He turned and rushed to the door, the spurs on his boots jingling with every step, saying, "God, I hope to hell I'm not too late!"

Then, remembering something, Amos stopped abruptly at the door and turned, a perplexed look on his face. He glanced at Jenny, then asked Joel, "When you said the hotel was full, did you mean all the rooms, too?"

"Yep, sure did."

"Do you think I could bribe someone for one of those rooms for my fiancée?"

"Even if you could, I wouldn't leave the little lady here, not with all the riff-raff that's been drifting in from the brush, and all the liquor that's flowing. Why there probably won't be a keg of White Mule left in town by tonight, and you know how potent that stuff is. She'd be safer with you at Las Cuevas."

"Are you crazy?" Amos counted. "There's a war

about to start down there. She could get shot!"

"Naw, there's a big crowd of people hanging around down there, and quite a few men brought their womenfolk with them. The soldiers are making them keep back from the river, but the Army is keeping an eye on things, which is more than I can say for here. Why, by nightfall, this town will probably have more hair on it than Abilene."

It was the first time Jenny had interrupted, but her curiosity got the better of her. "Excuse me, but did you say hair on it?"

"Sorry, little lady," Joel apologized, noting that Jenny had an eastern clip to her voice. "I guess that does sound peculiar to a stranger. It's a local cowhand saying. It means wild and lawless."

Cole could see Amos was chomping at the bit and knew what was frustrating him. It wasn't so much that the rancher didn't want to take Jenny along, as his fear she would slow him down. He had no idea how fast Jenny could ride when she had to. "Why don't you go ahead, if you're in such a hurry? I'll bring Jenny."

Amos had gone to great lengths to keep Jenny and Cole apart. He certainly didn't want to leave them alone. Seeing his hesitation and sensing his thoughts, Joel said, "Yeah, go ahead. I was planning on riding back down there myself to see what's really going on. Too many wild rumors going on around here. I'll ride along with Cole and the little lady. That ought to be enough protection for her, if that's what's worrying you. I'm a pretty mean shot with that Winchester of mine."

Amos could hardly come out and say what was worrying him, that he was afraid of competition for Jenny's affections. He didn't particularly like the idea, but he consoled himself with the thought that the two couldn't get too chummy with Joel around. "All right, I'll ride ahead," he agreed, then looked Jenny directly in the eye and said, "But you let me know as soon as you get there."

Jenny resented Amos's directive. She had no idea that he was jealous of Cole and feared him. In her estimation, he was treating her as if she were a child. She made no comment, but as he turned and stepped out the door, she gave him a murderous look that brought a grin to Joel's freckled face and made Cole's spirits soar with hope.

Twenty-five

As soon as Amos had disappeared, Cole formally introduced Joel and Jenny; then hearing Amos and his gunslingers ride off, the trio walked from the warehouse. As they strolled along the wharf, Cole glanced around him, then asked Joel, "Don't you usually keep at least one steamboat docked here?"

"Yep. The company hid it upstream, in case anyone got any bright ideas of trying to steal it and use it to get across the river for their own purposes."

"So the crowd here can't take things into their own hands?" Cole surmised.

"Both here, and across the river. There's a big, ugly mob forming in Camargo, armed with anything they can get their hands on. When the wind is right, you can hear them yelling, *"Maten los gringos,* kill the Americans," he added for Jenny's benefit. "Word also has it that the Mexican Army has arrived."

"Undoubtedly dispatched by General Cortinas,"

Cole commented in disgust, bringing a nod of agreement from Joel.

Jenny had been looking around also. "Is that where the ferry is, too?" she questioned Joel. "Hidden upstream?"

"Nope, the army confiscated it, since it belongs to the Mexican that runs it."

"For the same reason your company hid their boat, or to use themselves?" Cole asked, thinking it would be easier to transport horses and artillery on a ferry than a steamboat.

"I reckon that remains to be seen," Joel answered with a shrug.

The three mounted and rode down the rutted road that followed the river downstream, the men protectively placing themselves at each side of Jenny. When Jenny saw the palisade of Ringgold's Barracks in the distance, she asked, "Would it be too much trouble to stop at the fort, so I can send a wire back east?"

"It wouldn't be any trouble at all, ma'am," Joel drawled, "but it wouldn't do us any good. They ain't taking any personal wires for the time being, for fear of tying up the lines and keeping an important message from Washington from coming through. I know that for a fact. One of my drinking buddies is an operator."

Cole wondered if the operator was where Joel had gotten his information. The guard had said he had contacts he refused to reveal, and telegraph operators were privy to military messages and were just as human as the next person. Many gossiped about what they transmitted, which was one reason why the army sent really confidential messages by courier or secret code, that plus the fact that telegraph messages could be intercepted by anyone who knew Morse code and how to tap into the wires. The telegraph was fast, but not always private.

When they reached the short road that veered off from the river road and led to the fort, they saw a crowd of civilians outside the palisade. "I reckon Alexander hasn't left yet," Joel remarked, "or else all those people wouldn't be hounding those poor sentries at the gate for information. They closed the fort to civilians, you know."

Judging from the harassed expressions on the pickets' faces, Cole imagined they were wishing they were behind the walls, too. It was pointless for the civilians to badger them. Even if the troopers knew, they weren't at liberty to divulge information.

When they had ridden a little further down the road, Cole asked Joel, "How long have you ridden shotgun for the steam company?"

"For about four years now. Worked as a cowhand before that, until some steer put his horn in my hip. Never did heal right. Cut up something awful anytime I spent a lot of time in the saddle. I tried riding shotgun for a stage company, but all that jostling and bouncing was just as bad. Then I found this job, where the ride is just as smooth as silk. Reckon I'll stay with it just as long as I can."

"Why do they have guards on steamboats?"

Jenny asked.

"Sometimes we carry a lot of money, and the bandits have been known to attack us, particularly down at that spot where the river makes a wide U-turn, about thirty-five miles above Brownsville. And then there have been times when they took potshots at us just for the hell of it."

"And you shot back?" Jenny asked.

"You're damn tooting I did, if you'll excuse my language."

"I've been thinking about something you said that I'd appreciate you clarifying for me," Cole said, changing the subject.

"What's that?"

"You said you thought McNelly read more into the Army's promise to give him support than the officers meant. What made you think that?"

"Well I didn't want to say anything in front of Wright. As far as I'm concerned, he's still an outsider, and this is Texas business, kinda personal."

"If this is confidential, I can drop back," Jenny offered. "I'm a Yankee, too."

"No, ma'am, that's not necessary. I was thinking more in the lines of Wright being so critical of everything and you don't strike me as being that way. You see, we Texans are kinda proud of our Rangers. For a long time, they were the only thing that stood between us and the Indians and the criminals, and a lot of times when they were out in the wilderness, they made their own justice, because they had to. They kinda got used to doing it that way, setting themselves above the law, but they

371

got results. Rangering and stepping out of line a little kinda go hand-and-hand, and we Texans accept that, but outsiders might not. I just didn't want to have to get defensive if Wright started getting critical."

Jenny smiled, thinking Texans were a lot like Irishmen. Even wrong, they defended their own. "I understand," she answered. "Please go on with your story."

Joel looked directly at Cole, saying, "McNelly got real thick with Lieutenant Kells, who commanded the U.S. gunboat, *Rio Bravo*. Kells was always spouting off about how he'd been sent down here to bring this thing to a head, which was a bunch of hogwash. Hell, he was only twenty years old, still green behind the ears. He was just a rabble-rouser and a glory seeker who harbored crazy dreams about launching a war of conquest on Mexico. He talked to everybody that would listen to him. He even cornered me one day. He proposed McNelly and his Rangers go into Mexico around the vicinity of Las Cuevas and open fire on his boat to make it look like the bandits were attacking him, thereby giving him the excuse to bombard them with his howitzers and cannons and thus bring on a war. Then the pipsqueak ran his boat onto a sandbar he'd been warned about by veteran rivermen and was relieved of his command."

"And you think McNelly was actually taking this Kells's proposition seriously?"

"I sure do. He and Kells ain't the first ones to dream of an empire across the border. That temptation has been teasing men's minds for well over a hundred years, starting with those who coveted Texas when it still belonged to Spain. And when Kells disappeared from the scene, I don't think McNelly gave up on it either. That's why he was so eager to jump in and volunteer to bring the cattle back. He wasn't interested in those cattle. He saw his opportunity to involve the Army in his scheme. Yep, I believe McNelly went into Mexico knowing full well he'd get himself in a fix and hoping the Army would come bail him out."

Cole strongly suspected Joel was correct. McNelly wasn't a foolish man, or a man that would endanger his men by attacking a force much larger than his own for a few stolen cattle. "I think you're right, Joel. He was gambling on a much bigger stake. And I think attacking that ranch by mistake was the only thing that saved his men. If he had attacked Las Cuevas, his force would have been massacred, with all the artillery the bandits have there."

"Yeah, and that's something I've been wondering about. How do you know so much about that hideout?"

Cole glanced at Jenny and knew he couldn't answer truthfully without giving himself away. Jenny saw how perplexed he looked and assumed Cole didn't want his old acquaintance to know he had become an outlaw. "Maybe I can answer that question, Joel," she said, having decided to rescue Cole from his predicament. "Cortinas' men took me hostage last spring when I was traveling to Brownsville, and Cortinas held me prisoner at his ranch. Amos hired Cole to rescue me, but it took a little while, since Cole didn't know just what ranch I was being held at. That's why I don't have appropriate riding apparel. I had to leave all my clothing behind when we escaped."

Not knowing the entire story, Joel wondered why Wright didn't just pay the ransom Cortinas was demanding. "Well, little lady, don't you fret over what you're wearing. I know several ranchwomen who dress just like you're dressed. It's the only practical way to ride a horse. And while we're on the subject, I've been meaning to compliment you on how well you ride."

"Thank you," Jenny replied with pleasure. "Cole taught me."

"Well, he did a good job of it." Joel directed his conversation once more to Cole, saying, "So that's how you know so much about Las Cuevas? You were nosing around looking for the little lady here."

"Yes," Cole answered, for lack of a better story.

"You were damn lucky you didn't get caught."

"Yes, I know."

"Well, I don't imagine you feel too kindly about those bandits, either," Joel remarked to Jenny.

"I certainly don't!" Jenny answered angrily. "I personally hope the Army *does* invade Mexico and gives them and the arrogant General the thrashing they deserve."

"Well, I agree with you, little lady. And I reckon every man, woman, and child in Texas does, too.

Those thieving bastards deserve punishing, if you'll forgive my language, and have for a good long while. How about you, Cole? Don't you agree?"

"I don't know, Joel. If it was a matter of going in, punishing the bandits, and coming back out, I'd say sure, since the Mexican government hasn't been able to control them. But I don't think it's all that simple. If McNelly's true intention is to incite war, then we've got an entirely different tiger by the tail."

"We fought the Mexicans before, and licked them," Joel pointed out. "Twice, for us Texans."

"That was a different Mexico, Joel. We aren't the only ones that fought a major war recently. They just beat the tar out of what was reputed to be the most powerful army in the world—Napoleon's. Europe is still reeling from the shock of it. I think we'd be making a gross error to underestimate them, like the French did."

Joel mused for a long moment over everything Cole said, then admitted reluctantly, "You might have a point there, particularly with Diaz at the helm. There's no telling how he will react."

"Then he was successful in overthrowing the government?" Cole asked in surprise.

"Yeah. You didn't know that?"

"No, I was down in Mexico for the better part of the last six months. Mexicans rarely talk about national politics. The government changes hands so often, it's hardly worth their taking note."

"Well, Diaz is in, and did it with very little fighting, too."

Cole saw Jenny looking back and forth as he and Joel talked. "I'm sorry," he apologized. "We didn't mean to leave you in the dark. We're talking about Porfirio Diaz. He was a powerful general during Mexico's war with France, noted for his fierce determination and savage fighting, which wasn't surprising. He's a full-blooded Indian. He's declared himself President of Mexico, and I personally don't think he's going to show any weakness, in this matter or any other. I definitely don't think it's the right time for our Army to be flexing their muscles."

Jenny had meant what she had said about the bandits and Cortinas needing a thrashing, but agreed that war was too high a price to pay. "I see. In that case, I hope whoever is making the decisions in this matter makes the right one."

"Amen," Joel muttered.

Since the three knew Major Alexander and his troopers would have to pass them on their way to Las Cuevas crossing, they didn't rush. When they came near to the place late that afternoon, they were detoured by sentries barring the road, and directed to an area about fifty yards from the road where the other sightseers had been curtailed. As they rode to the woods where the civilians waited, some standing on their wagon beds and peering at the river, others impatiently pacing, and some taking the opportunity in the lull of events to take a nap on the ground, Jenny noted that there were indeed a few women among them, even a few children.

"I'm surprised to see families here," Jenny remarked.

"The men wouldn't want to leave them at home alone, not with the Apaches on the warpath," Joel answered.

"But they left their homes unprotected," Jenny pointed out.

"Yep, but what's happening here is so important to them that they'll take that risk. What you're seeing ain't just the big ranchers and their cowhands, but the little ranchers, the farmers, the goatherders. Almost all of them have been hit at some time by the bandits. They've been waiting a long time for justice to be done."

"The Mexicans stole goats, too?" Jenny asked in surprise.

"They sure did. They might not be all that valuable, but the Mexicans have a real fondness for goat meat."

Cole reined in, stood in his stirrups, and peered out at the river, bringing Joel and Jenny to a halt also. Just barely, he could see the men on the river bank on the Mexican side, and since a good half of them wore blue, knew the calvary was still there with McNelly and his Rangers. He studied the line of thick brush above the bank, but could see no sign of the enemy. Then he directed his eyes to the American bank and saw an equal number of troopers there, as well as two Gatling gun batteries set up on the bank, their muzzles facing south.

"What do you see?" Joel asked.

"The Army is still over there," Cole answered. "Other than that, not much."

"The Mexicans have made several charges since noon," a man standing next to them informed them, "but they were repulsed. Rumor has it there are at least four-hundred Mexican troops over there, plus the bandits. I sure hope Alexander brings enough men with him to swing the odds in our favor."

Cole, who had kept his eyes peeled on the Mexican bank, said, "The Mexicans have raised a flag of truce."

Both Joel and Jenny strained their eyes to see, but neither had Cole's keen sight. Then Cole said, "That must be Randlett and McNelly going to meet the bearer."

"Damn, I wish I had your eyes," Joel said. "But mine ain't that good in broad daylight, and the light is fading pretty fast." When Cole remained silent for so long he asked impatiently, "What's going on?"

"Randlett took a piece of paper from the Mexican delegation, read it, and now he's talking to them." He paused for a long moment, then said, "Now McNelly is talking to them, and Randlett is walking back to the river."

The sound of hoofbeats in the distance caught everyone's attention. "Here comes Alexander!" someone in the crowd yelled.

By that time, the sun had slipped beneath the horizon, and it wasn't until the horsemen rode into the light from the campfires lit by the calvary that Cole could see the Major and his adjutant leading the column of troopers. "Don't look to me like he's got many men with him," Joel commented. "What would you guess, fifty or so?"

"Yes," Cole answered, "hardly an invasion force."

They watched as Major Alexander dismounted, walked to the river's edge, and yelled something across to the captain on the opposite bank.

"Could you hear what he said?" Jenny asked Cole.

"Yes. He ordered Randlett and his troopers back. Immediately!"

When it dawned on the spectators that the Army was retreating, a cry of furor was raised. Many cursed the soldiers, and wild threats were made. Alexander ordered pickets placed between the crowd and his troops and sent a spokesmen to inform the crowd that a truce had been agreed on until the morning, then urged the sightseers to go home.

But like almost everyone else, Cole, Jenny, and Joel didn't budge. They watched until the last soldier disembarked, although all they could see was the troopers climbing from the little Mexican canoe that had transported them back to the U.S. The Mexican side of the river and the river itself was obscured in darkness. Randlett and Alexander disappeared into a little tent that had been set up as a command post.

"Well, I guess McNelly and his men are staying,"

Joel remarked.

"Does that surprise you?" Cole asked.

"Nope."

Amos suddenly appeared beside them, saying angrily to Jenny, "I thought I told you to let me know as soon as you arrived."

It was Joel who answered, fabricating smoothly, "We did just arrive. They closed the road off, until Alexander left the fort."

Amos couldn't dispute him, since he had no idea if what he said was true or not. "Did you see what that damn Alexander did?" he asked Joel and Cole, completely ignoring Jenny. "He pulled the troops back. The sniveling coward!"

"It wasn't his decision," Cole answered in a hard voice. "He was following orders."

"The hell with orders!" Amos spat back. "If he was any man at all, he would have done what McNelly did, or tried to do, teach those bandits a lesson. And now, he's left the Rangers over there at the mercy of the Mexicans."

"There's a truce until tomorrow morning," Joel pointed out.

"Since when do Mexicans honor truces, particularly bandits?" Amos countered.

It was a point that neither Joel or Cole could dispute. The bandits were notorious for breaking their word. "Well, the Army is sticking around, aren't they?" Joel pointed out. "That ought to make them think twice."

"And if you're really worried about the Rangers, you can go over and give them a hand," Cole suggested.

"That isn't my job!"

"Well, if it isn't yours, and it isn't the Army's, then whose job is it?" Cole asked.

It was one of those questions to which there was no answer, and Amos knew it. He glared at Cole furiously for a moment, then wheeled his horse, saying, "We've pitched camp this way."

Much later that night, Jenny lay on the cot in the tent and half-heartedly listened to a conversation between Joel and Cole from where they sat, away from Amos and the others, just a few feet from her tent. Most of the conversation concerned old acquaintances and, therefore, held little interest for her. Then, after a lull, she heard Cole say, "I've made a decision, Joel. If the Mexicans break their truce tonight and attack the Rangers, I'm going over there."

"Why are you gonna do that? I thought you didn't approve of what McNelly is doing?"

"I didn't approve of his trying to incite war, but I think he knows by now that idea has bit the dust. There's only one reason I can figure he's still over there, to show the bandits he means business. That may not have been his original intention, but I think that's his purpose now. He's trying to salvage something out of that mess. He's making a stand for Texas, for what's right, and I can't stand back and watch him and his men massacred."

"Yeah, but you ain't gonna stop it either."

"I know it would be suicide, but I feel like I have to do it."

There was a long pause before Joel said, "You know, I never could figure out how come those fellas from Gonzales went to the aid of the Alamo there at the end. They had to know by then it was suicide. It was already surrounded by thousands of Mexicans. I guess they must have been like you. They just couldn't turn their backs on them, act like they weren't there. A man has to live with his conscience." Again, Joel paused, then said in an ominous voice, "I'll go with you."

Jenny's heart raced with fear. She didn't sleep a wink the entire night. She cursed Cole, knowing in her heart that if she went to him and begged him not to go, he wouldn't listen. He was a noble fool, just like her father. Then she did something she hadn't done for a long, long, time. She prayed. She prayed with her whole heart and soul that the Mexicans would keep their word — and spare the life of the man she loved.

Twenty-six

Jenny's prayers were answered, at least throughout the night. At dawn the sun rose over the grey-green river valley, and the truce flag still flew between the Mexicans in the brush and the Rangers on the river bank. Feeling a little more secure in the light of day, Jenny took the opportunity to catch a few hours of much-needed sleep before the mid-morning deadline that signaled the end of the truce, or so she had planned. She overslept by several hours and, realizing what she had done, rushed from the tent without even putting on her boots.

She found Cole and Joel sitting alone beside the fire and drinking coffee. Before they even noticed her, she asked, "What's going on down at the river?"

Joel turned, a big grin crossing his freckled face before he answered, "Morning, ma'am."

Before Jenny could respond, Cole commented, "It's more like good afternoon." He gave her a piercing look, then said, "I've never known you to sleep so late. I was afraid you might be ill."

"No, I had trouble going to sleep last night," Jenny answered, then hoped he wouldn't ask why.

"Probably too much excitement," Joel contributed. He looked down at Jenny's tiny bare feet and said, "I wouldn't go barefooted around here, if I were you. There are a lot of rocks laying around that scorpions like to hide under."

Jenny frowned. That was one of the first things Cole had taught her, never walk around without your shoes, and always shake them out before putting them on. "I forgot. I was in a hurry to find out what was happening."

Cole rose and came to his impressive height in a long fluid motion that looked so graceful to Jenny it took her breath away. "There's nothing going on," he informed her, tossing out the coffee dregs from the bottom of his cup. "What we've got out there is a true Mexican standoff." He picked up the coffeepot and poured the dark liquid in the cup, then handed it to her, saying, "Have a cup of coffee. I'll get your boots for you."

As Cole walked away, Jenny took a sip and then made a face.

Joel laughed, saying, "I reckon Cole should have warned you that stuff is strong enough to walk on. It's been on the fire since dawn."

"Well, I like strong coffee, but this is a little too strong," Jenny admitted, tossing the coffee out. She looked around. "Where did everyone else go?"

"Oh, about a hour ago a rider came flying in from Ringgold. I imagine he was bringing a telegram for the Major. Everyone here ran down to the camp to see if they could find out anything, but the Army still has its pickets out and are keeping everyone away. We did hear some news this morning, though. McNelly sent his horses back during the night and came over to the north bank himself to make arrangements to have coffee and food delivered by that Mexican with the canoe. Then he had his men dig a long trench a little further down the river, where the bank isn't so high. It doesn't look like he's aiming on going anywhere."

"How long can this stalemate continue?"

"Who knows? Maybe he's hoping if he sits there long enough the Army will change its mind."

Cole walked up and handed Jenny her boots. As Jenny sat on a nearby log and started pulling on her socks, another group of riders coming from the direction of the fort were heard. Joel came to his feet, and both he and Cole watched as the party approached the army camp, noting that there was a civilian with the troopers.

"I know that man," Joel commented. "He's Lewis Avery, Commercial Agent at Camargo."

"Commercial Agent? Isn't that some kind of consular title?" Cole asked.

"Yep. Hell, now the diplomatic corps is in on this. It's getting serious if the State Department has been called in."

They watched in silence as the troopers wrestled the crowd to clear the way for Avery. When the man disappeared in the command tent, Cole said, "After Jenny has a bite to eat, let's go over there.

Maybe we can get wind of what's going on from someone."

A little later, Cole, Jenny, and Joel walked to the encampment. The cavalry had strung a crude rope fence to mark its perimeters, but sentries still had to patrol it to keep the curious civilians out. As Cole studied the Mexican bank from where they stood in the crowd, Jenny, who couldn't see a thing over the men standing in front of her, asked, "Can you see the Rangers?"

"Yes. They've entrenched themselves, just like we were told."

"Hey, look!" Joel said excitedly. "Avery's being taken over to them."

Jenny craned her neck, but still couldn't see anything. She waited as patiently as she could, then asked, "What's happening now?"

"Avery is talking to McNelly," Cole answered. "Now he's handing McNelly a paper. It looks like it might be a telegram."

The crowd around them had become quiet, also listening to what Cole said, since the majority of those men didn't have his keen eyesight either.

"They seem to be arguing," Cole said after a few minutes.

Jenny waited, and waited; then someone to the left of them yelled, "He's coming back!"

"Who? McNelly or Avery?" Jenny asked, fervently wishing she had a stool to stand upon.

"Avery," Cole answered. He turned, encircled Jenny's tiny waist with his hands, and lifted Jenny up in the air, so she could see.

"Avery doesn't look very happy," Cole commented, from where he was peering around her.

Jenny could barely see the canoe with the two men, much less Avery's face. Then she started when she heard an angry voice, asking, "What in the hell do you think you're doing?"

Jenny glanced down and saw Amos, his face beet-red with fury.

"I'm holding her up so she can see what's going on," Cole answered in a deceptively calm voice.

"Put her down this instant!"

"Maybe she's not through looking yet," Cole answered between clenched teeth.

Jenny was aware of everyone in the crowd looking at them. A flush of mortification rose on her face. "No, I've seen enough. Put me down."

As Cole lowered her to the ground, Amos caught her arm and jerked her to his side, saying furiously to Cole, "Don't you ever touch her again!"

Cole didn't like the rough way Amos was handling Jenny. "That's up to her, not you. And watch how *you* handle her!"

Amos was so angry he didn't even notice the murderous gleam in Cole's eyes. "No, it is up to me! She's my fiancée, and you're in my employ. Now, keep away from her! That's an order!"

Cole had had all he could take of the arrogant carpetbagger. "And if I refuse?"

"Then you're fired!"

"That's fine with me," Cole ground out.

It was then that Amos took note of the angry glitter in Cole's golden eyes. A shiver of fear ran over Amos when he realized how close he had come to dying. The gunman looked like he wanted to tear him apart with his bare hands. Amos stepped back, putting distance between them, then forced his own anger down before saying, "We'll settle up what I owe you when we get back to town."

Still holding Jenny's arm tightly in his hand, Amos turned and hurried away, shouldering his way through the crowd.

Joel issued a low whistle, then said to Cole, "For a minute there, I thought that son-of-a-bitch was a dead man. You had one hell of a mean look on your face. Remind me never to cross you."

"I shouldn't have let my anger get the better of me," Cole replied. "Now I don't have any excuse to be around her."

"Hell, she ain't married to him yet. You said yourself, it's up to her, not him."

Cole didn't tell Joel *that* was the problem, that it was Jenny's resistance holding him back more than Amos's. And another element had come into play. Time was running out. "Yeah," Cole answered half-heartedly.

As the day wore on and nothing happened, the crowd on the river bank became more and more impatient. Some people became verbally abusive to the sentries, calling them insulting names and demanding information. Amos was the worst offender.

Cole and Joel stood a little to the rear and watched in disgust as the carpetbagger hounded a sentry, first wheedling, then trying to bribe the man, and finally saying, angrily, "I demand to talk Major Alexander. Immediately!"

"I'm sorry, sir. The major is seeing no one."

"Do you know who I am?" Amos demanded, sticking his face into the hapless trooper's face. "I'm Amos Wright! Not only do I own one of the largest ranches in this area, but I have important contacts in Washington. If you know what's good for you, you'd damn better let me see your commanding officer. Now!"

From where he stood before the command tent, the major's adjutant walked up to the sentry and Amos and said to the rancher, "Move back, sir. You've crossed the line."

"Who do you think you're talking to, Lieutenant?" Amos demanded.

The lieutenant didn't even flinch. "I'm talking to you, sir."

"Do you know who I am?" Amos asked in a haughty voice.

"No, sir, and I don't care to. Now, step back, before I have to arrest you."

"Arrest me?" Amos thundered indignantly.

"Yes, sir. This area is a designated army post and off limits to civilians at the present time."

"What about that man who rode in earlier?" Amos argued. "He's a civilian."

"He's here on official government business. Now, step back."

As the lieutenant pushed Amos back, he noticed Cole standing a few feet away and said to him, "Excuse me, Mr. Benteen. I didn't see you standing there." Motioning with his arm, he said to those standing in front of Cole, "Clear the way for this man."

Cole realized the officer thought he was there in an official capacity, but before he could respond, Amos spat, "What the hell! Why are you letting him in?"

"He's here on official business for the Governor."

"You've got rocks in your head if you think that." Amos pointed an accusing finger at Cole, saying angrily, "That man is an outlaw, a bank robber and thief. There are wanted posters out all over the state for him. He's the one you should arrest."

"You are mistaken, Mister Wright," the adjutant informed Amos in a tone of voice that brooked no argument. "Mr. Benteen is no longer a wanted man. He has been completely vindicated of all the charges brought against him and is currently an agent working for the governor of Texas."

"Vindicated?" Amos asked in surprise. "When in the hell did that happen?"

"Last spring." The lieutenant's hand moved to the pistol at his side. "Now, move aside."

Cole had been watching Jenny during the exchange and had seen the fleeting expressions on her face, first shock, then hurt, and finally anger when she realized he had lied to her. He cursed the Lieutenant silently for giving him away, then remembered that he had said himself that it was no longer necessary to keep his true identity or his mission secret. The poor adjutant had no way of knowing he was still pretending to be an outlaw for personal reasons.

Amos moved aside and glared at Cole. Cole realized the damage had been done, and this was neither the time nor place to try to repair it. Since he was just as curious as anyone else, he decided to play along with the adjutant. "I'll see you later," he muttered to Joel, who was staring at him in astonishment, then walked through the path that had been cleared for him.

As soon as they were away from the picket line, the lieutenant said to Cole, "I'm sorry about that nasty incident, sir. I suppose you want to see Major Alexander."

"That would be nice," Cole replied noncommittally.

The Lieutenant took Cole to the command tent where he found Major Alexander alone, sitting behind a makeshift desk, looking haggard and very worried. After the Major had dismissed his adjutant, Cole said to him, "I'm afraid I'm here on false pretenses, Major. I'm no longer working for Governor Coke. I finished my assignment when I turned my report over to you. Your adjutant saw me in the crowd, assumed I was here on official business, and let me in. I'm here because I want to know what's going on."

An angry look came over the Major's face. He started to rise from his chair, but before he could say anything, Cole said, "I wouldn't have tried this with anyone else, but I figured after that conversation we had back at Ringgold the day I reported in, you'd be honest with me, like you were that day, man-to-man, without the hindrance of formality or rules."

Major Alexander realized he had spilled his guts that day and taking the role of an outraged officer now would make him look stupid and hypocritical. He sat back down and answered wearily, "Sit down, Mr. Benteen. To be perfectly honest, I could use someone to just talk to right now. Actually what's going on isn't all that confidential. It's just that I don't know how it would affect that crowd out there. I feel like I'm sitting on a powder keg with them, as well as that situation across the river."

"In other words, you have news you don't think they're going to like?"

"Precisely. I know they're hoping that the Army will still give the Rangers support, if nothing else from this side of the river with our artillery. But that is not going to happen. This morning I received a telegram from Colonel Potter telling me to advise McNelly to return to this side of the river and to inform him that I was not to support him in any way while he remained in Mexico. My orders explicitly say that if McNelly is attacked by Mexican forces while on Mexican soil, I am *not* to render him any assistance."

"That's going to be hard to do, isn't it? Sit right here and watch his command annihilated?"

The color drained from the Major's face. "Yes, it

will be very difficult, but that's precisely what I'll do, what I've been ordered to do."

Cole didn't envy the Major his position. Being a good officer was never easy — he knew that from his own experiences in the late war — but it seemed to him this officer was being severely put to the test, particularly in view of the fact that he knew the Major's true feelings. "I assume McNelly knows this and still refuses to retreat."

"He does. I showed him the telegram. He has also informed his men of my orders and given them the option of staying or leaving. They chose to stay, to the man."

Cole remembered what Joel had said about the Alamo, and thought this, too, sounded familiar. "What was Avery doing here?"

"The State Department has made arrangements with the Mexican government for McNelly's surrender. Naturally, they want to get him and his men out of Mexico in one piece. Avery had a telegram from the American consul at Matamoros instructing him to go to McNelly and advise him to surrender to the Mexican federal authorities who have been sent to the scene. Avery was to go along with the group to make sure nothing happened to the Rangers on the way to Matamoros. McNelly turned Avery down cold."

Cole wasn't surprised. "So he won't retreat and he won't surrender?"

"Not until he gets those blasted cows back and the thieves that took them. That's what he's demanding of the Mexicans." Alexander paused for a moment, then exclaimed in utter exasperation, "I can't believe what that man is doing! Before I arrived, Captain Randlett agreed with the Mexican officials to withdraw and then discuss the matter, but McNelly refused to accept those terms. He's setting his own terms. Not the Army, not the State Department, but one stubborn man is running this show. The rest of us are completely at his mercy. Do you know that he even had the audacity to tell the Mexicans he would give them an hour's notice before he commenced operations—an hour to prepare to defend themselves against thirty Rangers! My God, he's outnumbered at least fifteen to one! And the Mexicans have repeating Winchesters. He's sitting over there with singleshot buffalo guns. God, I wish I had the authority to order him back!"

Cole didn't comment. He knew the Major was just airing his frustrations. He wondered if McNelly's superiors knew what was going on, for a Ranger captain was given a lot of leeway for making decisions while operating in the field, but they were eventually answerable to their senior officers.

At that minute, the adjutant rushed into the tent, saying, "McNelly just sent word that he's given the Mexicans an hour to accept his demands, or he'll advance."

"My God! He actually did it!" Major Alexander said in a rush of words, then jumped to his feet and hurried from the tent, followed by Cole.

As they rapidly walked to the river, Cole thought the Major was not only sitting on a powder keg, but a powder keg with the fuse lit and burning, and he knew by the grim expression on the officer's face that he was well aware of that fact. When they reached the water's edge, Alexander and Cole stood and peered across, noting there was very little activity going on in the trench, but a great deal happening in the Mexican line of defense. Then several Mexican officials walked across the small field where the truce flag was still flying, and McNelly walked out to meet them.

"What do you suppose they're talking about?" Alexander asked Cole.

"The Mexicans might be trying some more delaying tactics," Cole suggested. "They're experts at that."

They watched as McNelly and the Mexican officials turned and walked back to their respective lines. Then McNelly motioned for the canoe to be brought across to him, before saying something to his men in the trench.

Everyone watched anxiously as McNelly and three of his men were poled back across the river, two of the Rangers bailing water from the leaky boat the entire trip. When the canoe grounded on the muddy bank, the frail-looking Captain stepped from it, his bearded face as expressionless as a stone wall. Then when Major Alexander walked up to him, the Ranger Captain drawled as casually as if he was giving a routine weather report, "The Mexican officials have agreed to deliver to me the stolen cattle and as many of the thieves as they can catch, tomorrow morning at ten, in Rio Grande

City. I accepted their promise and am withdrawing my men."

Everyone listening—the officers, Avery, Cole, any troopers within hearing distance—breathed an audible sigh of relief. Major Alexander congratulated McNelly, albeit rather stiffly, then turned to his adjutant and said, "Tell that crowd to disperse. The cattle and the Rangers are coming home. It's over!"

As soon as the unexpected news was announced, a loud cheer rang out, accompanied by a few gunshots in the air and a lot of back-slapping. McNelly had won an amazing victory, one which had no precedent. It would be the first time stolen cattle would be returned by the Mexicans. Before that it had always been a one-way trip for Texas beef. Then, because the sun would be setting in a few hours, the crowd quickly broke up, the majority of the spectators heading either for their homes or Rio Grande City.

When Cole walked from the camp, Amos was waiting for him. Without preamble, the rancher demanded, "Was that information the Lieutenant divulged true? You're an agent for the Governor?"

"I was, but I'm not now. I did an investigation on bandit activity for him."

"Why in the hell didn't you tell me?" Amos demanded.

"Because when you first approached me at Bagdad, I wasn't at liberty to. I was on the job at the time and using my reputation as an outlaw for my cover. When I delivered Jenny to you, I saw no purpose in telling you. You were hiring my gun, not me. Being vindicated of all the crimes I was falsely accused of didn't change my marksmanship."

"Then you were working for the Governor when you rescued Jenny?" Amos asked, a suspicious gleam in his eyes.

"I wasn't looking for her. I'll admit that. I had an investigation to make. I just happened upon her. By the time we made our escape, I had finished my investigation. I could hardly leave her to her fate." Cole had been very careful to keep his answers truthful, yet evasive, more to protect Jenny than anything. He felt it was her place to inform Amos why she hadn't told him the truth of her escape. "Look, if you don't think I earned that money for bringing Jenny out of Mexico, just say so."

A small crowd had gathered around Cole and Amos almost as soon as Cole had walked from the Army camp. Some of the men listening had ranches or businesses in the area, and Amos didn't want to appear to be a man who didn't keep his end of a bargain, not if he was going to be running for office. "No, of course not. Even if I hadn't known the young lady personally, I would have posted the reward for her return. Any God-fearing Christian would have."

Cole knew Amos was playing politics. It disgusted him. "Well, that's mighty wide of you," he answered sarcastically. "Now, why don't we ride into town, and you can pay me the rest of what you owe me."

Amos gave Cole an angry look, then smiled tightly and answered, "Of course. I'll be at the hotel, if I arrive there before you do."

Amos turned and walked to where Jenny and his gunslingers were waiting, already mounted, a short distance away. As they rode off, Jenny shot Cole a furious glance that told him she hadn't forgiven him for deceiving her.

Joel was one of those who had listened to the exchange between Amos and Cole and witnessed Jenny's look. When the other men walked away, he remarked to Cole, "I don't think I've ever seen a female look as furious as that little gal did, like she could skin you alive with her bare nails."

"She didn't know the truth, either," Cole informed Joel. "She thought I was an outlaw still on the run."

"Is that why you didn't tell me about you working for the Governor, 'cause she was standing there?"

"Yes. Believe it or not, I had my reasons for deceiving her."

Joel pulled their horses forward and handed Cole his reins, saying, "Well, I sure hope they were good reasons. Otherwise you can kiss any hopes of winning that little gal goodbye."

Cole frowned, wondering if his reasons were going to be good enough. Damn, he'd never known working to win a woman could be so difficult.

The sun was casting long shadows on the dusty main street when Cole and Amos rode into Rio Grande City. The news of the Rangers' success had preceded them, and a boisterous celebration was going on in every saloon and had spilled into the street itself.

After the two men had finally managed to thread their way across the street to the hitching post in front of the hotel, Joel said to Cole, "Wright must have sent his men off someplace. I don't see any sign of them in this crowd." He started at the sound of a gunshot, then turned in his saddle and glared at the drunk taking potshots at a hapless chicken down the street. "Damn fool!" he muttered, then turned and said to Cole, "You go on in and take care of your business with Wright. I'll stay out here and make sure no one stampedes our horses."

Cole dismounted and walked into the hotel. Joel waited in the street, turning down several friendly offers to have a swig from someone's bottle before Cole returned. When Cole walked from the hotel, Joel asked. "Well? Did Wright give you any trouble?"

"No, he had it ready for me. Just handed me this sack of gold coins without a word. Of course, the look he gave me could have killed. Now he's in there promising to buy everyone drinks and trying to bribe the desk clerk for a couple of rooms for him and Jenny."

"Did you count the money? I wouldn't put it

past him to cheat you."

"No, but I did look in the sack. They're twenty dollar gold pieces, and it feels heavy enough. He must have been carrying it in a money belt on his person to produce it that fast."

"Well, how about getting it out of sight? No use advertising it with all this riff-raff around." Then a thought came to Joel. "Which reminds me. You're not hauling around that money Amos paid you for rescuing Jenny, are you?"

"Ten thousand dollars?" Cole asked incredulously. "Do you think I'm crazy? No, I had him write me a draft for a bank in Fort Worth."

Cole stepped down from the boardwalk and slipped the sack of money into his saddlebags. Then he glanced around him, asking, "Have you seen Jenny?"

"Nope."

"Well, I guess she's somewhere in that crowd in the hotel, after all. Do you mind waiting a bit longer? I need to talk to her."

"No, go ahead," Joel grumbled. "As far as I know, my evening's free."

Cole chuckled, saying, "I won't be *that* long."

Cole walked back into the crowded hotel. After seeing no sign of Jenny in the small lobby, he walked back into the dining room and scanned the area. He saw Amos at the back of the room, talking to someone, then spied Jenny sitting at a table there, almost obscured from view by a coat rack on which several of the ranchers had hung their hats, along with a few of the waiters' aprons. He watched while Amos handed her a key, then stepped behind a couple of men waiting for a table while Amos walked towards the door, then past him.

As soon as Amos had stepped outside with a group of men he had promised to buy drinks for, Cole weaved his way around the dining tables to where Jenny was just rising.

Jenny saw him coming, and had her path been clear, would have run. His deception seemed a terrible betrayal. If he had lied about himself, what else had he lied about? Had their entire relationship been nothing but a sham, the relationship she had thought so open, so beautiful that she had placed the memories of it in the treasure chest of her heart? She felt a complete fool. Because she had thought they were so much alike, she had bared her soul to him, as well as her body, and he had been lying the entire time. Lying, and probably laughing up his sleeve.

Cole came to a stop before Jenny. Jenny drew herself up to her full height, raised her chin proudly, and glared at him, determined she wouldn't give him the satisfaction of saying one word or let him know how much he had hurt her.

"Jenny, I'm sorry you found out the truth the way you did, but I had reasons," Cole said softly. "I need to talk to you. I want to explain."

The hurt and fury came boiling to the surface like lava in a volcano. "You bastard! You lied to me!" Jenny hissed, her blue eyes blazing. "I was completely honest with you. I told you everything

401

about myself; I told you things I had never told anyone. I hid nothing." Tears glittered in her eyes. "I trusted you! But you deceived me."

"I never meant to hurt you, Jenny. Never! That's why I need to explain." Cole looked around him, then said, "But not here. Somewhere private. Meet me later tonight."

"No, I won't!" Jenny answered adamantly, doubly furious because she had almost broken down in front of him. "I don't want to hear your explanations. I don't ever want to see you again!"

Although Jenny had striven to keep her voice down, some of the diners were beginning to take notice. Seeing them staring at her, a flush rose on her face. "You're making a scene and embarrassing me," Jenny whispered. "Now, step aside."

"No, I won't, Jenny. Not until you promise to meet me."

Jenny knew Cole meant what he said. He'd stand there until doomsday, if need be. He could be unbelievably obdurate when he set his mind to it. She glanced around and saw there was no other avenue for escape, then agreed angrily, "All right! Where?"

"I'll meet you at the foot of the back stairs at nine tonight."

Jenny nodded her head curtly, having absolutely no intention of keeping the meeting. She could play at deception just as well as he did, she thought, or better.

Cole suspected what Jenny was planning. "Don't back out on me, Jenny. If you do, I'll really create a scene. I'll stand in the hallway outside your door and shout everything for God and all mankind to hear. I'm going to have my say, no matter what."

Jenny knew Cole was not a man to make idle threats. He'd humiliate her and himself, if that's what it took to attain his goal. And she could just imagine what Amos's reaction to that spectacle would be. Damn Cole! He'd outmaneuvered her again.

"I'll be there," she answered tightly.

Cole moved aside, and Jenny hurried away, furious and dangerously close to tears.

Twenty-seven

Cole was waiting at the bottom of the stairs behind the hotel at the specified time, occasionally wincing at the loud noises coming from the main street on the other side of the hotel. The celebration had progressed into a wild, drunken free-for-all, with dancing in the streets, fist fights, horse races, and shooting matches. Ironically, since the local cowhands had left for their ranches, those doing the most celebrating were the criminals who had drifted in from the brush — the very men the Rangers would be chasing if they weren't so occupied with the bandits — which made the situation all the more dangerous. Even sober, the outlaws were a mean, unpredictable lot.

When ten minutes passed and Jenny didn't appear, Cole started up the stairs, grim-lipped and determined. He was on the fourth stair from the bottom when the door at the top of the landing opened. In the feeble light of the stars, he saw a figure step outside, and for a moment thought it must be one of the Mexican maids, because of the woman's dress and the shawl wrapped around her head and shoulders to ward off the chill of the November night air. Then as the woman descended the stairs, he saw how pale her face was and knew it was Jenny.

When Jenny reached him, Cole commented, "I didn't recognize you at first in those clothes."

Jenny had changed into her Mexican clothing for that very reason, thinking she would look just like any other Mexican woman with the *rebozo* Rosa had given her to cover her light hair. "Good!" she replied coldly. "Hopefully no one else will recognize me, either, while we're standing out here. Now, say what you have to say, and get it over with. I plan to retire early tonight."

"I'm not going to talk to you here. I said someplace private."

"This is private enough."

"The hell it is! People go up and down these stairs all night long, to say nothing of the risk of us getting shot by a wild bullet with all these crazy drunks running amuck." Cole took her arm firmly in his hand and said, "Come on. We'll go down to Joel's place. It's quieter and safer down there."

Jenny didn't trust herself to be alone with Cole. Nor did she trust him. "No!" she answered adamantly. "You say what you have to say right here."

"What I have to say is going to take some time, and where I'm going to say it is at Joel's place. Now, you can either come along quietly by your own steam, or I'll carry you there."

"I'll scream!" Jenny threatened.

"Go ahead," Cole answered calmly. "Who do you think is going to hear you over all that racket out there? And even if they do hear you and come to your aid, what are you going to tell them? That you agreed to meet me out here, then changed your mind? Amos is going to love that."

"You bastard! You're blackmailing me!"

"No, Jenny, all I want is the opportunity to explain. Is that really asking too much? The chance to tell my side of the story?" When Jenny maintained her silence, Cole said, "I gave you credit for being a lot more fair than you are. I didn't think you'd sentence and hang me without even giving me a trial."

Cole's appeal to Jenny's sense of fairness worked. "All right," she relented. "I'll go with you. But you'd better not try anything!"

Cole made no promises, a point that Jenny noticed and that added to her unease. He led her to the river by the back way to avoid the mayhem taking place in the streets, the loud sounds fading as they put distance between them and the revelers. As they passed through the Mexican part of town, Jenny noted that there wasn't any celebrating going on there. Not a soul was out; the doors of every home were closed tight, and there wasn't a light to be seen. Jenny had been in Texas long enough to know why. The Mexicans were going to great lengths to avoid bringing attention to themselves, for fear the liquor-crazed *gringos* would use them for target practice.

When Jenny and Cole stepped into the warehouse, Jenny looked around in the light coming from the kerosene lamp on the dresser, then asked, "Where's Joel?"

"He's gone upriver with the rest of the steamboat crew to bring the boat back down at first light tomorrow morning. They're planning on starting their run to Brownsville as early as possible, so they won't be in the way when the Mexicans deliver the stolen cattle to McNelly."

Cole walked to Joel's 'quarters,' saying, "Come over here, where it's warmer. I lit the stove to get the damp chill from the river out of the air." He motioned to the bed, saying, "Make yourself comfortable."

"No, thank you," Jenny said tightly. "I'll just sit on that barrel again." She glanced around her, then asked, "Where is it?"

"The cook for the steamer took it. It contained lard."

"Then I'll just stand."

Cole knew Jenny feared he was going to make sexual overtures. He shook his head, saying, "You have a suspicious mind, Jenny."

"Not suspicious enough," Jenny tossed back, thinking how she had let him fool her.

Cole jerked a blanket from the bed, folded it double, then placed it on the floor in front of the stove. "Is that an acceptable chair? This is going to take awhile."

"That will do, thank you," Jenny replied stiffly, then walked to the blanket and sat, primly tucking her skirts around her legs, then pushing the shawl back from her head.

Jenny had let her hair hang loose and it looked like a glittering silken waterfall hanging on both sides of her face in the lamplight. Cole's eyes caressed it before he said softly, "You have the most beautiful hair."

The husky tone of his voice and the warm look of admiration on his face made Jenny feel weak and trembly. "We didn't come here to discuss my hair!" she answered, the alarming feelings he was arousing making her voice unnecessarily sharp.

"No, we didn't," Cole agreed. "I'm sorry. I didn't mean to get distracted." He sat on the side of the bed, stared at her for a moment, then said, "Now that I have you here, I don't know where to begin. I guess the best place to start is how I came to be a wanted man. Do you remember me telling you about going to live with my uncle in East Texas after my parents died?" Jenny nodded. "Well, he grew cotton."

That's where she had gotten the idea Cole came from farm stock, Jenny realized. Cole had said something about losing the land.

Cole continued. "When I came back from the war, the Federal government confiscated all the cotton that had been raised and set aside for the Confederacy. The men that grew it were supposed to be paid a portion of its worth, since they'd never been paid by the Confederate government; however, there were a lot of crooked Federal cotton agents that pocketed the full amount from the sales, then filed false reports. That's what happened to my uncle. The agent took the cotton, sold it, but never gave my uncle a penny. Then the agent had the audacity to come back and claim some of the cotton my uncle grew after the war was Confederate. My uncle was furious when the agent showed up with his wagons to cart the cotton away. He called him a thief and bastard and threatened to get his gun. When he turned to go into the house, the agent pulled his gun and aimed it at my uncle's back. As soon as I saw the man going for his gun, I pulled mine and shot. I was hoping to beat him to the draw, and keep him from harming my uncle, but his bullet got off before mine hit him. I didn't think I had aimed to kill, but I did. After so many years in the war, shooting for keeps just came automatically. When it was over, both he and my uncle were dead."

"And you became a hunted man?" Jenny interjected.

"No, not then. I turned myself in to the local sheriff and went on trial. My lawyer maintained the agent was trespassing with the intent to steal, meant to kill my uncle in cold blood, and that I was trying to protect my home and family. The jury found me not guilty, but the military commander of that district overruled them, saying they didn't have jurisdiction in my case, since the victim was a Federal Treasury Agent. I knew I didn't have a chance in hell with military trying my case. They were sending people to prison right and left who had done much less than I had. I didn't wait for them to come get me. I fled. That's when I became a hunted man."

Cole paused for a moment, then said, "At first, it wasn't so bad. I found odd jobs here and there. I even got a job with the Army as a scout for a few months, using an alias. Then Davis became Governor and set up his state police force. The man I had killed had been a personal friend of his, and he came after me with a vengeance. Hell, practically every crime in South or West Texas was placed at my feet, some hundreds of miles apart on the same day. But they didn't care if their claims were ludicrous. They had the entire state in a vise. No one dared to defy them. Justice was totally non-existent."

Cole continued. "I was with that crowd that marched on the state capitol when Davis refused to give up the governorship. I held one of the ladders while the legislators, who had been locked out of the capitol building by Davis, climbed in through a second floor window, so they could get on with the business they had been elected to. I helped stand guard with some old Ranger friends while Coke was inaugurated."

"But wasn't that dangerous?" Jenny interrupted.

"What if someone had recognized you?"

"A lot of men *did* recognize me," Cole admitted, "old friends and acquaintances, men I had served with during the war. They weren't a threat to me. They were just as determined as I was to see the end of the reign of terror and Coke in his rightful place. Coke recognized me, too. He and my uncle had been good friends. He knew my entire story, and more important, he knew only too well how biased the military had been during the Reconstruction. He'd been a justice of the Supreme Court of Texas until General Sheridan had him removed as an impediment to Reconstruction. Coke was determined to set things to right, not only in my case, but in many others. There were a lot of Texans who had been victims of injustice. He had all the false charges dropped against me and upheld the civil jury's verdict. He wiped the slate clean for me, so I couldn't refuse when he asked me to do a secret investigation on the bandits for him, even though I was sick to death of running and hiding and living among criminals. I was the perfect candidate, since I was still considered an outlaw in these parts, the man least likely to come under suspicion. That's why I lied to you Jenny, to protect myself. And until my mission was completed, I wasn't at liberty to reveal the truth. That didn't happen until we reached Texas and I sent in my report."

"All right, so you had good reason not to tell

me at first," Jenny conceded, "but why didn't you tell me then?"

"Because by then I had fallen in love with you. Not the woman Amos thought you were, but the real Jenny, the Jenny you're afraid to show him because you don't think he'll want you. But I want you, Jenny, just the way you are, with all your strengths and all your faults. And I wanted you to love me just as strongly, just as unconditionally, to accept and love me at my worst. And being an outlaw, a hunted man was my worst. That was important to me, Jenny. That you'd love me regardless of who I was, or wasn't."

Jenny knew that was how her mother had loved her father, unconditionally, regardless of who he was. It was a pure love, untainted by selfishness, one that came from the heart and the soul, a total giving that knew no restraint and had no boundaries. And she was just like her mother. She had fought tooth and toenail against loving a man so totally, so completely, but she was as helpless as her mother had been. It seemed they both had a weakness for big, good-looking, smooth-talking, noble bastards who could break their hearts.

Cole knew by the expression on Jenny's face that her feelings towards him had softened. He rose from the bed, then knelt on the blanket in front of her, saying softly, "I love you, Jenny. I didn't want it to happen, either, but it did. Some things were just meant to be; they're written in the stars. And in my heart, I know you love me, too."

Jenny opened her mouth to deny it, but the words wouldn't come. She shook her head, desperately fighting the tears that were gathering in her eyes. Cole caught her shoulders in his hands and shook her lightly, pleading, "Say you love me." When Jenny remained silent, Cole demanded, "Dammit, say it!"

Jenny could no longer hold back the words or the emotion. They came from her in a flood, as if a dam had burst. "All right! I love you!" Then the tears came, streaming down her cheeks. "Damn you!" she sobbed. "Are you happy now?"

Cole smiled, a smile so warm and loving it wrenched her heart. "Yes, I'm the happiest man on earth."

He sat down beside her, cupped her face in his hands, and kissed away the tears on her cheeks and eyelashes, then nibbled at her lips, teasing, softly playing, until Jenny was trembling for want of his warm, mobile mouth on hers. Finally he kissed her, at first achingly sweet as he told her of his love, then masterfully and deeply as he told her of his passion for her. And Jenny answered him fervently, kissing him back with equal passion, her tongue performing an erotic dance around his.

Cole cupped her breast in his hand and teased the nipple with his thumb through the material of her clothes, making it harden and rise, just as his flesh was doing. His mouth left hers to nuzzle the length of her throat, then kiss the frantic pulse beat at the base, before moving lower. Pushing her blouse and chemise strap from her shoulder, he bared the breast he been caressing. His tongue swirled around the creamy mound before his lips closed over the sensitive peak and his mouth hungrily tugged at it, bringing a moan of delight from Jenny.

Jenny's other breast ached with longing, jealous of its mate. When Cole tugged her blouse loose from her skirt, Jenny eagerly helped him strip the blouse and chemise from her. Cole nuzzled the warm valley between her breasts, breathing deeply of her fragrance, then brought her to her feet, his fingers loosening the buttons on her skirt. Jenny followed suit, working on the buttons on his shirt.

When the last article of clothing had been removed, they stood and avidly devoured each other with their eyes. "You're beautiful, so very beautiful," Cole muttered, his eyes dark with passion as they caressed every curve and hollow.

Jenny's eyes drifted over Cole's superb physique, then lingered on his blatant arousal shamefully long before she looked him in the eye and answered thickly, "So are you."

Cole chuckled, stepped forward and kissed the tip of her saucy nose before saying, "Men aren't beautiful, particularly there."

"That's a matter of personal opinion," Jenny

answered pertly. Then as Cole took her into his arms and she felt of electric brush of his erection against her hip, she gasped, reached for him, and asked, "Is magnificent more acceptable to you?"

A long shudder ran through Cole as Jenny ran her hands up and down him, and he lengthened yet another inch.

"Or splendid?" Jenny suggested.

Cole cut Jenny's compliments to his manliness short by sealing her lips with a torrid kiss that seemed to scorch her lungs and melt her bones. As her knees buckled, he sank to the blanket with her and rolled her on her back, still locked in that devouring kiss, kissing her as if he was trying to crawl into her, and leaving Jenny swirling in a maelstrom of sensation.

Cole quit his tender violence at her mouth, and placed a trail of searing kisses down her throat, across her shoulder, then over the rise of her breasts. Again, he adored the soft, swollen mounds in a torment of delight for Jenny, then proceeded to kiss and caress every inch of her body, from her head to the soles of her tiny feet.

His return trip was an agony of anticipation for Jenny, for as he nipped and licked his way slowly up her leg, lingering on the soft sensitive skin of her inner thighs, Jenny knew what his ultimate destination was. She was trembling like a leaf in the storm, hot and wanton, so ready for the feel of his mouth and tongue there she thought she would burst. She was whimpering with need. She cried out, partly in relief and partly in ecstasy, when he finally gave her what she wanted, what she needed, submitting eagerly to his demanding mouth and hot, probing tongue, glorying in her lover's skill as he drove her frantic excitement higher and higher, bringing her to a glorious release, then again, and again, until Jenny wondered if it was possible for someone to die from too much pleasure.

When Cole raised his head and hovered over her Jenny saw the smile on his lips and knew just how wantonly she had behaved. She'd begged him to stop with one breath, then urged him to continue with the next. But she didn't regret it. She knew he revelled in her abandon. "That was wonderful," she sighed in utter bliss. "Absolutely wonderful."

"I'm glad you enjoyed it," Cole answered, with just a hint of amusement in his voice. "I'd be happy to oblige any time."

As he moved over her and Jenny felt the hot tip of his manhood at her portal, she pushed him to his back, saying, "No! Not until I've had my way with you."

As Jenny placed hot kisses over his throat and chest, then dallied at his nubby male nipples, her tongue teasing and tantalizing just as his had done, Cole thought how often he had fantasized about her loving him this way. It seemed fitting that it should come after they had pledged their love. But only Jenny, in her own novel manner, would call it "having her way." Not that her description took any of the excitement out of it for him. The feel of her lips and tongue on his feverish skin was a torment of pleasure as she kissed and tongued every inch of his torso, then deliberately drew out the agony on his rock-hard thighs. Then as her long golden hair fell like a silken curtain over his lap and she lowered her head, he knew the moment had finally arrived. He trembled all over in anticipation. But Cole wasn't prepared for Jenny's erotic loveplay. Her tongue was like a flame, darting here and there, jarring nerve endings on his ultra-sensitive flesh, setting him on fire, an intense, sweet torture that rapidly brought him to the brink. A roaring filled his ears and a red haze filled his vision. He caught her and jerked her up, then rolled her to her back.

"I wasn't finished!" Jenny objected, glaring up at him.

Cole's breath was coming in short gasps. "I couldn't take any more, Jenny. I was about to explode. I didn't want it to end that way."

Jenny didn't either. She wanted him inside her when it happened, so she could feel his explosion as well as her own.

When Cole had regained control, he entered her slightly, then rubbed the bud of her desire with the hot tip of his rod until Jenny was writhing and begging for release. He bent his head and licked her heaving breasts, then buried his full length in her welcoming heat. He paused, so they could both relish the wonderful sensations of their joining. "I love you," he whispered in her ear, then kissed it.

The words had so much feeling in them that they brought tears to Jenny's eyes. "I love you, too," she answered, her voice choked with emotion.

He moved then, slowly at first, making her quiver from head to toe, then faster, snatching her breath away and stilling her heart, then with a sweet fury that flooded her body and consumed her soul, taking her to the shuddering peak of ecstasy over and over and over, until his own floodgates of passion burst and he filled her with his life-force and his love.

Their passion spent, they drifted in the warm afterglow, then dozed for a few moments, with Cole's dark head pillowed on her breasts. Finally, he lifted himself from her and rolled to his side, cradling her in his arms.

"Do you have any idea of the hell I've gone through these past weeks, not being able to love you, watching Amos touch you?" Cole asked. "There were times when I wanted to kill him, and others when all I wanted to do was just snatch you up and ride off with you, keep you a prisoner for life, if I had to. I never knew love could make a man so irrational, nor have I ever felt so helpless." He kissed the top of her head. "You've brought me to my knees."

He rose on one elbow, looked deeply into her

eyes, and said, "I love you, Jenny, more than I ever dreamed was possible. Marry me. I promise I'll take good care of you."

Cole caught Jenny off guard. She had not expected a marriage proposal. "And how would you do that?" she blurted.

Cole was determined he wasn't going to bribe Jenny to marry him, any more than he would buy her love. That, too, would have to be for himself and nothing more. "I'm not a wanted man any more. I can get a job to support us somewhere, maybe as a sheriff, since I'm so good with my gun."

Cole had succeeded in bringing out the soft spot in Jenny's heart, too well. For once, her thoughts weren't mercenary, but Cole's random pick of a job had been his downfall. Jenny remembered the terrible fear she had lived with the night before, and knew if he became a law officer, she would live in constant terror, then if he did get killed — being noble, naturally — it would break her heart and her spirit, just as her father's death had done her mother. She'd be left broken, probably with a parcel of children to feed, since she and Cole were so passionate and the Irish were so damn fertile.

For Jenny, the beauty of the moment was gone. She couldn't live that way, she thought. It would be a living hell, waiting, wondering if every time he walked out the door it would be the last time she saw him alive. She had been a fool to let herself get emotionally entangled with him. She had been right all along. Love was a folly, a painful folly. She pushed away from Cole, rose to her feet, and started to dress.

"Jenny?" Cole asked in bewilderment. "Did you hear what I said? I asked you to marry me."

"I heard," Jenny answered tightly, "and the answer is no. I'm marrying Amos."

For a moment Cole was too shocked to respond. Then he angrily reminded her, "You love me!"

"Love has nothing to do with it! Unlike you, I don't believe you have to love someone to marry them. In fact, I think it's better if you don't."

"Then nothing has changed?"

"Nothing."

Jenny wrapped her *rebozo* around her and started for the door. "Wait until I dress," Cole said, coming to his feet. "I'll walk you back."

"That's not necessary."

"I said I'd walk you back!" Cole said in a voice that brooked no argument.

Jenny kept her back to him while Cole dressed, fighting to maintain her composure, and telling herself over and over that she was doing the right thing. Her silent litany continued as they walked back to the hotel, the streets quiet and deserted at that late hour, for the revelers had succumbed to the powerful liquor that had been flowing so freely.

When they reached the foot of the stairs, Cole

stopped her and said, "I've done everything in my power to win you over, things I never dreamed I would do for any woman, but I won't beg anymore. There's a limit to what a man can do and still maintain any self-respect. I'm going to hope you'll change your mind. If you do, I'll be at the river until dawn. If you don't show up by then, I'll know it's over and leave. You can forget me — or try to."

Jenny knew she would never forget, but she wouldn't admit that to Cole. "I won't come," Jenny answered with determination. "You're just wasting your time."

Undaunted by her firm answer, Cole responded. "That's still over three hours away. Wars have been won in less time than that. I'll wait."

With that, he turned and walked away with that self-assured stride that was so much a part of him.

Twenty-eight

Cole's wait for Jenny's return seemed an eternity. He sat in the warehouse for well over two hours, then nervously paced the wharf, stopping to anxiously peer down the main street every time he reached that end of the dock. Over and over he told himself that Jenny *would* come, that her love was powerful enough to triumph over her mercenary tendencies. When she still didn't appear, he stood and stared down the dark, deserted street, every muscle in his long body taut as he tried to will her to come to him. When Cole saw a pearly flush in the eastern sky, he was forced to face the grim realization that he had failed. Somehow he had won all the battles, but lost the war.

With his shoulders slumped in defeat, he walked into the warehouse to pack his saddlebags, feeling an aching in his chest and a lump in his throat. Then, instead of packing, he sat on the side of the bed, staring out into space, his full concentration on the unbelievable pain he was feeling.

A sound at the doorway caught his attention. He turned his head and saw Jenny standing there, holding her saddlebags in her hands. When Cole just stared at her, Jenny said sheepishly, "I changed my mind. I guess the women in my family just have an incurable weakness for not doing what's good for them."

Dazed, wondering if his mind was playing tricks on him, Cole rose and walked to her, then stopped and stared. Finally, he blurted, "What took you so long?"

Jenny bristled. "So long? Damn you! You were awfully sure of yourself, weren't you?"

Cole scoffed, saying, "No, not at all. What I meant was, it seemed an eternity." Then the full realization hit him, and Cole caught her in a fierce embrace, muttering, "I thought you would never come. Never!"

Jenny endured the bone-crushing embrace for a moment, savoring her happiness, then squirmed away and admitted, "Well, I guess I did take a little while to make my decision. I went to my room and did a lot of thinking. No matter how much I twisted and turned everything, it all came down to one thing. Life without you would be a bigger hell than any kind of hell living with you could possibly be. I just can't bear to lose you, to walk out of your life, or have you leave mine."

Cole chuckled. "Did it ever occur to you that our life together might not be a hell of any kind? That we might have a bit of heaven?"

It was the promise of a bit of heaven that had made Jenny change her mind. Just being with Cole was heaven, and she'd hang on to it for as long as she could, live each day as it came and refuse to worry about what the future might bring. She'd done too much of that her entire life. "Yes, I thought of that," she admitted. "Even my parents' marriage wasn't all bad. They had some good times, too." Then, in her usual business-like manner, she said, "So, then I went to see Amos and told him the truth about myself and what I had decided."

"Alone?" Cole asked in surprise. "I could have gone with you."

"I was the one engaged to him," Jenny pointed out, "not you. And you didn't help get me in that mess, so why should you help get me out? Besides, I didn't need your help," Jenny said candidly, asserting her independence. "He was furious at first and called me a few names, which I figured I deserved. I reminded him that he hadn't been particularly honest with me either. He'd never told me how dangerous it was out here. Then I told him exactly what I thought of him." Jenny laughed. "I wish you could have seen the look on his face. It was priceless. He was horrified that I even knew such words, to say nothing of how well I used them. And just for sheer meanness, I used every shocking word I ever heard."

"Was my name even mentioned?" Cole asked.

"Yes. I told him I loved you and was going to marry you. He didn't say a word." Jenny laughed again. "By then, I think he was glad to get rid of me." She looked Cole directly in the eye, hers twinkling with mischief, saying, "You're not getting any big prize, you know."

"The hell I'm not!" Cole responded with fervor, then kissed her with equal enthusiasm.

The sound of a steamboat whistle in the distance interrupted the kiss. "We've got to hurry if we're going to board that boat before the crowd," Cole said, walking Jenny to the bed where his saddlebags lay. "Joel said they anticipated quite a few passengers, since the steamer hasn't sailed for several days."

Cole quickly packed his saddlebags, and the two walked out on the wharf just as the boat appeared. It came around a small bend in the river, the paddle wheel at its stern throwing muddy water and churning the light fog that hugged the river. Seeing that there was already a line at the ticket office, Cole hurried there and, as soon as he had purchased tickets, returned to where Jenny was standing.

He tossed Jenny's saddlebags over his shoulder with his, and said, "Let's get our horses."

Jenny fell in beside him as he walked down the ramp from the wharf. They really were going to have to hurry if they were going to walk all the way to the stables and then make the return trip before the steamer left. To her surprise, Cole circled to the back of the wharf. There, tied to a willow tree, were both his horse and Princess.

Jenny turned, an irritated look on her face, and asked, "If you weren't so damn sure of yourself, how do you explain this?"

"I just wanted to be ready if you said yes," he

answered, tossing their saddlebags on the horses' backs. "If you didn't, I figured I could always drop her off at the stables on my way out of town."

Cole handed Jenny Princess's reins, and they walked their horses back up the ramp and out on the wharf. The steamboat had been tied to the dock during their absence, and several people were already walking up the gangplank. Cole and Jenny stood in line and waited their turn to board.

When the two stepped from the gangplank, Joel was waiting for them, grinning from ear to ear. "I was hoping I'd see you two here this morning. And just in case, I reserved the private cabin for you."

"When they told me it wasn't available, I assumed someone in front of me had gotten it," Cole answered. "Thanks." He reached inside his vest. "How much do I owe you?"

"Just consider it an early wedding gift." He turned to Jenny and said with a twinkle in his eye, "There is going to be a wedding, ain't there?"

Jenny laughed and answered, "Yes, providing you'll give me away."

A pleased look came over Joel's face and then he answered soberly, "I'd be honored, little lady."

He turned to Cole, saying, "Here's the key to the cabin. The door is on the other side of the boat. I'll take your horses back to the pen for you. It's on my way to the stairs."

"Thanks, Joel, for everything," Cole answered.

After Joel had led their horses away, Cole and Jenny walked to the front of the boat. They stood at the railing there while the rest of the passengers boarded and the gangplank was pulled in. The sun was just coming over the trees when the whistle blew and the steamer chugged away.

Cole and Jenny stood at the railing and watched the scenery slide by. One by one, the other passengers deserted the deck for the public cabin, where it was warmer, for there was a cool nip in the river air. When they were alone, Cole stepped behind Jenny and slipped his arms around her.

"Where are we going after we get married?" Jenny asked.

"We'll take a steamer to Galveston, then another up the Brazos River to our home."

Jenny thought it strange that Cole was already calling their destination home. "What town is that?"

"There's no town there."

"Then how can you be sheriff, if there's no town?" Jenny asked, becoming more and more confused.

"I said I could be sheriff someplace, Jenny, not that I necessarily planned to do that. We're going back to my land, the land my uncle left me."

"But I thought you said you lost it."

"I did. What I forgot to tell you was that Coke helped me regain title to it, once I paid off the back taxes. It took everything I could scrape up, plus what some old friends loaned me, but I managed it."

Jenny was immensely relieved to learn she wouldn't have to live with the constant fear of Cole being killed in the line of duty. With that terrible burden removed, she'd be glad to undergo any trials or tribulations life on a farm might present, particularly if she didn't have to go hungry. "I've heard farming is hard work, but you eat well, since you can raise your own food."

Cole realized that Jenny had no idea that he was talking about a plantation, a "farm" of considerable size. Even when he had told her they grew cotton, she hadn't made the connection, probably because she had never traveled through east Texas and seen the sugar and cotton plantations there, many of which had survived Reconstruction and still thrived. Like many easterners, she equated plantations with the deep south, and cattle, Indians, and wilderness with Texas. She had no idea that a gracious, genteel manner of living existed in Texas the same as it had in the rest of the South.

Cole wondered if he should enlighten Jenny and decided against it. He was enjoying the heady knowledge that she had chosen him for himself. After his long battle, it was something he wanted to savor just a while longer. He decided to save the news for a wedding present. Jenny might be miffed at him for keeping more secrets, but he felt sure she would forgive him, particularly when he told her the house was still standing, albeit in need of some repairs and some paint to make it beautiful again, but sound. There was even some furniture left.

Cole was aware that Jenny was awaiting an answer. "I promise you, spitfire, you will never go hungry."

"Good, because you know what a big appetite I have."

Cole chuckled at her forthright admission. He wondered what his friends would think of Jenny. Undoubtedly, she'd set some of the more sedate back on their ears, but Cole didn't want her to change. Jenny was Jenny, the woman he loved, and if the rest of the world didn't like the way she was—to hell with them! Jenny was all he needed in this life, and the next.

Jenny had been doing her own musing. "As soon as we get to Brownsville, I've got to wire Carla and John and tell them I'm alive. Then I've got to write them a long letter. They're never going to believe all that's happened to me."

"Since I'll be assuming your debts as your husband, how much do you owe them?"

"Eight hundred dollars. I still have two hundred left from the thousand they loaned me." Jenny looked up over her shoulder and asked playfully, "Do you think I'm worth it?"

Cole drew her closer and nuzzled the top of her head. "Most definitely."

Jenny breathed a deep sigh of contentment. She had never known such happiness. She had an outstanding man, who offered her an extraordinary love, a powerful love she knew would never falter or fade or grow tedious. She felt truly blessed.

She turned in the circle of Cole's strong arms and faced him, then slid her hands under his vest. Running her palms up and down his chest, she smiled up at him seductively and said in a husky voice, "I'm chilled. Why don't we go to the cabin, so you can warm me?"

Cole felt an answering warmth flood his loins, and his heart pounded in anticipation. Yes, he thought, his little Yankee temptress wasn't shy. Life would never be dull with her. She was an absolute delight. He smiled and answered, "I think that can be arranged."

Above them, standing on the ledge outside the pilothouse, Joel watched as Jenny and Cole walked to the cabin. He grinned in approval, then turned his attention to the Mexican bank where a herd of cattle were being driven upstream by a dozen well-armed Mexicans. He strained his eyes to make out the brand on one cow's flank, then seeing it was the Santa Gertrudes "running W," grinned again. The Texas cattle were really going home.

And so were Cole and his future bride.

Historical Note

McNelly's foray into Mexico made the bandits take pause, but the wholesale thievery across the border continued. Help came from an unexpected source: the new President of Mexico, Porfirio Diaz. It turned out, much to everyone's surprise, that Diaz stood for law and order. The following year, in 1876, Diaz had Cortinas removed to Mexico City where he could keep an eye on the bandit king and kept him there a virtual prisoner until his death. Diaz created a national police force, the *rurales,* who were just as hard-riding, hard-shooting and fierce as the Texas Rangers and were determined to rid Mexico, and particularly the border, of its *bandidos.* So much pressure was inflicted on the outlaws by the *rurales* that the bandits actually sought refuge in Texas!

The bandit problem on the border remained at a low ebb during Diaz's entire thirty-five year dictatorship, then flared anew. Once again the entire border was in flames. This time the bandits were under a new chief, Francisco Villa. The hostilities on the bloody border continued until General John Pershing and his men crossed into Mexico and crushed Villa's army of bandits in 1916.